Rose Mather

A tale

Mary Jane Holmes

Alpha Editions

This edition published in 2023

ISBN : 9789357941808

Design and Setting By
Alpha Editions
www.alphaedis.com
Email - info@alphaedis.com

Contents

CHAPTER I.
THE WAR MEETING.

The long disputed point as to whether the South was in earnest or not was settled, and through the Northern States the tidings flew that Sumter had fallen and the war had commenced. With the first gun which boomed across the waters of Charleston bay, it was ushered in, and they who had cried, "Peace! peace!" found at last "there was no peace." Then, and not till then, did the nation rise from its lethargic slumber and shake off the delusion with which it had so long been bound. Political differences were forgotten. Republicans and Democrats struck the friendly hand, pulse beat to pulse, heart throbbed to heart, and the watchword everywhere was, "The Union forever." Throughout the length and breadth of the land were true, loyal hearts, and as at Rhoderic Dhu's command the Highlanders sprang to view from every clump of heather on the wild moors of Scotland, so when the war-cry came up from Sumter our own Highlanders arose, a mighty host, responsive to the call; some from New England's templed hills, with hands inured to toil, and hearts as strong and true as flint; some from the Empire, some the Keystone State, and others from the prairies of the distant West. It mattered not what place had given them birth; it mattered little whether the Green Mountains of Vermont, the granite hills of New Hampshire, or the shadowy forests of Wisconsin had sheltered their childhood's home; united in one cause they rallied round the Stars and Stripes, and went forth to meet, not a foreign foe, but alas, to raise a brother's arm against another brother's arm in that most dreadful of all anarchies, a national civil war.

In the usually quiet village of Rockland the utmost interest was felt, and though there, as elsewhere, were many whose hearts beat as warmly for their Southern friends as when the sun shone on a nation at peace, all felt the necessity of action, and when at last the evening came in which the first war meeting of that place was to be held, a dense and promiscuous crowd wended its way to the old brick church, whose hallowed walls echoed to the sound of fife and drum, strange music for the house of God, but more acceptable, in that dark hour, than songs of praise sung by vain and thoughtless lips. In the centre of the church, the men were mostly congregated, while the seats nearest the door were occupied by the women,—the wives and mothers and sisters who had come with aching hearts to see their brothers, sons and husbands give their signatures to what seemed their sure death warrant. Conspicuous among these was Widow Simms, whose old-fashioned leghorn, with its faded green veil, was visible at all public gatherings, its broad frill of lace shading a pair of sharp grey eyes, and a rather peculiar face. It was very white now, and the thin lips were firmly compressed as the widow tried to look resolute and unconcerned when two of her sons went forward, their faces glowing with youthful enthusiasm, as they heard the President repeat their names, "John Simms,—Eli Simms." The widow involuntarily said it after him, her mother's heart whispering within her, "Isaac won't go. He's too young. I can't give Isaac up," and her eye wandered to where her youngest boy was sitting, twirling his old cloth cap, and occasionally exchanging a word with the young man next to him, William Baker, who, together with his brother, arose, to follow John and Eli Simms.

Scarcely, however, had they risen to their feet, when a woman occupying the same seat with Widow Simms, uttered a cry more like the moaning howl of some wild beast, than like a human sound.

"No, Harry, no, Bill—no, no," and the bony arms were flung wildly toward the two young men, who, with a dogged, indignant glance at her, fell back among the crowd where they could not be seen, muttering something not very complimentary to "the old woman," as they called her.

But the old woman did not hear it, and if she had, it would have made no difference. It mattered not to her that they had ever been the veriest pests in the whole village, the planners of every grade of mischief, the robbers of barns and plunderers of orchards,—they were *her* boys, and she didn't want them shot, so she continued to moan and cry, muttering incoherently about the rich treading down the poor, and wondering why Judge Warner didn't send his own white fingered sons, if he thought going to war was so nice.

"I wouldn't make such a fuss, let what would happen to me," said the Widow Simms, casting a half contemptuous glance upon the weeping woman, whom she evidently considered far beneath her, and adding, "They had 'nough-sight better be shot than hung,' as an aside to the young woman just behind her,—sweet Annie Graham, who was holding fast to her husband's hand, as if she would thus keep him in spite of the speaker's eloquent appeals, and the whispers of his companions, who were urging him to join the company forming so rapidly before the altar.

There was a terrible struggle going on in Annie Graham's breast,—duty to her country and love for her husband waging a mighty conflict, the former telling her that if the right would triumph, somebody's husband must go, and the wife-heart crying out, "Yes, somebody's husband *must* go, I know, but not mine, not George."

Very tenderly George Graham's strong arm encircled the girlish form, and when he saw how fast the tears came to the great dreamy eyes of blue, and thought how frail was the wife of little more than a year, he bent down until his chin rested on her pale brown hair, and whispered softly to her,

"Don't, Annie, darling, you know I will never go unless you think I ought, and give your free consent."

Had George Graham wished, he could not have chosen a more powerful argument than the words, "Unless you think I ought."

Annie repeated them to herself again and again, until consciousness of all else around her was forgotten in that one question of *duty*. She heard no longer the second speaker, whose burning eloquence was stirring up hitherto reluctant young men to place their names beside others already pledged to their country's cause. Leaning forward so that her forehead rested on the railing in front, she tried to pray, but flesh and strength were weak, and the prayer ended always with the unuttered cry, "I cannot let George go," while the fingers twined more and more closely around the broad, warm hand, which sought awhile to reassure her, and then was withdrawn from her grasp as George arose and politely offered his seat to a lady who had just arrived, and who, after glancing an instant at his *coat*, accepted his civility as a matter of course, but withheld the thanks she would have accorded to one whom she considered her equal.

Spreading out her wide skirt of rich blue silk so that it nearly covered poor Annie, she threw her crimson scarf across the railing in front, hitting Widow Simms, and so diverting the attention of Mrs. Baker, that the latter ceased her crying, while the widow turned with an expression half curious, half indignant. Annie, too, attracted by the heavy fringe and softly-blended colors of the scarf, a part of which had fallen upon her lap, as the widow shook it from her shoulder with a jerk, stole a glance at the new comer, in whom she recognized the bride, the beauty, the envied belle of Rockland, Rose Mather, from Boston,—and wife of the wealthy and aristocratic William Mather, who three months before had ended the strife between the Rockland ladies as to what fair hand should spend his gold, and drive his iron greys, by bringing to his elegant mansion a fairy little creature with whose exquisite beauty even the most fastidious could not find fault. Childish in proportions, and perfect in form and feature, she would have been handsome without the aid of the dancing brown eyes, and chestnut curls which shaded her girlish brow. Rose knew she was pretty,—knew she was stylish,—knew she was fascinating,— knew she was just then *the rage*, and as such could do and say what she pleased. Sweeping back her chestnut hair with her snowy hand, she gave one rapid glance at the sea of heads around her, and then, in a half petulant tone, exclaimed to her companion!

"I don't believe Will is here. I can't see him anywhere."

"Didn't you know he had enlisted?" asked a young man, who had made his way through the crowd, and joined her.

For an instant the bright color faded from Rose Mather's cheek, but it quickly returned as she read in Mr. Wentworth's eye, a contradiction of his words.

"Will enlisted!" she repeated. "Such people as *Will* don't go to the war. It's a very different class, such, for instance, as that one going up to sign. Upon my word, it's the boy who saws our wood!" and she pointed at the youth, offering himself up that just such people as Rose Mather, radiant in silks and diamonds, and lace, might rest in peace at home, knowing nothing of war, and its attendant horrors, save what came to her through the daily prints.

Widow Simms heard the remark, and with a swelling heart turned toward the boy who sawed Rose Mather's wood, for *she* knew who it was, and it did not need the loud whisper of Mrs. Baker to tell her that it was *her* boy, the youngest of the three, the one she loved the best, the baby, who kept the milk of human kindness from turning quite sour within her breast by his many acts of filial love, and his gentle, caressing ways. How could she give him up, her darling, her idol, the one so like his father, dead ere he was born? Who would comfort her as he had done? Who would give her the good-night kiss, timidly, stealthily, lest the older ones should see and laugh at his girlish weakness? Who would bring his weekly earnings, and empty them slily into her lap? Who would find her place in the prayer book on Sunday, and pound her clothes on Monday, long before it was light? Who would split the nice fine kindlings for the morning fire or bring the cool fresh water in the summer from the farther well, and who, when her head was aching sadly would make the cup of tea she liked so much? Homely offices, many of them, it is true, but they made up the sum of that mother's happiness, and it is not strange that, for a moment, the iron will gave way, and the poor widow wept over her cruel bereavement, not noisily, as Mrs. Baker had done, but silently, bitterly, her body trembling nervously, and her whole attitude indicative of keen, unaffected anguish.

Rose did not know the relationship existing between the widow and the boy who sawed her wood, but her better nature was touched always at the sight of distress, and for several minutes, she did not speak except to tell Mr. Wentworth how much *Brother Tom* had paid for the crimson scarf, one end of which he was twirling around his wrist. To Annie it seemed an enormous sum, and a little over-awed with her close proximity to one who could sport so expensive an article of dress, she involuntarily tried to move away, and avoid, if possible, being noticed by the brilliant belle. She might have spared herself the trouble, for Rose was too much absorbed with the group of admirers gathering around her to heed the shrinking figure at her side, and, after a time, as Widow Simms recovered her composure, she resumed her gay badinage, bringing in Will with every other breath, and showing how completely her heart was bound up in her husband, notwithstanding the evident satisfaction with which she received the flattering compliments of the gentlemen who, since her arrival at Rockland, had made it a point to admire and flirt with the little Boston belle, laughing loudly at speeches which, from one less piquant and attractive, would have been pronounced decidedly silly and meaningless.

Rose was not well posted with regard to the object of that meeting. She knew that Sumter or Charleston had been fired upon, she hardly could tell which, for she was far too sleepy when Will read the news to comprehend clearly what it was all about, and she had skipped every word which Brother Tom had written about it in his last letter, the one in which he enclosed five hundred dollars for the silver tea-set she saw in Rochester, and wanted so badly. Rose was an accomplished musician, a tolerable proficient in both French and German, and had skimmed nearly all the higher branches, but like many fashionably educated young ladies, her knowledge of geography comprised a confused medley of cities, towns and villages, scattered promiscuously over the face of the earth, but *which* was *where* she could not pretend to tell; and were it not that Brother Tom had spent three winters in Charleston, leaving at last his fair-haired wife sleeping there beneath the Southern sky, she would scarcely have known whether the waters of the Atlantic or of Baffin's Bay, washed the shore of the Palmetto State. And still Rose was not a fool in the ordinary acceptation of the term. She knew as much or more than half the petted belles of modern society, and could say smart foolish things with so pretty an air of childishness, that even those of her own sex who were at first most prejudiced against her, confessed that she was certainly very captivating, and possessed the art of making everybody like her, even if she hadn't common sense!

On this occasion she chatted on in her usual style, provoking from George Graham more than one good-humored smile at remarks which evinced so much ignorance of the matter then agitating the entire community.

"Will wouldn't go to the war, of course," she said, 'supposing there were one, which she greatly doubted. Northern men, particularly those of Rockland, were so hateful toward the South. She didn't believe Boston people were that way at all. At least, Brother Tom was not, and he knew; he had lived in Charleston, and described them as very nice folks. Indeed, she knew they were, herself, for she always met them at Newport, and liked them so much. She didn't credit one word of what the papers said. She presumed Mr. Anderson provoked them. Tom knew him personally.

"You have another brother besides Tom—won't *he* join the army?" asked Mr. Wentworth, a smile curling the corners of his mouth.

Rose sighed involuntarily, for on the subject of *that other brother* she was a little sore, and the mention of him always gave her pain. He was not like Brother Tom, the eldest, the pride of the Carleton family. He was *Jimmie*, handsome, rollicking, mischievous Jimmie, to those who loved him best, while to the Boston people, who knew him best, he was "that young scapegrace, Jim Carleton, destined for the gallows, or some other ignominious end," a prediction which seemed likely to be verified at the time when he nearly broke a comrade's head for calling him a liar, and so was expelled from college, covered with disgrace. Something of this was known to Mr. Wentworth, and he asked the question he did, just to see what Rose would say. But if he thought she would attempt to conceal anything pertaining to herself, or any one else, for that matter, he was mistaken. Rose was too truthful for anything like duplicity, and she frankly answered:

"We don't know where Jimmie is. They turned him out of college, and then he ran away. It's more than a year since we heard from him. He was in Southern Virginia, then. Mother thinks he's dead, or he would surely write to some of us," and a tear glittered in Rose's eyes, as she thought of recreant Jimmie, sleeping elsewhere than in the family vault at beautiful Mt. Auburn. Rose could not, however, be unhappy long over what was a mere speculation, and after a few moments she resumed the subject of her husband's volunteering.

"She knew he wouldn't, even if he did vote for Lincoln. She was not one bit concerned, for no man who loved his wife as he ought, would want to go and leave her," and the little lady stroked her luxuriant curls coquettishly, spreading out still wider her silken robe, which now completely covered the plain shilling calico of poor Annie, whose heart for a moment beat almost to bursting as she asked herself if it were true, that no man who loved his wife as he ought, would want to go and leave her. In a moment, however, she repelled the assertion as false, for George had given too many proofs of his devotion for her to doubt him now, even though he had expressed a desire to join the army. Then she wished she was at home, where she could not hear what Rose Mather said, and she was about proposing to George that they should leave, when Mr. Mather himself appeared, and she concluded to remain. He was a haughty-looking man, very fond of his little wife, on whose shoulder he laid his hand caressingly, as he asked "what she thought of war now?"

"I just think it is horrid!" and Rose's fat hand stole up to meet her husband's; "Mr. Wentworth tried to make me think you had volunteered, but I knew better. The idea of your going off with such frights! Why, Will, you can't begin to guess what a queer-looking set they are. There was our milkman, and the boy who sawed our wood, and canal-drivers, and peddlers, and mechanics, and"——

Rose did not finish the sentence, for something in her husband's expression stopped her. He had caught the quick uplifting of Annie Graham's head,—

had noted the indignant flashing of her blue eye, the kindling spot on her cheek, and glancing at George, he saw at once how Rose's thoughtless words must have wounded her. He had seen the disgusted expression of Widow Simms, as she flounced out into the aisle, and knowing that the "boy who sawed his wood," was her son, he felt sorry that his wife should have been so indiscreet. Still, he could not be angry at the sparkling little creature chatting so like a parrot, but he felt impelled to say:

"You should not judge people by their dress or occupation. The boy who saws our wood has a heart larger than many who make far more pretensions."

Rose tried to pout at what she knew to have been intended as a reprimand, but in the excitement of the jam as they passed out of the church, she forgot it entirely, only once uttering an impatient ejaculation as some one inadvertently stepped upon her sweeping skirt, and so held her for a moment, producing the sensation which nearly every woman experiences when she feels a sudden backward pull, as if skirt and waist were parting company.

With the hasty exclamation, "Who *is* stepping on me, I'd like to know?" she turned just in time to hear Annie Graham's politely-spoken words of apology:

"I beg your pardon, madam; they push me so behind that I could not help it."

"It isn't the least bit of matter," returned Rose, disarmed at once of all resentment, by Annie's lady-like manner, and the expression of the face, on which traces of tears were still lingering.

"Who is that, Will?" she whispered, as they emerged into the moonlight, and George Graham's tall form was plainly discernible, together with that of his wife.

Will told her who it was, and Rose rejoined:

"He has volunteered, I 'most know. Poor, isn't he?"

"Not very rich, most certainly," was Mr. Mather's reply.

"Then I guess he's going to the war," was Rose's mental comment, as if poverty were the sole accomplishment necessary for a soldier to possess, a conclusion to which older and wiser heads than hers seemed at one time to have arrived.

Annie Graham heard both question and answer, and with emotions not particularly pleasant she whispered to herself:

"Rose Mather shall see that one man at least will not go, even if he is a mechanic and poor!" and clinging closer to George's arm, she walked on in silence, thinking bitter thoughts of the little lady, who, delighted with having *Will* on one side of her, and Mr. Wentworth, his partner, on the other, tripped gaily on, laughing as lightly as if on the country's horizon there were no dark, threatening cloud, which might yet overshadow her in its gloomy folds, and leave her heart as desolate as that of the Widow Simms, or the wailing mother of Harry and Bill.

CHAPTER II.
ROSE AND ANNIE.

Rose Mather's home was a beautiful place, containing everything which love could devise, or money purchase, and Rose was very happy there, dancing like a sunbeam through the handsome rooms of which she was the mistress, and singing as gaily as her pet canary in its gilded cage by the door. No shadow of sorrow or care had ever crossed her pathway, and the eighteen summers of her short life had come and gone like so many pleasant memories, bringing with them one successive round of joys, leaving no blight behind, and bearing with them, alas, no thanks for the good bestowed, for Rose was far too thoughtless to think that the Providence which shielded her so tenderly, might have dealt more harshly with her. But the shadow was creeping on apace, and Rose was conscious that the war meeting had awakened within her a new and uncomfortable train of thought. Like many others, she had a habit of believing that nothing very bad could happen to her, and so, let what might occur, she was sure her husband would be spared. Still, in spite of her gaiety, an undefined something haunted her all the way from the church, and even when alone with her husband in her tasteful sitting-room, with the bright gas-light falling cheerily around her, and adding a fresh lustre to the elegant furniture, she could not shake it off, nor guess what it was that ailed her. At last, however, it came to her, suggested by the sight of her husband's evening paper, and laying her curly head upon his knee, she gave vent to her restlessness in the expression:

"I wish there wouldn't be any war. What is it all for? Tell me, please."

It was the first interest she had evinced in the matter. And glad to talk with any one upon the subject which was beginning to occupy so much of his own thoughts, Mr. Mather drew her into his lap, and endeavored, as far as possible, to explain to her what it all was for. Much of what he said, however, was Greek to Rose, who only gained a vague idea that the North was contending for a bit of cloth, such as she had often seen floating over the dome of the old State House in Boston, and with the remark, that men's lives were far more valuable than all the Stars and Stripes in the world, she fell away to sleep leaving her husband in the midst of an argument not quite clear to himself, for, like his wife, he could not then see *exactly what the war was for.* Still, inasmuch as there was war, he would not play the coward's part, nor shrink from the post of duty if his country should need his services. But this Rose did not know, and secure in the belief that whatever might happen, Will would never go, she soon resumed her wonted cheerfulness, and if she said anything of the war, was sure to startle her hearers with some remark quite unworthy of a New England daughter. She did wish they would stop having so many meetings, she said, or if they must have them, she wished they'd get

Brother Tom to come and set them right. He had lived in Charleston. He could tell them how kind the people were to Mary, his sick wife, and were it not that 'twas beneath him to lecture, she'd surely write for him to come. Rose Mather was growing unpopular by her foolish speeches, and when at last she was asked to join with other ladies of the town in making articles of clothing for the volunteers, she added the last drop to the brimming bucket, by tossing back her chestnut tresses, and "guessing she shouldn't blister her hands over that coarse stuff. She couldn't sew much any way, and as for making bandages and lint, the very idea was sickening. She'd give them fifty cents if they wanted, but she positively couldn't do more than that, for she must have a new pair of lavender kids. She had worn the old ones three or four times, and Will preached economy every day."

With a frown of impatience, the matron who had been deputed to ask help from Rose, took the fifty cents, and with feelings anything but complimentary to the silly little lady, went back to the hall where scores of women were busily employed in behalf of the company, some of whom would never return to tell how much good even the homely housewife, with its pins and needles, and thread, had done them when far away where no mother or sister hand could reach them, nor yet how the thought that perhaps a dear one's fingers had torn the soft linen band, or scraped the tender lint applied to some gaping wound, had helped to ease the pain, and cheer the homesick heart. It was surely a work of mercy in which our noble women were then engaged, and if from the group collected in Rockland Hall, there was much loud murmuring at Rose Mather's want of sense or heart, it arose not so much from ill-nature, as from astonishment that she could be so callous and indifferent to an object of so much importance.

"Wait till her husband goes, and she won't mince along so daintily, taking all that pains to show her Balmoral, when it isn't one bit muddy," muttered the Widow Simms, pointing out, to those near the window, the lady in question, tripping down the street in quest of lavender kids, perhaps, or more likely, bound for her husband's office, where, now that everybody worked all day long at the Hall, she spent much of her time, it was so lonely at home, with nobody to call. "I hope he'll be drafted and have to go, upon my word!" continued the widow, whose heart was very sore with thinking of the three seats at her fireside, so soon to be vacated by her darling boys, Eli, John, and Isaac. "Yes, I do hope he'll be drafted, don't you, Mrs. Graham?" and she turned toward Annie, who was rolling up bandages of linen, and weaving in with every coil a prayer that the poor soldier, whose lot it should be to need that band, might return again to the loved ones at home, or else be fitted for that better home, where war is unknown.

Annie shook her head, but made no answer. There was no bitterness now in her heart against Rose Mather. She had prayed that all away, and only hoped the anguish which had come to her, making her brain giddy, and her heart faint, might never be borne by another, if that could be. George had volunteered—was to be second lieutenant, and Annie, oh, who shall tell of the gloom which had fallen so darkly around the cottage she had called hers for one brief year. It was a neat, cozy dwelling, and to Annie it never seemed so cheerful as on that memorable night of the war meeting, when she had lighted the lamp, and sat down with George upon the chintz-covered lounge he had helped her make when first she was a bride. It is true the carpet was not of velvet, like that Rose Mather trod upon; neither was there in all the house one inch of rosewood or of marble, but there was domestic love, pure and deep as any Rose ever experienced, and there was something better far than that, a patient, trusting faith in One who can shed light upon the dreariest home, and make the heaviest trial seem like nought. It was this trusting faith which made Annie Graham the sweet, gentle being she was, shedding its influence over her whole life, and softening down a disposition which otherwise might have been haughty and resentful. Annie was naturally high-spirited and proud, and Rose's remarks concerning volunteers in general, and George in particular, had stung her to the quick, but with the indignant mood there came another impulse, and ere the cottage had been reached, the bitter feeling had gone, leaving nothing but sorrow that it had ever been there. Like Rose, she wished there would be no war, but wishing was of no avail, and long after George Graham was asleep and dreaming, it may be, of glories won on battle-fields, Annie lay awake, questioning within herself, whether she ought, by word or deed, to prevent her husband's going, if he felt as he seemed to feel, that it was as much his duty as that of others to join in his country's defence. Annie was no great reasoner, logically; all her decisions were made to turn upon the simple question of right and wrong, and on this occasion she found it hard to tell, so evenly the balance seemed adjusted. More than once she stole from her pillow, and going out into the fresh night air, knelt in the moonlight, and asked for guidance to choose the right, even though that right should take her husband from her.

"If I knew he would not die, it would not be so hard to give him up," she murmured, as sickening visions of fields strewn with the dead, and hospitals filled with the dying, came over her, and for an instant her brain reeled with the thought of George dying thus, and leaving her no hope of meeting him again, for George's faith was not like hers.

Anon, however, something whispered to her that the God she loved was on the field of carnage, and in the camp and in the hospital, and everywhere as much as there in Rockland, that prayers innumerable would follow the brave volunteers, and that the evil she so much feared might be the means of working the great good she so desired. And thus it was that Annie came to a decision. Stealing back to her husband's side, she bent above him as he lay sleeping, and with a heart which throbbed to its very core, though the lip uttered no sound, she gave him to his country asking, if it could be, that he might come back again, but if it were ordered otherwise—"God's will be done." There was no shrinking after that sacrifice was made, though when the morning came, the death-white face and the dark circle beneath the eyes, told of a weary vigil, such as many and many a woman kept both North and South, during the dark hours of the Rebellion. But save the death-white face, and heavy eyes, there was no token of the inner struggle, as with a desperate effort at self-command, Annie wound her arms around her husband's neck, and whispered to him, "You may go,—I give my free consent," and George, who cared far more to go than he had dared express, kissed the lips which tried so hard to smile, little dreaming what it cost his brave young wife to tell him what she had. To one of his temperament, there was no danger to be feared for himself. The bullet which might strike down a brother at his side would be turned away from him. Others would, of course, be killed, but he should escape unharmed. In the language of one speaker, whose eloquent appeal had done much to fire his youthful enthusiasm, "He was not going to be *shot*, but to *shoot* somebody!"

This was his idea, and ere the clinging arms had unclasped themselves from his neck, his imagination had leaped forward to the future, and in fancy George Graham wore, if not a Colonel's, at least a Captain's uniform, and the cottage on the hill, which Annie so much admired, and for the purchase of which a few hundreds were already saved, was his,—bought with the money he would earn. The deed should be drawn in her name, too, he said, and he pictured her to himself coming down the walk to meet him, with the rose-blush on her cheek, just as she looked the first time he ever saw her. Something of this he told her,—and Annie tried to smile, and think it all might be. But her heart that morning was far too heavy to be lightened by a picture of what seemed so improbable. Still, George's hopeful confidence did much to reassure her, and when, a few days after, she started for the Hall, she purposely took a longer walk for the sake of passing the cottage on the hill, thinking, as she leaned over the low iron fence, how she would arrange the flower-beds more tastefully than they were now arranged, and teach the drooping vines to twine more gracefully around the slender columns supporting the piazza in front. She would have seats, too,—willow-twisted chairs beneath the trees, where she and George could sit at twilight, and watch the shadows creeping across the hollow where the *old* cottage was, and up the opposite hill, where the cupola of Rose Mather's home was plainly visible, blazing in the April sunshine. It was a very pleasant castle which Annie built, and for a time the load of pain which, since George volunteered, had lain so heavy at her heart, was gone; but it returned again when, as she passed a turn in the road, her eye wandered down to the hollow, and that other cottage standing there so brown and small, and looking already so desolate, because she knew that ere many days were over, she should wait in vain for the loved footsteps coming down the road,—should miss the pleasant, cheery laugh, the teasing joke and words of love which made the world all sunshine. The cottage on the hill became a worthless thing as poor Annie forced back her tears, and with quickened steps hurried on to join the group of ladies busy at the Hall.

Taking her seat by the window, she commenced the light work imposed on her, that of tearing and winding bandages for those who might be wounded.

"Maybe there'll never be no fight, but it's well enough to be prepared," was the soothing remark of the kind-hearted woman who gave the work to Annie, noting, as she did so, how the lip quivered and the cheek paled at the very idea.

"What if George should need them?" kept suggesting itself to her as she worked industriously on, hoping that if he did, some one of the rolls she was winding might come to him, or better yet, if he could only have the bit of soft linen she had brought herself,—a piece of her own clothing, and bearing on it her maiden name, Annie Howard. He would be sure to know it, she said, it was written so plainly with indelible ink, and it would make him feel so glad. But there might be other Annie Howards, it was not an uncommon name, was suggested next to her, as she tore the linen in strips, and quick as thought, her hand sought the pocket of her dress for the pencil which she knew was there. Glancing around to see that no one observed her, she touched the pencil to her lips and wrote after the name, "It's *your* Annie, George. Try to believe I'm there. Rockland, April, 1861."

There were big tear-drops on that bit of linen, but Annie brushed them away, and went on with her rolling, just as Widow Simms called her attention to Rose Mather, as mentioned several pages back.

Annie could not account for it to herself, but ever since Rose's arrival at Rockland, she had felt a strange inexplicable interest in the fashionable belle; an interest prompted by something more than mere curiosity, and now that there was an opportunity of seeing her without being herself seen, she straightened up and smoothing the soft braids of her pale brown hair, waited for the entrance of the little lady, who, with her pink hat set jauntily on her chestnut curls, and her rich fur collar buttoned gracefully over her handsome cloth cloak, tripped into the room, doing much by her sunny smile and pleasant manner to disarm the ladies of their recent prejudice against her. She was nothing but a child, they reflected; a spoiled, petted child; she would improve as she grow older, and came more in contact with the sharp corners of the world, so those who had the honor of her acquaintance, received her with the familiar deference, if we may be allowed the expression, which had always marked their manner toward William Mather's bride. Rose was too much accustomed to society to be at all disconcerted by the hundred pair of eyes turned scrutinizingly toward her. Indeed, she rather enjoyed being looked at, and she tossed the coarse garments about with a pretty playfulness, saying that "since the ladies had called upon her she had thought better of it, and made up her mind to martyr herself one afternoon at least, and benefit the soldiers. To be sure there wasn't much she could do. She might hold yarn for somebody to wind, she supposed, but she couldn't knit, and she didn't want to sew on such ugly, scratchy stuff as those flannel shirts, but if somebody would thread her needle, and fix it all right, she'd try what she could do on a pair of drawers."

For a time no one seemed inclined to volunteer her services, and Widow Simms's shears clicked spitefully loud as they cut through the cotton flannel. At last, however, Mrs. Baker, who had more than once officiated as washerwoman at the Mather mansion, came forward and arranged some work for Rose, who, untying the strings of her pink hat, and adjusting her tiny gold thimble, labored on until she had succeeded in sewing up and joining together a long leg with one some inches shorter, which had happened to be lying near. Loud was the shout which a discovery of this mistake called forth, nor was it at all abated when Rose demurely asked if it would not answer for some soldier who should chance to have a limb shot off just below the knee.

"The little simpleton!" muttered the widow, while Mrs. Baker pointed out to the discomfited lady that one division of the drawers was right side out and the other wrong!

There was no alternative save to rip the entire thing, and with glowing cheeks, Rose began the task of undoing what she had done, incidentally letting out, as she worked, that Will might have known better than to send her there,—she shouldn't have come at all if he had not insisted, telling her people would call her a secessionist unless she did something to benefit the soldiers. She didn't care what they called her; she knew she was a democrat, or used to be before she was married; but now that Will was a republican, she hardly knew what she was; any way, she was not a secessionist, and she wasn't particularly interested in the war either; why should she be?—Will was not going, nor Brother Tom, nor any of her friends.

"But somebody's friends are going,—somebody's Will, somebody's Tom; as dear to them as yours are to you," came in a rebuking tone from a straight-forward, outspoken woman, who knew from sad experience that "somebody's Tom was going."

"Yes, I know," said Rose, a shadow for an instant crossing her bright face, "and it's dreadful, too. Will says everything will be so much higher, and it will be so dull at Saratoga and Newport next summer, without the Southern people. One might as well stay at home. The war might have been avoided, too, by a little mutual forbearance from both parties, until matters could be amicably adjusted, for Brother Tom said so in his letter last night, and a heap more which I can't remember."

Here Rose paused quite exhausted, with the effort she had made to repeat the opinion of Brother Tom. She had read all his last letter, fully indorsing as much of it as she understood, and after a little she went on:

"Wasn't it horrid, though, their firing into the Massachusetts boys?—and they were from right 'round Boston, too. Tom saw them when they started. They were fine looking men, he says, and Will thinks I ought to be proud that I'm a Bay State girl, and so I am, but it isn't as if my friends had gone. Tom is a democrat, I know, but it's quite another kind that join the army."

Widow Simms could keep silent no longer, and brandishing her polished shears by way of adding emphasis to what she said, she began:

"And s'posin' 'tis folks as poor as poverty struck, haint they feelin's, I'd like to know? Haint they got bodies and souls, and mothers, and wives, and sisters? And s'posin' 'tis *democrats*,—more shame for t'other side that helped get up the muss. Where be they now, them chaps that wore the big black capes, and did so much toward puttin' Lincoln in that chair? Why don't they help to keep him settin' there, and not stand back with their hands tucked in their trouses' pockets? Both my boys, Eli and John, voted t'other ticket, and Isaac would, but he wasn't twenty-one. They've all jined, and I won't say I'm sorry, for if there's anything I hate, it's a *sneak!* It makes me *so* mad!" and the big shears again clicked savagely, as Widow Simms resumed her work, after having thus delivered her opinion of the *black republicans*, besides having, in her own words, given "that puckerin Miss Mathers a piece of her mind."

Obtuse as Rose was on many points, she saw there was some homely truth in what the widow had said, but this did not impress her so much as the fact that she had evidently given offence, and she was about trying to extricate herself from the dilemma when George Graham appeared, ostensibly to bring some trivial message to the President of the Society, but really to see if his wife were there, and speak to her some kind word of encouragement. Rose recognized him as the young man she had seen at the war meeting, and the moment he left the hall, she broke out impetuously,

"Isn't he handsome?—so tall, so broad-shouldered, and such a splendid mark for a bullet,—I most know he will be shot?"

"Hush-sh!" came warningly from several individuals, but came too late. The mischief was done. Ere Rose could collect her thoughts a group of frightened women had gathered around poor Annie, who had fainted.

"What's the matter? do tell!" cried Rose, standing on tiptoe and clutching at the dress of Widow Simms, who angrily retorted,

"I should s'pose you'd ask. It's enough to make the poor critter faint clean away to hear a body talk about her husband's being a fust rate mark for a bullet!"

With all her thoughtlessness, Rose had the kindest heart in the world; and forcing her way through the crowd, she knelt by the white-faced-Annie, and taking the drooping head in her lap, pushed back the thick braids of hair, noticing, with her quick eye for the beautiful, how soft and luxuriant they were, how pure was the complexion, how perfect were the features, how small and delicate the fingers, and how graceful was the slender neck.

"I'm so sorry! I wish I'd staid at home; I *am* so sorry," she kept repeating; and when at last Annie returned to consciousness, Rose Mather's was the first voice she heard, Rose's the first face she saw.

With an involuntary shudder she closed her eyes wearily, while Rose anxiously asked of those about her how they should get her home. "Oh, Jake," she suddenly exclaimed, as, towering above the female heads, she saw her colored coachman looking for her, and remembered that her husband was to call and take her out to ride, "oh, Jake, lift this lady up, careful as you can, and put her in our carriage. Is Will there? Well, no matter, he'll just have to get out. Stand back, won't you, and let Jake come," she continued, authoritatively to the group of ladies who, half-amused and half-surprised at this new phase in Rose Mather's character, made way for burly Jake, who lifted Annie's light form as if it had been a feather's weight, and bore it down the stairs, followed by Rose, who, with one breath, told Annie not to be a bit afraid, for Jake certainly would not drop her, and with the next asked Jake if he were positive and sure he was strong enough not to let her fall.

Lazily reclining upon the cushions of his carriage, William Mather was smoking his Havana, and admiring the sleek coat of his iron greys, when Rose appeared, and seizing him by the arm, peremptorily ordered him to alight, and help Jake lift the lady in.

"I don't know who 'tis, but it's somebody I made faint away with my silly talk," she replied in answer to Mr. Mather's question, "Who have you there?"

"*You* made faint away!" he repeated, as he found himself rather unceremoniously landed upon the flagging stones, his Havana rolling at his feet, and his wife preparing to follow Annie, whom Jake had placed inside.

"Yes; I talked about her husband's being a splendid mark for a bullet, and all that, without ever thinking she was his wife. He looked so tall, and big, and nice, that I couldn't help thinking his head would come above all the rest in a fight, but I don't believe it will. There Jake, we are ready now, drive on," said Rose, while poor Annie groaned afresh at this doubtful consolation.

"Drive whar?" asked Jake. "I dun know whar they lives."

"To be sure, nor I either," returned Rose, turning inquiringly to her husband, who gave the information, adding, as he glanced down the street,

"Mr. Graham himself is coming, I see. I think, Rose, you had best give your place to him."

Rose, who was fond of adventures, wanted sadly to go with Annie, but George, when he came up, seemed so concerned, and asked so many questions, that she deemed it best to leave it for his wife to make the necessary explanations, merely saying, as she stepped upon the walk,

"I am so sorry, Mr. Graham; I really did not mean anything wrong in saying I knew you'd be shot, for you are so———"

"Rose, your dress is rubbing the wheel," interrupted Mr. Mather, by way of diverting Rose from repeating the act for which she was expressing sorrow.

"No, it ain't rubbing the wheel, either. It isn't any where near it," said Rose, wondering what Will could mean; while George, taking a seat by Annie, smiled at what he saw to be a ruse.

Bent upon reconciliation, Rose pressed up to the carriage, and said to Annie, "You *won't* be angry at me always, will you? I shouldn't have thought of it, only he does look so———"

"Go on, Jake," Mr. Mather called out, cutting short Rose's speech, and the next moment Annie was driving down the street in Rose Mather's carriage, and behind the iron greys, an honor she had never dreamed in store for her when she saw the stylish turnout passing the door of her cottage in the Hollow.

CHAPTER III.
THE DEPARTURE.

The 13th Regiment was ordered to Elmira, and the day had arrived for the departure of the volunteers. Bright was the sun, and cloudless the sky which shone on Rockland, that spring day; but cloudless sky nor warm spring sun could comfort the hearts about to part with their treasures, some forever, and some to meet again, but when, or where, or how, none could tell save Him who holds the secrets of the future.

There were mothers who had never felt a pang so keen or a pain so sore, as when with hearts too full of anguish for the dry, red eyes to weep, they watched their sons pass from the threshold of the door, and knew that when the golden sunlight, falling so brightly around them, was purple in the west, they would look in vain for that returning step, and listen in vain for tones which were the first, perhaps, to stir the deep fountains of maternal love. Fathers, too, were there, with heads bent down to hide the tears they deemed it weak to shed, as they gave the farewell blessing to their boy, praying that God might be over and around him, both when the deafening battle roar was sounding in his ear, and when in the stilly night he wrapped his blanket about him, and laid him down to rest, sometimes with the southern star shining upon him, and sometimes with the southern rain falling on his unsheltered head, for all these vicissitudes must come to a soldier on the field. Wives and sisters, too, there were, who shuddered as they thought how the dear ones to whom they said good-bye, would miss the comforts they were leaving, miss the downy pillow, the soft, warm bed made with loving hands, and the luxuries of home never prized one half so much as now, when they were to be exchanged for a life within the camp. And there were maidens, from whose cheeks the roses faded, as they gave the parting kiss, and promised to be faithful, even though the manly form the lover bore away should come back to them all maimed and crushed and crippled with the toil of war. Far better so than not to come at all. At least so Annie Graham thought, as, winding her arms around her husband's neck, she whispered to him:

"If the body you bring back has my George's heart within it, I shall love you just the same as I do now," and with her fair head lying on his bosom, Annie wept piteously.

Not till then had she realized what it was to let him go. She had become somewhat accustomed to thinking of it,—accustomed to seeing him pass in and out, dressed in his stylish uniform, which made him look so handsome, and then she had hoped the regiment would not be ordered for a long, long time, never perhaps; but now that dream was over; the dreaded hour had come, and for a moment Annie felt herself too weak to meet it. Through the livelong night she had prayed, or if perchance sleep for a moment shut the swollen lids, the lips had moved in prayer that her husband might come back to her again, or failing to do so, that he might grasp, even at the eleventh hour, the Christian's faith, and so go to the Christian's home, where they would meet once more. She had given him her little Bible, all pencil-marked and worn with daily usage,—the one she read when first the spirit taught her the meaning of its great mysteries,—and George had promised he would read it every day,—had said that when he went to battle he would place it next his heart, a talisman to shield him from the bullets of the foe. And Annie, smiling through her tears, pointed him again to the only One who could stand between him and death, asking that when he was far away, he would remember what she said, and pray to the God she honored.

"It's time, now, darling," he said, at last, as he heard in the distance the beat of the drum.

But the clinging arms refused to leave his neck, and the quivering lips pressed so constantly to his, murmured:

"Wait a little minute more. 'Tis the last, you know."

Again the drum-beat was heard mingled with the shrill notes of the fife; the soldiers were marching down the street, and he must go, but oh, who can tell of the love, the pain, the grief, the tears mingled with that parting,—or the agony it cost poor Annie to take her arms from off his neck, to feel him putting her away, to hear him going from the room, across the threshold, down the walk, through the gate, and know that he was gone.

As a child in peril instinctively turns to the mother who it knows has never failed to succor, so Annie turned to God, and with a moaning cry for help, sank on her knees just where George had left her. Burying her face in the lounge she prayed that He who heareth even the raven's cry, would care for her husband, and bring him home again if that could be. So absorbed was she as not to hear the gate's sharp click, nor the footstep coming up the walk. Impelled by something he could not resist, George had paused just by the garden fence, and yielding to the impulse which said he must see Annie's face once more, he stole softly to the open door, and stood gazing at her as she knelt, her hands clasped together, and her face hidden from his view, as she prayed for him.

"Will the kind Father keep my George from peril if it can be, but if,—oh, God, how can I say it?—if he must die, teach him the road to Heaven."

That was what she said, and George, listening to her, felt as if it were an angel's presence in which he stood. He could not disturb her. She was in safer hands than his, and he would rather leave her thus,—would rather think of her when far away, just as he saw her last, kneeling in her desolation and praying for him.

"It will help to make me a better man," he said, and brushing aside the great tears swimming in his eyes, he left his angel Annie, and went on his way to battle.

Just off from Rockland's main street, and in a cottage more humble than that of George Graham, the sun shone on another parting,—on Widow Simms giving up her boys, and straining every nerve to look composed, and keep back the maternal love throbbing so madly at her heart. Rigid as if cut in stone were the lines upon her forehead and around her mouth, as she bustled about, doing everything exactly as it should be done, and coming often to where Isaac sat trying to look unconcerned and whistling "Dixie" as he pulled on the soft, warm pair of socks she had sat up nights to knit him. Eli and John had some too, snugly tucked away in their bundle, but Isaac's were different. She had ravelled her own lamb's wool stockings for the material composing his, for Isaac's feet were tender; there were marks of chilblains on them; they would become sore and swollen from the weary march, and his mother would not be there with soothing lint and ointment made from the blue poke-berries. Great pains had the widow taken with her breakfast that morning, preparing each son's favorite dish and bringing out the six china cups and damask cloth, part of her grandmother's bridal dower. It was a very tempting table, and John and Eli tried to eat, exchanging meaning smiles when they saw their mother put in Isaac's cup the biggest lump of sugar, and the largest share of cream. They did not care,—for they too loved the fair-haired, smooth-faced boy sipping the yellow coffee he could not drink for the mysterious bunches rising so fast in his throat. The breakfast was over now. Isaac was trying on his socks, while Eli and John, knowing their mother would rather be alone when she said good-bye to her baby, prepared to start, talking quite loud, and keeping up stout courage till the last moment came, when both the tall, six-foot young men put their arms around the widow's neck, and faltered a faint "Good-bye, mother, good-bye."

There were no tears in the mother's eyes, nor in the sons', but in the breast of each there was a whirlpool of raging waters, hurting far more than if they had been suffered to overflow in torrents. Eli was the first to go, for John lingered a moment. There was something he would say, something which made him blush and stammer.

"Mother," he began, "I saw Susan last night. We went to Squire Harding's together; and,—and,—well, 'taint no use opposing it now,—Susan and I are one; and if I shouldn't come back, be good to her, for my sake. Susan's a nice girl, mother," and on the brown, bearded cheek, there was a tear, wrung out by thoughts of only last night's bride, Susan Ruggles, whose family the widow did not like, and had set herself against.

There was no help now, and a sudden start was all the widow's answer. She was not angry, John knew; and satisfied with this, he joined his brother in the yard, where he was cutting his name upon the beech tree. Thrice the widow called them back, failing each time to remember what she wanted to say. "It was something, sure," and the hard hands worked nervously, twisting up the gingham apron into a roll, smoothing it out again and working at the strings, until Eli and John passed from the yard, and left her standing there, watching them as they walked down the road. They were a grand-looking couple, she thought, as she saw how well they kept step. They were to march together to the depot, she knew, and nobody in town could turn out a finer span, but who would go with Isaac?—"Stub," his brothers called him. She hoped it might be Judge Warner's son,—it would be such an honor; and that brought her back to the fact that Isaac was waiting for her inside; that the hardest part of all was yet to come, the bidding him good-bye. He was not in the chair where she had left him sitting, but was standing by the window, and raising often to his eyes his cotton handkerchief. He heard his mother come in, and turning toward her, said, with a sobbing laugh:

"I wish the plaguy thing was over."

She thought he meant the war, and answered that "it would be in a few months, perhaps."

"I don't mean that, I mean the telling you good-bye. Mother, oh, mother!" and the warm-hearted boy clasped his mother to his bosom, crying like a child; "if I've ever been mean to you," he said, his voice choked with tears— "if I've ever been mean to you, or done a hateful thing you'll forget it when I'm gone? I never meant to be bad and the time I made that face, and called you an old fool, when I was a little boy, you don't know how sorry I felt, nor how long I cried in the trundle-bed after you were asleep. You'll forget it, won't you, when I am gone, never to come back, maybe? Will you, mother, say?"

Would she? Could she remember aught against her youngest born, save that he had ever been to her the best, the dearest, most obedient child in the world? No, she could not, and so she told him, caressing his light brown hair and showering upon it the kisses which the compressed lips could no longer restrain. The fountain of love was broken, and the widow's tears dropped like rain on the upturned face of her boy.

Suddenly there came to their ears the same drum-beat which had sounded so like a funeral knell to Annie Graham. Isaac must go, but not till one act more was done.

"Mother," he whispered, half hesitatingly, "it will make me a better soldier if you say the Lord's Prayer with me just as you used to do, with your hand upon my head. I'll kneel down, if you like," and the boy of eighteen, wearing a soldier's dress, *did* kneel down, nor felt shame as the shaky hand rested once more on his bowed head, while his mother said with him the prayer learned years ago, kneeling as he knelt now.

Surely to the angels looking on there was charge given concerning that young boy,—charge to see that no murderous bullet came near him, even though they should fall round him thick and fast as summer hail. It would seem that some such thought as this intruded itself Upon the Widow Simms, for where the swelling pain had been there came a gentle peace. God would care for Isaac. He would send him home in safety, and so the bitterness of that parting was more than half taken away.

Again the drum beat just as Annie heard it. Another pressure of the hand, another burning kiss, another "good-bye, mother, don't fret too much about us," and then the last of the widow's boys was gone.

Turn we now to the shanty-like building down by the mill, where the mother of Harry and Bill rocked to and fro upon the unmade bed, and rent the air with her dismal howls, hoping thus to win at least one tender word from the two youths, voraciously devouring the breakfast she, like Widow Simms, had been at so much pains to prepare, watching even through her tears to see "if they wan't going to leave her one atom of the steak she had spent her yesterday's earnings to buy."

No they didn't. *Harry* took the last piece, growling angrily at Bill, who, kinder hearted than his brother, suggested that "*Hal* shouldn't be a pig, but leave something for the old woman."

"Leave it yourself," was Harry's gruff response, and turning to his mother, he told her "not to make a fool of herself, when she knew she was glad to be rid of them. At any rate, if she were not, the whole village were;" adding, by way of consolation, that "he should probably end his days in State Prison if he staid at home, and he had better be shot in a fair fight, as there was some credit in that."

Around Harry Baker's childhood there clustered no remembrance of prayers said at the mother's knee, or of Bible stories told in the dusky twilight, and though reared in New England, within sight of the church spire, he had rarely been inside the house of God, and this it was which made the difference between that scene and the one transpiring in the house of Widow Simms. All the animal passions in Harry Baker's case were brought to full perfection, unsubdued by any softer influence, and rising from the table, after having filled his stomach almost to bursting, he swaggered across the room, and opening his bundle began to comment upon the different articles, he having been too drunk to notice them when given to him on the previous night.

"What in thunder is this for?" he exclaimed, holding up the calico housewife, and letting buttons, scissors and thread drop upon the floor. "Plaguy pretty implements of war, these!" and he began to enumerate the articles. "Fine tooth comb, black as the ace of spades. Good enough idea that; hain't used one since I can remember;" and he passed it through his shaggy hair, whose appearance fully verified the truth of his assertion. "Half a paper of pins. Why didn't the stingy critters give us more? An old brass thimble, too. Here, mother, I'll give you that to remember me by," and he tossed it into her lap. The drawers then took his attention; the identical pair Rose Mather made, and though they were better than any he had ever worn, he laughed at them derisively. Trying them on he succeeded in making quite a long rip in one of the seams, for Rose's stitches were none the shortest. Then, with a flourish, he kicked them off, uttering an oath as he felt a sharp scratch from the needle which Rose had broken, and failed to extricate. The woolen shirt came next, but any remarks he might have made upon that, were prevented by his catching sight of the *little brown book* which lay at the bottom of the bundle.

"Hurrah, Bill, if here ain't a Testament, with 'Harry Baker' inside. Rich, by George! Wonder if they s'posed I'd read it. Let us see what it says. 'Come unto me all ye that labor.' Mother, that means *you*, scrubbin' and workin', you know. Keep the pesky thing. I enlisted to lick the Southerners, not to sing *himes* and psalms!" and he threw the sacred book across the floor, just as the first drum-beat sounded. "That's the signal," he exclaimed, and hastily rolling up the shirt and drawers, he started for the door, carelessly saying, "Come Bill take your Testament and come along. Good-bye, old lady. You needn't wear black if I'm killed. 'Twon't pay, I guess."

"Oh, Harry, Harry, wait. Wait, Billy boy, do wait. Give your old marm one kiss," and the poor woman tottered toward Harry, who savagely repulsed her, saying "he wan't going to have her slobberin' over him."

"You, Billy, then, you'll let me kiss you, won't you?" and she turned toward Bill, who hesitated a moment, for Harry was in the way.

Bill was afraid of Harry's jeers, and so he, too, refused, while the wailing cry rose louder.

"Oh, Billy, do just once, and I've been so good to you! Just once, do, Billy."

"Shan't do it," was Bill's reply, as he followed Harry, who, as a farewell parting had hurled a stone at a cow across the street, set the dog on his mother's kitten, stepped on the old cat's tail, and then left the yard, slamming after him the rickety gate his mother had tried in vain to have him fix before he went.

Billy, however, waited. There was something more human in his nature than in his brother's. He had not thrown his Testament away, and the sight of it in his bundle had touched a tender chord, making him half resolve to read it. Watching his brother till he was out of sight, he went back to where his mother sat, moaning dolefully,

"Oh that I should raise sich boys!—that I should raise sich boys!"

"Mother," he said, and Mrs. Baker's heart fairly leaped at the sound, for there was genuine sympathy in the tone. "Mother, now that Hal has gone, I don't mind kissin' you, or lettin' you kiss me, if you want to."

The doleful moan was a perfect scream as the shrivelled arms clasped Bill, while the joyful mother kissed the rough but not ill-humored face.

"There, now, don't screech so like an owl," he said, releasing himself from her, and adding, as he glanced at a huge silver watch, won by gambling, "Maybe seein' I've a few minutes to spare, I'll drive a nail or so into that confounded gate, and I dun know, but while I'm about it, I'll split you an armful of wood. I had or'to have cut up the hull on't I s'pose, but when Hal is 'round I can't do nothin'."

It was strange how many little things Bill did do in these few minutes he had to spare—things which added greatly to his mother's comfort, and saved her several shillings, beside making a soft warm spot in a heart which knew not many such. Glancing at the tall clock brought from New England, when Mrs. Baker first moved to Rockland, Bill remarked:

"The darned thing has stopped agin. I or'to have iled it, I s'pose. It would kind of been company for you, hearin' it tick. I *vum*, if I hain't a mind to give you this old turnep," and again he drew out the silver watch. "You'll lay abed all day without no time. Like enough I'll nab one from some tarnal rebel,— who knows?" and with his favorite expression, "*Nuff said*," Bill laid the watch upon the table, his mother moaning all the while,

"Billy boy, Billy boy, I never sot so much store by you before. How can I let you go? Stay, Billy, do, or else run away the first chance you git. Will you, Billy boy?"

"Not by a jug full!" was the emphatic response. "I ain't none of that kind. I'll be shot like a dog before I'll run. The Baker name shall never be disgraced by my desertin'. It's more like Hal to do that; but don't howl so. I'm kinder puttin' on the tender, you know, 'cause I'm goin' away. I should be ugly as ever if I's to stay to hum. So stop your snivelin'," and having driven the last nail into a broken chair, Bill gathered up his bundle, and with the single remark, "Nuff said," darted through the open door, and was off ere his mother fairly comprehended it.

There was a great crowd out that morning to see the company off. Fathers, mothers, wives, and sisters,—those who had friends in the company and those who had none. The Mather carriage was there, and from its window Rose's childish face looked out, now irradiated with smiles as its owner bowed to some acquaintance, and again shadowed with sympathy as the cries of some bereaved one were heard amid the throng.

Widow Simms, too, was there, drawn thither by a desire to see if Isaac *did* march with Charlie Warner, as she hoped he would, notwithstanding that he had told her he was probably too short. She didn't believe that,—he was taller than he looked, and inasmuch as Charlie was the most aristocratic of the company, she did hope Isaac would go with him. So there she stood waiting, not far from Mrs. Baker, who had dried her eyes, and come for a last look at her boys.

Onward the soldiers came, slowly, steadily onward, the regular tread of their feet and the measured beat of the drum making solemn music as they came, and sending a chill to many a heart; for 'twas no gala day, no Fourth of July, no old-fashioned general training, they were there to celebrate. Every drum-beat was a note of war, and they who kept time to it were going forth to battle. Onward, onward still they came, George Graham's splendid figure towering above the rest, and eliciting more than one flattering compliment from the lookers on.

There were John and Eli, side by side,—John eagerly scanning the female forms which lined the walk for a sight of last night's bride, and Eli looking for his mother, if perchance she should be there. She was there, and what to John was better yet, she stood with her hand on *Susan's* shoulder, showing that thus early she was trying to mother her.

"That's him,—that's John," and Susan's voice faltered as she pointed him out to the widow, whose heart gave one great spasm of pain as she saw him, and then grew suddenly still with wrath and indignation; for alas, her Isaac, who was to have gone with Charlie Warner, son of Rockland's Judge, was marching with *William Baker,—Bill,*—who had been to the workhouse twice, to say nothing of the times he had stolen her rare-ripes and early melons! She had not looked for anything like this, and could scarcely believe her senses. Yet there they were, right before her eyes, Isaac and Bill, the former hoping his mother would not see him, and the latter trying not to see his mother, who was quite as much delighted to see him with Isaac Simms as the widow would have been had Isaac been with Charlie Warner, just in front.

Mrs. Baker had followed her sons to the hall, had heard the reasons for the captain's decision, and she called out in a loud, exultant tone,

"Miss Simms! Miss Simms do you see your Ike with Billy? Cap'n Johnson would have put him with Charlie Warner if he hadn't fell short two inches. Look kinder nice together, don't they? only Ike stoops a trifle, 'pears to me."

It didn't "'pear" so to Widow Simms, but then her eyes wore blurred so that she could not see distinctly, for, strange to say, the sharpest pang of all was the knowing that Isaac, so pure, so gentle, so girl-like, must be a companion for reckless, swearing, gambling Bill, and for a time she could not quite forgive her youngest born that he had not been just two inches taller. Blind, ignorant Widow Simms, the hour will come when, on her bended knees, she'll thank the over-ruling hand which kept her boy from growing *just two inches taller!*

Onward, still onward they moved, until they turned the corner and paused before the depot.

A little apart from the rest George Graham stood, wishing that the cars would come, and building airy-castles of what would be when he returned, covered with laurels, as he was sure to do if only opportunities were offered. He would distinguish himself, he thought, with many a brave deed, so that the papers would talk of him as a gallant hero, and when he came back to Rockland, the people would come out to meet him, a denser crowd than was assembled now. Their faces would not then be so sad, for they would come to do him honor, and in fancy he heard the stirring notes of the martial music, and saw the smile of joy steal over the weather-beaten features of the leader of the band, the man with the jammed white hat, as he fifed that welcome home. There would be carriages there, too, more than now, and maybe there would be *a carriage expressly for him,* and the dreamer saw the long procession moving down the street,—saw the little boys on the walk, the women at the doors, and heard the peal of the village bells. It would be grand, he thought, if he could have a crown just as the Roman victors used to do,—it would please Annie so much to see him thus triumphant. *She* would not come up to the depot, he knew. She would rather be alone when she met him, while he, too, would prefer that all those people should not be looking on when he kissed his little wife. Just then the train appeared, and the confusion became greater as the crowd drew nearer together, and the man with the jammed white hat who was to fife George's welcome home, redoubled his exertions, and tried his best to drown his own emotions in the harsh sounds he made. But above the fife's shrill scream, above the bass drum's beat, and above the engine's hiss, was heard the sound of wailing, as one by one the Rockland volunteers stepped aboard the train.

Bill was the last to go, for as a parting act he had fired the old cannon, which almost from time immemorial had heralded to Rockland's sleeping citizens that twelve o'clock had struck and it was Independence day. Some said it was no good omen that the worn-out gun burst in twain from the heavy charge with which Bill had seen fit to load it, but Bill cared not for omens, and with three cheers and a *tiger* for Uncle Sam, he jumped upon the platform just as the final all aboard was shouted.

There was a ringing of the bell, a sudden puffing of the engine, a straining of machinery, a sweeping backward of the wreaths of smoke, and then, where so lately one hundred soldiers had been, there was nothing left save an open space of frozen ground and iron rails, as cold and as empty as the hearts of those who watched until the last curling ring of vapor died amid the eastern woods, and then went sadly back to the homes left so desolate.

CHAPTER IV.
WILL AND BROTHER TOM.

"A letter from brother Tom,—I am so glad. It's an age since he wrote, and I've been dying to hear from home. Dear old Tom!" and dropping parasol in one place, gloves in another, and shawl in another, Rose Mather, who had just come in from shopping, seized the letter her husband handed her, and seating herself upon an ottoman near the window, began to read without observing that it was dated at *Washington* instead of Boston, as usual.

Gradually, however, there came a shadow over her face, and her husband saw the tears gathering slowly in her eyes, and dropping upon the letter she had been "dying to get."

"What is it, Rose?" Mr. Mather asked, as a sob met his ear.

"Oh, Will," and Rose cried outright, "I didn't believe Tom would do that! I thought people like him never went to the war. I 'most know he'll be killed. Oh, dear, dear. What shall I do?" and Rose hid her face in the lap of her husband, who fondly caressed her chestnut hair as he replied,

"You'll bear it like a brave New England woman. We need just such men as your brother Tom, and I never respected him one half so much as now that he has shown how truly noble he is. He was greatly opposed to Lincoln, you know, and worked hard to defeat him; but now that our country is in danger, he, like a true patriot, has thrown aside all political feeling and gone to the rescue. I honor him for it, and may success attend him."

"Yes," interrupted Rose, as a new idea struck her, "but what will his Southern friends think of him? and he has got a heap of them. There are the Birneys and Franklins from New Orleans, the Richardsons in Mobile, and those nice people in Charleston,—what will they say when they hear he has taken up arms against them? and he always used to quarrel so with those stiff Abolitionists in Boston, when they said the Southerners had no right to their slaves. Tom insisted they had, and that the North was meddling with what was none of its business, and now he's turned abolitionist, and joined too,— dear, dear."

Mr. Mather smiled at Rose's reasoning, and after a moment, replied, "I have no idea that Tom has changed his mind in the least with regard to the negroes, or that he loves his Southern friends one whit the less than when defending them from abuse. Negroes and Southern proclivities have nothing to do with it. A blow has been struck at the very heart of our Union, and Tom feels it his duty to resent it. It's just like this: suppose you, in a pet, were trying to scratch your mother's eyes out, and Tom should try to prevent it. Would you think him false to you, because he took the part of his mother?

Would you not rather respect him far more than if he stood quietly by and saw you fight it out?"

"It is not very likely I should try to scratch out mother's eyes," said Rose, half laughing at her husband's odd comparison, and adding, after a moment, "I don't see how folks can fight and love each other too."

Mr. Mather didn't quite see it either, and without directly replying to Rose, he asked, by way of diverting her mind from the subject of her brother's volunteering, if she noticed what Tom said about the Rockland Company in general, and George Graham and Isaac Simms in particular?

This reminded Rose of Annie, who had been ill most of the time since her husband's departure.

"I meant to have called on Mrs. Graham right away," she said. "The poor creature has been so sick, they say, but would not let them send for George, because it was his duty to stay where he was. I'd like to see duty or anything else make me willing to part with you. I don't believe Mrs. Graham loves her husband as I do you, or she would never consent to be left alone," and Rose nestled closer to her husband, who could not find courage to tell her what he meant to do when he handed her Tom's letter. It would be too much for her to bear at once, he thought, as he saw how greatly she was pained because her brother had joined the army, and was even then in Washington.

To Rose it was some consolation that Tom was captain of his company, and that his soldiers were taken from the finest families in Boston. This was far better than if he had gone as a private, which of course he would not do. He was too proud for that, and she could never have forgiven him the disgrace. Still, viewed in any light, it was very sad, for Tom had been to Rose more like a father than a brother. He was the pride, the head of the Carleton family, upon whom herself and mother had leaned, the one since the day of her widowhood, and the other since she could remember. He it was who had petted and caressed, and spoilt her up to the very hour when, at the altar, he had given her away to Will. He it was, too, who had been the arbiter of all the childish differences which had arisen between herself and *Jimmie*, teasing, naughty *Jimmie*, wandering now no one knew where, if indeed he were alive. And at the thought of Jimmie, with his saucy eyes and handsome face, her tears flowed afresh. What if he were living and should join the army, like Tom? It would be more than she could bear, and for a long time after her husband left her, Rose sat weeping over the picture she drew of both her brothers slain on some bloody battle-field. The shadow of war was beginning to enfold her, and brought with it a new and strange sympathy for those who, like herself, had brothers in the army.

Again remembering Annie Graham, she sprang up, exclaiming to herself,

"I'll go this very afternoon. She'll be so glad to know what Tom thinks of George!" and ere long Rose was picking her way daintily through the narrow street which led to the cottage in the Hollow. It was superior to most of the dwellings upon that street, and Rose was struck at once with the air of neatness and thrift apparent in everything around it, from the nicely painted fence to the little garden with its plats of flowers just budding into beauty.

"They have seen better days, I am sure, or else Mrs. Graham's social position was above her husband's," was Rose's mental comment, as she lifted the gate latch and passed up the narrow walk, catching a glimpse, through the open window, of a sweet, pale face, and of a thick stout figure, flying through the opposite door, as if anxious to avoid being seen.

Poor Annie had been very sick, and more than once the physician who attended her had suggested sending for her husband, but Annie, though missing him sadly, and longing for him more than any one could guess, always opposed it, begging of Widow Simms, who of her own accord went to nurse her, not to write anything which would alarm him in the least. So George, ever hopeful, ever looking on the sunny side, thought of his blue-eyed wife as a little bit sick, and nervous it might be, but not dangerous at all, and wrote to her kind, loving, cheering letters, which did much to keep her courage from dying within her. Annie was better now,—was just in that state of convalescence when she found it very hard to lie all day long, watching Widow Simms as she bustled out and in, setting the chairs in a row with their six backs square against the wall, and their six fronts opposite the table, stand and bureau, also in a row. She was just wishing some one would come, when the swinging of the gate and the widow's exclamation, "Oh, the land, if that stuck up thing ain't comin'," announced the approach of Rose Mather.

"I'll make myself missin', for mercy knows I don't wan't to hear none of your *secession* stuff. It fairly makes my blood bile!" was the widow's next comment; and gathering up her knitting she hurried into the kitchen, leaving Annie to receive her visitor alone.

Not waiting for her knock to be answered, Rose entered at the open door, and advanced at once into the room where Annie was, her fair hair pushed back from her forehead, her blue eyes unusually brilliant, and her face scarcely less white than the pillow on which it lay.

Rose had an eye for the beautiful, and after the first words of greeting were over, she broke out in her impulsive way—

"Why, Mrs. Graham, how handsome you are looking! just like the apple blossoms. I wish your husband could see you now. I'm sure he wouldn't stay there another hour. I think it's cruel in him, don't you?"

The tears came at once to Annie's eyes, and her voice was very low as she replied:

"George does not know how sick I have been, neither do I wish to have him. It would only make his burden heavier to bear, and I try to care more for his comfort than my own."

This was a phase of unselfishness wholly new to Rose, and for an instant she was silent, then remembering Tom's letter, she seated herself upon the foot of the bed, and throwing aside her bonnet, took the letter from her pocket, telling Annie as she did so that she, too, was now interested in the war, and in every one whose friends had gone.

"I never knew how it felt before," she said; "and I've made a heap of silly speeches, I know. Don't you remember that time in the Hall, when I talked about your husband being shot? I am sorry, but I *do* think he's more likely to be picked off than Tom, who is not nearly as tall. You are faint, ain't you?" she added, as she saw how deathly pale Annie grew, while the drops of perspiration stood thickly about her lips.

"Simpleton, simpleton!" muttered Widow Simms, listening through the keyhole in the kitchen, while Annie whispered:

"Please don't talk that way, Mrs. Mather. I know George is very tall, but unless God wills it otherwise, the bullets will pass by him as well as others."

Rose saw she had done mischief again, by her thoughtless way of speaking, and eager to repair the wrong, she bent over Annie and said:

"I am sorry. I'm always doing something foolish. You are faint; shan't I tell the servant to bring you some water? She's in the kitchen, I suppose," and ere Annie could explain, Rose had darted into the neat little kitchen where Widow Simms was stooping over the stove and kindling a fire, with which to make the evening tea.

"Girl, girl, Mrs. Graham wants some water. Hurry and bring it quick, will you?"

Rose called out a little peremptorily, for there was something rather suggestive of defiance in the square, straight back which never moved a particle in answer to the command.

"Deaf or hateful," was Rose's mental comment, and as it might possibly be the former, she wished she knew the girl's name, as that would be more apt to attract her. "Most every Irish girl is Bridget," she thought to herself, "and I guess this one is. Any way she acts like the girl that used to order mother out doors, so I'll venture upon that name."

"Bridget, Bridget!" and this time the voice was decidedly authoritative in its tone, but what more Rose might have added was cut short by the widow, who dropped the griddle with a bang, and turning sharply round, replied:

"There's no Bridget here, and if it's me you mean, I am *Mrs. Joseph Simms!*"

Rose had good reason for remembering Mrs. Simms, and coloring crimson, she tried to apologize:

"I beg your pardon; I did not see your face. I supposed everybody kept a girl; and your back looked like——"

"Don't make the matter any worse," interrupted the widow, smiling in spite of herself at Rose's attempt to excuse her blunder. "You thought from my dress that I was a hired girl, and so I was in my younger days, and I don't feel none the wus for it neither. Miss Graham's faint, is she? She's had time to get over it, I think. Here's the water," and filling a gourd shell she handed it to Rose, who, in her admiration of the (to her) novel drinking cup, came near forgetting Annie.

But Annie did not care, for the rencounter between the widow and Rose had done her quite as much good as the water could, and Rose found her laughing the first really hearty laugh she had enjoyed since George went away.

"It's just like me," Rose said, as she resumed her seat by Annie, listening intently while she told how kind the Widow Simms had been, coming every day to stay with her, and only leaving her at night because Annie insisted that she should.

"I like Mrs. Simms!" was Rose's vehement exclamation, "and I am glad Tom said what he did about Isaac, who used to saw our wood. I did not tell you, did I? And there's something real nice about your husband, too. I mean to call her in while I read it," and Rose ran out to the wood-shed, where the widow was now splitting a pine board for kindling, the newspaper she at first had used, having burned entirely out.

Rose's manner and voice were very conciliatory as she said:

"Please, Mrs. Simms, come in and listen while I read what brother Tom has written about Mr. Graham and your Isaac,—something perfectly splendid. Tom has volunteered and gone to Washington, you know."

It was strange how those few words changed the widow's opinion of Rose. The fact that Thomas Carleton, whom the Rockland people fancied was a Secessionist, had joined the Federal army, did much toward effecting this change, but not so much as the fact that he had actually noticed her boy, and spoken of him in a letter.

"Miss Mather ain't so bad after all," she thought, and striking her axe into the log, she followed Rose to the sitting-room, listening eagerly while she read the few sentences pertaining to George and Isaac. They were as follows:

"By the way, Will, I find there's a company here from Rockland. Fine appearing fellows, too, most of them are, and under good discipline. I am especially pleased with the second lieutenant. He's a magnificent looking man, and attracts attention wherever he goes."

"That's George, you know," and Rose, quite as much pleased as Annie herself, nodded toward the latter, whose pale cheek flushed with pride at hearing her husband thus spoken of by Rose Mather's brother.

"Yes, but Isaac," interrupted the widow. "Whereabouts does he come in?"

"Oh, pretty soon I'll get to him. There's more about George yet," answered Rose, as she resumed her reading.

"I had the pleasure of talking with him yesterday, and found him very intelligent and sensible. If we had more men like him, success would be sure and speedy. He has about him a great deal of fun and humor, which go far toward keeping up the spirits of his company, and some of the poor fellows need it sadly. There's a young boy in the ranks, Isaac Simms, who interests me greatly."

"Oh-h!" and the widow drew a long sigh as Rose continued:

"I wonder he was ever suffered to come, he seems so young, so girl-like and so gentle. Still he does a great deal of good, Lieut. Graham tells me, by visiting the sick and sharing with them any delicacy he happens to have. He's rather homesick, I imagine, for when I asked him if he had a mother, his chin quivered in a moment, and I saw the tears standing in his eyes. Poor boy, I can't account for the interest I feel in him. Heaven grant that if we come to open fight he may not fall a victim."

"Yes, yes, my boy, my darling boy," and burying her face in her hard hands, the widow sobbed aloud. "I thank you, Miss Mather, for reading me that," she said, "and I thank your brother for writing it. Tell him so will you. Tell him I'm nothing but a cross, sour-grained, snappish old woman, but I have a mother's heart, and I bless him for speaking so kindly of my boy."

Rose's tears fell fast as she folded up the letter, and Annie's kept company with them. There was a bond of sympathy now between the three, as they talked together of the soldiers, Mrs. Simms and Annie devising various methods by which they might be benefited, and Rose wishing she, too, could do something for them.

"But I can't," she said, despairingly. "I never did anybody any real good in all my life,—only bothered them," and Rose sighed as she thought how useless and aimless was her present mode of life.

"You'll learn by and by," said the widow, in a tone unusually soft for her; then, as if the sock she held in her lap had suggested the idea, she continued, "Can you knit?"

Rose shook her head.

"Nor your mother, neither?"

Again Rose shook her head, feeling quite ashamed that she should lack this accomplishment.

"Well," the widow went on, "'taint much use to learn now. 'Twould take a year to git one stocking done, but if when winter comes, that brother of yours wants socks and mittens, or the like of that, tell him I'll knit 'em for him."

"Oh, you are so kind!" cried Rose, thinking to herself how she'd send Widow Simms some pineapple preserves, such as she had with dessert that day.

They grew to liking each other very fast after this, and Rose staid until the little round table was arranged for tea and rolled to Annie's bedside. There was no plate for Rose, the widow having deemed it preposterous that she should stay, but the table looked so cosy, with its tiny black teapot, and its nicely buttered toast, that Rose invited herself, with such a pretty, patronizing way, that the widow failed to see the condescension it implied. It did not, however, escape Annie's observation, but she could not feel angry with the little lady, touching her bone-handled knife as if she were afraid of it, and looking round in quest of the napkin she failed to find, for Widow Simms had banished napkins from the table as superfluous articles, which answered no earthly purpose, save the putting an extra four cents into the pocket of the washerwoman, Harry Baker's mother.

It was growing late, and the sunset shadows were already creeping into the Hollow when Rose bade Annie good-bye, promising to come again ere long, and wondering, as she took her homeward way, whence came the calm, quiet peace which made Annie Graham so happy, even though her husband were far away in the midst of danger and death. Rose had heard that Annie was a Christian, and so were many others whom she knew, but they were much like herself,—good, well-meaning people, amiable, and submissive when everything went to suit them, but let their husbands once join the army and they would make quite as much fuss as she, who did not profess to be anything. And then, for the first time in her life, Rose wished she, too, could learn from Annie's teacher, and so have something to sustain her in case her husband should go. But he wouldn't go,—and if he did, all the religion in the world could not make her resigned,—and the tears sprang to Rose's eyes as she hurried up the handsome walk to the piazza, where *Will* sat smoking his cigar in the hazy twilight. She told him where she had been, and then sitting upon his knee told him of Annie, wishing she could be like her, and asking if he did not wish so too.

Will made no direct reply. His thoughts were evidently elsewhere, and after a few minutes he said, hesitatingly:

"Would it break my darling's heart if I should join Tom at Washington?"

There was a cry of horror, and Rose hid her face in her husband's bosom.

"Oh, Will, Will, you shan't, you can't, you mustn't and won't! I didn't know you ever thought of such a cruel thing. Don't you love me any more? I'll try to do better, I certainly will!" and Rose nestled closer to him, holding his hands just as Annie Graham had once held her husband's.

"You could not be much better, neither could I love you more than I do now, Rosa, darling," Mr. Mather replied, kissing her childish brow. "But, Rosa, be reasonable once, and listen while I tell you how, ever since the fall of Sumter, I have thought the time would come, when I should be needed, resolving, too, that when it came, it should not find me a second *Sardanapalus!*"

The sudden lifting of Rose's head, and her look of perplexed inquiry, showed that notwithstanding the fanciful ornament styled a *Diploma* lying in her writing-desk, Sardanapalus had not the honor of being numbered among her acquaintances. But her heart was too full to ask an explanation, and her husband continued:

"Besides that, there was a mutual understanding between Tom and myself, that if one went the other would, and he has gone,—nobly laying aside all the party prejudice which for a time influenced his conduct. Our country needs more men."

"Yes, yes," gasped Rose; "but more have gone. There's scarcely a boy left in town, and it's just so every where."

Mr. Mather smiled as he replied:

"I know the boys have gone,—boys whose fair, beardless faces should put to shame a strong, full-grown man like me. And another class, too, have gone, our laboring young men, leaving behind them poverty and little helpless children, whereas I have nothing of that kind for an excuse."

"Oh, I wish I had a dozen children, if that would keep you!" cried Rose, the insane idea flashing upon her that she would at once adopt a score or more of those she had seen playing in the muddy Hollow that afternoon.

Mr. Mather smiled, and continued:

"Suppose you try and accustom yourself to the idea of living a while without me. I shall not die until my appointed time, and shall undoubtedly come back again. Don't you see?"

No, Rose didn't. Her heart was too full of pain to see how going to war was just as sure a method of prolonging one's life as staying at home, and she sobbed passionately, one moment accusing her husband of not loving her as he used to, and the next begging of him to abandon his wild project.

Mr. Mather was a man of firm decision, and long before he broached the subject to his wife, his mind had been made up that his country called for *him*,—not for somebody else,—but for *him* personally; that if the rebellion were to be crushed out, men of wealth and influence must help to crush it, not alone by remaining at home and urging others on, though this were an important part, but by actually joining in the combat, and by their presence cheering and inspiring others. And Mr. Mather was going, too,—had, in fact, already made arrangements to that effect, and neither the tears nor entreaties of his young wife could avail to change his purpose. But he did not tell her so that night; he would rather come to it gradually, taking a different course from that which George Graham had pursued, for where George had left the decision wholly to his wife, Mr. Mather had taken it wholly upon himself, making it first and telling Rose afterwards. It was better so, he thought, and having said all to her that he wished to say on that occasion, he tried to divert her mind into another channel. But Rose was not to be diverted. It had come upon her like a thunderbolt,—the thing she so much dreaded,—and she wept bitterly, seeing in the future, which only a few hours before looked so bright and joyous, nothing but impenetrable gloom, for she could read her husband tolerably well, and she intuitively felt that she had lost him,—that he was going from her, never to come back, she knew. She should be a widow before she was nineteen, and the host of summer dresses she meant to buy when she went back to Boston, changed into a widow's sombre weeds, as Rose saw herself arrayed in the habiliments of mourning. What a fright she looked to herself in the widow's cap, with which her vivid imagination disfigured her chestnut hair, and she shuddered afresh as she thought how hideous she was in black.

Poor, simple little Rose! And yet we say again Rose was not a *fool*, nor yet an unnatural character. There are many, many like her, some who will recognize themselves in this story and more who will not. Gay, impulsive, pleasure-seeking creatures, whom fashionable education and too indulgent parents have done their utmost to spoil, but who still possess many traits of excellence, needing only adverse circumstances to mould and hammer them into the genuine coin of true-hearted womanhood. Such an one was Rose.

Reared by a fond mother, petted by an older brother, and teased by a younger, flattered by friend and foe, and latterly caressed and worshiped by a husband, Rose had come to think far too much of her own importance as Mrs. Rose Mather,—*née* Miss Rose Carleton, of Boston, an acknowledged belle, and leader of the *ton*.

There was a wide difference between Rose and Annie Graham, for while the latter, in her sweet unselfishness, thought only of her husband's welfare, both here and hereafter, Rose's first impulse was a dread shrinking from being alone, and her second a terror lest the years of her youth, now spread out so invitingly before her, should be passed in secluded widowhood, with nothing from the gay world without wherewith to feed her vanity and love for admiration. Still, beneath Rose's light exterior there was hidden a mine of tenderness and love, a heart which, when roused to action, was capable of greater, more heroic deeds, than would at first seem possible. And that heart was rousing, too,—was gradually waking into life; but not all at once, and the tears which Rose shed the whole night through were wrung out more from selfishness, perhaps, than from any higher feeling. It would be so stupid living there alone in Rockland. If she could only go to Washington with Will it would not be half so bad, but she could not, for she waked Will up from a sound sleep to ask him if she might, and he had answered "*No*," falling away again to sleep, and leaving Rose to wakefulness and tears, unmingled with any prayer that the cloud gathering so fast around her might sometime break in blessings on her head.

It was scarcely light next morning when Rose, determining to prevail, redoubled her entreaties for her husband to abandon the decision be now candidly acknowledged, but she could not. He was going to the war, and going as a private. Rose almost fainted when he told her this, and for a time refused to be comforted. She might learn to bear it, she said, if he were an officer, but to go as a common soldier, like those she worked for at the Hall, was more than she could bear.

It was in vain that Mr. Mather told her how only a few could be officers, and that he was content to serve his country in any capacity, leaving the more lucrative situations to those who needed them more. He did not tell her he had declined a post of honor, for the sake of one who seemed to him more worthy of it. He would rather this should reach her from some other source, and ere the day was over it did, for in a small town like Rockland it did not take long for every other one to know that William Mather had enlisted as a private soldier, when he might have been *Colonel* of a regiment, had he not given place to another because that other had depending on him a bed-ridden mother, a crazy wife, and six little helpless children.

How fast William Mather rose in the estimation of those who, never having known him intimately, had looked upon him as a cold, haughty man, whose loyalty was somewhat doubtful, and how proud Rose felt, even in the midst of her tears, as she heard on every side her husband's praise. Even the Widow Simms ventured to the Mather mansion, telling her how glad she was, and offering to do what she could for the volunteer, while Annie, unable to do anything for herself, could only pray that God would bring Mr. Mather back safely to the child-wife, who was so bowed down with grief. How Annie longed to see her,—and, if possible, impart to her some portion of the hopeful trust which kept her own soul from fainting beneath its burden of anxious uncertainty. But the days passed on, and Rose came no more to the cottage in the Hollow. Love for her husband had triumphed over every other feeling, and rousing from her state of inertness, she busied herself in doing, or rather trying to do, a thousand little things which she fancied might add to *Willie's* comfort. She called him *Willie* now, as if that name were dearer, tenderer than *Will*, and the strong man, every time he heard it, felt a sore pang,—there was something so plaintive in the tone, as if she were speaking of the dead.

It was a most beautiful summer day, when at last he left her, and Rose's heart was well nigh bursting with its load of pain. It was all in vain that she said her usual form of prayer, never more meaningless than now when her thoughts were so wholly absorbed with something else. She did not pray in faith, but because it was a habit of her childhood, a something she rarely omitted, unless in too great a hurry. No wonder then that she rose up from her devotion quite as grief-stricken as when she first knelt down. God does not often answer what is mere lip service, and Rose was yet a stranger to the prayer which stirs the heart and carries power with it. The parting was terrible, and Mr. Mather more than half repented when he saw how tightly she clung to his neck, begging him to take her with him, or at least to send for her very soon.

"What shall I do when you are gone? What can I do?" she sobbed, and her husband answered:

"You can work for me, darling,—work for all the soldiers. It will help divert your mind."

"I can't I can't," was Rose's answer. "I don't know how to work. Oh, Willie, Willie! I wish there wasn't any war.

Willie wished so too, but there was no time now for regrets, for a rumbling in the distance and a rising wreath of smoke on the western plain warned him not to tarry longer if he would go that day. One more burning kiss,—one more fond pressure of the wife he loved so much,—a few more whispered words of hope, and then another Rockland volunteer had gone. Gone without daring to look backward to the little form lying just the same as he had put it from him, and yet not just the same. He had felt it quivering with anguish when he took his arms away, but the trembling, quivering motion was over now, and the form he had caressed lay motionless and still, all unconscious of the dreary pain throbbing in the heart, and all unmindful of the loud hurrah which greeted William Mather, as he stepped upon the platform of the car and waved his hat to those assembled there to see him off. Rose, who had meant at the very last to be so heroic, so brave, so worthy the wife of a soldier, had fainted.

CHAPTER V.
JIMMIE.

There were loving words being breathed into Rose's ear, when she came back to consciousness, and there was something familiar in the touch of the hand bathing her brow, and smoothing her tangled hair, but Rose was too weak and sick to notice who it was caring for her so tenderly, until she heard the voice saying to her

"Is my daughter better?"

And then she threw herself with a wild scream of joy into the arms which had cradled her babyhood, sobbing piteously:

"Oh, mother, mother, Willie has gone to the war! Willie has gone to the war!"

It was very strange, Rose thought, that her mother's tears should flow so fast, and her face wear so sad an expression just because of Will, who was nothing but her son-in-law. Then it occurred to her that Tom might be the occasion of her sadness, but when she spoke of him, asking why her mother had not prevailed on him to stay at home, Mrs. Carleton answered, promptly:

"I never loved him one half so well, as on that night when he told me he had volunteered. He would be unworthy of the Carleton blood he bears, were he to hesitate a moment!" and the eye of the brave New England matron kindled as she added: "If I had twenty sons, I would rather all should die on the Federal battle-field than have one turn traitor to his country! Oh, *Jimmie, Jimmie*, my poor misguided boy!"

It was a piteous cry which came from the depths of that mother's aching heart,—a cry so full of anguish that Rose was startled, and asked in much alarm what it was about Jimmie. Had she heard from him, and was he really dead?

"No, Rose," and in the mother's voice there was a hard, bitter tone. "No, not dead, but better so, than what he is. Oh, I would so much rather he had died when a little, innocent child, than live to bear the name he bears!"

"What name, mother? What has Jimmie done? Do tell me, you frighten me, you look so white!" and Rose clung closer to her mother, who, with quivering lip and faltering voice, told her how recreant runaway Jimmie had joined the Confederate army under Beauregard, and was probably then marching on to Washington to meet her other son, in deadly conflict, it might be; his hand, the very one, perhaps, to speed the fratricidal bullet which should shed a brother's life-blood!

No wonder that her heart grew faint when she thought of her boy as a *Rebel*,—aye, a rebel of ten times deeper dye than if he had been born of

Southern blood, and reared on Southern soil, for the roof-tree which sheltered his childhood was almost beneath the shadow of Bunker Hill's monument, and many an hour had he sported at its base, playing directly above the graves of those brave men who fell that awful day when the fierce thunders of war shook the hills of Boston, and echoed across the smoky waters of the bay. Far up the lofty tower, too, as high as he could reach, his name was written with his own boyish hand, and the mother had read it there since receiving the shameful letter which told of his disgrace. Climbing up the weary, winding flight of stairs, she had looked through blinding tears upon that name,—JAMES MADISON CARLETON,—half hoping it had been erased, it seemed so like a mockery to have it there on Freedom's Monument, and know that he who bore it was a traitor to his country. Yet there it was, just as he left it years ago, and with a blush of shame the mother crossed it out, just as she fain would have crossed out his sin could that have been. But it could not. She knew that Jimmie was in the Southern army, and not wishing to speak of it at home, where he already bore no envied name, she had come for sympathy to her only daughter; and it was well for both she did, for it helped to divert Rose's grief into a new and different channel; to set her right on many points, and gradually to obliterate all marks of what so he had called Secession.

Tom had been her pride; the brother she honored and feared, while Jimmie, nearer her age, was more a companion of her childhood; the one who teased and petted her by turns, one day putting angle worms in her bosom just to hear her scream, and the next spending all his pocket-money to buy her the huge wax doll she saw in the shop window, down on Washington street, and coveted so badly. Such were some of Rose's reminiscences of Jimmie, and while time had softened down the horrid sensations she experienced when she felt the cold worms crawling on her neck, it had not destroyed the *doll*, the handsomest she had ever owned, nor made her cease to love the teasing boy. She could not feel just as her mother did about him, for she had not her mother's strong, patriotic feeling, but her tears flowed none the less, while she, too, half wished him lying beneath the summer grass, in beautiful Mt. Auburn.

"How did you hear from him?" she asked, when her first burst of grief was over, and her mother replied by taking out a letter, on which Rose recognized her brother's handwriting.

"He sent me this," Mrs. Carleton said, and tearing open the letter, she read it aloud to Rose.

"RICHMOND, VA., *June, 1861.*

"DEAR MOTHER: Pray don't think you've seen a ghost when you recognize my writing. You thought me dead, I suppose, but there's no such good news as that. I'm bullet-proof, I reckon, or I should have died in New Orleans last summer when the yellow fever and I had such a squabble. I was dreadfully sick then, and half wished I had not run away, for I knew you would feel badly when you heard how I died with nobody to care for me, and was tumbled into the ground, head sticking out as likely as any way. I used to talk about you, old Martha said, and about Rose, too. Dear little Rose. I actually laid down my pen just now, and laughed aloud as I thought how she looked when I treated her to those worms; telling her I had a necklace for her! Didn't she dance and didn't Tom thrash me, too, till I saw stars! Well, he never struck me a blow amiss, though I used to think he did. I was a sorry scamp, mother,—the biggest rascal in Boston. But I've reformed. I have, upon my word, and you ought to see how the people here smile upon and flatter me, telling me what a nice chap I am, and all that sort of thing.

"In short, mother, to come at once to the point, and not spend an hour in arguing, as Tom used to do when he took me up in the attic where he kept the *gads*, you know,—in short, I've been naturalized,—have sworn allegiance to the future Southern monarchy, and am as true a Southern blood as you would wish to see. I've got a Palmetto cockade on my cap,—a tiny Confederate flag on my sleeve, and what is best of all, I've joined the Southern army under Beauregard, and shall shortly bring the war to the threshold of the Capitol, licking the Yankees there congregated like fun. It's about time now, mother, for you to ring for Margaret. You'll want the camphor, and make a fuss, of course, so while you are enjoying that diversion, I'll go and practice a little with my gun. You know I could never hit a barn without shooting twice, but I'm improving fast, and shall soon be able to pick off a Yankee at a distance of a mile!

"*2 o'clock*, P.M.

"Well, mother, I take it for granted you are nicely tucked up in bed, with the curtains drawn and a wet rag on your head, as the result of what I've told you. I'm sorry that you should feel so badly, and wish I could see you for an hour or so, as I could surely convince you we are right. We have been browbeaten and trodden upon by the North until forbearance has ceased to be a virtue, and now that they've thrown down the gauntlet we will meet them on their own terms. I dare say they have made you believe that we struck the first blow by firing into Sumter, but, mother, those northern papers do lie so, all except the *Herald*, and a few others, which occasionally come within a mile of the truth, but even they have been bribed recently, or something. If you want the unbiased truth of the matter subscribe for the Richmond *Examiner*, or better yet, the Charleston *Mercury*, whose editor is a

New England man, and of course is capable of judging right. He knows what has brought on this war. He'll tell you how the South Carolinians generously bore the insult of the Federal flag flying there defiantly in their faces until they could bear it no longer, and so one day we pitched in.

"I say *we*, for I was there in Fort Moultrie, and saw the fight, but did not join, for the brave fellows, out of compliment to my having been born near Bunker Hill, said I needn't, so I mounted a cotton bale and looked on, feeling, I'll admit, some as I used to on the Fourth of July, when I saw how noble old Sumter played her part. And once, when a shell burst within ten feet of me, turning things generally topsy turvy, and blowing shirt sleeves and coat sleeves, and waistbands and boots, higher than a kite, I was positively guilty of hurrahing for the Stars and Stripes. I couldn't help it, to save me.

And yet, mother, I believe the North wrong,—and the South right, but so generous a people are we, that all we ask now, is for you to *let us alone*; and if the Lincolnites won't do that, why, then we must stoop to fight the mudsills. It's all humbug, too, about the negroes being on the verge of insurrection. A more faithful, devoted set, I never saw. They'll fight for their masters until they die, every man of them. Tom will tell you that. What are his politics? Bell and Everett, I dare say, so there's no danger of my meeting him in battle, and I'm glad of it, for to tell the truth, I should feel rather ticklish raising my gun against old Tom. May be, though, he is humbugged like the rest, and forms a part of that unit said to exist at the North. What sort of a thing is that, mother? What does it look like? Democrats and Republicans, Abolitionists and Garrisonites, all melted in one crucible and bearing *Abraham's* image and superscription! I wish I could see it. Must have changed mightily round Boston from what they used to be when they quarreled so, some against and some for Southern rights and Southern people. But strange things happen nowadays, and it may be Tom, too, has turned his coat, and taken sides with the Federals. If so, all I can say, is, Tommie, oh, Tommie, beware of the day, when Southern bloods meet thee in battle array; for a field of weak cowards rushes full on my sight, and the ranks of the Yankees are scattered in flight. Won't we rout them, though! I shall fight next time. I've played pollywog long enough. I am regularly enlisted now. Am a *Rebel*, as you call us at home. Nothing very bad about that, either, as I can prove to you, if you'll take the trouble to hunt up my old dog-eared History of the United States, where Washington is styled by the British the *Rebel Chief*.

"The South are only doing what the Thirteen did in '76, trying to shake off the tyrant's yoke. It's the same thing precisely, only the shoe is on the other foot, and pinches mightily. We did not at first intend to subjugate the North, but maybe they'll provoke us to do it, if they keep on. Now, however, we only want, or rather did want a peaceable separation, and you may as well yield to it first as last. What do you intend doing with us, any way, suppose you succeed in licking us? Hold us as a conquered province, just as England holds Ireland? Much good that will do you. It will be some like keeping a mad dog chained so tightly that he cannot get away, but is none the less snappish and non-come-at-able for that. No, no, acknowledge our independence, and call home the chaps you have dragged from Poor Houses and State Prisons, lanes and ditches, and sent to fight against Southern gentlemen. This, to me, is the most humiliating feature of the whole; and if I must be *shot* or taken prisoner, I hope it will be by some one worthy of my steel. This last I'm writing for old Tom's benefit. Give him my compliments, and tell him nothing would please me more than to welcome him to our camp some day.

"Dear little Rose,—perhaps she would not let a Rebel kiss her, and I don't know but I'd turn Federal for half an hour or so for the sake of tasting her sweet lips once more. I do love Rose, and I feel a mysterious lump in my throat every time I look at her picture, taken just before I left home. I never show it, for somehow it would seem like profanation to have the soldiers staring at it. So I wear it next my heart, and when I go into battle I shall keep it there. Perhaps it will save my life, who knows?

"I am getting tired, and must close ere long. Now, mother, please don't waste too many tears over me. The time will come when you'll see we are right; and if it will be any consolation, I will say in conclusion, that I have written a heap worse than I really believe. I am not a fool. I understand exactly how the matter stands, but I like the Southern side the best. I think they are just as near right as the North, and I'm going to stick to them through thick and thin. We shall have a battle before long, and this may be the last time I'll ever write to you. I've been a bad boy, mother, and troubled you so much, but if I'm shot you will forget all that, and only remember how, with all my faults, I loved you still,—you and Tom and little Rose,—more than you ever guessed.

"By the way, I believe I'll send you a lock of my hair, cut just over my left ear, where you used to think it curled so nicely. Perhaps it will enhance its value if you know I severed it with a bowie knife, such as I now carry with me. Tell Rose I'll send her a calico dress by and by. It will be the most costly present I can make her if the blockade is carried out, but it won't be; that old Bull across the sea will be goring you with his horns first you know. Then you'll have a sweet time up there, beset before and behind, and possibly annexed to Canada. But I don't want to make you feel any bluer than you are probably feeling, so good-bye, good-bye.

"Your affectionate Rebel,

"James M. Carleton."

"P. S.—I shall send this to Washington by a chap who is going to desert, you know, and join the Federals with a pitiful story about having been pressed into the Rebel service, telling them, too, how poor and weak and demoralized we are,—how a handful of troops can lick us, and so draw them into our web, as a spider tempts a fly, don't you see? They offered me that honor, knowing that a son of George Carleton, twice M. C. from Massachusetts, and now defunct, would be above suspicion, and would thus gather a heap of items. But hang me, if I could turn spy on any terms. So I respectfully declined. You see I am quite a somebody, owing to my having had sense enough to wait until I was twenty-one, ere I ran away, and so bringing a part of my property with me. Money makes the mare go here as elsewhere, but I'm about running out. I wish you could send me a few thousand, can't you?"

And this was Jimmie's letter, over which the mother had wept far bitterer tears than any she shed when her eldest born bade her his last farewell, giving to her, just as Jimmie had done, a lock of his brown hair. She had it with her now, and she laid them both on Rose's hand,—the dark brown lock, and the short black silken curl, which twined itself around Rose's finger, as if it loved the snowy resting-place. Rose's first impulse was to shake it off as if it had been a guilty thing; but the sight of it recalled so vividly the handsome, saucy face, and laughing, mischievous black eyes it once had helped to shade, that she pressed it to her lips, and whispered sadly, "Dear Jimmie, I cannot hate him if I try, nor see how he is greatly at fault," while in her heart was the unframed prayer that God would care for the Rebel-boy, and bring him back to them.

Mrs. Carleton was proud of her family name,—proud of her family pride,—and she shrank from having it known how it had been disgraced, so after Rose's first grief was over she bade her keep it a secret, and Rose promised readily, never doubting for a moment her ability to do so. Rose had already borne much that morning. Excessive weeping for her husband, added to what she had heard of Jimmie, took her strength away, and she spent that first weary day in bed, sometimes sobbing bitterly as the dread reality came over her that *Will* was really gone, and again starting up from a feverish, broken sleep with the idea that it was all a dream, or a horrid nightmare, from which she should at last awake. Callers were all excluded, and with a delicious feeling that she was not to be disturbed, Rose, late in the afternoon, lay watching the western sunlight dancing on the wall, when a step upon the stairs was heard, and in a moment Widow Simms appeared, her sharp face softening into an expression of genuine pity when she saw how white and wan Rose was looking.

"They tried to keep me out," she said, "that brawny cook of yours and that filigree waiting-maid, but I would come up, and here I am."

Then sitting down by Rose she told her Annie had sent her there. "She's sorry for you," the widow said, "and she sent this to tell you so," and the widow handed Rose a tiny note, written by Annie Graham. Once Rose would have resented the act as implying too much familiarity, but her heart was greatly softened, while, had she tried her best, she could not have regarded Annie Graham in the light of an inferior. Tearing open the envelope she read:

"MY DEAR MRS. MATHER—I am sure you will pardon the liberty I am taking. My apology is that I feel so deeply for you, for I understand just what you are suffering,—understand how wearily the hours drag on, knowing as you do that with the waning daylight *his* step will not be heard just by the door, making in your heart little throbs of joy, such as no other step can make. I am so sorry for you, and I had hoped you at least might be spared, but God in his wisdom has seen fit to order it otherwise, and we know that what He does is right. Still it is hard to bear,—harder for you than for me, perhaps, and when this morning I heard the car signal given, I knelt just where I did when my own husband went away, and asked our Heavenly Father to bring your Willie back in safety, and, Mrs. Mather, I am sure He will, for I felt, even then, an answer to my prayer,—something which said, 'It shall be as you ask.'

"Dear Mrs. Mather, try to be comforted; try to see the brighter side; try to pray, and be sure the darkness now enveloping you so like a pall will pass away, and the sunshine be the brighter for the cloud. Come and see me when you feel like it, and remember, you have at least two friends who pray for you, one at the Father's right hand in Heaven, and one in her cottage in the Hollow.

"ANNIE GRAHAM."

Rose had not wept more passionately than she did now, as she kissed the note, and wished she were one half as good as Annie Graham.

"But I am not," she said, "and never shall be. Tell her to keep praying until Will comes home again."

"I will tell her," returned the widow, "but wouldn't it be well enough to try what you can do at it yourself, and not leave it all for her?"

"Try what I can do at praying?" Rose exclaimed. "I can't do anything, only the few words I always say at night, and they have nothing in them about Will."

"Brought up like a heathen!" muttered the widow, feeling within herself that to the names of her own sons and Captain Carleton, William Mather's must now be added, when, as was her daily custom, she took her troubles to One who has said, "Cast your burdens upon the Lord, for He careth for you."

"We'll both remember your husband, Miss Graham and I, so don't fret yourself to death," she said, soothingly, as Rose broke into a fresh burst of tears.

"It isn't him so much," Rose sobbed, "though that is terrible and will kill me, I most know, but there's something else that ails me a great deal worse than that; at least, mother has made me think it is, though I can't quite see how having one's brother join the Rebel army is so very bad."

Rose forgot her promise of secrecy, just as her mother might have known she would. The story of the Carleton disgrace was told, and perfectly aghast, the horrified widow listened to it.

"Your brother a rebel?" she almost shrieked, "a good-for-nothing, ill-begotten rebel! I thought you said he was a captain of a company;" and mentally the widow struck from her list of names that of poor, scandalized Tom, that very moment perspiring at every pore as he went through with his evening drill within the Federal camp.

"No, no," Rose cried, vehemently, "not Tom; I have another brother, a younger one,—Jimmie we call him. Did you never hear of Jimmie, who ran away more than a year ago?"

"Never!" and the staunch patriot of a widow pursed up her thin lips with an expression which plainly said the Carleton family had fallen greatly in her estimation, in spite of all Tom had said of Isaac.

Rose, however, was not good at reading expressions, and taking it for granted the widow wanted to hear all about it, she told her what she knew, marvelling much at the rigid silence her auditor maintained.

"Isn't it shameful?" she asked, when she had finished.

"Shameful? Yes. I hope he'll be catched and hung higher than Haman. I'll furnish rope to hang him!" was the indignant widow's reply, and ere Rose could quite make out what ailed her, she had said good-afternoon, and banging the door behind her, was hurrying off, muttering to herself, "Somethin' wrong in their bringin' up. Needn't tell me. I'd like to see my boys turnin' traitor! The rascal!" and as by this time the widow had reached the shop where she was to stop for burning-fluid, she turned into the little store, and catching up the can with a jerk, spilt a part of its contents upon her clean gingham dress, and then hurried off again with rapid strides toward the cottage in the Hollow.

The Carletons, Tom and all, were below par in her opinion, and kept sinking lower and lower, until she reached the cottage, where she gave vent to her wrath as follows:

"A pretty how d'ye do up to *Miss Martherses*. Her brother *Jim* has jined the cowardly, sneakin', low-lived, contemptible Rebels, and is comin' on to take Washington! The scalliwag! If things go on at this rate, I'll jine the army myself, and tar and feather every one on 'em! Needn't tell me."

Annie was no lover of gossip, and knowing that the widow was terribly excited, she made no reply except to pass her a letter bearing the Washington postmark. This had the desired effect, and utterly oblivious of Jimmie, the widow tore open *Isaac's* letter, in which he spoke of Captain Carleton as being very kind to him, and very popular with the soldiers.

"I would fight for him till the very last," Isaac wrote; "he has been so good to me, always noticing me with a bow when he comes into our regiment, as he sometimes does, and when he can, speaking to me a pleasant word. He knows I sawed his sister's wood, for I told him so. It seemed so mean-like to be passing myself off for better than I am, and you know a soldier's dress does improve a chap mightily, giving him kind of a dandy air. Why, even Harry Baker and Bill look like gentlemen, though Harry gets drunk awfully, and has been in the guard-house twice, But, as I was saying, Captain Carleton didn't appear to think a bit less of me, though he struck me on the shoulder, and laughed kind of queer when I said why I told him I sawed Mrs. Mather's wood, and the next day I saw him talking with our colonel, and heard something about sergeant, and *Isaac Simms*, and 'too young to be expedient.' Then, when I met him again, he asked me wasn't I twenty-one, in such a way that I knew he wanted me to tell him yes; but, mother, I thought of that prayer we said together, the morning I came away, 'Lead us not into temptation,' and I couldn't tell a lie, though the answer stuck in my throat and choked me so, but I out with it at last. I said, 'No, sir, I was only eighteen last Thanksgiving,' and then his face had the same look it wore when I told him I was a wood-sawyer. 'And so I suppose you'll be nineteen next Thanksgiving' he said, adding 'You don't know what you lost by telling the truth so frankly, but the moral gain is much greater than the loss. You are a brave boy, Isaac Simms, and worthy of being a second George Washington.' I do like him so much! Can't you send him something, mother, if it's nothing more than the nice cough-candy you used to make, or some of that poke-ointment? I notice he coughs occasionally, and I heard him say his feet were sore. I'd like to give him something, just to see his handsome white teeth when he laughed, and said 'Thank you, my boy.' Oh, I would almost die for Captain Carleton."

Surely, after reading this, the widow could feel no more animosity against the Carletons, on account of Jimmie's sin.

"Every family must have a black sheep," she said to Annie, though where hers was she could not tell. It surely was not John, nor Eli, nor Isaac, so she guessed it must have been the girl baby that died before 'twas born, and for whom she shed so many tears. She shouldn't do it again, she'd bet, for if it had lived, it would most likely have cut up some rusty or other, just as Jim Carleton had,—married *Bill Baker*, like as not; and with this consolatory reflection, the widow took up Isaac's letter for a second time, resolving in her own mind that she would send that Captain Carleton something if she set up nights to make it.

"I'm glad my boy didn't tell a lie," she whispered softly to herself, as she came again to that part of the letter, poor, weak human nature creeping in with the same thought, and suggesting how grand it would be to have him "Sergeant Simms, with the increased wages per month it would have brought." This was the old Adam counselling within her, while the new Adam said, "Better never to be promoted than lose his integrity," and with a silent prayer for the boy who would not tell a lie, the widow folded up the letter, and then repeated to Annie the particulars of Jimmie Carleton in a much milder manner than she would have done an hour before. So much good little acts of kindness do, stretching on link after link, until they reach a point from which they recoil in blessings on the doer's head. Thus Captain Carleton's friendly words to Isaac Simms were the direct means of saving his mother and sister from the bitter prejudice the Rockland people, in their then excitable state, might have felt toward them, had Widow Simms told the story of Jimmie in the spirit she surely would have told it, had it not been for Isaac's timely letter. This, together with a little judicious caution from Annie, changed her tactics, and though she, that very night, had several opportunities for telling how "Miss Martherses brother was a rebel, and that Miss Marthers couldn't see the mighty harm in it if he was," she kept it to herself, speaking only of the noble Tom, so kind to her boy Isaac.

CHAPTER VI.
FINDING SOMETHING TO DO FOR THE WAR.

The next morning the Mather carriage, containing both Mrs. Carleton and Rose, drove down the Hollow, and stopped in front of Annie's gate. Mrs. Carleton's business was with Widow Simms, who was mixing bread in the kitchen, and who experienced considerable trepidation when told "the grand Boston lady" had asked for her.

"I'm pesky glad I hain't tattled about Jim," she thought, as washing the flour from her hands and hooking her sleeves at the wrist she entered the sitting-room, and with a low courtesy, waited to hear the lady's errand.

Mrs. Carleton had come with a request that the widow should not repeat what Rose had so heedlessly told her the previous night.

"You may think it strange that I care so much," Mrs. Carleton said, "and until you are placed in similar circumstances you cannot understand how I shrink from having it known that my son could fall so low, or do so great injustice to his early training."

If the widow had possessed one particle of prejudice against the Carletons, this would have disarmed her entirely, but she did not. Isaac's letter had swept that all away, and she replied that "Jimmie's secret was as safe with her as if locked up in an iron chest."

"I did feel blazin' mad at you, though, for a spell," she said, "for I thought you might have brung him up better; but this cured me entirely," and she handed Isaac's letter to Rose, bidding her read it aloud.

"Noble boy. You must be proud of him," was Mrs. Carleton's comment, while Rose, ever impulsive, seized upon a new idea.

It would be so nice for the Rockland ladies to fit up a box of things and send to Company R, reserving a corner for Tom and Will. She should do it, anyway, on her own responsibility, if nobody chose to help her, and she whispered to Annie that George should have a large share of the delicacies she would provide.

"You may send that candy to Tom, if you choose," she said to the widow, "though I think cod liver oil would be better. And the ointment too,—only it mustn't sit near my preserves, for fear the two will get mixed."

Rose had found something to do, and so absorbed was she in a plan which every one approved, that she forgot to cry *all* the time for *Will*, as she had fully intended doing. Up the streets and down she went, sometimes walking, sometimes riding, but always in a flurry, always excited, now tumbling over dry-goods boxes in quest of one large enough to hold the many articles preparing in Rockland for the then ill-fed, suffering soldiers of the 13th Regiment, now up at the express office, bargaining about the expense, which she meant to bear herself, and now down at the Hall, adroitly smoothing over little bickerings frequently arising among the ladies assembled there, concerning the articles sent in, some declaring the fried apple pies brought by Mrs. Baker should not go, nor yet the round balls of Dutch cheese she had saved sour milk two weeks to make, just because "Billy relished it so much, 'long with apple turnovers."

Poor old Mrs. Baker! It was the best she could do, and when Rose saw how the tears came at the prospect of Billy's losing the feast she had prepared with so much care, she declared the cheese should go if she had to send it in a separate box. It was just so with the widow's poke ointment, some of the ladies wondering what next would be brought in and what it could be for. Rose knew exactly what 'twas for; Tom had corns, and the despised salve was for him, so that should go if nothing else. But when Susan Ruggles Simms, her thoughts intent on *John*, brought in a round of roasted veal, which her mother-in-law said would be in a most lively condition by the time it reached Washington, Rose, after suggesting that it be packed in ice and put in a refrigerator, yielded for once, and persuaded the girl-wife to carry home her veal, which would most surely be spoiled ere John came to see it.

"You can write him a nice long letter," she said, when she saw how disappointed Susan looked. "You can tell him your intentions were good until we old experienced married ladies persuaded you out of them."

So Susan, with a sigh, carried back her nice stuffed roast, the widow muttering in an aside tone, "That's all them shiftless Ruggleses know! Might as well send *maggits* and done with it."

It was a strange medley that huge box contained, for every member of Company R was remembered, thanks to the indefatigable Rose, who procured a list of the names, and when she found any without friends in that immediate vicinity, she supplied the deficiency from her own store of luxuries. Of course *Will* and *Tom* fared the best, while next to them came Lieutenant Graham and Isaac Simms, Rose writing a tiny note to the latter, telling him how much she liked him for speaking so of Tom, and sending him a pair of her fine linen sheets, because she couldn't think of anything else, and thought these would be cool to sleep in on hot summer nights. Dear little Rose! how fast she grew in popularity, the people wondering they had never seen before how good she was, and imputing some portion of her present interest to the presence of her mother, who had made arrangements to remain for an indefinite length of time in Rockland, and who, far less demonstrative than her active daughter, did much by her sensible advice to keep the wheel in motion, and Rose from overdoing the matter so zealously taken in hand.

The box was packed at last;—every chink and crevice was full. Mrs. Baker's Dutch cheese and fried apple pies were there, wrapped by Rose Mather in innumerable folds of paper, tied around with yards of the strongest twine she could find, and safely stowed away where they could not be harmed; Widow Simms's ointment too, and the candy she had made, occupied a corner, together with her daguerreotype sent to *Isaac*, and a letter to Captain Carleton. That letter was a mammoth undertaking, but the widow felt it her duty to write it, groaning and sweating, and consulting Perry's old leathern-bound dictionary for every word of which she felt at all uncertain, and driving poor Annie nearly distracted with asking "if this were grammar, and if that were too lovin' like, for a widder to send a widower." Not a little amused, Annie gave the required advice, smiling in spite of herself, as she read the note the widow handed her, and which ran as follows:

"MY DEAR MR. CAPTIN CARLETON:—I can't help puttin' *dear* before your name, you seem so nigh to me since Isaac told how kind you was to him. I'm nothin' but a shrivelled, dried up widder, fifty odd years old, but I've got a mother's heart big enough to take you in with my other boys. I know you are a nice, clever man, but whether you're a *good* one, as I call good, I don't know, though bein' you come from Boston I'm afraid you're a Unitarian, and I'll never quit prayin' for you till I know. That's about all I can do, for I'm poor a'most as Job's turkey; but if there's any shirts or trouses, or the like o' that wants makin', let me know, for I don't believe your mother or sister is great at sewin'. Mrs. Marthers ain't, I know, though as nice a little body as ever drawed the breath. Your wife is dead, too, they say, and that comes hard agin. I know just how that feels, for my man died eighteen years ago last October, a few weeks before Isaac was born.

"I send you some 'intment for your feet, and some bits of linen rags to bind round your toes; also, some red pepper candy, and my likeness to Isaac. He'll let you see it if you want to. It don't 'pear to me that my eyes is as dull as that, or my lips so puckered up, but we can't see as others see us, and I ain't an atom proud. Heaven bless you for being kind to Isaac, and if an old woman's prayers and blessin's is of any use, you may be sure you have mine. If you come to battle, be so good as to oversee him, won't you, and git him put way back, if you can. Excuse haste and a bad pen.

"Yours with regret,

"MRS. BELINDA SIMMS,"

This was the widow's letter, sent with Tom's parcel to Washington, where the box was greeted by the company with exclamations of joy, and could those who sent it have seen the eager, happy faces of each one as he found he was remembered, they would have felt doubly repaid for all the trouble and annoyance it had cost them. Only one growl of dissatisfaction was heard, and that from Harry Baker, who, with a muttered oath, exclaimed, as he undid his paper parcel,

"Apple turnovers, by jing! Sourer than swill, and mouldier than the rot. Halloo, Bill, got some too, I see. What in fury is this? *Dutch cheese*, as I'm alive. Make good bullets for Secesh, so here goes!" and the next moment there whizzed through the air the cheese poor old Mrs. Baker had found so hard to smuggle in. The apple pies followed next, and then the reckless Harry amused himself with jeering at Bill, who, after carefully stowing away in his pocket, the large, strong twine Rose Mather had bound around the paper parcel, seated himself upon the ground, and was munching away at his pie, not because he liked it, but because his mother had sent it, and Billy's mother was dearer to him now than when he was at home.

Meanwhile, in another part of the camp, Tom Carleton was opening his parcel, while around him stood a group of officers, some his personal friends whom he had known in Boston.

"There must be some mistake," he said, as he daubed his white fingers with the sticky candy. But Rose had packed his things in a separate box, and directed it herself. There could be no mistake, and he continued his investigations, coming next upon the widow's picture, which Rose had carelessly placed in his parcel.

It would be impossible to describe Tom's look of amazement and perplexity, as his eye fell upon the face which looked out upon him from its glass covering. Precise, puckered, and prim, with a decided best-clothes air. Who could it be? Tom asked this question aloud, while his companions laughingly declared it some lady love he had left behind, suggesting at last that he read the note which lay just beneath it, as that might explain the mystery. So Tom did read it, with a fellow-officer looking over his shoulder, and reading too. But there was too much of the anxious, genuine mother-tone about that letter to cause more than three or four hearty laughs at the expense of Tom and the widow. Tom knew now for whom the picture was intended, and he carried it to Isaac, but it was many a day ere Tom Carleton heard the last of *Mrs. Belinda Simms!*

Numerous were the thanks sent by Company R to Rose for her kind thoughtfulness in setting afloat a plan which brought them so much good, and Rose, as she received the messages, wished it was all to be done again, and wondered what she could find to do next. One of Will's letters told her at last what to do. She could be kind to the soldiers, if there were any in Rockland. She could visit their families, speak to them words of comfort, and supply, if needful, their necessities. This was just what suited her, and she commenced her task with a right good will, startling many an awkward youth wearing a soldier's dress, by accosting him in the street, inquiring into his history, and frequently ending the interview by offering him her soft white hand, and leaving in his rougher one a piece of money, which affected him less than the brightness of the brilliant eyes he remembered long after the silver was spent. Every soldier's wife and every soldier's mother was looked after, and the Mather carriage was oftener seen in the muddy Hollow and by lanes in Rockland, than at the gates of more pretentious dwellings. Harry's mother and Bill's, and others of her standing, blessed the little lady, for the sunshine brought so often to their squalid homes, while Annie and Widow Simms prayed from a full heart that no evil should befall the husband or the brother of the heroic Rose.

CHAPTER VII.
THE BATTLE.

Brightly, beautifully the Sabbath morning broke over all the hills of the Northland, covering them with floods of rosy light, burnishing the forest trees with sheens of gold, and cresting each tall spire with colors which seemed born of Paradise, so radiantly bright they looked, flashing from their lofty resting-place, and glancing off across the valleys where the fields of waving corn and summer wheat were growing. To the westward, too, where prairie on prairie stretches on into almost interminable space, the same July sun was shining, as quietly, as peacefully, as if in the hearts of men there burned no bitter feeling of fierce and vindictive hate,—no thirsting for each other's blood. Oh, how calm, how still it was that Sunday morning both east, and north and west, and as the sun rose higher in the heavens, how soothingly the bells rang out their musical chimes. From New England's templed hills to the far-off shores of Oregon, the echoes rose and fell, ceasing only when ceased the tramp of the many feet hastening up to worship God in his appointed way. Old and young, rich and poor, father and mother, sister and brother, husband and wife, assembling together to keep the holy day, that best day of the seven, praying not so much for their own sins forgiven as for the loved ones gone to war,—the dear ones far away,—and little, little dreaming as they prayed, how the same sun stealing so softly up the church's aisle, and shining on the church's wall, was even then looking down on a far different scene,—a scene of carnage, blood and death. For, off to the southward, near where the waters of the Potomac ripple past the grave of our nation's hero, another concourse of people was gathered together; their Sunday bell the cannon's roar; their Sunday hymn the battle-cry.

Long before the earliest robin had trilled its matin song, they had been on the move, their bristling bayonets glittering in the brilliant moonlight like the December frost, as with regular, even tread they kept on their winding way, knowing not if the pale stars watching their course so pityingly, as it were, would ever shine on them again. Onward,—onward,—onward still they pressed; over the hills, through the ravines, down the valleys, across the fields, till the same sun which shone so softly on their distant homes rose also over the *Federal Fly*, as it has been aptly termed, moving onward to the *Web* which lay beyond, so well concealed and so devoid of sound that none could guess that the treacherous woods, wearing so cool, so inviting a look, were sheltering a mighty, expectant host, watching as eagerly for the advancing foe as ever ambushed spider waited for its deluded prey. Backward,—backward, stretched the Confederate army, line after line, rank after rank, battalion after battalion, until in numbers it more than quadrupled that handful of men steadily moving on. From out their leafy covert the enemy peered, exulting that the fortunes of the great Republic, their whilom mother, were so surely within their power, and pausing for a time in sheer wantonness, just as a kitten sports with the mouse she has already captured, and knows cannot escape. Onward,—onward,—onward swept the Federal troops; their polished arms and glittering uniforms flashing in the morning sunlight just as the flag for which they fought waved in the morning breeze. They were weary and worn, and their lips were parched with feverish thirst, for hours had passed since they had tasted food or water. But not for this did they tarry; there was no faltering in their ranks, no faintly beating heart, no wild yearning to be away, no timid shrinking from what the woods, now just before them, might hold in store, and when the whisper ran along the lines that the enemy was in view, there was nought felt save joy, that the long suspense was ended and the fray about to commence.

There was a halt in the front ranks, and while they stand there thus, let us look once more upon these those whom we have known. Just where the good-humored faces of the Irish regiment, and the tall caps of the Highlanders are perceptible, the 13th appears in view, our company marching decorously on, no lagging, no faltering, no cowards there, though almost every heart had in it some thought of home and the dear ones left behind. Prayers were said by lips unused to pray, and who shall tell how many records of sins forgiven were that morning written in heaven? Bibles, too, were pressed to throbbing hearts, and to none more closely than to George Graham's broad chest. He had prayed that morning in the clear moonlight, and by the same moonlight he had tried to read a line in Annie's well-worn Bible, opening to where God promises to care for the widow and the fatherless. Was it ominous, that passage? Did it mean that he, so strong, so vigorous, so full of life, should bite the dust ere many hours were done? He could not believe it. He was too full of hope for that. He could not die with Annie at home alone, so he buttoned her Bible over his heart, and prayed that if a bullet struck him it might be there, fondly hoping that would break its force.

There was a shadow on his handsome face, and it communicated itself to Isaac Simms, who was glancing so stealthily at him, and guessing of what he was thinking. Isaac, too, had prayed in the moonlight, and he, too, had thought, "What if I should be killed!" wondering if his mother ever would forget her soldier boy, even though she might not weep over his nameless grave. This to Isaac was the hardest thought of all. The boy that would not tell a lie for the sake of promotion, was not afraid to die, but he preferred that it should not be there 'mid piles of bloody slain. He would rather death should come to him up in the humble attic, where he had lain so oft and listened to the patter of the rain on the roof above, or feigned to be asleep when his mother stole noiselessly across the threshold to see if he were covered from the cold and shielded from the snow, which sometimes found an entrance through a crevice in the wall. 'Tis strange when we are in danger what flights our fancy often takes, gathering up the minutest details of our past life, and spreading them out before us with startling distinctness. So Isaac, with possible death in advance, thought of his past life; of every object connected with his home, from the grass-plat in the rear, where his mother bleached her clothes in spring, to the blue and white checked blanket hung round his attic bed to protect him from the winter storm. That widow, so stern, so harsh, so sharp to almost every one, had been the tenderest of parents to him, and a tear glistened on the cheek of the fair-haired boy as he remembered the only time he ever was hateful to her. He had asked her forgiveness for it, and she surely would not recall it when she read the letter Eli or John would send, bearing the fatal line, "Mother, poor Isaac is dead." He knew they would call him "poor Isaac," for though they sometimes teased him as his "mother's great girl baby," they petted him quite as much as she, only in a different way, and he felt now that both would step between him and the bullet they thought would harm him. Eli would any way, but John, perhaps, would hesitate, as he now loved Susan best. Isaac was proud of his brothers, and he glanced admiringly at them as they marched side by side, keeping even step just as they did down Main street, with his mother and Susan looking on. One now was thinking of Susan, and one of his widowed mother.

Close by Isaac walked Bill, quiet and subdued. He had not prayed that morning,—he never prayed; but when he saw Isaac kneeling on his blanket he had said to him, "Manage to get in a word or two for me and Hal; we need it, mercy knows." And surely if ever poor mortal needed prayer it was *Hal*, as his brother styled him. Half stupefied with the vile liquor he had constantly managed to get, he trudged on, boasting of what he could do; "only give him a chance and he'd lick the entire Secession army. He'd like to see the ball that could kill him; he was good at dodging; he'd show'em a thing or two in the way of fight; he'd take the tuck out of the Southern gentlemen,—yes, he would," and so he went thoughtlessly boasting on to death!

Will Mather was not there. Indisposition had detained him at Washington, and with a hearty God speed he had sent his comrades on their way, lamenting that he, too, could not join them, and bidding his brother-in-law do some fighting for him.

At the head of his company Capt. Carleton moved. Firm, erect, and dignified, as if born to command, he did full justice to the Carleton name, of which he was justly proud; but his face was paler than its wont, and a tinge of sadness rested upon it as his regiment halted at last in front of what was supposed to be the hidden foe. Thomas Carleton had wept bitter tears when he laid his Mary to rest beneath South Carolina's sunny skies, and had thought he could never be reconciled to the loss, but he was half glad now that she was dead, for she was born of Southern blood, and he would rather she should not know the errand which had brought him to Virginia, where first he met and loved her,—rather she should not know how he had come to war with her people. There was another thought, too, which made him sad that July day. The green, beautiful woods standing there so silently before him probably sheltered more than one with whom he had in bygone days struck the friendly hand and bandied the friendly joke, for his home was once in Richmond, and there were there those who once held no small place in his heart. And they were dear to him yet. He was not fighting against them personally, he was contending only for his nation's rights, his country's honor. He bore no malice toward his Southern brethren, and like many of our staunchest, bravest Northern men, he would even then have met them more than half way with terms of reconciliation. He knew they were no race of bloodthirsty demons, as some fanatics had madly termed them. They were men, most of them, like himself,—warm-hearted, impulsive men, generous almost to a fault in peace, but firm and terrible in war. *Tom* had lived among them,—had shared their hospitalities,—had seen them in their various phases, and making allowance for the vast difference which education and habits of society make in one's opinions, he saw many points wherein the North had misunderstood their actions, and not made due concessions when they might have done so without yielding one iota of their honor. But time for concession was over now. Political fanatics had stirred up the mass of the people till nought but *blood* could wash away the fancied wrong. And they were there that Sabbath morn to spill it. Tom, however, did not know that the green, silent woods sheltered his *brother*, for his mother had purposely withheld from him the fact that Jimmie had joined the Southern Army. She knew the struggle it had cost him to take up arms against a people he liked so much, and she would not willingly add to his burden by telling him of Jimmie's sin, and it was well she did not, for had he known how near he was to Jimmie, he could not have stood there so unmoved, awaiting the first booming gun which should herald the opening of the battle.

It came at last, a bellowing, thunderous roar, whose echoes shook the hills for miles, as the hissing shell went plowing through the air, bursting harmlessly at last just beyond its destined mark. The enemy were in no hurry to retort, for a deep silence ensued, broken ere long by another heavy gun, which did its work more thoroughly than its predecessor had done, for where several breathing souls had been there was nought left save the bleeding mutilated trunks of what were once human forms. The battle had commenced. Sherman's Brigade, in which was the N. Y. 13th, did its part nobly, overrunning in its headlong charges battery after battery, and recking little of the shafts of death falling so thick and fast. Louder and more deafening grew the battle din, hoarser and heavier the battle thunder, denser, deeper the battle smoke, dimming the brightness of that Sabbath morn. Louder, shriller grew the Gaelic scream, fiercer rose the Celtic cry, wilder rang the yells of the 13th, as its members plunged into the thickest of the fight their demoniacal shouts appalling the hearts of the foe far more than the rain of shot so vigorously kept up, and causing them to flee as from a pack of fiends.

Steady in its place George Graham's giant form was seen; no thought of Annie now; no thought of home; no thought of Bible buttoned over the heart; thoughts only of the fray and victory.

Not far away, and where the fight was thickest, the widow's boys, Eli and John, stood firm as granite rocks, the beaded sweat dropping from their burning brows, begrimed with battle smoke, as with unflinching nerve and hands that trembled not, they took their aims, seeing more than one fall before their sure fire.

White as the winter snow one boyish face gleamed amid the excited throng; the fair hair pushed back from the girlish forehead, and the scorching sun falling upon the unsheltered head, for Isaac's cap had been shot away, and the ball which shot it lay swimming in the dark life blood of poor Harry Baker, just behind, and *just two inches taller* than the widow's youngest born. Poor Harry! He had done his best to keep the promise made so boastfully. In all the 13th Regiment there was not one who played a braver part than he, firing off with every gun a timely joke, which raised a smile even in that dreadful hour. But Harry's work was done, and Mrs. Baker had but one boy now, for her first-born lay upon the ground so blackened and disfigured, with the thick brains slowly oozing from his mangled head, and the purple gore pouring from his lips, that only those who saw him fall, could guess that it was Harry. Poor Harry! We say it again, sadly, reverently, for rude and reckless though he was, he fell fighting for his country; and to all who perish thus we owe a debt of gratitude, a meed of praise. Sacred, then, be the memory of those whose graves are with the slain, far away beneath Virginia's sky, and sacred be the memory of poor Harry Baker. His own worst enemy, he lived his life's brief span, and died at last a soldier's death.

"Shot plump through the upper story! Won't the old woman row it, though?" was Bill's characteristic comment, as the whizzing and the death shriek met his ear, and the falling, bleeding figure met his view.

Spite of his jeering words there was a keen pang in Billy's heart as he shrank away from the gory mass he knew had been his brother,—a sudden upheaving of something in his throat and a blur before his vision, as he began to realize what it was to go to war. But there was then no time to waste over a fallen brother. The dread work must go on, and with the whispered words, "Poor Hal, I'll do the tender for you when we get the varments licked," he marked the position by signs he could not miss, and then pressed closer to his comrade, saying, as he did so—

"Ike, Hal's a goner. Shot right through his top-knot, with a piece of your cap wedged in his skull. If you'd been a leetle taller you'd been scalped instead of Hal. So much you get for bein' 'Stub.'"

Isaac shuddered involuntarily, but ere he could look back the crowd behind pushed him forward, and so he failed to see the ruin which, but for his short stature, would have come to him. There were no marks upon him yet,—nothing, save the uncovered head, to tell where he had been. The balls which struck down others passed him by, the wind they made lifting occasionally his fair hair, but doing no other damage. Above, around, before, behind, at right, at left, the grape shot fell like hail, but left him all untouched, and Billy, grown timid since poor Harry's fate, pressed closer to the boy who would not tell a lie, as if there were safety there.

Onward, onward they pressed, Isaac wondering sometimes how Tom Carleton fared, and looking again in quest of their young Lieutenant Graham, still towering above them all, in spite of Rose's prediction. The ball for which he was the mark had not been fired yet, but it was coming. An Alabamian volunteer had singled out that form, yelling exultingly as he saw it reel and totter like a broken reed. They were well matched in size, the two combatants, both splendid marks, as Rose had said, and Bill Baker's sure aim froze the laugh upon the Alabamian's lips and sent him staggering to the ground, just as Isaac received his captain's orders to lead the fainting, wounded George to a place of comparative safety.

"It's only my arm they've shattered," George whispered, glancing sadly at the disabled limb over which Isaac's tears were falling. "Will it kill me, think?" was the next remark, prompted by a thought of Annie.

Isaac did not believe it would, and with all a woman's tenderness he bound it up and held his canteen to the lips of the fainting, weary man, whispering,

"Water, boy, water."

Isaac had not, like many others, thrown his canteen away, and he gave freely to the thirsty George, who, with each draught, felt his pulse grow stronger, while his eyes kindled with fresh zeal as the noise of the battle grew louder, and seemed to be coming nearer. The onslaught was terrible now. Cannon after cannon belched forth its terrific thunder, ball after ball sped on its deadly track, battery after battery opened its blazing fire, shell after shell cut the summer air, and burst with murderous hiss; shout after shout rent the smoky sky, shriek after shriek went down with the rushing wind, officer after officer bit the dust, rank after rank was broken up, soul after soul went to the bar of God, and then there came a pause. The firing ceased, the stifling smoke rolled gradually away, and showed a dreadful sight,—men mutilated and torn, till not a vestige of their former looks was left to tell who they had been. Mingled together, in one frightful mass, the dead and dying lay, smiles wreathing the livid lips of some, and frowns disfiguring others. Arms, hands, and feet, heads, fingers, toes, and clots of human hair, dripping red with blood, were scattered over the field,—parts of the living mass we saw but a few hours agone moving on so hopefully beneath the morning moonlight, "Like leaves of the forest when autumn hath blown," they lay there now, their mangled remains crying loudly to Heaven for vengeance on the heads of those who brought this curse upon us.

CHAPTER VIII.
THE RETREAT.

The day was ours, nobly won with sweat and toil and blood, and the brave men who won it were thinking of the laurels so laboriously earned, when suddenly the entire scale was turned, and ere they knew what they were doing, the tired, jaded troops found themselves rushing headlong from the battle-field, never so much as casting a backward glance, but each striving to out-run the other, and so escape from they knew not what! How that panic happened no one can tell. Some charged it to the reckless conduct of a band of Regulars sent back for ammunition, and others upon the idle lookers on, the curious ones, who had come "to see the Rebels whipped," and who at the first intimation of defeat joined in the general stampede, making the confusion worse, and adding greatly to the fright of the flying multitude.

It was a strange retreat our soldiers made. All law and order were at an end, company mixed with company, regiment with regiment, and together they rushed headlong down the hill, many in their dismay fording the creek regardless of the shot and shell sent after them by the astonished foe, now really in pursuit.

Some there were, however, who made the retreat more leisurely, and among these, Bill Baker. Remembering the mark he had fixed in his own mind, he sought among the slain for Harry, finding him at last, trampled and crushed by the flying troops, and wholly unrecognizable by any save a brother's eye. Bill knew him, however, in a moment, but there was no time now to "do the tender," as he had purposed doing. There was danger in tarrying long, and with a shudder Bill bent over the mangled form, and with his jack-knife severed a lock of matted, bloodwet hair, taking also from the pockets whatever of value they contained, not from any avaricious motive, but rather from a feeling that the rebels should get nothing save the body.

"A darned sight good Hal's carcass will do ye!" he said, shaking his fist defiantly in the direction of the foe, "but the wust is your own this hot weather, if you don't bury him decently;" then turning to the lifeless gore, he continued: "Poor Hal! I'm kinder sorry you are dead. You had now and then a streak of good about you, and I'm sorry we ever quarreled, I be, upon my word, and I wish you could hear me say so; but you can't, knocked into a cocked up hat as you are, poor Hal. If there was a spot on your face as big as a sixpence that wasn't smashed into a jelly, I'd kiss you just for the old woman's sake, but I swan if I can stomach it! I might your hands, perhaps," and bending lower, Bill's lips touched the clammy fingers of the dead.

There was something in the touch which brought to Bill's heart a pang similar to the one he felt when he saw his brother fall, and rising to his feet, he said, mournfully:

"Good-bye, old Hal, I'm going now; I wish you might go, too. Good-bye," and wiping away a tear which felt much out of place on his rough cheek, Bill walked away, saying to himself, "Poor Hal. I didn't s'pose I had such a hankerin' for him. Didn't s'pose I cared for nobody; but such a day's work as this finds the soft spot in a feller's heart if he's got any. Poor Hal! Mother'll nigh about raise the *ruff*!"

Thus soliloquizing Bill moved on, not rapidly as others did, but rather leisurely than otherwise. He seemed to be benumbed, and did not care much what became of himself. Wading the stream he trudged on, now wondering "What the plague they all were running for, when they'd got the rascals licked," and again anathematizing the shot which fell around him.

"S'pose I care for you," he said, hitting a spent ball a kick. "S'pose I care if I do get killed? better do that than to run."

Then reflecting that to be shot in the *back* was not considered a distinguished mark of honor, he hastened his lagging steps until the shelter of the wood was reached. Bill was very tired, and feeling comparatively safe, determined not to travel farther until he had had some rest. Hunting out a thick clump of underbrush near a stream of water, where he would be sheltered from observation, he crawled into its midst, and was ere long sleeping soundly, wholly oblivious to the strange sights and sounds around him, as squad after squad of soldiers hurried by.

Meanwhile George Graham was sitting faint and weary beneath the tree, when the first token of the retreat met his view.

"See, they are running," Isaac said, grasping his sound arm in some affright. "Let us run, too. You lean on me, and I'll lead you safely through."

"With a bitter groan, George attempted to rise, but sank back again from utter exhaustion. A species of apathy had stolen over him, and he would rather stay there and die, he said, than make the attempt to flee. He did not think of Annie, until Isaac, bending down, said, entreatingly:

"It will be horrid for Annie to know you died, when you might have got away. Try for Annie's sake, can't you?"

Yes, for Annie's sake he could, and at the mere mention of her name, the dim eye kindled, and the pale cheeks glowed, while the wounded man made another effort to rise. He succeeded this time, and with slow steps the two commenced their retreat. It was a novel sight, that tall, muscular man, towering head and shoulders above the frail boy, upon whom he leaned heavily for support,—the generous Isaac, who would not leave him there alone, even though he knew the danger he was incurring for himself.

"They'll treat us decent if we're taken prisoners, won't they, think?" he asked, as the possibility of such a calamity was suggested to his mind. Not till then had George thought of that. They would not murder a wounded man, he was sure, but they might take him prisoner, and death itself was almost preferable to days of captivity and sickening suspense away from Annie. The very idea roused him into life, and with a superhuman effort, he hastened on, almost outrunning Isaac, until they, too, had reached the friendly woods where Bill had already taken shelter. Just then a loaded wagon passed them, its frightened, excited occupants paying no heed to Isaac's cry for help, until one whose uniform showed him to be an officer, sprang up, exclaiming:

"The strong must give place to the wounded. I can find my way to Washington better than that bleeding man!" and *Tom Carleton* seized the reins with a grasp which brought the foaming steeds nearly to their haunches. The vehicle was stopped, and the next instant Tom had leaped upon the ground, spraining his ankle severely, and reeling in his first pain against the astounded Isaac, who cried out, joyfully:

"Oh, Captain Carleton, save Lieutenant Graham, won't you? We can walk, you and I."

Tom had not the least suspicion as to whom he was befriending until then, and now, unmindful of his own aching foot, he assisted George to the seat he had vacated, and watched the party without a pang as they drove rapidly away, leaving him alone with Isaac.

"We'll do the best we can, my boy," he said, cheerily, as he met the confiding, inquiring look bent upon him by Isaac, who, relieved of his former charge, felt now like leaning for protection and guidance upon Captain Carleton.

Alas, his hopes were short-lived, for a groan just then escaped from Tom's white lips, wrung out by the agony it cost him to step. Isaac saw him stagger when he sprang to the ground, and comprehending the case at once, he resumed his burden of care, and kneeling before poor Tom, who had sunk upon the grass, he rubbed the swollen limb as tenderly as Rose herself could have done.

"If we could only find some water," Tom said, scanning the appearance of the woods, and judging at last by indications which seldom failed, that there must be some not very far away. "There where the bushes are," he said, pointing toward the very spot where Bill lay snoring soundly, and dreaming of robbing Parson Goodwin's orchard, in company with Hal. "There must be water there, and human beings too, for I hear singing, don't you?"

Isaac listened till he, too, caught a strain of melody, as sad and low as if it were a funeral dirge some one was trilling there.

"What can it mean?" Tom said. "Lend me your hand, my boy, and I'll soon find out."

It was a harder task to move than he anticipated, for the ankle was swelling rapidly, and bearing the least weight upon it made the pain intolerable. Leaning on Isaac's shoulder, he managed to make slow progress toward the stream bubbling so deliciously among the grass, and toward the music growing more and more distinct.

It was reached at last, and the mystery was solved. Leaning against a tree was a Confederate officer, whose white face told plainer than words could tell that never again would he be seen in the pine-shadowed home he had left so unwillingly but a few months before. Beside him upon the grass lay a boy, scarcely more than twelve years old, a drummer in a company of New England volunteers, both little hands shot entirely off, and the bleeding stumps bound carefully up in the handkerchief of the Rebel, who had smothered his own dying anguish for the sake of comforting that poor child, sobbing so piteously with pain.

"I didn't s'pose any of you was so good, or I shouldn't have come to fight you. Oh, mother, mother, they do ache so,—my hands,—my hands!" he said, the cry of contrition ending in a childish wail for the mother sympathy never more to be experienced by that drummer boy.

A smile flitted across the officer's face as he replied, "Had we all known each other better, this war would not have been," and the noble foe held the boy closer to his bleeding bosom, dipping his hand in the running stream, and laving the feverish brow where the drops of sweat were standing.

"What makes you so kind to me?" the dying boy asked, his dim eyes gazing wistfully into the face bending so sadly over him.

"I have a boy about your size,—Charlie we call him," the stranger said.

"And I am Charlie, too," the child replied, "Charlie Younglove, and my home is in New Hampshire, right on the mountain side. Father is dead, and we are poor, mother and I. That's why I came to the war. I wanted to go to college, sometime. Do you think I'll die? Will I never go home again?—never see mother nor little sister either?"

The soldier groaned, and bent still closer to the drummer boy, asking so earnestly if he must die. How could he tell him yes, and yet he felt he must; he would not be faithful to his trust if he withheld the knowledge, or failed to point that dying one to the only source of life.

"Yes, Charlie," he answered, mournfully, "I think you will. Are you afraid to die? Did your mother never tell you of the Saviour?"

"Yes, yes, oh yes!" and the little face lighted up as at the mention of a dear friend. "I went to Sunday School, and learned of Jesus there. I've prayed to him every night and every morning since I came from home. I promised her I would,—mother, I mean,—and she prays, too. She said so in her letter, right here in my jacket pocket. Don't you want to read it?"

The officer shook his head, and Charlie went on:

"I didn't want to fight to-day, because I knew it was Sunday, but I had to, or run away. Will God punish me for that, think? Will he turn me out of Heaven?"

"No, no, oh no!" and the North Carolinian's tears dropped like rain upon the troubled face, upturned so anxiously to his. "God will never punish those who put their trust in Jesus."

"I do, I do, I do!" and the trembling voice grew fainter, adding, after a pause: "You are a good man, I know. You have been to Sunday School, I guess, and you prayed this morning, didn't you?"

The soldier answered, "Yes," and the child continued:

"You are dying, too, I 'most know, for there's blood all over us. We'll go together, won't we, you and I? Will there be war in Heaven, between the North and South?"

"No, Charlie. There is naught but peace in Heaven," and again the white hands laved the feverish forehead, for the soldier would fain keep that little spirit till his could join it company, and speed away to the land where trouble is unknown.

But it could not be, for Charlie's life was ebbing away; the last sand was dropping from the glass. Closer the fair curly head nestled to its strange pillow,—the bleeding bosom of a foe,—and the lips murmured incoherently of the elm-trees growing near the mountain home, and the mother watching daily for tidings of her boy. Then the train of thought was changed, and Charlie heard the *bell*, just as it pealed that morning from his own village spire. How grand the music was echoing through the Virginia woods, and the blue eyes closed, as with a whisper he asked:

"Don't you hear the old bell at home, calling the folks to church? It has stopped now, and the children are singing before the organ, 'Glory to God on high.' I used to sing it with them. Do you know it, *'Gloria in excelsis'*?"

"Yes, yes!" the soldier eagerly replied, glad to find they were both of the same faith,—that little Yankee boy, born among the granite hills, and he a North Carolinian, born on Southern soil.

"Then sing it," Charlie whispered; "sing it, won't you? Maybe I'll go to sleep. I don't ache any now."

With a mighty effort the soldier forced down his bitter grief, and in a low, mournful tone, commenced our beautiful church chant, the dying child for whom he sang, faintly joining with him for a time, but the sweet voice ceased ere long, the curly head pressed heavier, the bleeding stumps lay motionless, and when the chant was ended, Charlie had gone to his last sleep.

Carefully, reverently, the North Carolinian laid the little form upon the grass, and kissed the stiffened lips for the sake of the mother, who might never know just how Charlie died.

Just then footsteps sounded near. Tom and Isaac were coming, and the face of the soldier darkened when he saw them, as if they had been intruders upon him and his beautiful dead. Their appearance, however, disarmed him at once, and with a faint smile he pointed to his companion, and said:

"He was in the Federal army two hours ago; he has joined God's army now. Poor Charlie! I would have done much to save him!" and with his hand he smoothed the golden hair, on which the flecks of western sunshine lay.

Isaac knew it was a Rebel speaking to him, and for an instant he experienced the same sensation he had felt in the midst of the fray, but only for an instant, for though he knew it was a sworn foe, he knew, too, that 'twas a noble-hearted man, and with a pitying glance at the dead, he asked if aught could be done for the living.

"No," and the soldier smiled again; "my passport is sealed; I am going after Charlie. Some one of your men did his work well—see!" and opening his coat, he disclosed the frightful wound from which the dark blood was gushing.

Then, in a few words he had told them Charlie's story, adding in conclusion,

"You will escape; you will go home again: and if you do, write to Charlie's mother, and tell her how he died. Tell her not to weep for him so early saved. Her letter is in his pocket: take it as a guide where to direct your own."

This he said to Isaac, for he saw Tom was disabled. Isaac did as he was bidden, and the letter from Charlie's mother, written but a week before, was safely put away for future reference, and then Isaac did for the North Carolina soldier what the North Carolina soldier had done for the Yankee boy: he staunched the flowing blood as best he could, bathed the throbbing head, and held the cooling water to the dry, parched lips, which feebly murmured their thanks.

The stranger saw the distinction there was between his new-found friends, and feeling that Tom was the one to whom he must appeal, he turned his glazed eyes upon him, and said:

"Whose government will answer for all this, yours or the one that I acknowledge?"

"Both, both!" Tom replied vehemently; and the stranger rejoined:

"Yes, both have much to answer for,—one for not yielding a little more, and the other for its rash impetuosity. Oh, had we, as a people, know each other; could we have guessed what brave, kind hearts there were both North and South, we should never have come to this; but we believed our leaders too much; trusted too implicitly in the dastardly falsehoods of a lying press; and it has brought us here. For myself I am willing to die in a good cause; and of course I think *ours* is just; exactly as you think of yours; but who will care for my poor Nellie I left in my Southern home? What splendid victory can repay her for the husband she will lose ere yonder sun has set, or what can compensate my daughter Maude or my boy Charlie for their loss?"

The North Carolinian paused from exhaustion, and Tom essayed to comfort him.

Bending over him, and supporting the drooping head which dropped lower and lower, the lips whispering of *Nelly*, of Maud and Charlie, and of the Tar River winding past their door, until there seemed no longer life in that once vigorous frame.

"He's dead," Isaac was about to say, but the words froze on his lips, for in the distance he caught sight of two other men coming towards them,—one strong and powerful, the other slight and girlish-looking. Tom saw them, too, and turning to Isaac, said hurriedly,

"Run, my boy, and leave me. They will think far more of capturing an officer than a private. You can escape as well as not,—run, quick."

But Isaac would share Capt. Carleton's fate, whatever that might be, and with a deep flush on his boyish face, he drew nearer to his companion and stood gazing defiantly at the Rebels as they came up.

"We have nothing to hope," Tom whispered, "but we'll sell ourselves dearly as possible," and bracing himself against the tree, he prepared to do battle, refusing at once the bullying Rebel's command,

"Surrender or die."

"Never!" was the firm response, and while Isaac engaged hand to hand with the smaller of the two, Tom parried skillfully each thrust of his antagonist, who accused him of having murdered the North Carolina officer lying near.

Both Tom and Isaac had thought the stranger dead, but at this accusation the white lips quivered, and whispered faintly, "No, no, they were kind to me, the officer and the boy."

For an instant the Rebel's uplifted hand was stayed, and it is difficult to say what the result might have been had not another voice called through the leafy woods, "No quarter to the Yankee!"

Tom's cheek blanched to an unnatural whiteness, as with partial lips and flashing eyes he watched the new comer hastening to the rescue, the handsome, graceful stranger, whose appearance riveted Isaac's attention at once, causing him to gaze spell-bound upon the face of the advancing foe, as if it were one he had seen before. How handsome that young man was, with his saucy, laughing eyes of black, his soft, silken curls of hair, and that air of self-assurance, which bespoke a daring, reckless spirit. Isaac could not remove his eyes from the young Rebel, and his late antagonist met with no resistance, as he passed his arms around him and held him prisoner at last. Isaac did not even think of himself; his thoughts were all upon the stranger, at whom poor Tom sat gazing, half bewildered, and trying once to stretch his arms toward him, while the lips essayed to speak. But the words he would have uttered died away as a sudden faintness stole over him, when he saw that he was recognized. There was a violent start,—a fading out of the bright color on the Rebel's cheek, and Isaac, still watching him, heard him exclaim, "No, no, not him, leave him alone," while at the same time he attempted to free Tom from the firm grasp the enemy now had upon him.

With an oath the soldier shook him off, then rudely bade his half-senseless victim rise and follow as a prisoner of war. And Tom, unmindful of the pain, arose without a word, and leaning heavily upon his captor, hobbled on, caring little now, it would seem, what fate was in reserve for him. He seemed benumbed, and only an occasional groan, which Isaac fancied was wrung out by pain, told that he was conscious of anything.

"He's lame," Isaac cried, the hot tears raining over his face, while he begged of them to stop, or at least to *carry* poor Capt. Carleton, if they must go on. "I won't run away," he said, imploringly to his own captor, feeling intuitively that his was the kinder nature. "Don't be afraid of me. I'll help you carry him if necessary. Do have some pity. He's fainting, see!" and Isaac almost shrieked as poor Tom sunk upon the grass, utterly unable to move another step. They must carry him now or leave him there, and anxious for the honor a captured officer of Tom Carleton's evident rank in life would confer upon them, the Rebels availed themselves of Isaac's proffered aid, and the three, bearing their heavy burden, moved slowly on until far beyond the bushes by the stream, where the other soldier sat upon the ground, his laughing black eyes heavy with tears, and his heart throbbing with a keener pain than he had ever known before.

"I was wrong to let him go," he said aloud. "Three against two would surely have carried the day, and that boy at his side was brave, I know. But it cannot now be helped. He is their prisoner, and all that remains for me to do is to see that the best of treatment comes to him until he is released. But what! are the dead coming back to life?" and the soldier started up as he caught a sound of bending twigs near by.

CHAPTER IX.
THE REBEL AND THE YANKEE.

Bill Baker was awake at last, and from his hiding-place had seen Capt. Carleton and Isaac disappear beneath the trees in the distance.

"They are goners," he muttered to himself, "Won't that snap dragon of a widow be mad, though, when she hears how they've got Ike. Poor Ike, I'd help him if I could, but 'taint no use interferin' now," and with this reflection, Bill turned his attention toward the stranger, watching him for several minutes, first to decide his politics, and second, to calculate his probable strength. The soldier was at least a head taller than Bill, who nevertheless far exceeded him in strength of muscle and power of endurance.

"I can manage him," was Bill's contemptuous comment, and feeling in his pocket for the strong cord *Rose Mather* had bound round his paper parcel of turnovers and cheese, he prepared to spring upon his foe in the rear and take him by surprise.

The cracking twigs betrayed him, and changing his tactics he walked directly in front of the astonished young man, who, with heightened color, haughtily demanded "what he was doing there,—and whether he were a friend or foe."

"What am I doin' here?" Bill repeated, sticking his cap a little more to one side, and half shutting one of his wicked grey eyes, "Kinder peekin' round to see what I can find. Be I friend or foe? You must be green to ask that. Don't you re-cog-nize my *regimentals*, made after the cut of Uncle Sam, *siled* some, to be sure, but then I've been at a dirty job,—been lickin' jest such scamps as you. Now, then, corporal, seein' I answered you civil, what are *you* doin' here? You won't answer me, hey?" he continued, as the stranger deigned him no other reply than a look of ineffable disdain. "Wall, then, if you're so 'fraid of your tongue, s'posin' we try a rastle, rough and tumble, you know; and the one that gits beat is t'other's prisoner. That's fair, as these dead folks will witness;" and Bill's glance for the first time fell upon the bodies lying near them,—upon Charlie's childish face, with the golden curls clustering around it.

The sight touched a tender chord in Bill, and forgetting for a moment his new acquaintance, he bent over the drummer boy, murmuring,

"Poor child, your folks or'to have been ashamed to let you come to war."

Now was the Rebel's time. He felt intuitively that he was no match for the thick-set, brawny Bill. Safety lay alone in flight, and with a sudden bound he fled like a deer.

"Nuff said," dropped from Bill's lips, and the next instant he, too, was flying through the woods in pursuit of the foe.

It proved an unequal race, and Bill's strong arms ere long closed like a vice around the struggling soldier, who resisted manfully, until resistance was vain, and then sullenly stood still, while Bill fastened his hands behind him, with the cords unwittingly furnished by Rose Mather!

"Don't squirm so, corporal," Bill said, as he bound the knots securely, with his knee upon the back of the stranger, whom he had thrown upon his face. "Don't squirm so like an eel and I'll be done the quicker. I calkerlate to tie you so you can't git away, and you may as well hold on. Got kinder delicate hands, haint you? Never done nothin', I guess, but lick niggers and shute your betters. There, you may stan' up now if you want tew."

The young man struggled to his feet, saying, proudly:

"What do you intend doing next, sir?"

"What do I intend doin'?" Bill replied, with imperturbable gravity. "I intend leadin' you by this string inter camp, and showin' you up for to'pence a sight. What d'ye s'pose I intended doin'?"

The young man made one more desperate struggle to free himself, but the twine only cut into his flesh, making the matter worse, so he finally submitted to his fate, and suffered Bill to take him where he listed. Bill was in no hurry to get to camp. He rather enjoyed being alone with his prisoner, and leading him to a little thicket he made him sit down, and placing one of his feet upon him he began to ask him innumerable questions,—what was his name, where did he come from, what company was he in, and so on, to none of which did the stranger vouchsafe a reply.

With a haughty look upon his handsome face, he maintained a rigid silence, while Bill continued:

"Needn't talk unless you want to. Speech is free with us, you know; but seein' you won't tell who you be, maybe you wouldn't mind hearing my geneology. It'll make you feel better, mabby, to know my reputation and standin' in society. Corporal, did you ever hear of a *Yankee*, a real live mudsill Yankee, such as Southern gentlemen feel above fightin' with? Wall, I'm that critter. What do you think of me, take me as a hull?"

The stranger groaned in disgust, and Bill continued:

"Them cords hurt you, I guess. Like enough I'll ease 'em up a trifle, if you say so. I ain't hard-hearted, if I be rough as a nutmeg-grater. Shall I loosen 'em so's not to hurt them soft, baby hands of yourn?"

"Thank you, sir. I don't mind it in the least," was the soldier's answer, though all the while the coarse twine was cutting cruelly into the tender flesh.

This Bill suspected, and muttering to himself:

"Good grit, if he is a Rebel," he went on: "Considerable top-lofty, ain't you, corporal? And as chaps of your cloth like to meet with their equals, I'll go on with my history. I was born in Massachusetts, not over a day's ride from Boston. Ever been to Boston?"

No answer from the stranger, save a heightened color, and Bill proceeded:

"Tall old town. Got a smashin' monument out to Charlestown. Heard on't I s'pose, as I take it some of you Southern dogs can read. Wall, father died in State's Prison down there to Charlestown, and then we moved to Rockland, the old woman, Hal and me. Hal's lyin' up there where the hottest of the fight took place, and I'm here tormentin' you by tellin' you my character. I've been to the workhouse twice,—I have, I swan,—once for gettin' drunk, and once for somethin' else a good deal wus. How do you feel now?" and Bill leered wickedly at the young man, who seemed bent on keeping silence.

Only the expression of his face told the extreme contempt he felt for his companion, and how it did wound to the quick one of his nature to be held a prisoner by such as William Baker. But there was no help for it; he must submit to be taken to Washington by the despised Bill, and then,—oh, how his heart sank within him as he thought, what then? Was there no method of escape? Couldn't he get away, or better yet, couldn't he hire Bill to let him go? Strange he had not thought of this before. Yankees were proverbially avaricious, and almost every man had his price. He could try, at all events, and unbending his dignity, he inquired what Bill would ask to let him go?

"What'll I ask?" repeated Bill, placing both feet instead of one upon his prisoner. "I dun know. Le'ss dicker a spell and see. What'll you give, and where do you keep your traps?"

"In my pockets," the unsuspecting soldier answered; "there's my watch and chain, worth over three hundred dollars."

"Whew-ew!" whistled Bill, his face lighting up instantly, while hope crept into the stranger's heart. "A gold watch worth over three hundred! Let's see the critter."

"You forget that my hands are tied," the stranger suggested.

"So they be, but mine ain't," and the next moment Bill was holding to his ear an elegant Parisian watch, and asking if the stranger were positive sure it cost more'n three hundred dollars. "I had an old pewter thing that I gin to mother," he said, "and this concern jest comes in play. It's mine, you say, if I'll let you cut stick and run?"

"Yes, sir; I give you that in exchange for my liberty."

"Wall, now, kind a generous, ain't you? But I want you should fling in something to clinch the bargain. A chap of your cloth is of more valley than three hundred. What else have you got, corporal?" and laying the watch carefully upon the grass, Bill's hand a second time sought the stranger's pocket, bringing out an expensive and exquisitely wrought quizzing-glass.

"Wall, now, if these ain't the curisest spetacles!" he exclaimed. "I'll jest see how a Reb looks through 'em," and adjusting them to his eyes, Bill walked demurely around his prisoner, and then standing at a little distance inspected him minutely, as if he had been some curious monster. "Hanged if I can see in 'em, but mabby they'll suit the old woman to hum," he said, placing the glass beside the watch, and adding: "Watch and spetacles ain't enough, corporal. What more have you got? Ain't there a ring on one of your hands?"

"Yes, a costly diamond," was the faint response, and Bill ere long was trying in vain to push it over his large joints.

"It don't fit me, but I guess 'twill my gal, when I git one," he said, laying that, too, with the watch and eyeglass.

A silver tobacco-box and handsome cigar-case followed next, the stranger groaning mentally, as a faint suspicion of Bill's real intentions crossed his mind. There remained now but one more article, the dearest of all the young Rebel possessed, and the perspiration started from every pore as he felt the rough hand again within his pockets, and knew he could not prevent it.

"Oh, no, no, no, not that! Spare me that. Do not open it, please!" and the haughty tone was changed to one of earnest supplication, as Bill drew forth a small daguerrean case, and placed his dirty thumb upon the spring.

Something in the stranger's voice made him pause a moment, but anything like delicacy of feeling was unknown to the rough Bill, and the next instant he was feasting his rude gaze upon the features which the Rebel youth had guarded almost religiously, even from his equals in camp. How beautiful that girlish face was, with its bright laughing eyes, and soft chestnut curls falling in such profusion around the childish brow, and upon the smooth, white neck. Even Bill was awed into silence, while a feeling of bewilderment crept over him as if he had seen that face before, and mingled with this feeling came remembrances of that last day at home, when fair hands, which, ere he was a soldier, would have scorned to touch such as he, had waved him an adieu.

"Whew-ew!" he whistled, at last. "Ain't she pretty, though? Your sweetheart, I guess," and he leered at the stranger, who made him no reply; only the lips quivered, and in the dark eyes there was a gathering moisture; but when Bill asked, "May I have this, too, if I'll let you go?" the stranger answered, promptly:

"Never! I'll die a thousand deaths before I'll part with that! Liberty is not worth that price. Give me back the picture, and I'll go with you willingly wherever you please. Do give it back," he added, in an agony of fear, as Bill continued gazing at it, and making his remarks.

"Can't a feller look at a gal on glass if he wants to? I wouldn't hurt the little critter if I could as well as not. So you won't give her to me, nor tell me who 'tis, neither?"

"Stranger," said the Rebel, "have you any feelings of refinement?"

"Nary feelin'," and Bill shook his head, but did not withdraw his eyes from the picture.

"Well, then, have you a wife?"

"Nary wife. Nobody would have Bill Baker."

"Nor sister?"

"Nary sister but a dead one that I never seen."

"Nor mother? You surely have a mother," and the soldier's voice shook with strong emotion.

"You've got me there," and Bill's eyes turned upon his prisoner. "I have a mother, and you ought to hear the old gal take on when she comes home from washin' from Miss Martherses or some of the big bugs and finds Hal dead drunk on the trundle-bed, and me not a great sight better. Handsome old gal,—one of the kind that don't wear hoops, but every time she steps takes her gownd up on her heels, you know."

The Rebel groaned aloud. There was no tender point upon which his captor could be touched, and the tears rained over his handsome face as he begged of Bill to give him at least the ambrotype.

"It's the only thing which has prevented me from being a perfect villain," he said. "It has kept me from the wine cup, and from the gambler's den."

"Pity it hadn't kept you out of the Southern army," was Bill's dry response, and the stranger answered, eagerly:

"I wish it had, I wish it had! Please give it back, and I'll swear allegiance to the veriest minion in Lincoln's train."

"I never thought no great of a turncoat," Bill replied, closing the case, and still holding it in his hand. "If you're a Southern dog, stay so, not go to barkin' on both sides. We don't want no traitors. Honest, though, corporal, where *was* you born? There's a kind of nateral look in your face, as if I'd seen it afore," and Bill laid the ambrotype upon the grass.

But with regard to his birthplace, the stranger was non-committal; and Bill continued:

"If I let you go, you'll give me the watch?"

"Willingly, willingly."

"And the spetacles?"

"Yes, oh yes."

"And the glass bead ring?"

"Yes, everything but the picture."

"Don't be so fast," Bill rejoined. "I'll get to that bimeby. Watch, spetacles, glass bead ring, tobarker-box, and this other thingumbob, but not the picter, if I'll let you go? And you'll go with me to Washington, and be showed up like a caravan if I'll give up the picter? Them's the terms as I understand."

"Yes," the stranger gasped, a shadow of hope stealing into his heart.

Alas, how soon it was erased by Bill's continuing:

"Yankees ain't generally very green. We can make you Southern bloods buy wooden cowcumber-seeds any time of day, and do you s'pose I'm goin' to let you off at any price? *No* SIR! If you go to war, you must take the chances of war. I ain't a-goin' to hurt you, and I'll ease up them strings if you say so, but, corporal, you're my prisoner; and these traps," laying his hand upon the various articles upon the grass, "these traps, picter and all, I *con-fis-cate* as *con-tra-band!* How do you feel now?" and Bill coolly pocketed his contrabands, all save the watch, which he adjusted about his neck.

There was a fierce storm of tears, and sobs, and wild entreaties, and then the poor discouraged soldier was still, his white face wearing again its look of cold, haughty reserve, and his whole manner indicative of the aversion he felt for the vulgar Bill, upon whom the feeling was entirely lost, for though Bill knew the proud Southerner felt above him, he could not appreciate the feelings which made the young man shrink from him as from a loathsome reptile. Bill had no intention of treating him cruelly, and as by this time the night shadows were creeping into the woods, he sought out a dryer and more sheltered spot, and bade his prisoner sleep while he sat by and watched. It seemed preposterous that the stranger should sleep under so great excitement, but human nature could endure no longer without rest, and when at last the stars came out, they shone down upon that tired soldier, sleeping upon the grass, with Bill sitting near, and watching as he slept. There were visions of home, and of the battle, too, it would seem, mingled in the young man's dreams, for he talked sometimes with his mother, asking her to forgive her boy, and take him back again to her love; then he was pleading for another, a captive it would seem, asking that nought but the best of care should come to the wounded officer; and then the picture flitted across his mind, for he held converse with the original, and Bill, listening to him, muttered:

"'Twas his gal, or sister, sure; I'm sorry for him, I *vum*, but hanged if I'll give it up. It's *contraband* according to war. He needn't of jined the army."

And so the weary night wore on, the deep stillness of the Virginia woods broken occasionally by the shouts of riders as they passed by, in search of whatever there was to find. Once, as the shouts came near, the soldier started up, but ere the scream for help had passed his lips, Bill's hand was laid firmly upon them, and Bill himself whispered fiercely.

"One yelp, and I gag you with the handkerchief the old woman took from her pocket and gin me the mornin' I come from home. She takes snuff, too, the old woman does!"

There was a gesture of disgust, and then the stranger became quiet again, while the shouts died away in the distance and were not heard again that night. The morning broke at last, and just as it was growing light, Bill, aroused by the falling rain from the slumber into which he had inadvertently fallen, awoke his prisoner, and led him safely through the pickets of the enemy without encountering a human being. They were a strange looking couple, and when, on the following day, they reached Washington, they attracted far more attention than the prisoner desired, for he shrunk nervously from the curious gaze fixed upon him, refusing to answer all questions as to his name or birthplace, and appearing glad when at last he was relieved from Bill's surveillance and led to his prison home.

CHAPTER X.
NEWS OF THE BATTLE AT ROCKLAND.

Great Battle at Manassas!

Total Rout of the Federal Army!

3,000 killed and as many more taken prisoners!

Fire Zouaves all cut to pieces!

Only three or four escape alive!

N. Y. 13th completely riddled!!!

Sherman's Battery, and hosts of guns in the hands of the Rebels!

Frightful Panic at Washington!

The Capitol in imminent danger!

Gen. Scott in convulsions, the President crazy, and Seward threatened with softening of the brain!

Women and children fleeing for their lives!

Beauregard marching on with 500,000 men!

The Baltimoreans in ecstasies, and the Philadelphians in despair!

Such were some of the exaggerated reports which ran like lightning through the streets of Rockland on the first arrival of the news, throwing the people into a greater panic than was said to exist in Washington. Hints of some terrible disaster, the exact nature of which could not be known until the arrival of the evening papers, had early in the afternoon found their way from the telegraphic station into the village, creating the most intense excitement. Men left their places of business to talk the matter over, while groups of women assembled at the street corners, discussing the probabilities of the case, and each hoping that *her* child, *her* husband, *her* brother had been spared.

Prominent among these was Widow Simms, holding fast to Susan's hand, and occasionally whispering a word of comfort to the poor child, whose eyes were red with weeping over the possible fate of John. Rose Mather's carriage drove up and down, and from its window Rose herself looked anxiously out, her face indicative of the anxiety she felt to hear the worst, if worst there were. She knew her husband could not have been in battle, for he was still in Washington, but she was conscious of a feeling as if some dire calamity were impending over her, and among the crowd collected in the street there was none who waited more impatiently for the coming of the evening train than she. She had taken Annie Graham to ride with her, and the two presented a most striking contrast, for where Rose was nervous, impatient and excited, Annie, though feeling none the less concerned, was quiet, submissive and resigned, exhibiting no outward emotion until the shrill whistle was heard across the plain, when a crimson flush stole into her cheek, deepening into a purple as the carriage drew up in front of the office, where the throng was growing denser,—men pushing past each other, and elbowing their way to a stand-point near the door, where they could catch the first item of news, and scatter it among the eager crowd. The papers came at last, and the damp sheets were almost torn asunder by the excited multitude.

"Me one,—me, please," and Rose Mather's hand was thrust from the window in time to catch a paper destined for some one farther in the rear, but ere she had found the column sought, she heard from those around her that the worst was realized.

There had been a battle. Our troops were utterly defeated, and worse than all, disgraced.

"But the 13th?" Annie whispered faintly. "Does it speak of the 13th?"

Rose did not know. Her interest just then was centered in the "Massachusetts——," and in her eagerness to hear from Tom, she forgot for a moment that such a regiment as the N. Y. 13th existed. But there were others who did not forget, and just as the question left Annie's lips, the answer came in the despairing cry which rent the air as some reckless person shouted aloud,

"The 13th a total wreck! Not a man left of Company R."

"Oh, George," poor Annie cried, and the next moment Rose held the fainting form upon her lap.

"Drive home,—to Mrs. Graham's I mean," she said to Jake, who, with some difficulty made his way through the crowd, but not until the story so cruelly set afloat was contradicted by those who had more coolly read the sad intelligence.

The news was bad enough, but the Rockland company was not mentioned, and its friends had no alternative but to wait until the telegraph wires should bring some tidings of the saved. Rose was the first to be remembered. Will did his duty faithfully.

"A terrible battle," his message ran. "Soldiers are arriving every hour, but Tom has not come yet."

A telegram for the Widow Simms came next, the mother's quick eye taking in at a glance that only Eli's name and John's were appended to it. Isaac's was not there. Where was he then, oh where? She asked this question frantically, refusing to read the note lest it should confirm her fears.

"I'll read it, mother. Let me see," Susan said, wresting the paper from her hands, and reading with trembling tones,

"Eli and I are safe. Isaac was last seen leading Lieut. Graham from the field."

Oh what a piteous wail went up to Heaven then, for Widow Simms, when she received the news, was sitting in Annie's door, and Annie was kneeling at her side. George was wounded, of course, and if wounded, dead, else why had he not thought of her ere this? Locked in each other's arms the two stricken women wept bitterly, the mother sobbing amid her tears, "My boy, my boy," while Annie moaned sadly, "My George, my husband."

Well was it for both that ere that dark hour came they had learned to follow on, even when their Father's footsteps were in the sea, knowing the hand which guided would never lead them wrong. Annie was the first to rally.

"It might not after all be so bad," she said. "George and Isaac were prisoners, perhaps, but even that was preferable to death. It would surely save them from danger in future battles. The Southerners would not maltreat helpless captives. There were kind people South as well as North."

Thus Annie reasoned, and the widow felt herself grow stronger as hope whispered of a brighter day to-morrow.

To Annie it was brighter, for it brought her news of George, wounded in his right arm, an inmate of the hospital, and at present too weak to write. This was all, but it comforted the young wife. He was not dead. He might come home again, and Annie's heart overflowed with grateful thanksgiving that while so many were bereaved of their loved ones she had been mercifully spared. The next mail brought her a second letter from Mr. Mather, more minute in its particulars than any which had preceded it. He had obtained permission to stay with George, had removed him to a private boarding-house, far more comfortable than the crowded hospital; and, at his request he wrote to Annie that her husband, though badly wounded and suffering much from the terrible excitement of the battle, was not thought dangerous, and had strong hopes of ere long receiving his discharge and returning home where she could nurse him back to life.

This was Annie's message, read by her eagerly, while the Widow Simms, forgetting all formality in her anxiety to hear if there was aught concerning her boy, looked over her shoulder, her eye darting from line to line until she caught *his name*. There was something of him, and grasping Annie's arm, she whispered,

"Read what it says of Isaac."

And Annie read how brave Tom Carleton had generously given place to the poor wounded George, and staid behind him with Isaac, hoping to make his way to Washington in safety. They had not been heard from since, and the widow's heart was sick as heart could be with the dread uncertainty. Anything was preferable to this suspense, and in a state of mind bordering upon distraction she walked the floor, now wringing her hands and again declaring her intention to start at once for somewhere. She knew not whither, or cared, provided she found her child.

In the midst of her excitement the gate swung open, and Mrs. Baker rushed up the walk, her sleeves above her elbows, and her hair pushed back from her bonnetless head, just as she had left her washing at a neighbor's when she received *Bill's letter*, which told of Hal's sad fate, and unravelled the mystery of Tom Carleton's silence.

"He's took! The Rebels have got your Ike!" she shrieked, brandishing aloft the soiled missive, and howling dismally. Then, putting her hand into her bosom, she drew forth the lock of hair, and thrusting it almost in to the widow's face, cried out, "Look, 'tis Harry's hair, all there is left of Harry. That's what I git for havin' a boy two inches taller than Ike, who stood in front, and would of been shot instead of Harry, only he was shorter. Read it, Miss Graham," and tossing the letter into Annie's lap, the wretched woman sank upon the doorstep, and covering her face with her wet apron, rocked back and forth, while Annie read aloud as follows:

"WASHINGTON, *July 24th*, 1861.

"DEAR MOTHER: We've met the rascals, and been as genteelly licked as ever a pack of fools could ask to be. How it happened nobody knows. I was fitin' like a tiger, when all on a sudden I found us a-runnin' like a flock of sheep; and what is the queerest of all, is that while we were takin' to our heels one way the Rebels were goin' it t'other, and for what I know, we should of been runnin' from each other till now if they hadn't found out the game, and so turned upon us.

"But wust of all is to come. *Hal* is dead,—shot right through the forehead, and the ball that struck him down took off Ike Simmses cap, so if Ike had been only a little taller, Hal would of lived to been hung most likely."

"Oh, I wish he had, I wish he had!" poor Mrs. Baker moaned, still waving back and forth and kissing the lock of hair, while the widow involuntarily thanked her Heavenly Father that the two inches she once so earnestly coveted for her boy had wisely been withheld.

Then followed Bill's account of cutting away the hair he inclosed, of his flight into the woods, his sleep by the brook, and his waking just in time to see

Capt. Carleton and Isaac Simms disappear beneath the trees, in charge of rebel soldiers.

Now that she knew the worst the widow sat like one stunned by a heavy blow, uttering no sound, as Annie read Bill's account of capturing his prisoner. Ere she reached this point, however, she had another auditor, Rose Mather, who had come with a second letter from her husband, and who, passing the weeping woman in the door, came and stood by Annie, and listened with strange interest to the story of that captive parting so willingly with everything save the picture.

"Poor young man!" she sighed, when Annie finished reading. "I don't suppose it's right, but I *do* feel sorry for him. What if it had been Jimmie? Perhaps he has a sister somewhere weeping for him just as I cried for Tom. Dear Tom, Will writes he is a prisoner with Isaac Simms. I'm glad they are together. Tom will take care of Isaac. He had a quantity of gold tied around his waist," and Rose's soft hand smoothed caressingly the widow's thin, light hair.

The widow had not wept before, but at the touch of those little fingers the flood gates opened wide, and her tears fell in torrents. They were bound together now by a common bond of sympathy, those four women, each so unlike to the other, and for a time they wept in silence, one for her wounded husband, one for a child deceased, one for a captured brother, the other for a son.

Now, as ever, Annie was the first to speak of hope, and her words were fraught with comfort to all save Harry's mother. She could not comfort her, for from reckless, misguided Harry's grave, there came no ray of consolation, but to the others she spoke of One who would not desert the weary captives. Neither bolt nor bar could shut Him out. God was in Richmond as well as there at home, and none could tell what good might spring from this seeming great evil. For a long time they talked together, and the afternoon was half spent when at last they separated, Rose going back to her luxurious home where she wrote to her mother the sad news concerning Tom, blurring with great tears the line in which she spoke of Jimmie, wondering what his fate had been.

Slowly, disconsolately poor Mrs. Baker returned to her day's work so long neglected, but the suds she left so hot two hours before had grown cold, the fire burned out, and with that weary, discouraged feeling which poverty alone can prompt, she was setting herself to the task of bringing matters up again, when her employer, touched with the sight of the white, anguished face, kindly bade her leave the work until another day, and seek the quiet she so much needed. Poor old woman! How desolate it was going back to the squalid house where everything, even to the bootjack he had once hurled at her head, reminded her of the Harry who would come back no more! She did not think of his unkindness now. That was all forgotten, and motherlike, she remembered only the times when he was good and treated her like something half way human. He was her boy,—her first-born, and as she lay with her tear-stained face buried in the scanty pillows of her humble bed, she recalled to mind the time when first he lisped the sweet word mother, and twined his baby arms about her neck.

He was a bright, pretty child, easily influenced for good or evil, and the rude mother shuddered as she felt creeping over her the conviction that she had helped to make him what he grew to be, laughing at his fierce temper and at times provoking him on purpose, just to see him bump his little round, hard head against the oaken floor. Then, as he grew older, it was fun to hear him imitate the oaths his father used, and she had laughed at that until the habit became so firmly fixed that neither threats nor punishment could break it. And when the Sabbath bells were pealing forth their summons to the house of prayer, she had suffered him to stay away, offering but slight remonstrance when the robin's nest just without the door was pilfered of its unfledged occupants, the mother-bird moaning over its murdered young, just as she was moaning now over her ruined boy. Poor Harry! There was some excuse for him, some apology found in the nature of his early training, but for her who reared him,—none. She might have taught him better. She might have sent him to the Sunday school across the way, where Sunday after Sunday she had heard the hymns the children sang swelling on the Sabbath air, Harry sometimes joining in as he sat in the cottage door, adjusting the bait with which to tempt the unsuspecting fish playing in the brook nearby. A mother's fearful responsibility had been hers. She had not fulfilled it, and it rolled back upon her now, stinging as only remorse can sting, and making her wish amid her pain that the boy, once so earnestly desired, had never been given her, or else had died in its cradle bed, and so gone where she knew the hardened in sin never could find entrance.

So absorbed was she in her grief as not to hear the sound of wheels stopping near her gate, nor the tripping footstep upon the floor. Rose Mather, restless at home and wishing for something to do, had remembered the miserable woman, and knowing how desolate her comfortless house must seem that summer night, she had conquered her aversion to the place and come to speak, if possible, a word of cheer. Mrs. Baker's howls always had the effect of making her laugh, they seemed so forced, so unnatural; but there was something so new, so real in the stillness of that figure crouching upon the bed, that Rose for a moment was uncertain how to act. It was no feigned sorrow of which she was a witness now, and advancing at last towards the untidy bed, she laid her hand upon the disordered, uncombed hair, and whispered soothingly, "I am so sorry for you, Mrs. Baker, and I'll do all I can to help you. I'll give you money to make your cottage pleasanter, and by and by you won't feel so badly, maybe."

This was Rose's idea of comfort. Money, in her estimation, was to the poor a panacea for nearly every evil, but all her wealth could not avail to quiet the feeling of remorse from which Mrs. Baker was suffering. With a sob she thanked the kind-hearted Rose, and then continued, "'Tain't the poverty so much, nor the knowin' that he's dead, though that is bad enough. It's the something that tells me I or'to have brung him up better. I never sent him to meetin', never went myself, never had him baptized, though I did try once to learn him 'Now I lay me—' but he, that's my man, laughed me out of it. He said there wasn't any God, that we all come by chance, but I knew better. *I* had a prayin' mother, and though I forgot what she learnt me, it 'pears to come back to me now. Oh, Harry, I wish I'd done different, I do, I do," and the repentant woman buried her face again in the scanty pillows, while Rose looked pityingly on.

Here was a case she could not reach. Money would not cure that aching heart, or quiet that guilty conscience. "Mrs. Graham would know exactly what to say," Rose thought, wishing more and more that she, too, possessed the wisdom which would have told her what it was poor Mrs. Baker needed. Sitting down beside her, Rose talked to her of *Bill*, who, her husband said, was highly complimented for having captured a rebel. Will had not seen the prisoner, she said, or heard his name; he only knew the fact, and that Bill was greatly praised. This was some consolation to Mrs. Baker, but it did not take the pain away, and as she was not inclined to converse, Rose soon bade her good-bye and left her there alone in her deep sorrow.

The following Sunday, just as the notes of the organ were dying away in the opening service, a bent, shrinking figure stole noiselessly in at the open door, and Rose Mather recognized beneath the thin black veil, the haggard face of Widow Baker, who, except on funeral occasions, had never before been seen within the walls of the church. Annie saw her, too, and while Rose, touched with the humble attempt she had made to put on something like mourning for her child, thought how she would give her an entire new suit of black, Annie thought how she would daily pray that the blow which had fallen so crushingly might result in everlasting good to the now stricken mother.

Scarcely less keen, but of a far different nature, was the grief of Widow Simms. There was no black upon her leghorn bonnet. She would not have worn it if Isaac had been dead, but every expression of her stern face told how constantly her heart was going out after her darling boy, her captured Isaac languishing in his sultry prison, sick perhaps, and pining for his mother. How savage she felt toward Beauregard and all his clan, resolving at times to start herself for Richmond, and beard the lion in his den.

"She'd tell them what was what," she said. "She'd let them know what an injured mother could do. She'd turn a second *Charlotte Corduroy*, if necessary, and free the land from such vile monsters," and she actually sharpened up her shears as a weapon of offence in case the pilgrimage were made!

This was the Widow Simms excited, but the Widow Simms when calm was a very different woman, praying then for her boy, and even asking forgiveness for the stirrers up of the rebellion. At Annie's request she had at last come to live altogether at the cottage in the Hollow, and it was well for both that they should be together, for the widow's stronger will upheld the weaker Annie who, in her turn, imparted much of her own trusting, childish faith to the less trusting widow.

Greatly Annie mourned as the days went on, because no line came to her from George himself, nothing in his own handwriting, when he knew how she desired it, if it were but just his name. What made him always deputize Mr. Mather to write his letters for him? Annie put this question once to *Rose*, but the twilight was gathering over them, and so she failed to see the heightened color on Rose's cheek and the moisture in her eye. Rose did not now, as formerly, bring her William's letters, and read to her every word he said of George. She only told her how cheerfully George bore his illness, and how Will read to him every day from Annie's Bible, choosing always the passages she had marked, but the rest was all withheld and Annie never dreamed the reason, or of the effort it cost the talkative little Rose to keep back what William said she must until the worst were known.

Thus the August days glided by, one by one, until the summer light faded from the Rockland hills, and September threw over them her rich autumnal bloom, and then one day there came a note for Annie, written as of old by William Mather, but signed by George himself. Poor Annie, how she cried over and kissed that signature, to which George had added, "God bless you, darling Annie." Every letter was unnaturally distorted, and few could have deciphered the words; but to the eye of love they were plain as noonday, and Annie's kisses dropped upon them until they were still more blurred than when they came to her.

It was very hard for Rose to keep from telling the dreadful story of what had followed the penning of those brief words, "God bless you, darling Annie." But Will had said she must not, so she made no sign, only her arms clung closer around Annie's neck, and her lips lingered longer upon the snowy forehead as she said good-night, and went away with the secret which Annie must not know then.

CHAPTER XI.
THE WOUNDED SOLDIER.

How those polished, cruel-looking instruments sparkled, and glittered, and flashed; and how the sick man shuddered as he glanced toward the table where they lay, asking, with quivering lip, if there were no other alternative save the one their presence suggested.

"None but speedy death!" was the response of the attending surgeon, who was too much accustomed to just such scenes as this, to appreciate the feelings of that poor soldier, shrinking so painfully from what they told him must be if he would live.

"None but speedy death,"—George repeated the words slowly to himself, dwelling longest upon the last, as if to accustom himself to thoughts of it.

"Wait a little, wait till I think the matter over," he said, in reply to the question, "are you ready?" and turning his face to the wall, so that those about him should not see the fearful conflict going on, he thought long and earnestly. Wasn't it better to die than go back to Annie maimed and disfigured for life? Better die than lose a portion of the manly beauty of which he had been so proud. Would Annie love him just the same, even though the strong right arm, which had toiled for her so cheerfully, could never work for her again, never encircle her in its embrace? Would the scarred stump be as dear to her as the well-moulded limb had been? He did not know, and the tears, which all through the weary days of his sickness had been kept back, now fell like rain upon the pillow, as he fancied the meeting between his sweet young wife, and her poor, crippled husband. The cottage on the hill so earnestly coveted, would never be theirs now. He could not earn it. He could not earn *much* any way, with his left arm, and he groaned aloud, as he thought of the poor unfortunate seen so often in the Rochester depot, peddling daily papers. Would he ever come to that? He, who, but a few months ago had so bright hopes for the future? Would the delicate Annie he had meant to shield so carefully from every ill of life, yet be compelled to earn the bread she ate? It was a sad, sad picture the excited soldier drew of what the future might bring, and the fainting spirit had almost cried out, "I would rather die!" when there came stealing across his mind the memory of Annie's parting words,

"If the body you bring back has in it my George's heart, I shall love you all the same."

Yes, she would love him just the same, for, as it was not her fair, sweet face alone which made her so dear to him, so it was not his splendid form which made him dear to her. Annie's love would not abate, even though he went back to her the veriest cripple that ever crawled the earth. But how different his going home would be from what he had fondly hoped. No papers heralding his arrival; no dense crowd out to meet him; no fife trilling a jubilee; no drum beating a welcome; no bell ringing its merry peal; no carriage, no procession; nothing but the curious gaze of the few who might come out to see how George Graham looked without an arm, and whisper softly to each other, "Poor fellow, how I pity him!" He didn't want to be pitied; he would almost rather die; and he did not want to die either, when he thought calmly of it. He was not prepared; and forcing back the bitter tears, he turned his white, worn face to William Mather, bending so sadly over him, and whispered:

"Tell them they may cut it off, but not till you've written to Annie, and I have signed my name. You know how she has begged for a word from me. Tell them to keep away; they shall not intrude on my interview with Annie."

George was growing excited, but he became calm again when he found himself alone with Mr. Mather, who wrote the letter which gave Annie so much joy. There was nothing in it of the expected amputation; nothing but encouragement that he should ere long come home to stay with her always.

"There, give me the pen," he said, when the letter was finished, and the trembling fingers grasped it eagerly, but quickly let it fall as the purple, festered flesh above the elbow throbbed and quivered with the pain the sudden effort caused. "Once more; I'll do it if it costs my life!" he whispered, nerving himself with might and main, and then, with Mr. Mather guiding his hand, he wrote his name, and the words, "God bless you, darling Annie!" "It's done, and she must never know the agony it cost me," he moaned, as his bandaged arm fell heavily at his side, while with his other hand he wiped away the sweat which stood so thickly upon his face. "Bring Annie's Bible," he said, "and lay it on my pillow. It will make me bear it better. Oh, Annie, Annie, if you could be here to pray for me! Can't *you*?" and the dim eyes turned imploringly toward Mr. Mather who shook his head hesitatingly.

Man of the world as he had been, he had not yet learned to pray, but he could not resist that touching appeal, and bending down he answered:

"I never learned to pray, but while the operation is going on, I'll do the best I can. Shall I call them now?"

George nodded, and William admitted the two surgeons, who were growing somewhat impatient at the delay. They were not naturally hard-hearted men, but years of practice had brought them to look on amputations in a mere business point of view. Still there was something about this case which touched a chord of sympathy, and they spoke kindly to the sufferer, telling him it would soon be over, and was not half so bad as losing a leg would be.

George made no reply except to shudder nervously as he saw the cold, polished steel so soon to cut into his flesh.

"You'll need bandages," he said, his mind flashing backward to the day when he had looked in at Rockland Hall, where Annie, with others, sat working for just such a scene as this.

"It's here," Mr. Mather answered, pointing to a table where lay a ball prepared for Company R.

Without knowing why he did so, Mr. Mather took it up and began mechanically to unroll it, pausing suddenly as traces of a pencil met his view. There was something written there,—something which made him start as he read, "Annie Howard. It's your Annie, George. Try to think I'm there. Rockland, April, 1861."

Was it a happen so, or a special providence that this bit of linen, over which Annie's prayers had been breathed, should come at last to him for whom it was intended? Mr. Mather believed the latter, and pointed it out to George, who, comprehending the truth at a glance, uttered a wild, glad cry of joy as he pressed it to his lips.

"Yes, Annie, I know you are here. I can feel your presence, and it will help to ease the pain. Begin without delay. Don't wait, if it must be done."

There was a moment's silence, a shutting of both William's and George's eyes, and a shriek of anguish rang through the room as George cried out, "Oh, Annie, Annie, stand up closer to me,—it makes me faint, it hurts me so bad! Pray, Mr. Mather, pray!" and Mr. Mather did pray, the first prayer which had passed his lips since his early boyhood,—not aloud, but silently; and the writhing victim grew still at last, only shivering once as the sharp saw glided through the splintered bone. Carefully they bound up the bleeding stump with the soft linen Annie had sent, speaking comforting words to the sufferer, who seemed to be stupefied, for he did not notice what they said.

It was done at last; and after few directions the operators hurried off to do for others, what they had done for George. Poor George, how long and weary were the days and nights immediately succeeding the amputation, and how horrible the sensation which prompted him to fancy the severed limb was there; to feel the hot blood tingling through his finger tips, throbbing through his wrists, streaming into his elbow joints, and then to know 'twas all a mere delusion, for the right arm once so full of vigor, was nought now, save a putrifying mass buried away beneath the sod. He would not have Annie know it yet, he said. He would rather spare her as long as possible, and so the news was withheld from her, while day after day George waited and watched for the favorable change which should make it safe for him to undertake the tedious journey. Three times was the travelling-bag packed, with the hope of going to-morrow, and as often did the doctor's stern mandate bid him wait a little longer.

At last the terribly nervous sensation passed away, taking with it all the pain, and leaving no feeling save one of intense uneasiness and languor, which the once strong man strove in vain to shake off, trying day after day to sit up, if only for a moment, and as often falling back upon his pillows from sheer exhaustion. He was only tired; he had never been rested since the battle, he said, and if he could once go home to Annie, and lie upon the lounge, where he last saw her kneeling, he should get well so fast. Often in his troubled sleep he talked of her, begging her not to spurn her poor, crippled husband, but to love him just the same.

"I never can work for you as I used to do," he would say, "never can buy that cottage on the hill, but God won't let us starve, and I shall love you so much, so much, when I find you do not shrink away from poor, mutilated George."

It was a sad, but not unprofitable lesson, which William Mather was learning by that bedside. At home in Rockland, where their positions were so different, he had always respected George Graham, but he had learned to love him now with a brother's love, and gladly would he have saved him for the sweet wife in whom his own darling Rose was so deeply interested, and whose letters were silently working good in him as well as George. Greatly his personal friends marvelled that he should stay so closely immured within that sick-room, when he might, had he chosen, have mingled much in the world without, and many were the attempts they made to drag him away. But he withstood them all, and clung the closer to his friend, who leaned upon him with all the trustful confidence of a little child. Hour after hour he sat by his patient, reading to him from Annie's well-worn Bible, and when at last the heavy cloud was lifted, and the pathway through the valley of death was divested of its gloom, he was the first to whom the sick man imparted the joyful news, that whether he lived or died, all was well,—all was peace within.

In silence and in tears Mr. Mather listened to the story of what was so strange to him, and in the next letter sent to Rose, he told her of the new resolves awakened within him, tracing them back to that humble cottage in the Hollow, where Annie Graham, unknown save to a few, was wielding a mighty power for good. Everything which he could do for George he did, and Annie herself could scarcely have been more gentle or kind; and George,—oh how grateful he was to his noble friend, blessing him so often for the kindly deeds.

"God will surely let you go home unharmed," he said one day when Mr. Mather had been more than usually attentive. "I pray to Heaven every hour, that you may never know the dreary heart-pang it costs one to die away from home, and all that we hold dear, for I am dying. I have given up the delusion that to-morrow will find me better. I shall never be better until I wake in Heaven,—shall never go back to Annie,—never see my old home again. It is a humble home, Mr. Mather, but you can't begin to guess how dear it is to me, because it is the spot where I brought Annie after she was mine. How well I remember that first night of housekeeping; how proud I felt, knowing it was my home, my table, my wife sitting opposite—that her own darling hands had made the tea, and cut the bread she passed me, and that I had earned it, too. The poor have many joys to which the rich are strangers, and I've sometimes thought we love each other more because there is little else to divide our love. True it is that mortal man never loved a creature better than I have loved my Annie. She was of gentler blood than I,—was far more delicately reared, and I know it was an unequal match. She was far above me in social position. Highly educated and accomplished, too; she was a belle and favorite everywhere, while I was only George Graham,—a mechanic and engineer. She kept nothing from me, and she told me of a childish fancy when she was a mere girl of fourteen, but if she ever sent a regret after the handsome, black-eyed boy,—the object of that fancy,—it was not perceptible to me. Still, I think that may have had its influence,—that, and the fact that her life was very wretched with her proud, hard aunt, on whom she was dependent, and who wanted her to marry a white-haired millionaire. But Annie chose me, and I have worshipped her with an idolatry which I know was sinful in the sight of Heaven, who will have the first place in our hearts. I have told you all this because your wife has been a friend to Annie, and I want her to know that Annie is her equal, if she did marry a poor mechanic. I am not blaming any one. I know the distinctions there are in social life. I should feel just so, too, perhaps, if I was rich and had been educated as you were. Even as it is I always was proud to think my wife was a lady-born, and I hoped one day to raise her to the position she ought to fill. But that dream is over now. It matters little what becomes of the body after the soul has left it, though I should rather lie in Rockland graveyard, where Annie can sometimes come to see me, and I do so want to hear her voice once more before I go,—to tell her with my own lips that if in Heaven I find a place, she has led me there."

"Suppose we send for her," Mr. Mather said, the glad thought flashing upon his mind of the joy it would be to see his own darling once more, for if Annie came, Rose, he knew, was sure to come also. "I'll send for both Annie and Rose at once. They can come on together."

Mr. Graham made no objection, and Mr. Mather set himself to the task of writing the letter, which he hoped was to bring not only Annie, but his own precious Rose.

"Don't say a word about my *arm*. I'd rather tell her myself. She won't mind it so much when she sees how sick and weak I am," George suggested; and so Mr. Mather bade Rose keep the amputation to herself as heretofore.

"You will defray Mrs. Graham's expenses," he wrote, "and come as soon as possible, for her husband is nearer death than you imagine."

The letter was finished and read aloud to George, who faintly nodded his thanks, and then the message was sent on its way to the North.

CHAPTER XII.
GETTING READY.

"Oh, I've such perfectly splendid news this morning. We are going to Washington right away, you and I, for Will says so in his letter. You see George is a great deal,—George can't,—well, *George isn't very well*," and quite delighted with the happy turn she had given her words, Rose skipped around Annie's cottage like a bird, lighting at last upon a stool at Annie's feet, and asking if she were not glad. "Why, how white you are!" she exclaimed, as she observed the paleness of Annie's cheek. "What makes you? Don't you want to go?"

Annie was not deceived by Rose's abrupt turn. She knew that George was worse, else he had never sent for her: and hence the sudden faintness, which Rose's gay badinage could not shake off at once.

"Did your husband write, or mine?" she asked, and Rose replied,

"Will, of course. George has never written, you know."

"Yes, I know;" and in Annie's voice there was a tone approaching nearer to bitterness than any that Rose had ever heard from her. "Where is the letter? Let me read it for myself."

But Rose had found it convenient to leave the letter at home, and so she answered,

"I did not bring it with me. I can tell you all there is in it."

"But will you?" and Annie grasped her shoulder firmly. "Will you tell me all? Tell me what it is about my husband, and why he never writes? Is George dying, and is that the reason why he sends for me? Tell me, Mrs. Mather, for I will not be put off longer."

There was a look in the blue eyes before which Rose fairly quailed, and turning her face away she answered truthfully,

"Yes, George is very sick. He will never come home again; and he wants you there when he dies."

Softly the quivering lips repeated, "When he dies!" poor Annie wondering if it could be George who was meant. *Had* the evil she most dreaded come upon her at last? Must she give her husband up and live without him? How dark, how cheerless the future looked, stretching before her through many years it might be! Was there no hope,—no help? It was Annie's darkest hour of trial, and for a moment the spirit fainted, refusing to bear the load which, though more than half-expected, had come so sudden at the last. But Annie was not one to murmur long, and Rose Mather never forgot the sweet submissive smile which played over her white face as she said,

"Whether George lives or dies, God will do all things well."

After this there was no more repining, no more bitterness of tone, nothing save humble submission to whatever might be in store for her.

Rose was very enthusiastic on the subject of the Washington trip, and Annie listened eagerly to her suggestions.

"It is absurd for two young ladies like us to travel alone," Rose said. "We must have some nice elderly woman to matronize the party. I mean to write to mother to send up one from Boston."

"Miss Marthers," interrupted the Widow Simms, who sat by the window knitting for some soldier boy, "Miss Marthers, don't be a simpleton, a sendin' down to Boston for somebody to marternize you and Miss Graham, when you can find forty of 'em nearer home. Let *me* go. Eli and John are there, you know; and 'tain't such a great ways to Richmond, where my poor Isaac is. Did I tell you I got a letter last night from a strange woman up in New Hampshire, whose boy was in the battle? The rascals let your brother write to her, because there was something between her Charlie and a rebel officer who was good to the child, when he was dyin'. There's now and then a streak of good amongst 'em."

"Yes; but what of *Tom?*" Rose asked eagerly, forgetting Washington in her anxiety to hear from her brother, of whom not one word had been known after his name had appeared in the paper as one of the prisoners at Richmond, together with that of a boy called "Isaac Simpson."

The more humane of Captain Carleton's captors had repeated what the dying officer said of Tom's kindness to him, and for this Tom had at last found opportunity for sending a note to Charlie's mother, telling her how her darling died, and asking her to write for him to his mother, his sister and the Widow Simms. This the grateful woman had done, but Rose had not received her letter yet, and she listened eagerly while the widow read the very words which Tom had written concerning himself and Isaac. There was but little said of suffering or privation. Tom, it would seem, was tolerably well cared for, but he told of days and nights when his heart went out in earnest longings for the loved ones at home, and then he spoke of Isaac, saying,

"Tell his mother that he does not bear prison confinement well, and she would hardly know her boy. He is very popular among his fellow prisoners, and does more good, I verily believe, than half our army chaplains. One poor fellow, who died the other day, blessed Isaac Simms as the means of leading him to Heaven."

"Oh, I'm so glad he's there, ain't you?" and the tears shone in Rose's eyes as she involuntarily paid this tribute to Christianity.

"On some accounts I am, and then again I ain't," was the widow's reply, as she wiped the moisture from her glasses and returned them to her pocket. "I'm glad he's doing good, but I don't want him sick there alone, without his mother. It's hard to see why these things are so, but that's nothin' to do with the goin' to Washington. Will you take me, Mrs. Marthers? I know I'm homespun and ignorant, but you may call me waitin maid, or anything you like, if you'll only take me."

The widow's voice was full of entreaty, and Rose could not resist it. It would be *grander*, she thought, to have a woman from Boston, but then Mrs. Simms wanted to go so badly, while Annie, too, preferred her, she was sure. So it was settled that as soon as the necessary arrangements could be made, Mrs. Simms, Annie and Rose were to start for the Federal Capital. Had the care of an entire regiment devolved upon Rose, she could not have been busier or have felt a greater responsibility than she did in planning and arranging the journey, and between times trying to initiate Widow Simms into the mysteries of travelling, telling her not to be frightened and think they'd run off the track each time the whistle blew,—not to show undue anxiety about her baggage, as she—Rose—should hold the checks, little brass pieces, which they would get at the depot,—not to bother the conductor by asking questions, or let the people know that she had never been further in the cars than Rochester.

To all these directions the widow gravely promised compliance, saying, in an aside to Annie, "It does me good to see the little critter patternize me, as if she s'posed I was a tarnal fool, and didn't know a steam *locofoco* from a canal boat."

The day before the one appointed for the commencement of the journey came at last. Rose's three trunks, of the size which makes the porters *swear*, were packed to their utmost capacity, for Rose meant to make a winter's campaign, and display her numerous dresses at parties and levees. So everything which she could possibly and impossibly need, even to her skating dress, was stowed away in the huge boxes, together with various luxuries for her husband and George, and then, as the afternoon was drawing to a close, she started for the cottage in the Hollow, to see that everything there was in readiness.

It had not taken the widow long to pack up her three dresses, and her small, old-fashioned hair trunk, locked and tied round with a bit of rope, was standing near the door ready for the morrow's early train. On Annie's face there was a hopeful, expectant expression, which told how glad she was at the prospect of meeting her husband so soon.

"Two days more and I shall see him," she thought, picturing to herself the meeting, and fancying what she would do, what she would say, and how carefully she would nurse him when once she was there with him. It was a bright picture she drew of that meeting with her husband,—of the kisses, the caresses, she would lavish upon him, and she was almost as impatient as Rose herself to have the November day come to an end, knowing that with the darkness she was nearer to the asked-for to-morrow.

Just as the sun was setting, Rose took her leave, saying, as she bade Annie good-bye, "I mean to drive round by the depot and get the tickets to-night, so as to save time in the morning."

Annie smiled at the little lady's restlessness, and after kissing her good-night, stood by the window watching her, as she drove down the street, and thinking to herself,

"When I see her again it will be *to-morrow.*"

Rapidly Rose Mather's iron greys bore her to the depot, where but a few idlers were lounging, as it was past the hour for the cars. The window between the ladies' sitting-room, and the office was closed, and Rose knocked against it in vain. The ticket agent had gone to his tea, and with a feeling of dissatisfaction Rose was turning away, when a sharp, clicking sound from an adjoining apartment reached her ear, and stepping to the open door, she stood looking in, while the telegraphic operator received a communication. What was it that made him start so, and utter an exclamation of surprise? Was it bad news the wires had brought to him? Had there been another battle? Was Washington in danger? Rose wished she knew, and she was about to inquire, when the operator turned upon her, and asked if she knew *Mrs. Graham*, wife of the Lieutenant?

"Yes, yes; has anything happened to him?" she answered, grasping the now written message, which the agent handed her, saying:

"Break it to her as gently as possible. He was the finest fellow in all the company," and the kind-hearted man, not yet accustomed to the horrors entailed by the war, wiped a tear away, as he muttered to himself, "Poor George!"

There was no need for Rose to open the envelope, for she knew well enough what it contained, but her fingers mechanically tore it apart, and with streaming eyes she read the fatal message which would break poor Annie's heart.

"Oh, I *cannot* tell her," she cried, sinking down upon the hard settee, and sobbing bitterly. "How can I take this to her, when I left her so happy half an hour ago?"

But it must be done, and summoning all her courage she bade Jake drive back to the Hollow, shivering as she saw the cheerful light shining from the window, and shrinking more and more from the task imposed upon her, when, as she drew nearer, she saw Annie's bright, joyous face as she put together the garments for to-morrow, pausing occasionally to speak to Widow Simms, who sat before the blazing fire, dreaming visions of what might be could she but get a pass to Richmond!

"Don't you hear wheels?" the widow asked as the carriage stopped before the gate.

Annie thought she did, and going to window she saw Rose as she came up she walk.

"Why, it's Mrs. Mather," she cried. "What can have brought her back to-night?" and hastening to the door she led Rose in, asking why she was there.

"Oh, Annie," Rose replied, winding her arms around Annie's neck, "I wish I did not have to tell, but I must, and I know it will kill you dead. I'm sure it would me, and I don't see why you should be served so either. We shall not go to-morrow, for Will is going to bring him home. Don't you know now? Can't you guess?" and Rose thrust the dispatch into the hands of the bewildered Annie, who clutched it eagerly, and bending to the lamplight, read what Rose had read before her.

It came to her like a thunderbolt, striking all the deeper because it found her so full of eager expectation; and the November wind, as it swept past the door, and down the lonely Hollow, took with it one wailing cry of anguish, and then all was still within the cottage, save the sobbing whispers of Widow Simms and Rose bending over the unconscious form which lay upon the bed, so white and still that a terrible fear entered the hearts of both lest the stricken Annie, too, were dead.

CHAPTER XIII.
THE DYING SOLDIER.

Backward now we turn, and stand again in the chamber where we saw the glitter of the polished steel, and heard the bitter cry forced out by pain from lips unused to give such sign of weakness. They were white now as the wintry snow which covers the Northern hills, and the breath came feebly from between them, as the sick man whispered faintly:

"I shall not be here if Annie comes, for when the drum beats on the morrow, calling my comrades to their daily drill, I shall be far away where sounds of battle were never heard but once. Oh the peace, the quiet, the rest, there is in Heaven. I hope you will one day come to share it with me; you who have been kinder than a brother," and the long, white fingers grasped the hand which for so many days and weeks had soothed the aching head and cooled the fevered pillows with all a woman's tenderness.

Never for an hour had that faithful friend deserted his post. Day and night had found him there, ministering to every want, and, as far as human aid could do, smoothing the pathway leading so surely down to death. But his vigils were almost over now; his release was just at hand, for, as George had said, the morrow's drum-beat would only find there the body, which was so worn by suffering and disease, that William Mather could lift it in his arms as easily as he could have lifted a little child. He was greatly changed from the days when he had been aptly called the Rockland Hercules. But as the outer man decayed, the inner life grew strong and bright, shining forth at the last with all the splendor which perfect faith in Christ's Atonement can shed around a death-bed. There was no repining now, no murmuring at the mysterious dealings of Providence, nothing but sweet, childish confidence, and a patient waiting for the end coming on so fast that George himself could feel the irregular beat of his wiry pulse, and mark the death hue as it came creeping on, settling first in purplish spots about his finger tips, and spreading its ashen coloring over his clammy hands.

A stormy November night had closed over Washington, and the rain beat dismally against the windows of the room where Mr. Mather bent over the dying soldier, listening to what he said.

"You can't tell Annie *all*," George whispered, looking fondly up into the face he had learned to love so well. "You must write it down so as not to lose a single word. Bring pen and paper, and then sit where I can see you, for the sight of you does me good; you have been so kind to me."

The writing utensils were brought, and then sitting where George could look into his face, Mr. Mather wrote as the dying man dictated:

MY DEAR, DEAR, DARLING ANNIE:—It will be days, perhaps, before you see this letter, and ere it reaches you somebody will have told you that your poor George is dead! Are you crying, darling, as you read this? Do the tears fall upon the words, '*poor George is dead?*' Don't cry, my precious Annie. It makes my heart ache to think how you will sorrow and I not there to comfort you. It's hard to die away from home, but not so hard as it would once have been, for I hope I am a different man from the one who bade you good-bye a few short months ago; and, darling, it *must* comfort you to know that your prayers, your sweet influence have led the wanderer home to God. We shall meet again in Heaven, Annie,—meet where partings are unknown. It may be many years, perhaps, and the grass upon my grave may blossom many times ere you will sleep the sleep which knows no waking but at the last you'll come where I am waiting you. I *know* I shall be there, Annie. All the harassing doubts and fears are gone. Simple faith in the Saviour's promise has taken them away, and left me perfect peace. God bless you, Annie darling, and grant that as you have guided me, so you may guide others to that home above, where I am going so fast. You have made me very happy since you have been my wife, and I bless you for it. It makes my death pillow easier to know that not one bitter word has ever passed between us,—nothing but perfect confidence and love. I was not good enough for you, darling. None knows that better than myself. You should have married one of gentler blood and higher birth than I, a poor mechanic. I have always felt this more than you, perhaps, and have tried so hard not to shame you with my homespun ways, had I lived, I should have improved constantly beneath your refining influence, but that is all past now, and it is well, perhaps, that it is so. As you grew older you *might* have felt there was a lack in me, a something which did not satisfy the cravings of your higher nature, and though you might not have loved me less, you would have seen that we were not wholly congenial. I am well enough in my way, but I am not a suitable companion for a girl of culture like yourself, and I've often wondered that you should have chosen me. But you did, and again I bless you for it. Never, never, was year so happy as the one I spent with you, my darling, darling Annie, and I was looking forward to many such, but God has decreed it otherwise, and what he does we know is right. I shall never see you again! and though they will bring me back to you, I shall not feel your tears upon my face, or see you bending over my coffin-bed! Still I know you will do this, and that makes it necessary for me to tell what, perhaps, has been too long withheld, because I would spare you if possible.

"Annie, had I lived, I never could have toiled for you as I once did, for where the right arm, which has held your light form so often, used to be, there is nothing now but a scarred stump, and this is why I have not written. Does it make you sicken and shrink away from me? Don't, Annie. Your crippled husband's heart is as full of tenderness now as ever. I was too proud of my figure, Annie, and the thought that you might love me less when you knew how maimed I was, hurt more than the cold, sharp steel, cutting into my throbbing flesh.

"And now, dear Annie, I come to the hardest part of all. I know just how you'll start and shudder at what you deem so cruel a suggestion,—know just how keen the pang will be, for I have felt the same and my spirit well nigh fainted as I thought of the time when another's caressess than mine would call the sweet love light to your eye and kindle the soft blushes on your cheek. Listen to me, Annie. You'll be glad one day to remember that I told you what I did. You are young and beautiful, and though you do not believe it now, the time will surely come when my grave will not be visited as often as at first, and the flowers you will plant above me when next spring's sun is shining will wither for want of care, and the rank grass growing there will not be trodden down by your dear little feet, for they will be waiting by another fireside than ours in the Hollow, and my Annie will bear another name than mine. Do you discredit me, darling? It will surely be, and I am willing that it should, but you will never know the anguish it costs me to be willing. It is the bitterest drop in all the bitter cup, but I drank it with tears and prayers, and now I can calmly say to you what I am saying,—can even from my death-bed give you to another, whoever he may be. You can never forget me, I know; never forget your soldier husband, who fell in his country's cause, but by and by thoughts of him will cease to give you pain, and our short married life will seem like some far-off dream.

"I cannot say how it would be with *me* were you taken and I left, but I am much like other men, and judging from their example I should do just as they do, so if in after years another asks you, as I once did, to be his guiding star, don't refuse for me. Think that from my low grave I bless you in your new relations, and will welcome you to Heaven all the same, though you come fettered and bound with other links than those my love has thrown around you.

"I am almost done now, Annie. There is a gathering film before my eyes, and I feel the death chill creeping through my veins. It would be sweet to have you here, as I go down the brink up which no traveler has ever come; but it cannot be, and I will not repine. There is One with me whose presence is dearer far than yours could be; One whose everlasting arm will be beneath me as I pass over Jordan. Leaning on Him I need no other stay, but shall go fearlessly down to death. There is another with me, too,—an earthly friend, who has been kinder than a brother, and my heart clings to him more fondly than he can ever guess. Always respect William Mather, Annie, for what he has been to me. Pray that prosperity may attend him all his days, and that at the last he may find a place in Heaven. He is thinking of these things, I know, and from the dreary hours spent with me there may yet spring up plants of everlasting growth.

"My mind begins to wander, darling. There's a rushing sound in my ears, while thoughts of you and thoughts of that terrible Sabbath battle are blended together. Good-bye, my precious one. Don't cry too much when you read this. It is not good-bye forever. A few more years of earth to you, a moment of heavenly bliss to me and then we meet again, where golden harps are ringing. I can almost hear them now,—almost see the shining throngs sent out to meet me, just as I once vainly dreamed the Rockland people would come to welcome me home from war. In fancy I put my arms around your neck just as I used to do; in fancy hold you to my bosom; in fancy kiss your girlish lips, and smooth your pale brown hair.

"I don't know how you'll live without me; don't know who will earn your bread, but the God of the widow and fatherless will surely care for my darling and keep her heart from breaking. With him I leave you, knowing you are safer there than elsewhere.

"Good-bye, good-bye."

There were great tear blots upon this letter, for Mr. Mather, as he penned it, had wept over it like a child, forming a resolution which he wondered had not suggested itself before. Kneeling by the dying George, he said, "God *will* care for your darling, and I shall be His instrument. So long as I have a home, Annie shall not suffer. Rose's love was given to her long ago and mine will follow soon. She shall be a sister to us both."

The glazed eyes lighted up with joy, and the white lips whispered the thanks which ended in a prayer for blessings on one who had proved himself so kind to the poor soldier.

"Come closer to me," they said; "take my hand in yours and keep it there while I thank you for what you've been to me. You'll forgive me, I know, that I ever thought you proud, for I did, and sometimes there was a bitter feeling in my heart when I saw your Rose surrounded with every luxury, and thought of Annie, as highly educated as she, taking a far lower place in Rockland, because her husband was a mechanic. There is more of that feeling among the working classes than you imagine, and you don't know how much good a familiar word or a little notice from such a you does to those who fill the humbler walks of life. Women feel this more than men, and again I bless you for the care promised my Annie. I do not ask that you should take her to your home as you suggest. You'll think differently of that bye and by, but see that she does not want; see that no winter night shall find her hungry, no winter morning cold. Oh, Annie, Annie, that you should ever come to this!"

It was a bitter, wailing cry, embodying all the mighty love the sick man had ever felt for his young wife. George had thought himself resigned, but weak human nature, which clings so tenaciously to life, was making one last effort for the mastery, and the worn spirit fainted for a time in the fierce struggle which ensued. The mind began to wander, and was in fancy back again at the cottage in the Hollow, where the soldier clasped his Annie to his bosom, begging of her in piteous tones not to love him less because he was a cripple. "I have only one arm to work with now, but I won't let you starve, for when there's but one crust left, I'll give it all to you, and laugh so merrily that you will never guess how the hunger pain is gnawing at my heart. I've felt it once, my darling. I know just what it's like. 'Twas on that terrible day when our brave boys met the foe, way up there at Manassas. There were hours, and hours, and hours, when we neither ate nor drank, and the July sun poured down so hotly, drying the perspiration which dropped from my hair like rain. 'Twas my very life I sweat away that awful day, fighting for the Union. Did you hear the battle, Annie,—hear the cannon's bellowing thunder as it echoed through the Virginia woods? Wasn't it grand the yell the Highlanders gave, as, with the 69th, they bore down battery after battery, and plunged into the enemy's midst! How bravely our company played their part, fighting their way through shot and shell, and blood and brains, wading ankle-deep in human gore! Hurrah for the Stars and Stripes, my boys! Three cheers for the Federal Flag! Yes, give us three times three; and when it floats again over all the land, remember the soldiers who helped defend it. Hurrah, hurrah!"

Mr. Mather shuddered as the wild shout rang through the room. It seemed so like a mockery, that dying soldier shouting for liberty, and trying in vain to wave aloft his poor, scarred stump. Anon, however, the patriotic mood was changed, and the voice was very sad which whispered:

"But hush! what sounds are these, mingling in the glad notes of victory? 'Tis the widow, the orphan, the mother, weeping over the slain! There's mourning East and West; there's weeping North and South, for the dead who will return no more! A crushed rebellion is hardly worth the fearful price. Oh, Annie, pray for the poor soldier,—everybody pray. Honor our memory,—forget our faults,—speak kindly of us when we are gone. We gave our life for freedom! 'Tis all that we can do. Speak kindly of the soldiers slain!"

Reason was struggling back again; and bending lower, Mr. Mather said:

"George, we *will* honor the soldiers dead, and care for the soldiers living."

"Yes, yes!" George answered, faintly. "They need it so much,—more than the people guess who stay at home and *read* about the war. It will be long, and the contest terrible. The North is strong, and the South determined, and both will fight like fiends. But right must conquer at last, and the Star Spangled Banner shall wave again even over misguided Charleston, whose sons and daughters shall weep for joy as they greet the joyful sight. God speed the happy day!"

Mr. Mather could only press the hand which lay again in his. He could not speak, for he knew there was a *third presence* now in the sick-room,—that its dark form was shading the bed whereon he sat, and with that feeling of awe death always inspires, he sat silently watching its progress, and thinking, it may be, of the future time when *William Mather* would be the dying one instead of George Graham. Slowly the marble pallor and the strange chill crept on, pinching the nose, contracting the lips, touching the forehead and moistening the soft brown hair which William smoothed caressingly, as he bent down to catch the last faint whisperings of a spirit nearly gone.

"We fought the battle bravely. Tell them not to be discouraged because of one defeat. Our cause is just. 'Twill triumph at the last. Don't be too bitter toward the South; there are kind hearts there as well as here, and its daughters weep as sadly as any at the North. God help and pity them all. Annie, darling, I am almost home; so near that I can see the pearly gates which stand open night and day. It is not hard to die,—no pain, no anguish now,—nothing but joy and gladness and everlasting *rest, rest,*—perfect rest for the Redeemed."

Drearily the November wind went sweeping down the street, and the sobbing rain beat against the window, whilst the misty daylight came struggling faintly into the silent room which held the living and the dead; the one cold, and white, and still, his features wearing a smile of peace as if he had indeed entered into everlasting rest,—the other kneeling by his side, and with his face buried in the pillows, praying that when his time should come, he, too, might die the death of the righteous, and go where George had gone.

CHAPTER XIV.
MATTERS IN ROCKLAND.

With quivering lip Mr. Mather told the members of Company R that their lieutenant was dead; and strong men as they were they did not deem themselves unmanly that they wiped the big tears away, and crowding around their informer anxiously asked for particulars of their departed comrade, all speaking kindly of him, and each thinking of the sweet girl-wife at home on whom the news would fall so crushingly. A soldier's dying was no novel thing in Washington, and so, aside from Company R, there were few who knew or cared that another soul had gone to the God who gave it,—that another victim was added to the list which shall one day come up with fearful blackness before the provokers of the war. The drums beat just the same,— the bands played just as merrily, and the busy tide went on as if the quiet chamber in —— street held no stiffened form, once as full of life and hope as the gay troops marching by.

But away to the Northward there was bitter mourning, and many a bright eye wept as the sad news ran along the streets that Rockland's young lieutenant, of whom the people were justly proud, lay dead in Washington, and many a heart beat with sympathy for the young wife who, ever since hearing the fatal news, had lain upon her bed, more dead than alive, with a look upon her white face which told better than words of the anguish she was enduring.

Nothing could induce Rose to leave her for a moment. "*Will* had staid by George," she said, "and she should stay by Annie."

With her sitting by, Annie grew stronger, and could at last talk calmly of what was expected on the morrow.

"It will be terrible," she said, "to hear the tramp of feet coming up the walk, and know they are bringing George! Oh, Mrs. Mather, you'll stay by me, won't you, even if your husband is among the number?"

Annie did not mean to be selfish. She was too much benumbed to realize anything fully, and she never thought what it would cost Rose to stay there, knowing her husband would seek her at home, and be so disappointed at not finding her there. Rose could not refuse a request so touchingly made, but just as the morning broke she went home for a few moments to see that all necessary preparations were made for Will's comfort; then, penning him a note to tell why she was not there to meet him, she returned again to the cottage, where Widow Simms was busily at work setting things to rights for the expected arrival, her tears falling upon the furniture she was dusting, and her chest heaving with sobs as she heard in the distance the sound of a gathering crowd, and thought,

"It may be my boy they'll go up next to meet."

Poor Annie, too, shuddered and moaned as she caught the ominous sounds, and knew what they portended.

"It would be better to bring him back quietly," she said. "It seems almost like mockery, this parade, which he can never know. I may be glad, by and by that they honored him thus, but it's so hard now," and covering her head with her pillow, Annie wept silently as she heard the mournful beat of the muffled drum, and knew the march to the depot had commenced.

How Rose wanted to be in the street and see her husband when he came; but with heroic self-denial, she forced down every longing to be away, and sitting down by Annie, busied herself with counting off the minutes and wondering if the clock would ever point to half-past ten, or the train ever arrive.

There was a great crowd out that morning to meet the returning soldier, and George's dream of what might be when he came back again was more than realized. There were men and carriages upon the street, and groups of women at the corners, while the little boys ran up and down. But in the beat of the muffled drum there was a tone which made the hearts of those who heard it overflow with tears, as they remembered *what* that dirgelike music meant. Around the jammed white hat of the man who played the fife there was a badge of mourning, and in the notes he trilled a mournful cadence far different from the patriotic strains he played as a farewell to Rockland soldiers, going forth to battle, with hopes so sanguine of success. One of that youthful band was coming back; not full of life and fiery ambition as when he went away, dreaming bright dreams of the glory he would win, and the laurels he would wear, when once again he trod the streets at home. Not as a conquering hero, with the crown of fame on his brow, though the crown indeed was won, and where the golden light of Heaven shines from the everlasting hills, he was wearing it in glory. But his ear was deaf to all earthly sounds, and the tribute of respect his friends fain would bestow upon him, awakened no thrill in his cold, pulseless heart. Still they felt that all honor was due to the dead, and so they had come up to meet him, a greater throng than any of which he had dreamed when ambition burned within his bosom. There was a carriage waiting, too, just as he hoped there might be; a carriage sent expressly for him, but the children on the sidewalk shrank away and ceased their noisy clamor as it went by, its sombre appearance somewhat relieved by the gay coloring of the Stars and Stripes laid reverently upon it.

Slowly up the street the long procession passed, unmindful of the rain which, mingled with the snow and sleet, beat upon the pavements, and dashed against the window-panes, from which many a tear-stained face looked out upon the gloomy scene, made ten times gloomier by the sighing of the wind and the rifts of leaden clouds veiling the November sky. Over the eastern hills there was a rising wreath of smoke, and a shrill, discordant scream told that the train was coming, just as the carriage sent for George drew up to its appointed place.

Gently, carefully, tenderly they lifted him out, and set him down in their midst; but no loud cheering rent the air, no acclamations of applause, nothing save that dreadful muffled beat, and the soft notes of the fife, telling to the passengers leaning from the windows that the dead, as well as the living, had been their fellow-traveller. The banner upon the hearse told the rest of the sad story, and with a sigh to the memory of the unknown soldier, the passengers resumed their seats, and the train sped on its way, leaving the Rockland people alone with their dead.

Reverently they placed him in the carriage which none cared to share with him. Carefully they wrapped around him the Stars and Stripes, and dropping the heavy curtains, followed through the streets to the cottage in the Hollow, which he had left so full of life and hope. Around that cottage there was a gathered multitude next day, and though on the unsheltered heads of those without, the driving rain was falling, they waited patiently while the prayer was said, and the funeral anthem chanted. Then there came a bustling moment,—people passing beneath the Star Spangled Banner, and pausing to look at the dead. There were sobs and tears, and words of fond regret, and then the coffin-lid was closed, and once more that muffled beat was heard, as with arms reversed the Rockland Guards marched up the walk, where, leaning upon their guns they stood, while strong men carried out their late companion, and placed him in the hearse, *the carriage sent for him.* There was no relative to go with him to the grave,—none in whose veins his blood was flowing, so Mr. Mather and Rose took the lead, followed by a promiscuous crowd of carriages and pedestrians, the very horses keeping time to the solemn music beaten by the drum, and played by the man in the jammed white hat.

Slowly through the November rain,—through the November sleet, and through the November mist they bore him on through the streets which he so oft had trodden; on past the cottage he meant to buy for poor Annie, whispering to herself with every note of the tolling bell, "George has gone to Heaven." Onward, still onward, till streets and cottage were left behind, and they came to where the marble columns, gleaming through the autumnal fog, told who peopled that silent yard. Just by the gate, the bearers paused, and stood with uncovered heads while the solemn words were uttered, "Earth to earth, ashes to ashes, dust to dust!" Then, when it was all over, the long procession moved through the spacious churchyard, past the tall monuments betokening worldly wealth; past the less imposing stones, whose lettering told of treasure in Heaven; past the group of cedar trees and pine;

past the graves of the nameless dead, and so out upon the highway, Rose Mather starting in alarm as the band struck up a quicker, merrier march, whose stirring, jubilant notes seemed so much like mockery. She knew it was the custom, but the music grated none the less harshly, and drawing her veil over her face, she wept silently, occasionally glancing backward to the spot of freshly upturned earth where Rockland's first soldier was buried,—the brave, self-denying George,—who gave all he had for his country, and died in her behalf.

Four weeks after George's death, Annie left the cottage in the Hollow, and went to live for a time with Mrs. Mather. Early orphaned, and thrown upon the charities of a scheming aunt, who, after her marriage with George, had cast her off entirely, there was now no one to whom she could look for help and sympathy save Rose, and when the latter insisted that her home should be Annie's also, while William, too, joined his entreaties with those of his wife, and urged as one reason his promise made to George, Annie consented on condition that as soon as her health was sufficiently restored, she should do something for herself, either as teacher, or governess in some private family.

Amid a wild storm of sobs and tears she had read her husband's dying message, growing sick and faint just as he knew she would when first she learned of his loss, and why it was he had never written to her himself. But this was naught compared to the horror which crept round her heart as she read what George had written of a coming time when the long grave by the gate would not be visited as often as at first, or he who slept there remembered as tearfully.

"Oh, George, George!" she cried, "it was cruel to tell me so," and sinking to her knees, she essayed to breathe a vow that other love than that she had borne for George Graham should never find entrance to her bosom. But something sealed her lips,—the words she would have uttered were unspoken, and the rash vow was not made.

Still there was an added drop to her already brimming cup of sorrow, and a sadder, more loving note in the tone of her voice when she spoke of her husband, as if she would fortify herself against the possibility of his prediction coming true. It was a sorry day when she finally left her cottage home, and only God was witness to the parting; but the dim, swollen eyes and colorless cheeks attested to its bitterness, as, with one great upheaving sob, she crossed the threshold and entered the carriage where Rose sat waiting for her, while the motherly Widow Simms wrapped around her the pile of shawls which were to shield her from the cold, and bade her god speed to her new home.

Rapidly the carriage drove away, while the widow returned to the cottage to perform the last needful office of fastening down the windows and locking up the doors, then, with a sigh at the changes a few short months had wrought, she went back to her own long deserted home. And the busy tide of life rolled on in Rockland just the same as if in the churchyard there was no new-made grave, holding the buried love of Annie, who, in Rose Mather's beautiful home, was surrounded with every possible comfort and luxury, and treated with as much consideration as if she were a born princess, instead of the humble woman, who, a few months before, was wholly unknown to the little lady of the Mather Mansion.

CHAPTER XV.
THE DESERTER.

Another had taken George's place in Company R, and both the Widow Simms and Susan Simms shed tears of natural pride when they read that *John* was the favored one, and bore the title of Lieutenant. It more than half atoned for his long absence to the young wife, who, greatly to her mother-in-law's disgust, was made the happy possessor of a set of furs bought with a part of the new lieutenant's increased wages.

"Better lay by for a wet day; but easy come, easy go. They will never be worth a cent. Tain't like them Ruggleses to save, and to think of the silly critter's comin' round in the storm just to show 'em, late on Saturday night; I'm glad I wan't to hum," was the widow's muttered comment, as on the Sunday following the receipt of the furs she pinned around her high, square shoulders, the ten years' old blanket shawl, and tying round her neck the faded tippet of even greater age, started for church, determining not to notice or speak to the extravagant Susan, if she appeared, as she was sure to do, in her new finery.

This was hardly the right kind of spirit for the widow to take to church, but hers was a peculiar nature, and the grace which would have sufficed to make Annie Graham an angel, would hardly have kept her from boiling over at the most trivial matter. This the widow felt, and it made her more distrustful of herself, more careful to keep down the first approaches of her besetting sin. But the furs had seriously disturbed her, particularly as they were said to have cost $35—"more than she had spent on her mortal body in half-a-dozen years," she thought, as, with her well-worn Prayer Book in hand, and a pair of Eli's darned, blue socks upon her feet to keep them from the snow which had fallen the night before, she walked rapidly on in the direction of St. Luke's.

There was an unusual stir about the doors, a crowd of eagerly talking people, and conspicuous among them was Susan, looking so pretty in her neatly fitting collar, and holding her little muff so gracefully that the widow began to relent at once, and to feel a kind of pride that "John's wife was as genteel lookin' as the next one, if she did come of them shiftless Ruggleses," but inasmuch as it was Sunday, she shouldn't flatter Susan by speaking of the furs; but the first chance she got on a week day she'd tell her "she was glad she got 'em, if they didn't make her vain; though I know they will," she added; "it's Ruggles natur' and she's standin' out there now, just to show 'em to the folks in the street goin' to the Methodis' meetin'."

But the widow was mistaken, for Susan had scarcely a thought of her furs, so absorbed was she in throwing what little light she could upon a mystery which was troubling the people and keeping them outside the door, while they talked the matter over. It seemed that the sexton, when, at about ten o'clock on the previous night, he came to see that the fire kindled in the furnace at sunset was safe, had stumbled over a human form lying upon the pile of evergreens gathered for the Christmas decorations, and placed for safe keeping in the cellar of the church. There was a cry between surprise and terror, and a muttered oath, and then the ragged, frightened intruder sprang to his feet, and bounding up the narrow stairway, fled through the open vestry door ere the sexton had time to collect his scattered senses.

This was his story, corroborated by Susan Simms, who said that when, at about seven o'clock the previous night, she was passing the church, she saw a dark-looking object, which she at first mistook for a woman, but as she came nearer she saw it was the figure of a man who, at the sound of her steps, dropped behind a pile of rubbish, and thus disappeared from view,—that feeling timid she did not return home that way, but took the more circuitous route past her mother-in-law's, where she stopped for a moment and repeated the circumstance to the neighbor she found staying there.

"Then she didn't come half a mile out of the way just to tell of her finery," thought the widow, coming nearer to Susan, and even smoothing the soft fur, which, half an hour before, had so provoked her ire.

Various were the surmises as to who the man could be, and why he had entered the lonesome cellar; and the morning services had commenced ere the knot of talkers and listeners at the door disbanded and took their accustomed places in the church. Rose Mather was there as usual, but she knelt in her handsome pew alone, for Will had been gone from her two whole weeks, and Annie was still too much of an invalid to venture out. With others at the door she heard of the intruder, and after asking a few questions she had passed into the aisle, with a certain wise air about her, as if she knew something which she should not tell! As one after another came in, it might have been observed that she turned often and curiously toward the door, glancing occasionally at the spot where Mrs. Baker, now a regular attendant, was in the habit of sitting. She was not there to-day, a fact which no one observed save Rose and the Widow Simms, the latter of whom only noticed it because Annie, she knew, was deeply interested in the repentant woman. "She's sick, most likely," the widow thought, while Rose, too, had her own opinion as to what kept Harry's mother from church that Sunday morning.

Meantime the object of their solicitude sat crouching over the fire of wet green wood she had succeeded in coaxing into a blaze, now looking nervously toward the half closed door of the small room her boys used to occupy, and again congratulating herself that it was Sunday, and consequently no one would be coming there to pry into the secret she was guarding as carefully as ever tigress guarded its threatened young. The half frozen, famished wretch, fleeing from the shadow of the church out into the wintry storm which had come up since nightfall, had gone next to the tumble-down shanty of a house which Mrs. Baker called her home. It was late for a light to be there, for Mrs. Baker kept early hours; but through the driving snow the wanderer, as he turned the corner, caught a friendly gleam shining out from the dingy windows, and waking in his breast one great wild throb of joy, such as some lost mariner feels when he spies in the distance the friendly bark and knows there's help at hand.

It was a desolate, dreary home, but to the wanderer hastening toward it, and glancing so timidly around as if behind each rift of snow there were bristling bayonets sent to stop his course, it seemed a splendid palace. Could he gain that shelter he was safe. His mother would shield him from the dreaded officers he fancied were on his track, and so, the sick, fainting man kept on until the old board fence was reached, where, leaning against the gate, he stood a moment, and with his feverish hand scooped up the grateful snow to cool his burning forehead. The tallow candle was burning yet within the cottage, but the fire was raked together on the hearth and the stranger could see the glow of the red embers and the broken shovel lain across the andiron.

"I wonder what she's doing up so late," he whispered, and moving cautiously up the walk to the uncurtained window, he started suddenly at the novel sight which met his view.

Years before, when he lived in New England, he remembered that one day when playing in the garret he had found in a chest of rubbish, a large, square book, which Hal had said was their grandmother's Bible. Afterward he had seen it standing against a broken light of glass, to keep out the snow which sometimes beat in upon himself and Hal, and that was the last he could remember concerning that Bible or any other belonging to his mother. How then was he astonished to see it lying on the old round stand, the dim tallow candle casting a flickering light upon the yellow leaves and upon the figure of his mother bending over them, and loudly whispering the words she was reading. It was not an entirely new business to Mrs. Baker, the reading of the Bible, for after the news of Harry's death she had hunted up the long neglected volume which had given her aged mother so much comfort. It might bring consolation to her, she thought, and so with tearful eyes and aching heart she had tried to read and understand the sacred pages, pencil-marked, some of them, by a sainted mother's hand, and fraught with so many memories of the olden time when she was not the hard, wrinkled, desolate creature people knew as Mrs. Baker. The way of life was still dark and dim to that half heathenish woman, but she was determinedly groping on, following the little light she had, and each night found her bending over the

Bible ere she sought the humble bed standing there in the dark corner, just where it stood that morning when her two boys went away.

It was far more comfortable-looking now than then, for there was a nice, warm blanket on it, while the outer covering was clean and new. Rose Mather had kept her promise given in the hour of the poor mother's bereavement, and scattered about the room were numerous articles which once did duty in the servants' apartments at the Mather mansion. But the intruder did not notice these; he was too much absorbed with the stooping figure, whispering a part of the 14th chapter of John, and occasionally wiping away a tear as she came to some passage more beautiful than the others. There were tears, too, in the eyes of the rough man outside, but he forced them back, and pressing closer to the window, watched the lone woman inside, as, sinking down upon her knees, with the flickering candle shining on her wrinkled face, she prayed first for herself and then for him, *the boy* standing without the door, and listening, while his heart beat so loudly that he almost feared she would hear and know that he was there. But she paid no heed, and the tremulous voice went on, asking that God would follow and bless, and care for the Billy boy far away, and bring him back to the mother who had never been to him what she ought. The name Billy boy touched a tender chord, and stretching out his hands toward her, the man who bore that name sobbed out,

"Oh, mother, mother, I'm here, I'm here!"

There was a sudden pause, and turning her head the startled woman listened.

Was it the wind moaning round her lonesome dwelling, or was it poor dead Harry calling to her, as in her superstitious imagination she sometimes believed he did when she was praying for Billy, reproaching her that no prayer had ever been said for him, the lost one? Again the sobbing cry, and a rustling movement by the door. It could not be the wind, for that only shook the loosened timbers or screamed through some gaping crevice, while this, whatever it might be, called:

"Mother, mother, come."

Was it a warning from the other world,—a summons to follow her first-born? Annie Graham had said there were no such messages sent to us, and Annie was always right; so the frightened woman listened again until the rattling of the latch, and a feeble, timid knock told her there was more than the winter wind or spirits of the dead about her house that night. There was a human being seeking to gain entrance, and tottering to the door she asked who it was, and what they wanted there.

"Mother, mother, let me in. I'm your Billy boy, come from the war."

The words were hardly uttered ere the door was opened wide, the frantic woman dragging rather than leading in the worn-out man, who, staggering forward, fell into her arms, sobbing piteously,

"I'm so sick and tired. I've been weeks on the road, hiding everywhere; for, mother,—shut the door tight, so nobody can hear,—I've run away; I've had enough of war, and so I left one night. You know what they do to deserters. They hang them, neck and heels. Oh, mother, mother, don't let them find me, will you? I've done my best in one dreadful battle. They musn't get me now. Will they, think?" and Billy cast a searching glance around the room to see that no officer was there with power to take him back.

Would they get him from her? She'd like to see them do it, she said, as she led the childish deserter to the hearth, he leaning heavily upon her, and falling, rather than sitting upon the chair she brought. Weary of a soldier's life, and satisfied with one taste of battle, he had stolen away one night when the rain and the darkness sheltered him from observation. Greatly magnifying the value put upon himself, as well as the chances for detection, he had not dared to take the cars, lest at every station there should be one of the police waiting to secure him. So he had made the entire journey from Washington on foot, travelling by night and resting by day, sometimes in barns, but oftener in the woods, where some friendly stump or leafless tree was his only shelter. He had reached his home at last, but his haggard face, his blood-shot eyes, his blistered feet and tattered garments bore witness to his long, painful journey.

With streaming eyes the mother listened to the story, then opening the bed of coals, she warmed and chafed his half-frozen limbs, handling tenderly the poor, blistered feet, from which the soles of the shoes had dropped, leaving them exposed. But all in vain did she prepare the cup of fragrant tea, sent her that afternoon by Mrs. Mather. Billy could do little more than taste it. He was too tired, he said; he should be better in the morning, after he had slept. So with eager, trembling hands his mother fixed the bed in the little room which had not been used since he went away, bringing her own pillows, and the nice rose blanket given by Mrs. Mather, together with a strip of carpet which she spread upon the floor so as to make it soft for Billy's wounded, bleeding feet. How sick he was, and how he moaned in his fitful sleep, now talking of *Hal*, now of being shot, and again of the Bible on the stand, and the prayer he heard his mother make.

Mrs. Baker was not accustomed to sickness, but she knew this was no ordinary case, and she suggested sending for the doctor; but Billy started up in such dismay, telling her no one must know that he was there unless she wanted him killed, that he succeeded in communicating a part of his terror to her, and she spent the entire Sunday by her child's bedside, doing what she could to allay the raging fever increasing so fast, and keeping watch to see that no one came near to drag her boy away.

The next morning it became absolutely necessary for her to leave him for a time, as she must procure the few necessaries he needed, and taking advantage of the heavy sleep into which he had fallen, she stole noiselessly out, hoping to return ere he should wake. Scarcely, however, had she left the lane and turned into Main Street, when Rose came tripping to the gate, drawn thither by a curiosity to see if her suspicions were correct. She had learned from her husband of Bill's exit from Washington, and for some days had been expecting to hear of his arrival in town. That he had come she was certain, and telling Annie where she was going, she had started rather early for Mrs. Baker's. As her knock met with no response she entered without further ceremony, and passing on through the low dark kitchen came to the door of the little room where Bill lay breathing heavily, and muttering about camps, and guard-houses, and deserters. The sight of suffering always awoke a chord of sympathy in Rose Mather's bosom, and without a thought of danger she bent close to the sick man, and involuntarily laid her soft, cool hand upon his burning forehead. The touch awoke him, but in the wild eyes turned upon her there was no glance of recognition, or look of fear. He evidently fancied himself back in Washington, and asked the name of her regiment.

"Oh, I know," he continued, still keeping his eyes fixed upon her, "you're the chap I took, but you've fell away mightily since then. Yankee fare don't set well on your Rebel stomach, I guess," and a wild, coarse laugh rang through the room, making Rose shudder and draw back, for she felt intuitively that Billy was mad.

She was not, however, afraid of him, and standing at a little distance, she tried to reason with him, telling him she was not a Rebel,—she was Mrs. Mather, come to do him good.

Bill only laughed derisively. "Couldn't cheat him. Guess he knew them eyes and them hands, white as cotton wool. I'll bet I've got a ring that'll fit 'em," he continued, and reaching for his pantaloons, which he had insisted should lie behind him on the bed, he took from the pocket the costly diamond once worn by his Rebel captive, and *confisticated* by him as *con-tra-band*. "Try it on," he said to Rose, who mechanically obeyed, wondering why it should look so familiar to her.

It was too large for her slender fingers, and dropping off, rolled upon the floor. Rose at once set herself to finding the missing ring, and had just returned it to its owner when Mrs. Baker came in, terribly alarmed at finding Mrs. Mather there. Rose, however, quieted her fears at once by telling her she had known for some days past of Bill's desertion, and had kept it from every one but Annie, because her husband thought it best. She did not believe he would be followed, she said, for Will wrote that he had become so reckless and discontented that his absence was no loss to the army, but for a while it might be well that his presence should not be known in Rockland, as the people might be indignant at a deserter, and perhaps in their excitement do him some injury.

"He ought to have medical advice, though," she added, "for I think he's very sick."

Mrs. Baker knew he was, and fear lest he should die overcame every other feeling, making her consent that Rose should call their family physician. It was nearly noon ere he arrived, and in the meantime Rose had reported the case to Annie, and then returning to Mrs. Baker's, took her place by Billy, who called her "his little Rebel," and ordered her about as if he had been a commanding officer, and she his subordinate. The novelty of the thing was rather pleasing to Rose, and notwithstanding that the physician pronounced the disease typhus fever in its most violent form, she persisted in staying, saying some one must help Mrs. Baker, and she was not afraid.

So day after day found her in that comfortless dwelling, while the frequent callers at the Mather mansion wondered where she could be. It came out at last that she was nursing William Baker, lying dangerously sick of typhus fever in his mother's dilapidated home, and then, as villagers will, the Rockland people wondered and gossiped, and wondered again how the aristocratic Rose Mather could sit hour after hour, in that poverty-stricken cottage, ministering to the wants of despised Bill Baker. Rose hardly knew, herself, and when questioned upon the subject could only reply—

"I guess it's because he's a soldier, and I must do something for the war. Will knows it. He says I'm doing right, and Annie Graham, too."

And so, with her heart kept brave by thinking that Will and Annie approved her course, Rose went every day to Mrs. Baker's, doing more by her cheerful presence and the needful comforts she supplied to arrest the progress of the disease and effect a favorable change, than all the physicians in the county could have done. Bill owed his life to her, and it was touching to witness his childish gratitude when reason resumed her throne, and he learned who it was he had sometimes called his "little Rebel," and again had fancied was some beautiful angel sent to cure and comfort him. He had often seen Mrs. Mather in the streets before he went away; but never as closely as now, and for hours after his convalescence he would lie looking into her face, which seemed to puzzle him greatly. Occasionally, too, he would take from his pocket a picture, which he evidently compared with something about her person, then, with a sly wink, which began to be very annoying, he would return it to its hiding-place, and ask her sundry questions, which, under ordinary circumstances, she would have resented as being too familiar.

At last, one afternoon, as she was sitting by him, while his mother did some errands in the village, he suddenly surprised her by dropping upon her lap an elegant gold watch, which Rose knew at a glance must have belonged to some person of taste and wealth.

"What is it? Whose is it?" she asked, and Bill replied:

"'Twas his'n, the chap's I took, you know. He's down to the old Capitol now, shet up. Didn't you never hear of him?"

"You mean the young man you captured," Rose replied. "Tell me about him, please. Who was he, and where was his home?"

"You tell," Bill answered, with one of his peculiar winks. "He gave it as *John Brown*; but a chap who knowd him said 'twas somethin' else. He wan't a Rebel neither—that is, it wan't his nater, for he came from Yankee land."

"A *traitor*, then," Rose suggested, and Bill replied:

"You needn't guess agin; and you and I or'to be glad that no such *truck* belongs to us."

Rose colored scarlet, but made no response, for recreant Jimmie flashed across her mind, and she shrank from having even the vulgar Bill know how intimately she was connected with a traitor. Bill watched her narrowly, and thinking to himself,

"I'm on the right track, I'll bet," he continued, "I hain't no relations in the Confederate army, I know, and I don't an atom b'lieve you have."

No answer from Rose, except a heightened bloom upon her cheek, and her inquisitor went on:

"Have you any friends there?"

Rose could not tell a lie, and after a moment's silence, she stammered out:

"Please don't ask me. Oh, Jimmie, Jimmie, I wish I knew where he was!" and the great tears trickled through the snowy fingers clasped over her flushed face.

"I'll be darned if I aint cryin' too," Bill said, wiping his eyes with his shirt sleeve, "but bein' I'm in for it I may as well see it through."

"What might be your name before it was Miss Marthers?"

"Carleton!" and Rose looked up quickly at Bill, who continued:

"You came from Boston, I b'lieve?"

"Yes, from Boston," and Rose leaned eagerly forward while Bill, with his favorite "Nuff said," plunged his hand into his pocket, and taking out the *picture*, passed it to Rose.

Quick as thought the bright color faded from her cheek, and with ashen, quivering lips, she whispered;

"*It's I!* It's mine, taken for Jimmie, just before he went away! How came you by it? Oh tell me!" and in the voice there was a tone of increasing anguish. "Tell me, was it,—was it,—*Jimmie*, my brother, whom you took prisoner and carried to Washington?"

"If James Carleton is your brother, I s'pose it was," Bill said; "and that's the very picter he stuck to like a chestnut burr, begging for it like a dog, and offerin' everything he had if I'd give it up."

"Why didn't you, then?" and Rose's eye blazed with anger, making Bill shrink before their indignant gaze.

"'Twas rotten mean in me, I know," he said timidly, "but they *was con-tra-band* according to law, and I felt so savage at the pesky Rebels then. I didn't know 'twas you he teased so for, actually cryin' when I wouldn't give it up. I'm sorry, I be, I swan, and I'll give you every confounded contraband. You've got the watch, and there's the ring, the spetacles, the tobarker box, and the thingumbob for cigars, the sum total of his traps, except a chaw or so of the weed that I couldn't very well bring back," and Bill's face wore a very satisfied expression as he laid in Rose's lap every article belongin' to her brother.

She knew now who the prisoner was in whom she had felt so strange an interest. It was *Jimmie*, and the mystery concerning his fate was solved. He was a captive at Washington, and her heart ached to its very core as she thought of both her brothers languishing so many weary months in prison. Very minutely she questioned Bill, eliciting from him little or nothing concerning Jimmie's present condition. He only knew that he was a captive still, that he was represented as maintaining the utmost reserve, seldom speaking except to answer direct questions, and that he seemed very unhappy.

"Poor boy, he wants to come home, I know," and Rose sobbed aloud, as she thought how desolate and homesick he must be. "I can't stay any longer to-day," she said, as she heard Mrs. Baker at the door, and bidding Bill good-bye, she hurried home, where, after a long passionate flood of tears, wept in Annie's lap, she wrote to her mother and husband both, telling them where Jimmie was, and begging of the former to come at once and go with her to Washington.

CHAPTER XVI.
NEWS DIRECT FROM JIMMIE.

That night, as Rose sat alone in her cheerful boudoir, musing upon the strange events which had occurred within the last few months, a letter was brought to her, bearing her mother's handwriting. It had passed hers on the road, and Rose tore it open, starting, as a soiled, tear-stained note dropped from the inside upon the floor. Intuitively she felt that it was from Jimmie, and catching it up, she read the homesick, heart-sick, remorseful cry of penitence and contrition which the weary Rebel-boy had at last sent to his mother. Stubbornness and proud reserve could hold out no longer and he had written, confessing his error, and begging earnestly for the forgiveness he knew he did not deserve.

"I am not all bad," he said; "and on that quiet morning, when beneath the cover of the Virginia woods I lay, watching the Union soldiers coming so bravely on, there was a dizziness in my brain, and a strange, womanly feeling at my heart, while a sensation I cannot describe thrilled every nerve when I saw in the distance the Stars and Stripes waving in the summer wind. How I wanted to warn them of their danger, to bid them turn back from the snare so cunningly devised, and how proud I felt of the Federal soldiers when contrasting them with ours. I fancied I could tell which were the Boston boys, and there came a mist before my eyes, as I thought how your dear hands and those of little Rose had possibly helped to make some portion of the dress they wore.

"You know about the battle. You read it months ago, and wept, perhaps, as you thought of *Jimmie* firing at his own brother, it might be, but, mother, *I did not.* I scarcely fired at all, and when I was compelled to do so to avoid suspicion, it was so high that neither the wounded nor the dead can accuse me as their murderer; and I'm glad now that it is so. It makes my prison bed softer to know there is no stain of blood upon my soul.

"Poor Tom, I dare say, has written to you of our encounter in the woods, but he does not know the shock it was to me to meet him there, and know I could not help him. Dear Tom, my heart aches more for him than for myself, for the Richmond Prison Guards are not like those who keep watch over us. There are humane people there,—kind, tender hearts,—which feel for any one in distress, but the jailers, the common soldiers, and the rabble, are not, I fear, as considerate as they might be. Many of them have been made to believe the war entirely of the North's provoking, that *Hamlin* is a *mulatto*, and Lincoln a foul-hearted knave, whose whole aim is to set the negroes free. But enough of Southern politics. It will all come clear at last, and the Star Spangled Banner wave again over every revolted State.

"Write to me, mother. Say you forgive your Rebel-boy. Say that, when I am exchanged, as I hope to be, I may come home, and that you will not turn away from your sinful, erring

"JIMMIE."

There was a message of love for Rose, and then the letter closed with one last, touching entreaty that the mother would forgive her child and take him back again to her confidence and love.

"Of course she'll do it," Rose said, vehemently, and seizing a pen and paper she wrote to Will, inclosing a note to Jimmie, full of pardon and tender love, bidding him when he should be released come directly to Rockland, where their mother should be waiting for him, and where she, forgetting all the past, would nurse him back to health.

Nearly a week went by, and then there came a letter from Will, telling how he had visited the Rebel Jimmie in his prison, and Rose wept frantically as she read the particulars of that interview when her brother first met the sister's husband, of whom he had never heard.

"I found him sitting apart from the others," William wrote, "apparently absorbed in disagreeable reflections, for there was an abstracted look upon his face and deep wrinkles upon his forehead. If he had not been pointed out to me, I should have known him by his striking resemblance to your family. The Carleton features could not be mistaken, particularly the proud curve about the mouth, and the arching of the eyebrows, while I recognized at once the soft, curling hair and brilliant complexion, which you will remember once attracted me toward a certain little girl, who is now all the world to the old bachelor Will.

"But this isn't a love letter, darling. I'm only going to tell you how sorry your brother looked sitting there alone in that noisy multitude, whose language and manners are not the most refined that could be desired, and how my heart warmed toward the solitary being, and forgave him at once for all his errors past. Very haughtily he bowed to me when I was introduced, and then in silence awaited to hear my errand, the proud curve around his mouth deepening as he surveyed me with a hauteur which, under ordinary circumstances, would have annoyed me exceedingly. As it was, I could almost fancy myself the prisoner and he the freeman, he seemed so cool, so collected, while I was embarrassed and uncertain how to act.

"'Is your visit prompted by curiosity to see how a so-called Rebel can bear confinement, or did you come on business?' he asked, and then all my embarrassment was at an end.

"'I came,' I said, 'partly at your sister's request, and partly to ascertain how much you are willing to do toward the attainment of your freedom.'

"I do not think he understood the last. He only caught at the words, 'your sister,' and grasping my arm, he whispered hoarsely, 'What of my sister? Have you seen her? Do you know her, and does she hate me now?'

"I told him I was your husband, and with quivering lip, he asked me, 'Is she well, my precious little Rose, whom I remember as almost a child, and mother—has she cast me off? Oh, if she only knew how I am punished for my sin, she would forgive her wayward boy.'

"Here he broke down in such a wild storm of sobs and tears, that the inmates of the prison gathered in groups around him, their looks indicative of their surprise at witnessing so much emotion in one who up to that moment had appeared haughtily indifferent to everything around him. With an authoritative gesture he waved them off, and then, passing him your note, I, too, walked away, leaving him alone while he read it, but even where I stood I could hear the smothered sobs he tried in vain to suppress. I am inclined to think he is right in saying that joining the Confederate army was the best lesson he ever learned. I am sure he must be greatly changed from the reckless, daring boy, whose exploits you have described so often. He is very anxious to swear allegiance to the Stars and Stripes, even though he should be doomed to prison life for five more weary months, and as I am not a mere private now, and have considerable influence in Washington, I hope, ere long, to write that he is free, and on his way to Rockland, whither he will go first.

"Jimmie expresses the utmost sympathy for Tom, and says he would gladly take his place, if that could be, for he fears the inmates of those Richmond tobacco houses are not always cared for, as he has been at Washington. Poor Tom, I hope he will be among the list of the exchanged, and if so, you may expect soon to welcome both your brothers."

No wonder Rose wept tears of joy over his letter, while her thoughts went after her rebellious, but repentant brother, nor tarried there, for, farther to the South, another weary captive pined, and every fibre of her heart bleed with sympathy for Tom—poor Tom, she always called him—and as the days of sickening suspense went by she grew so nervous and so ill that her mother came up from Boston to attend her, while Annie shook off her own feelings of weary languor, and did for Rose the same offices which Rose had once done for her.

"I do so wish you had been my sister," Rose said to her one day, when she had been kinder than usual "I know I should be a better woman, and so would all of us."

Annie made no reply, except to twine around her fingers the coils of chestnut hair, lying in such profusion upon the pillows. For a few moments Rose lay perfectly still, with her eyes fixed upon the paper bordering, as if counting the fanciful flowers, but her thoughts were intent upon a far different subject. Turning to her mother, she suddenly asked:

"How *old* is Jimmie, twenty-three, or twenty-four?"

"Twenty-three last May," was the reply, and, with rather a troubled expression upon her face, Rose continued, "*Will* is *thirteen* years older than I am," and the little curly head shook doubtfully.

"What are you talking about?" Mrs. Carleton asked, but Rose did not answer at once.

There was another interval of silence, and then starting quickly, Rose called out, "Mother, don't you remember that affair of Jimmie's ever so long ago, when he was a boy at school in New London? There was a little girl that he fancied, and you took him home for fear of what would come of it; when you found she was poor and nobody?"

Glancing quickly at Annie, who was attentively examining the hem-stitch of the fine linen pillow-case, Mrs. Carleton said, reprovingly:

"You should not parade our family matters before strangers, my daughter."

"Oh, Annie is no stranger," Rose answered, laughingly. "She's one of our folks now, besides, she is not enough interested in the love affair of a seventeen years old boy ever to repeat it."

"Love affair!" Mrs. Carleton rejoined, a little scornfully. "Not very much love about it, I imagine. She was stopping with her aunt at the Pequot House, and Jimmie saw her a few times, passing himself off by another name than his own. If he had cared for this child he would never have done that."

"He seems to have a *penchant* for assuming names," Rose rejoined, playfully. "He called himself *John Brown*, at Washington, while to this little Pequot girl he was, let me see, what was it? Can't you think, mother?"

Rose was bent on talking about Jimmie and his Pequot girl, and knowing that she could not stop her, Mrs. Carleton replied:

"Richard Lee, or something like that."

"Oh, yes, 'Dick!' I remember now; and her name was,—what *was* it, mother? It makes my head ache so trying to recall it."

"If I ever knew, I've forgotten," Mrs. Carleton said, and after trying in vain to think, Rose dismissed the name, but not the subject.

"How angry Jimmie was," she continued, "when you brought him home, and how awfully he swore. It makes you shudder, don't it?" and she turned to Annie, who had shivered either with cold or horror at Jimmie's profanity. "He was a bad boy once, but I most know he's better now. Maybe, mother, this was a real nice girl and if you'd let Jimmie alone he might have become attached to her, and she have been his wife by this time. Then he would not have joined the Rebel army. Don't you think you and Tom were a little too severe on Jimmie sometimes?"

"Perhaps so," was the faint response, as Mrs. Carleton looked out upon the wintry landscape, seeing there visions of a handsome, boyish, tearful face, flushed with anger and entreaty as its owner begged of her not to take him back to Boston, which he hated, but leave him where he was, saying that the little girl at the Pequot House had already done him more good than all the sermons preached from the pulpits of the Bay State Capital.

But she had disregarded Jimmie's wishes, and from that time forward he had pursued a course of recklessness ending at last in prison. With a half-regretful sigh Mrs. Carleton thought of all this, and in her heart she blamed herself for some of her boy's disobedience. But it could not now be helped, and with another sigh, she turned toward Rose, still speculating as to what the result might have been, had Jimmie been suffered to follow up his first, and so far as she knew, only fancy.

"What do you suppose would have happened if Jimmie had staid in New London, and this scheming aunt, whom mother feared far more than the Pequot, had staid there too?" she asked of Annie, forgetting that the particulars of the affair had not been repeated.

But it did not matter, for Annie answered all the same. She was sitting now with her back to Mrs. Carleton, while, so far as Rose was concerned, her face was in the shadow. Consequently Rose could not see its expression, as she replied:

"Nothing probably would have come of it. I imagine the *Pequot*, as you call her, was not more than fourteen, and you know how easily we forget the fancies of that age. She was undoubtedly pleased with the evident admiration of your handsome brother, and watched anxiously it may be, for the evenings when, with others of his comrades, he came to the hotel; but a closer acquaintance would have resulted in her knowing the deception about the name, and after that she would not have cared for him. If he really liked her he would not have imposed upon her thus. She's forgotten him ere this, and is probably a married woman."

"Perhaps so," Rose replied; "I wish I knew. Jimmie didn't mean to deceive her long. He took the name Dick Lee, partly in sport, and partly because he didn't wish his teacher to know how often Jim Carleton was at the Pequot House, when he thought him somewhere else. After he began to like her, and saw how pure and good and truthful she was, he hated to tell her, but had made up his mind to do so when mother took him away."

"He might have written," Annie said, "and she may have been silly enough to cry over his abrupt and unexplained departure."

"Mother wouldn't let him write," Rose rejoined, laughingly. "She watched him closely, and got Tom interested too. Poor Jimmie, I wonder if that girl ever thinks of him now?"

"She may, but I dare say she is glad your mother took him home. She has outlived all that fancy," and Annie's white fingers, on one of which the wedding ring was shining, worked nervously together.

As if bent on tormenting both her auditors by talking of Jimmie, Rose kept on, wondering how he looked, if she should know him, what he would say, how he would act, and if he ever would come.

"I'm so glad you are here, Annie," she said, "for you do everybody good you come in contact with, and I want you to talk to Jimmie, will you?"

Annie only smiled, but her cheeks burned with excitement, and Rose was about asking if her head didn't ache, when a letter was brought in bearing the Washington postmark. Eagerly Rose broke it open, screaming with joy as she read that Jimmie had been released,—had taken the oath of allegiance, and was coming home to Rockland.

"He'll be here,—let me see,—Thursday, on the three o'clock train. That's to-morrow. Oh, I'm so glad!" and in her delight the little lady forgot that for the last week she had been playing *sick*, and leaping upon the carpet, danced about the room, kissing alternately her mother and Annie, and asking if they were ever so pleased in their lives.

"Oh, I forgot!" she suddenly exclaimed, as she saw the great tears dropping from Annie's eyes, and guessed of what she was thinking. "I did not mean to make you sorry contrasting Jimmie's coming home with that of poor George. Dear Annie, don't cry," and the chubby arms closed coaxingly round the now sobbing Annie's neck. "Don't cry. You'll like Jimmie, I know, and if you don't, I know you'll like dear Tom. He's perfectly splendid, and he gave his place to George, you know."

Yes, Annie knew, but it only made her tears flow faster as she thought of Rose, so full of hope, her husband yet alive, and her brothers coming home, while she, without a friend on whom she could lean, was alone in her desolate widowhood. Excusing herself from the room, she sought her own pleasant chamber, and there alone poured out her grief into the ear of One who almost since she could remember had been the recipient of all her sorrows. And Annie had far more need of help than Rose suspected. She could not stay there and meet Jimmie Carleton face to face after what she had heard, while a return to the lonely cottage seemed impossible. Widow Simms's home suggested itself to her mind; but if the prisoners were exchanged, and Isaac came home, she might be an intruder there, and besides, what truthful reason could she give to Rose for her strange conduct? It was a sad dilemma in which Annie found herself so suddenly placed, and more than an hour of solitary and prayerful reflection, found her still uncertain as to the course duty would dictate in the present emergency. It seemed expedient that she should go away, and when in the evening she joined Rose, who chanced to be alone, she suggested leaving her house, at least during Jimmie's stay, and going either to the cottage in the Hollow, or to stay with Widow Simms.

In the utmost astonishment Rose listened to the proposal, and then replied:

"*You* go away because Jimmie is coming! Preposterous! Why, I want you here on his account, if nothing more. Besides, where will you go? Widow Simms has taken Susan to live with her at John's request, and that little *teenty* place will not begin to hold three women with *hoops!*"

"You forget the widow does not wear them," Annie suggested, her heart beginning to sink, notwithstanding her playful words.

"Yes, I know," Rose replied; "but you are not going there. If you are in the way here with Jimmie, you'd surely be more in the way there with Isaac. Don't you see?" and Rose looked as if this argument were altogether conclusive.

"I can go home," Annie said, faintly. "The cottage is mine till the first of April."

Rose colored, and hesitated somewhat, as if a little uncertain how what she had to say on this subject might be received; then, resolving to put a bold face upon it, she said:

"I ought to have told you before, I suppose. Don't you remember the day you had the sick headache, more than a week ago? Well, while you were asleep, a man came to know if you'd let him into the cottage till spring, as he was obliged to leave where he was, and could find no other place. I did not wish to wake you, and as I knew you would not care, I said yes on my own responsibility, and sent Bridget down to pack all your things in the chamber, as he only wanted the lower rooms. She put them away real carefully, Bridget did, for I've been myself to see," Rose added, quickly, as she saw the color mounting to Annie's cheeks, and feared she might be indignant at the liberty.

"And is he there?" Annie asked, conquering all emotion, and speaking in her natural tone.

"Yes, he's there," Rose answered. "You are not angry, are you? He's a nice man, and so is his wife."

"I am not angry," Annie replied, "but more sorry than I can express, though, had I been consulted, I should undoubtedly have done as you did."

"Oh, I'm so glad, for it has bothered me a heap, wondering what you'd say!" Rose cried, throwing her arms around Annie's neck. "And now you'll stay with us, for you see you have nowhere else to go; shan't she, mother?" and she appealed to Mrs. Carleton, who had just come in.

"Of course Mrs. Graham will stay" was Mrs. Carleton's reply; for, during the few days of her sojourn at Rockland, she had become greatly interested in the sweet young Annie, and already foresaw the benefit she would be to Rose, who needed some such influence to keep her in check.

Mrs. Carleton was proud, and at first her daughter's growing intimacy with the wife of a mechanic had given her pride a pang, but a closer acquaintance had dispelled the foolish prejudice, for she saw in the gentle Annie unmistakable marks of education and refinement, while she was not insensible to the charm thrown round the beautiful stranger by the lovely Christian character which shone so brightly now in the dark hour of affliction. Coming nearer to her, and laying her hand in a motherly way upon her pale brown hair, she said:

"We all want you, Mrs. Graham, and as Rose, by an act which I will admit was too presuming, has virtually closed your own doors against you, I see no alternative but for you to stay with us. Rose needs you, and as she says, you may do Jimmie good, while *Tom*, if he ever comes, will be glad to meet the wife of one in whom he was greatly interested."

After this, Annie offered no further remonstrance, though in her heart she hoped Jimmie's residence in Rockland would not be very long. Of Tom she had no dread. She rather wished to see him than otherwise, for he had been kind to George, and in fancy she had enshrined him as a middle-aged, greyish haired man, stooping a little, perhaps, and withal very fatherly and venerable in his appearance! This was *Tom*,—but *Jimmie*, handsome, saucy-eyed, mischievous Jimmie, putting angle worms in Rose's bosom, and frightening the little Pequot with a mud-turtle, found on New London beach, was a very different thing, and though trusting much to the lapse of years and change of name, Annie shrank nervously from the dreaded to-morrow, which was to bring the Rebel home.

CHAPTER XVII.
THE CONFEDERATE SOLDIER'S WELCOME TO ROCKLAND.

Rose had fretted herself into a headache, and as Mrs. Carleton could not think of meeting her returning prodigal in the presence of strangers, there was no one to go up to meet him unless *Annie* should consent to do so! But greatly to Rose's disappointment Annie obstinately refused, while Mrs. Carleton, too, said it would not be proper for Mrs. Graham to go alone and meet a stranger whom she had never seen.

"Couldn't she tell him she was Annie, my adopted sister?" Rose said, half poutingly. "What will he think when he finds nobody there but Jake, who, I verily believe, looks upon him as half a savage for having joined the Southern army? I heard him, myself, tell Bridget that *Ben Arnold* was coming to-day, meaning that horrid traitor that gave up *Yorktown*, or something," and having thus betrayed her ignorance of Revolutionary history, Rose bathed her aching head in eau-de-cologne, and lay back upon her pillows, wondering what Jimmie would say, and how he would manage to brave the gaping people who were sure to stare at him as if he were some monster. She hoped there would not be many there, and of course there wouldn't, for who knew or cared for Jimmie's coming?

More cared for Jimmie's coming than Rose suspected, and the streets were full of men and boys of a certain class, hastening to the depot to see the Rebel, as they persisted in calling him, in spite of Billy Baker's repeated suggestions that they soften it down somewhat by prefixing the word "*reformed*." Bill was very busy, very important, very consequential that day, and quite inclined to be very patronizing, and do the agreeable to the man he had captured at Manassas. "Folks or'to overlook him," he said, "and treat him half way decent, for the best was apt to stumble, and there should neither be hootin' nor hissin', if he could help it."

Indeed, so impressed was Bill with the idea that the responsibility of Jimmie's reception was pending upon himself, that he deliberately knocked down two of the ringleaders, who announced their intention to hoot and to hiss as much as they pleased. Bill's warlike propensities were pretty generally understood in Rockland, and this energetic demonstration had the effect of quelling, to a certain extent, the Babel which would otherwise have reigned, when at last the train stopped before the depot, and the expected *lion* appeared upon the platform, his identity proven by Bill, who whispered, "That's him, with the rowdy hat,—that's the chap;" then, with a proud air of self-assurance, he stepped forward and offered his hand to the embarrassed stranger, who was looking this way and that, in quest of a familiar face.

"Halloo, Corporal!" he called out with the utmost *sang froid*, "you re-*cog*-nize me, I s'pose. I'm the critter that took you in the Virginny woods. I've gin all them contrabands to your sister, Miss Marthers. She and I has got to be considerable intimate. I think a sight on her," he continued, as Jimmie showed no signs of reciprocating the coarse familiarity other than by rather haughtily offering his hand.

But Bill was not to be put down, for "wasn't he as good as Corporal Carleton? hadn't they sustained to each other the relation of captor and captive, and if there were any preference, wasn't it in his favor?" He thought so, and nothing abashed by Jimmie's evident disgust, he was about announcing to him that a carriage was in waiting, when Jake made his way through the crowd to the spot where Jimmie stood. The sight of him suggested a new idea to Bill, and bowing first to one and then to the other, he said, "Ah, Mr. Jacob Sullivan, allow me to introduce you to my friend, Corporal Carleton, late of the Confederate army, supposed to be fitin' for just such goods and chattels as you."

The African's teeth were plainly visible at this novel introduction, while the good-humored smile which broke over the hitherto cold, haughty features of the stranger, changed into a general laugh the muttered groans and imprecations which the words "Confederate Army," had provoked. It was strange what a difference that smile made in the looks of Jimmie's handsome face, removing its haughty, sarcastic expression, and softening to a great extent the feelings of the crowd, many of whom instinctively dropped the brick-bats, stones, and bits of frozen mud, with which they were prepared to pelt the Rebel's carriage so soon as they should be in the rear. Still they must have some fun, even if it were at *Bill's* expense, and just as the latter was button-holing the persecuted Jimmie, and escorting him to the carriage, one, more daring than the others, proposed "three groans and a tiger for the deserter."

Instantly, hats, caps, and fists were flourished aloft, and the air resounded with the most direful sounds imaginable, as groan after groan came heaving up from the leathern lungs of the crowd. With a fierce gesture of impatience Jimmie turned upon them, his black eyes flashing fire at what he deemed an insult offered to himself. Whatever his faults had been, desertion was not among the number, and he was about to say so, when Bill, with imperturbable gravity, whispered to him, "They don't mean you now, Corporal. It's me they're hittin' a dig. You see, I did leave Washington in a hurry. Don't mind 'em an atom; they're the off-scourin's of the town," and having piloted Jimmie safely to the carriage door, Bill took off his own cap, and swinging it around his head, shouted aloud, "Three cheers for Corporal Carleton!"

For an instant there was a silence, the crowd a little uncertain as to how far their loyalty might be impeached by cheering for a Rebel; but when the dark, handsome face, with its winning smile, was again turned toward them, and they saw in it a strong resemblance to the patriotic little lady whom even the lowest of them had learned to regard with respect, their doubts were given to the winds, and the ringleader, who carried in his pocket a quantity of questionable eggs, designed for use as the occasion might require, led off the cheers, making the depot ring with the loud huzzas, interlarded here and there by a groan or hiss from those not yet won over to the popular party.

Lifting his hat gracefully, Jimmie bowed an acknowledgment, and his lips moved as if about to speak, while cries of "Hear, hear!" "Give us a speech!" "Let's have your politics!" ran through the excited throng. Standing close to Jimmie, who would fain have dispensed with his suggestive presence, Bill whispered in his ear, "Let 'er slide, Cop'ral. Go in strong for Uncle Sam if you don't want this new coat of yourn sp'ilt. There ain't a rotten hen's nest in town but what was robbed this mornin' on your account, and if they once git fairly to work, it'll take mor'n me and Mr. Sullivan to stop em! Pitch in, then, to your sarmon."

Jimmie's natural disposition prompted him to brave the purloined contents of Rockland's hen's nests, but he would not endanger his sister's carriage, and besides that, he felt that submission to people so infinitely beneath him was a part of his merited punishment; so, forcing down his pride, he in a few well-chosen words, told his breathless audience that though he had once proved faithless to his country, none regretted it more than himself, or was now a firmer friend to the Stars and Stripes, the brief speech ending with the proposal of three cheers for the Star Spangled Banner.

In a trice the whole crowd responded with might and main, prolonging their yells with the cries of "Carleton! Carleton forever!" and promises to make him police justice in the spring, should he want to run for that very agreeable office!

"Couldn't of done much better myself," said the delighted Bill, hovering about the window of the carriage in which Jimmie had now taken his seat.

Thoroughly tired of the scene, Jimmie intimated to Jake his wish to go home, and the iron greys sprang quickly forward, but not until Jimmie had caught Bill's parting words, "Call round and see a feller, won't you? I'll show you the old gal. You know you asked me about her in the Virginny woods."

It seemed like a new world to Jimmie when, after they had left the noisy crowd, they turned into the pleasant, quiet street which wound up the hill to where the handsome Mather mansion stood, every blind thrown back and wreaths of smoke curling gracefully from every chimney, for Rose, wishing to do something in honor of her brother's return, had ordered the whole house to be opened as if for a holiday, while every flower which could possibly be spared from her conservatory, had been broken from its stem, and fashioned into bouquets by Annie's tasteful hands.

"Wouldn't it be splendid," Rose said, as she lay watching Annie at her task, "wouldn't it be splendid to hang the Stars and Stripes in festoons across the hall, where Jimmie will pass under them?"

Annie did *not* think it would. In her opinion Jimmie was not deserving of such honor, and she said so, as delicately as possible, adding that "were it Tom it would be a very different thing."

Rose knew that Annie was right, and so the Stars and Stripes were not brought out to welcome the young man now rapidly approaching. Annie was the first to catch the sound of the carriage wheels, and when Rose turned to ask if she really supposed Jimmie was there, she found herself alone.

"She's gone to meet him, of course," she said, "but I most wish she had staid here, for I wanted to introduce her myself. I hope she won't dislike him."

Meantime in the parlor below, Mrs. Carleton sat waiting for her boy,—not as Spartan mothers were wont to wait for their sons returning from the war, but with a yearning tenderness for the loved prodigal, blended with loyal indignation for his sin. He was not coming to her as a hero who had done what he could for his country, but with a traitor's stain upon his fair name, which she would gladly have wiped out. She heard the carriage as it stopped, and heard the step on the piazza, not rapid and bounding as it used to be, but slow and heavy, as if uncertain which way to turn.

"I must go out to meet him," she said, but all her strength forsook her, and sinking upon the sofa, she could only call out faintly, "Jimmie, my boy."

He heard her, and almost before the words had left her lips her *Jimmie boy* was kneeling at her feet, with his face buried for an instant in her lap; then, with one burning kiss upon her forehead, the proud James Carleton, who in his early boyhood was scarcely ever known to acknowledge that he was wrong, asked to be forgiven and restored again to the confidence and love he had forfeited, and with her hand upon his bowed head, the mother forgave her boy, bidding him look up, that she might see again the face she had once thought so handsome. It was tear-stained now, and worn, and Mrs. Carleton sighed as she detected upon it unmistakable marks of reckless dissipation. Still it was Jimmie's face, and it grew each moment more natural as the flush of excitement deepened on the cheeks, and lent an added brightness to the saucy, laughing eyes. The lines upon the forehead and about the mouth would wear away in time, Mrs. Carleton hoped, and parting the soft, black curls clustering around the broad, white brow, she told him why Rose was not there to meet him, and asked if he would go up then to see her.

Rose heard them coming, and at the sound of the familiar voice calling her name, the tears flowed in torrents, and with her face buried in her pillows she received her brother's first embrace. Very gently he lifted up her head, and taking in his the little hot hands, kissed again and again her childish face, and wiping her tears away, asked, half seriously, half playfully, "if they met in peace or war?"

"Oh, in peace, in peace!" Rose answered, and winding her arms around his neck, she hugged and cried over him, asking why he had been so naughty, when he knew how badly they would feel, and why he had not interfered to save poor *Tom* from a prisoner's fate.

He explained to her how that was impossible, but for his treachery he had no excuse; he could only answer that he was sorry, and ask again to be forgiven.

"I do not now believe the South *all wrong*," he said. "Many of them sincerely think they are fighting for their firesides; others hardly know what they are fighting for; while others again are impressed into the army and cannot help themselves. As for me, I would gladly blot out the past, for which I have no apology; but as that cannot be, I would rather talk as little of it as possible. Try, Rose, to forget that you ever had a rebel brother. Will you?"

Rose's kisses were a sufficient answer. She was too happy just then to remember aught save that he had always been the dearest brother imaginable; besides that Annie taught that we must forgive as we would be forgiven. Annie bore no ill will toward the South. She prayed for *them* as well as for the North, and cried most as hard over the sick, suffering soldiers captured by our army as over our own prisoners, and if she could forgive, Rose surely ought to do so too.

"You have not seen Annie yet," she said; "she ran away the moment she knew you had come. I thought she might be going to meet you, but it seems she did not. You must love her a heap, and I know you will. She's so beautiful in her mourning, and bears her trouble so sweetly. I wish everybody was as good as Annie Graham. She has never been heard to say one bitter thing against the South. She only pities and prays and says they are misguided."

"And pray, who is this paragon of excellence that I must love a heap?" Jimmie asked, when Rose had exhausted the list of Annie's virtues, and paused for a little breath.

"Who was she? Hadn't he heard of Annie? Had *Will* failed to tell him of her adopted sister?" Rose asked in some astonishment.

Will had proved remiss in that one particular duty, and never, until this moment, had Jimmie heard that Rose had an adopted sister; and if *Rose*, why not himself? Wasn't he Rose's brother?

"Certainly you are," Rose replied; "but I'm not sure Annie will let you call her sister, because you're,—you're,—well, you see, Annie is real good, and, as I told you, prays, just as hard for Southern soldiers as for ours, that is, prays that they may be Christians, and that their sick and wounded may be kindly cared for, but of course she wants us to beat, and knows we shall, but I guess she does not think of you just as she does of Tom, though she never saw either. She would not go up to the depot to meet you, and I wanted her to so much. She said, too, it was not good taste, or something like that, to hang out our banner on a *Rebel's* account, and she acts so funny generally about your coming home that I hope you'll do your best to be agreeable, and make her like you. Will you Jimmie?" and Rose looked up at her brother in such a comical, serious way, that he laughed aloud, promising to do his best to remove all prejudice from *Miss* Graham's mind, and asking who she was and where she came from.

"I'm sure I don't know where she came from," Rose replied, a little uncertain how to grapple with the Carleton pride, which existed in Jimmie as well as the rest of them. "She's a lady, as any one can see, and possessed of as much refinement as we often find in Boston. She can't help it, Jimmie, if she is poor. It don't hurt her one bit, and I'm getting over those foolish notions cherished by our set at home. Will says she came of a good family and might have married a millionnaire, old enough to be her father, but she wouldn't. She preferred a mechanic, George Graham, the most splendid looking man you ever saw. He's dead now, poor fellow. Will took care of him, and brought him home; that's why Annie lives with me."

Rose's explanations were not the plainest that could have been given, but Jimmie extracted from the medley of facts a very prominent one. It was not a *Miss* but a *Mrs.*, to whom he was to be agreeable. It had not seemed a very unpleasant duty to change a beautiful young girl's opinion of himself, but a Mrs. was a very different affair, and for the first time since his arrival his old, merry, half-sarcastic laugh rang through the room, as with a mocking whistle, he said,

"A widow, hey! How many children does she boast?"

"Not a single bit of a one," Rose answered, feeling that Jimmie had said something very bad of Annie.

He saw it in her countenance, and hastened to make amends by asking numberless questions about Annie, whose history from the time of Rose's first acquaintance with her up to the present hour, he managed at last to get, the result being that he was not as much interested in the Widow Graham, as he mischievously called her, as he might have been in *Miss Annie*. The easily disheartened Rose gave him up as incorrigible, and mentally hoping Tom would not prove as refractory as Jimmie had done, she turned the conversation upon Will, whose goodness she extolled until the supper bell rang and Jimmie arose to leave her for a time, as she was not prepared to go down that night and do the honors of the table.

The gas was lighted in the dining-room, and the heavy damask curtains were dropped before the long French windows. A cheerful coal fire was blazing on the marble hearth, while the table, with its snowy linen, its china, silver and cut glass, presented a most inviting appearance, making Jimmie feel more at home than he had through all the long years of his voluntary exile from the parental roof.

"This is nice," he said, with a pleasant feeling of satisfaction not unmingled with a certain degree of self-reproach, which whispered that after what had passed he was hardly worthy to be the recipient of so much luxury.

Thoughts like these were about shaping themselves into words, when he caught sight of a figure he had not before observed, and became aware that he was not alone with his mother, as he at first supposed. It was a delicate little figure, not as *petite* as his sister's but quite as graceful, with its sloping shoulders and rounded waist, almost too small to suit the theorems of a *Water Cure*, but looking vastly well to Jimmie, whose first thought was that he could span it with his hands. Around the well shaped head the heavy bands of pale brown hair were coiled, forming a large square knot which, falling low upon the neck, gave to the figure a more girlish appearance than Jimmie had expected to find in his sister's protégée, the *Widow Graham*. He knew it was Annie, by the mourning robe fitting so closely around the slender throat, and for an instant he wished she were not there as he preferred being alone with his mother. But one glance at the sweet face turned toward him as Mrs. Carleton repeated his name, dispelled all such desires, and with a strange sensation, which he attributed to pleasant disappointment, he took the soft, white hand which Annie extended toward him. It was a very small, a very pretty hand, and trembled perceptibly as it lay in Jimmie's broader, warmer one, while on the pale cheek there was a deep, rich bloom, which Mrs. Carleton herself had never observed before.

"I have heard of Mrs. Graham from my sister," Jimmie said, bowing to her with his usual gallantry, while Annie tried to stammer out some reply, making a miserable failure, and leaving on Jimmie's mind the impression that she was prejudiced against him, and so would not welcome him home.

A dozen times in the course of the supper Jimmie assured himself that he did not care what was the opinion held of him by such as Annie Graham, while he as often changed his mind and knew that he did care, wondering what it was about her face which puzzled him so much. She looked a little like Tom's wife, Mary, he thought, that is, as Mary had looked just before her departure for Charleston, when she bade him good-bye, whispering to him timidly of a world where she hoped to meet again the friends she loved so well. And as, whenever he thought of Mary, he felt that her angel presence was around him still, he now felt that another angel spirit looked out at him from the soft eyes of blue raised to his so seldom, and when raised withdrawn so quickly. What did she think of him? He would have given something to have known, but he was far from suspecting the truth or guessing what Annie felt, as she saw upon his face the lines of dissipation, and thought of the debasing scenes through which he must have passed since the days of auld lang syne, when, with the little Pequot of New London, he sat upon the rocks and watched the tide come in, telling her how, on the morrow night, his own fanciful little boat, named for her should bear them across the placid waters of the bay to where the green hill lay sleeping in the summer moonlight. The Pequot's reply had been that the morrow was the Sabbath, and not even the pleasure of a sail with him could tempt her to steal God's time, and appropriate it to such a purpose. He had called her a little Puritan then, asking where she learned so strict a creed, and adding, "but I half believe you're right, and if I'd known you sooner I should have been a better boy;" then kissing her blushing cheek, he had led her from the rocks over which the waves were breaking now, and that was the last the Pequot ever saw of him. There was no sail upon the bay, no more watching for the ebb and flow of the evening tide, no walks on the long piazza, or strolls upon the beach, nothing but news one night that the handsome, saucy-eyed boy was gone to his home in Boston, leaving no message or word of explanation for her, the little Pequot, whose step was slower for a few days, and whose headache was not feigned, as the harsh aunt said it was, when she refused to join the revellers in the parlor, and dance with the grey-haired man, four times her age, who sought her for his partner. They had not met since then till now, and Annie struggled hard to keep back the tears as she remembered all that had come to her since that summer at New London—remembered the childish fancy which died out so fast, and the later love which crowned her early girlhood, finding its full fruition at the marriage altar, and twining itself so closely around the fibres of her heart, that when it was torn away, it left them sore and bleeding with pain at every pore.

Surely, with this sad experience, Annie, young and beautiful though she was, could feel for Jimmie Carleton naught save the deference she would have felt for any stranger who came to her as the brother of her patroness. And still she was conscious of a deeper interest in him than if he had been a perfect stranger, and his presence awoke within her an uncomfortable feeling, making her wish more and more that she was away where she would not be obliged to come in daily contact with him. Under these circumstances it is not strange the conversation flagged, until for Rose's sake Annie felt compelled to make an effort. Suddenly remembering Isaac Simms, she asked if anything was ever heard at Washington of the Richmond prisoners?

"Yes," Jimmie replied; and eager to show his own willingness to talk of the war and the Federal Army, he told how only the day before he left for Rockland, news had come from Tom, saying he was well as could be expected, considering his fare, but the boy captured with him would surely die if not soon restored to purer air and better care than those tobacco prisons afforded.

"Oh,—it will kill Mrs. Simms if they should bring him back to her dead," and the hot tears gushed from Annie's eyes as she heard in fancy the muffled drum beating its funeral marches to the grave of another Rockland volunteer.

The tears once started could not be repressed, and Mrs. Carleton and Jimmie finished their supper alone, for Annie excused herself, and hastening to her room, poured out her grief in tears and prayers for the poor sick boy, pining in his dreary prison home, while mingled with her tears was a note of thanksgiving that to her had been given the comfort of knowing that the death pillow of her darling was smoothed with friendly hands, and that no harsh, discordant sounds of prison riot or discipline had disturbed his peaceful dying.

Meantime Jimmie had returned to his sister, whose first question was for Annie. "What did he think of her? Wasn't she sweet, and hadn't she the prettiest blue eyes he ever saw?"

"I hardly saw them, for she is evidently coy of her glances at a *Rebel*," Jimmie answered, half playfully, half bitterly, for Annie's manner of quiet reserve had piqued him more than he cared to confess.

"She's bashful," Rose replied; "and then, Jimmie, you can't expect her to forgive you as readily as your own sister, for you know she never saw you till to-night, and she's a true patriot; but say, did you ever see so sweet a face— one that made you think so much of an angel?"

"Rather too pale to suit my taste. I like high color better," and Jimmie pinched Rose's glowing cheek until she screamed for him to stop.

"It's all going wrong, I know," Rose began, poutingly. "You don't like Annie a bit, and she's so good, too. You can't begin to guess how good. And there's nothing blue about her, either. Why, she's a heap more cheerful than I could be if Will were dead, as George is. I'd die too,—I know I should; but Annie's a real Christian, and that does make a difference. It seems to be all through her, and she lives it every minute. I honestly believe I'm better than before she came. She has actually persuaded me not to get up big dinners on Sunday, as I used to do, but to let all the servants go to church, and every night she goes for half an hour into the kitchen and teaches old black Phillis how to read the Bible. She's so truthful, too. Why, she said she presumed that little Pequot girl would not have liked you any way after she heard that Dick Lee was not your name."

"The Pequot girl! How came Mrs. Graham to hear of her?" Jimmie asked, his face flushing crimson.

"Oh, I happened to ask mother something about her one day, right before Annie, and so, of course, explained a little. It would not have been polite if I hadn't," Rose replied, adding, as she saw her brother's evident chagrin, "you need not mind one bit, for Annie never tells anything."

It was not the fearing she would tell which affected Jimmie unpleasantly; it was the feeling that he would rather Annie Graham should not know of all his delinquencies, and so despise him accordingly. How unfortunate it was that she was there, and yet he would not have sent her away if he could, though he did wish she were not so well posted with regard to his affairs, both past and present. What made Rose tell her of the *Pequot*, and why had the Pequot haunted him ever since he came into that house? Something had brought her to his mind, and as the servant just then came in, bringing her mistress's supper, he left his seat by Rose, and walking to the window looked out upon the starry sky, wondering within himself where she was now, the little girl who had sat with him upon the rocks, and told him it was wicked to break God's fourth command. The scene which Annie saw at the supper table was present with him now, remembered, for the first time, since the battle at Bull Run. Then, as he lay waiting for the foe, he had in fancy heard again a sweet, girlish voice, bidding him keep holy the Sabbath day, and the tear which dropped upon his gun was prompted by the thought of all he had passed through since the happy school-boy days when the Pequot preached to him her gentle sermons.

In the hall there was a rapid footstep, and Rose called out:

"Annie, Annie, come here. Why, where are you going to-night?" she continued, in much surprise, as Annie looked in, hooded and shawled as for some expedition.

"Going to see Mrs. Simms. It is not far, you know," was Annie's answer, and the door closed after her in time to prevent her hearing Rose's reply.

"It's dark as pitch, and slippery too. Jimmie, do please see her to the gate, but don't go in, for the widow is awful against Rebels!"

The next moment Jimmie was half way down the stairs, calling to Annie, who held the door-knob in her hand.

"Mrs. Graham, allow me to be your escort,—Rose is not willing you should go out alone."

"Thank you, I am not at all afraid, and prefer going alone, as Mrs. Simms might not care to meet a stranger," Annie replied, with an air of so much quiet dignity, that Jimmie knew there was no alternative for him save to return to his sister's chamber, which he did, feeling far more crestfallen than he had supposed it possible for him to feel, just because a widow had refused his escort.

It was wholly owing to the taint of Rebeldom clinging to him, he knew, for he was not accustomed to having his attentions thus slighted by the ladies to whom they were offered, and all unconsciously the manner of reserve which Annie assumed toward him was punishing him for his sin quite as much as anything which had yet occurred, making him feel keenly that by his traitorous act he had, for a time at least, built a gulf between himself and those whose good opinion was worth the having.

"Why haven't you gone?" Rose asked, as he came into the room. "She wouldn't let you? I don't believe you asked her just as you should. Dear, dear, it's all going wrong between you two, and if Tom don't act any better when he comes home, what shall I do?"

"Send Mrs. Graham away," trembled on Jimmie's lips, but knowing, from what he had seen, that so far as Rose was concerned, Annie's tenure at the Mather mansion was stronger than his own, he wisely kept silent, and sitting down by the open grate, he went off into a fit of abstraction, mingled with sad regrets for the past and occasional thoughts of the little white-faced Annie, now essaying to comfort the Widow Simms, who had extorted from her the intelligence brought by Jimmie of her boy, and who, with her hard hands covering her face, was weeping bitterly, and sobbing amid her tears,

"My poor, poor boy! It's the same to me now as if he was dead. I'll never see him any more. Oh, Isaac, my darling!"

CHAPTER XVIII.
THE RICHMOND CAPTIVES.

How close, and dirty, and terrible it was on that third floor of the dingy tobacco house, where Isaac, as a private, was first confined, and as the summer days glided by and the August sun came pouring into the great, disorderly room, how the young boy panted and pined for a breath of sweet, pure air, such as swept over the far-off Eastern hills, and how full of wistful yearning were the glances he cast toward the grated windows, seeking to catch glimpses of the busy world without, in which he could not mingle. Not very near those windows did he dare approach, for more than one had already paid the penalty of such transgression, and in his dreams, Isaac saw yet the white death agony which stole over the face of the Fire Zouave shot by the inhuman guard while looking from the window.

No wonder that the homesick boy grew sadder, wearier each day amid such horrors as these, praying, sometimes, that he might die, even though he must be buried far from the quiet Rockland churchyard, where the cypress and the willow were growing so green and fair, and where a mother could sometimes come and weep over her soldier boy's grave. It would matter little where he slept, he thought, or what indignities were heaped upon his lifeless form, for his soul could not be touched; that would be safe with Him, whom Isaac, in his captivity, had found to be indeed the Friend which sticketh closer than a brother. The Saviour, honored since early childhood, did not desert the captive, and this it was which made him strong to bear, through the long summer days, during which there came to him no tidings of his home, and his eye was greeted with no sight of a familiar face, for Captain Carleton was yet an inmate of the hospital. Neither did any friendly message come to tell he was remembered by the man whose fortunes he had voluntarily shared, when he might, perhaps, have escaped, for though *Tom* thought often of the generous lad, and sent to him many a word of comfort through mistake or negligence only one brief message had ever reached its destination, and so forsaken by every human aid, poor Isaac looked to Heaven for help, finding there a peace which kept his heart from breaking.

But as the summer days glided into September, and the heat grew more and more intense, until at last September, too, was gone, and the Virginia woods were blazing in the light of the October sun, and still there was no token of relief, oh! who, save those who have felt it, can tell of the loneliness, the dreary despair, which crept into the captive's soul, driving out all hope, and making life as it existed in those walls a burden, which would be gladly shaken off. How Isaac paled and drooped as the weary hours stole on; how he loathed the sickening food; and how at night he shuddered with horror, and shrank away from the vermin-covered floor, his only pillow unless he substituted the coat, now scarcely less filthy than its surroundings! As Tom wrote to the New Hampshire woman, Mrs. Simms would scarcely have recognized her son in the haggard, emaciated boy, who, on one October afternoon, sat crouching in his corner, grasping the little Testament given by the Rockland ladies, and repeating its precious truths to the poor, sick, worn-out youth, whose head lay on his lap, and whose eyes, blistered with homesick tears, were fastened with a kind of hungry wistfulness upon the girlish face above him, the face of Isaac Simms, pointing the dying soldier to the only source of life. It was thus Tom Carleton found him, Tom, just released from the hospital, and transferred to the first floor of that dark prison.

With Tom it had fared better, for Yankee-like in his precautions, he had gone into the battle with a quantity of *gold* fastened securely around his person, and gold has a mighty power to unlock the hardest heart. As a commissioned officer, and a man of wealth and rank, many privileges were accorded to him which were denied the common soldiers, and his first act after entering the tobacco house was to seek out his late companion and ask after his welfare. He did not know him at first, though directed to that locality as the one where the *"Preacher"* would probably be found. He could not think he had ever seen either of these famished, miserable looking creatures, but touched by the impressive scene, he stood a moment listening, while Isaac read,

"I am the way, the truth, and the life. No man cometh to the Father but by me."

"Yes, but how shall I go to Him? Where is He?" the sick boy asked, and bending lower, Isaac answered:

"He's here. He's standing close by you. He hears all I say. He knows you want him, and he will not cast you off, for he has said he wouldn't. Only believe, and take him at his word, that's all."

There was an evident lifting up of both souls to God, and Tom felt that even in that horrid place, there were angels dwelling. He knew now that one was Isaac, and the great tears rolled down his cheeks as he saw the fearful change wrought in little more than two short months.

"Isaac," he said, softly, "Isaac, my boy, don't you know me?"

Not till then had Isaac observed the tall figure standing near, but at the sound of the well-remembered voice he looked quickly up, and putting gently from him the head of his comrade, sprang to his feet with a scream of joy, and threw himself into the open arms of Tom, who held and soothed him, while he sobbed out his delight.

"Oh, Captain Carleton!" he cried, his body quivering with emotion, "I am so glad! I thought you had,—I didn't know,—Oh, *why* haven't you come before, I'm so sick, so sick and tired, that I almost want to die! Will we ever be exchanged; have they forgotten us at Washington? Shall we never go home again?"

These were questions which more than one poor captive had asked, and which none could answer. Tom, however, did the best he could, and hushing Isaac as he would have hushed and quieted a grieving child, he spoke to him many a word of comfort, promising to care for him as for a younger brother, and speaking of various ways in which his forlorn condition should be bettered, now that he was an inmate of the same prison. It was a blissful interview, and its good effects were seen in the brightness of Isaac's face, and the cheerful smile which played around his mouth, even after Tom had gone to his quarters below.

Softer than downy pillow seemed the hard bare floor, that night, as with his arm thrown round his invalid friend, Isaac lay dreaming of the frost-tipped trees at home, and the brown nuts ripening on the hill, where he, perhaps, might pick them yet, for Tom had given some encouragement that an exchange would ere long be effected, and as each believed his own name would be upon the list, so Isaac hoped his would, and in slumber's fitful fancy he was at home again, and saw his mother come softly in to tuck the bed-clothes round him, or see if he were sleeping, just as she used to do. How still he lay to make her think he *was* asleep! How real seemed the vision, how life-like the kiss pressed upon his lips, and the tear-drop that came with it! In a corner of the room there were groans and imprecations, and with a nervous start the dreamer woke to find it all a horrid delusion. That stifling, fetid atmosphere had in it no odor of Rockland's healthful breezes, and the star, shining on him through the iron bars, though familiar to him, was not the same which he used to watch from the window beneath the eaves, facing to the north. No home, no mother, no soft feathery pillow for his head, or blanket for his body—nothing but that feverish hand still upon his forehead, and that tear on his cheek, for *these* were real, and the sick soldier at his side, who gave the kiss and tear, was whispering in his ear, that the way so tearfully sought was found at last; that the gloomy, desolate prison was like the gates of Paradise, and death disarmed of all its terror.

"If mother could only know it," he said, "I should be so glad, and you'll tell her, won't you, when you get home again? Tell her it wasn't very hard to die, even in this dingy hole; that Heaven and Jesus are as near to me here on the floor, as if I were lying on my own bed at home, with her standing by. Tell her I'm glad I fought for the Stars and Stripes, but sorry I ran away without her consent, for I did. I got out on the wood-shed roof, and so came off unseen. She's prayed for me every day and every night, and God has heard her prayers. He sent you here to lead me in the way, and after I am gone, he'll let you go back again."

There were a few more whispered words on either side, and then the exhausted but happy youth fell away to sleep, while Isaac wept with thankfulness that his confinement there had not been all in vain.

Faithful to his promise, Tom, as far as was possible, alleviated the hardships so long and so meekly borne by Isaac, and with his gold bought many a delicacy for Isaac's end, the poor, sick Massachusetts boy, who, one night ere the physician had fairly decided that he was in need of medical care, laid his head on Isaac's lap as he was wont to do, and with another whispered message for the mother far away, and another assurance of perfect peace, went where the wicked cease from troubling, and the weary are at rest!

While he lived there had been something to take Isaac's mind—something to excite his sympathy, and in ministering to Henry's wants, he had more than half forgotten his own, but now that he was gone, and the corner where he had sat or lain was empty, Isaac, too, faded rapidly, and not all Tom's efforts had power to save him from the apathy which came stealing over him so fast. Touched with pity at his forlorn, dejected appearance, his comrades made him a little bed in the corner where the dead boy had been, and there all the day long he lay, rarely noticing any one except Tom Carleton, who came often to his side, and whose own warm blanket formed the pillow for his head. From the first floor to the third there was not one who was not more or less interested in the pale invalid, bearing his pain so patiently, never complaining, never repining, but thanking those about him for any kindness rendered with such childlike, touching sweetness, that even the rough jailer regarded him with favor, and paused sometimes to speak to him a word of encouragement.

In this state of feeling it was not a difficult matter for Tom to obtain permission for Isaac to be removed from the dirty corner above to his own comparatively comfortable cot in the officers' apartments below. But this did not effect a cure. Nothing could do that save a sight of home and mother.

"Could I see *her*," Isaac said one day, "or even stand again beneath the Federal Flag, I might get better, but here I shall surely die, and if I do, oh, Captain Carleton, you'll get them to send me home, won't you? I don't care for myself where I am buried, but my mother—it would break her heart to hear I was put with the negroes. She's a rough woman, and folks who don't know her much, thinks she's cross and queer, but she's been *so* good to me, and I love her so much! Oh, mother, mother, I wish she was here now," and the sick boy turned his white face to the wall, sobbing out choking sobs which seemed to come from the lowest depths of his heart.

Cries for home and mother were not uncommon in that prison house, but there was something so piteous in his childlike wail that other officers than Tom bent over the poor lad, trying to comfort him by telling of an exchange which, it was hoped would ere long be effected, and by painting happy pictures of the glad rejoicing which would greet the returning captives. For an instant the great tears, dropping so fast from Isaac's lids, were staid in their course, and a smile of hope shone on his pallid face, but quickly passed away as he suggested,

"Yes, but who knows if *I* will be on the list?"

No one could tell him that. All would not go, they knew, and they could only wait patiently, each hoping *he* would be the favored one. At last there came a day, never to be forgotten by the inmates of that tobacco house, a day on which was read the names of those who were to be released and breathe again the air of freedom. Oh, how anxiously the sick boy listened as one after another was called. "Captain Thomas Carleton" was among the number, and a deep flush stole to the young man's face as uncertainty was thus made sure. *He* was going home, and like waves upon the beach, the throbs of joy beat around his heart, making him glad as a little child when returning to its mother after a long separation.

But oh, who shall tell Isaac's emotions as name after name was called, and none that sounded like his. Would they never reach it, never say *Isaac Simms?* Could it be he was not there? Larger and thicker grew the drops of sweat, quivering about his mouth, and standing upon his forehead. Whiter, more death-like grew his face: heavier, sadder, more mournful the eyes, fixed so wistfully upon the caller of that roll, growing less so fast. There could not be many more, and the head drooped upon the heaving bosom, with a discouraged, disheartened feeling, just as the last was read, not *his*, not Isaac Simms. *He was not there*, and with a moan, which smote painfully on Tom's ear, the disappointed boy turned away, and wept bitterly, while his pale lips moved feebly with the prayer for help he essayed to make. To be left there alone, with no kind Captain Carleton to soothe the weary hours, to be returned, most likely, to the noisy floor above, to die some night when nobody knew or cared,—it was terrible,—and Widow Simms would have shrieked in anguish could she have seen the look of despair settling down on her darling's face.

But though she did not see it, there was one who did, and guessing at the thoughts which prompted it, he walked away to be alone, and gather strength for the sacrifice he must make. Tom Carleton could not desert the boy who had clung so faithfully to him, and as Isaac had once staid by him in the Virginia woods, when he might have gone away, so he now would stay with Isaac. Still it was hard to give up going home, and for a moment he felt as if he could not. There was a fierce struggle between duty and inclination,—a mighty combat between Tom's selfishness and his better nature,—and then the latter conquered. He must stay. It would not be difficult to find some person to take his place clandestinely, for already were the unfortunate ones seeking to buy such chances, and offering every possible inducement to any who would accept. A young lieutenant about his age and appearance, and whose wife and child were suffering from his absence, was the one selected by Tom as his substitute, and the matter soon arranged. Then, with a forced cheerfulness he did not feel, Tom went back to Isaac, who was still weeping silently on his couch, and whispering to an unseen presence, "*You'll* never leave me, will you? and when I die you'll take me up to Heaven?"

Here was a faith, a trust, to which Tom Carleton was a stranger, and wishing himself more like that sick boy, he bent over the cot, and said cheerily,

"Isaac, are you asleep?"

In the tone of his voice there was something so kind and sympathetic, that Isaac started up, and winding his feeble arms around Tom's neck, sobbed out,

"Forgive me, Captain Carleton; I'm glad you are going home, but I wasn't at first; the bad, hard lumps kept rising in my throat as I thought of staying here alone without you, but they're gone now. I prayed them all away, and I am glad you are going. I shall miss you dreadfully, but God will not forsake me. And, Captain Carleton, if you ever do,—see—my,—my"——

Isaac's voice was choked with tears, and he could not at first articulate that dear word, but soon recovering, he went on—"see my mother, you'll tell her about me. Tell her everything except how I've suffered. That would do no good—'twould only make her cry, and when she hears, as she maybe will, that I am dead, tell I wasn't afraid, for the Saviour was with me. I'd rather you shouldn't say good-bye at the last. It would make me feel so bad, only sometime before you go I want to tell you how much I love you for your goodness, and to ask you to be a"——

He did not finish the sentence, for Tom knew what he would say, and wiping both sweat and tears from off the worn face, looking so lovingly at him, he answered, "I *will* try to be a better man. I never felt the need of it so much till I came here, and Isaac, I am going to stay till you, too, are exchanged. Did you think I would desert the boy who, but for me, would not have been a prisoner?"

Isaac did not reply; only the soft, blue eyes lighted up with sudden, eager joy; the lips trembled as if they would speak, there was a perceptible shudder, and then Tom held in his arms a fainting, unconscious form. The revulsion of feeling was too great, and for many minutes Isaac gave no sign of life, but when at last he was restored again, he tried to dissuade Tom from making so great a sacrifice, but all in vain. Tom silenced every objection, and when the 3d of January came, and prisoners were released, another than Tom Carleton answered to his name, and marched from Richmond in his stead.

Tom had once spent several months in Richmond, and in the higher circles he numbered many personal friends, who, until quite recently, were ignorant of the fact that he was a prisoner in their midst. Of these the more loyal to the new Confederacy ignored him entirely. Others, remembering his genial humor, and quiet, gentlemanly manner which had won their admiration for the elegant Bostonian and his gentle wife, threw their prejudice aside, and respecting him because he had stood firmly by his own State, visited him in his prison, while others sent playful messages that though they denounced him as an intruder upon their rights, they owned him as a friend, and would gladly ameliorate his condition. To these acquaintance it was soon known how great a sacrifice Tom had made for the sake of a young boy, and the result was a gradual abatement of the surveillance held over Tom, while many privileges hitherto denied by the strict jail discipline, were accorded to him. Isaac, too, was benefited through him, and more than one fair lady visited the invalid, growing strangely interested in the gentle "Yankee boy," and bringing many a delicacy with which to tempt his capricious appetite. But no amount of kindness could win him back to health so long as he breathed the atmosphere of prison walls. To go home was all he desired, and day after day the flesh shrivelled from his bones, and the blue veins stood out round and full upon his wasted hands until there came a night when the physician told the jailer, whom he met upon the stairs, that "the Yankee boy was dying."

There were not many now in prison, and ere long the sad news was known throughout the building, causing the riotous ones to hush their noisy revels, and tread softly across the uncovered floor, lest they should disturb the sufferer below. The jailer, too, remembering his own son, afar in Southern Tennessee, wiped a tear from his rough face, and drew nearer to the humble cot where Tom sat watching the panting and seemingly dying boy. There were moments of feverish delirium, when the prison, with its surrounding horrors, faded away, and Isaac was at home, bathing his burning brow with the snow covering the Northern hills, or talking to his mother of all that had transpired since the April morning when, followed by her prayers and tears, he left her for the battle. Then, reason came back again, as clear as ever, and with Tom Carleton's hand pressed between his own he dictated what Tom should say to the mother when he went back to her alone and left her boy behind.

"I shall never go home any more," he said, "and I've built such bright castles about it, too, fancying how nice it would seem to lie on mother's soft, warm bed, and watch the sun shining through the windows, or the grass springing by the door. The snow will melt from the garden before long, and the flowers I used to tend come up again, but I shan't be there to see them. I shall be lying here so quiet and so still that I shall not even hear the cannon's roar, or the loud huzzahs when peace is at last declared, and the cruel war is ended. Oh, if all the dead ones could know, it would be something worth fighting for, but when the troops are marching home, and the bells ring out a welcome, there'll be many a one missing in the ranks, and almost every graveyard, both North and South, will hold a soldier's grave, but you will not forget us, will you?" and the sunken eyes turned pleadingly on Tom. "When the bonfires are kindled at the North, and the glad rejoicings are made, you will think of the poor boys who fought and died that you might enjoy just such a holiday?"

Tom could only answer by pressing the thin hands he held, and Isaac continued:

"Tell mother not to fret too much for me. I guess she did love me best, because I was the youngest, but Eli and John will comfort her old age. Tell them, too, how much I love them, and how proud I was of them that day at Bull Run. They used to plague me sometimes, and call me a girl baby, but I've forgiven that, for I know they did not mean it. I hope they'll both be spared. It would kill mother to lose us all. Tell her how I bless her for the lessons of my childhood, the prayers said at her knee before I knew their meaning, the Sunday School she sent me to, and the Bible stories told in the winter twilight. Tell her I was not afraid to die, only I wanted her so much, but everybody's been good. There are kind folks here in Richmond, and God will bless them for it. Oh, Captain Carleton, I'm a poor ignorant boy, and you a proud, rich man, but you will heed me, won't you, and when I'm gone, you'll take my little Testament and read it every day. Read it first for Isaac's sake, but it won't be long before you'll read it for its precious truths, and you will come to Heaven where we can meet again—promise, won't you?"

There was a moment's silence, during which Tom choked down the tears he could scarcely suppress, so strongly this scene reminded him of another, when he sat by Mary's side, and heard her dying voice urging him to meet her. Four years the Southern sun had shone upon her grave, and he had made no preparation yet, but now he would put it off no longer, and bending over Isaac, he replied:

"I promise; and if you see my darling in the better land, tell her, God helping me, I'll find my way to where she has gone."

The white lips feebly murmured their thanks, and then suddenly asked:

"Do you think mother's got the letter you sent, and knows how sick I am? If so, she's praying for me now, and maybe her prayers will save. I'm not afraid to die, but if I could go home to Rockland first, it would not seem so bad. Pray, mother, pray—pray, pray hard," and too much exhausted to talk longer, the half-delirious boy turned upon the pillow furnished by some kind lady, and fell into a heavy sleep, from which the physician said he would never waken.

Midnight in Richmond, and Tom, counting off the strokes, bent lower to watch for the expected change. There was no color in the parted lips, and about the nose there was a pinched, contracted look, which Tom remembered to have seen in Mary's face, when by her bedside he had sat, just as he sat by Isaac's, but where Mary's hands were cold and dry Isaac's were moist and warm, while the rapid pulses were not as wiry, and irregular as hers had been. There was hope, and falling on his knees, Tom Carleton asked that the life almost gone out might be restored, and promised that if it were he would not forget this lesson as he had forgotten the one learned by Mary's death-bed. He would be a better man, he said, and God, as he sometimes does, took him at his word. Gradually the sharp expression passed away, the hair grew damp with a more healthful moisture, the pulses were slower, the breathing more regular, and when at last the heavy slumber was broken, and Isaac looked up again, Tom knew that he would live.

There was a murmured prayer of thanksgiving, a renewal of his pledge, and then he bent every energy to sustain the life coming so slowly back. Softly the morning broke over the prison walls, and they who had expected to look on Isaac dead, rejoiced to hear that he was better.

"It may be I shall see mother yet," he whispered, faintly, when Tom told him that the dreaded crisis was past; "and if I do, I'll tell her of your kindness."

"Would you like very much to go home to your mother?" Tom asked, and with a quivering lip and chin Isaac answered:

"Yes, oh, yes, if I only could! I was willing to die, but I guess we all cling to life at the last, don't you?"

Tom did not reply to this, but spoke instead of a rumor that all were soon to be discharged and sent back to Washington.

"We'll go together, then," he said, "you and I, for I shall visit Rockland first and see my sister Rose."

The prospect of release was meat and drink for Isaac who rallied so fast that when the joyful news of an exchange *did* come, he was able, with Tom's help, to walk across the floor of what had been his home so long.

Haggard, wasted, weary, and worn were those prisoners as they filed down the stairs and out into the streets, but with each moment which brought them nearer home, their spirits rose, and when at last they stood again on Federal soil and saw the Stars and Stripes waving in the morning breeze, long and deafening were the huzzas which rent the air as one after another gave vent to his great joy at finding himself free once more. Isaac, however, could neither shout, nor laugh, nor speak, and only the large eyes, brimming with tears, told of joy unutterable, but when arrived at Washington, his two stalwart brothers took him in their arms, hugging and crying over him as over one come back to them from the grave, his calmness all gave way, and laying his tired head on Eli's bosom, while John held and caressed his wasted hands, he sobbed out the happiness too great to be expressed in words. To him a full discharge from service was readily accorded, while to Tom a furlough of several weeks was given, and after a few days at Washington both started northward to join the friends waiting so impatiently for their arrival.

CHAPTER XIX.
TOM'S RECEPTION.

The people of Rockland had become somewhat accustomed to the "Rebel lion," as they had playfully called Jimmie Carleton, and the latter could now go quietly through the streets without attracting attentions which at first had been vastly disagreeable to the sensitive young man. Gradually, as he mingled more with the people, they had learned to like him, and were fast forgetting that he had ever joined the ranks of the foe and struck at his mother country. With the rabble who had met him at the depot on his first arrival at Rockland he was vastly popular, for forcing down his pride, he had been very conciliatory toward them, and they still adhered to their olden promise of making him their next police justice, provided he would consent to run.

With his usual impudence, Bill Baker continued to annoy the proud Bostonian with his good-humored familiarities, some of which Jimmie permitted, while others he quietly repulsed, for Bill's constant allusions to the past were exceedingly disagreeable, and as far as possible he avoided his quondam associate, who, without the least suspicion that his manner was disgusting in the extreme, would hail him across the street, addressing him always as "Corp'ral," and if strangers were in hearing, inviting him to "call 'round and see a fellar once in a while for old acquaintance sake."

At the Mather mansion matters remained about the same as when Jimmie first came home. Mrs. Carleton was still there, waiting for her other son, and Rose, as usual, was ever on the alert, seeking ways and means by which the soldiers might be benefited, compelling Jimmie to be interested in all her plans, dragging him from place to place, sending him on errands; and once, when in a great hurry to get a box in readiness for the hospitals at Washington, actually coaxing him into helping *tie* a *comfortable*, which was put up in her back parlor, and which she "must send immediately, for some poor fellow was sure to need it." "Jimmie could learn to tie as well as herself," she said, when he pleaded his ignorance as an excuse for refusing his services. "She didn't know how once, but Widow Simms and Annie had taught her a heap, and Annie would teach him, too. All he had to do was to put the big darning needle through twice, tie a weaver's knot, cut it off, and the thing was done; besides that, 'twas a real pretty quilt, made from Annie's calico dress, which she used to wear last summer and look *so* sweetly in. Annie was tying on one side and Jimmie must tie on the other; he needn't be so lazy. He ought to do something for the war."

By the time Rose had reached the last points in her argument, Jimmie had closed the book he was reading, and concluded that there might be duties required of him a great deal worse than tying a soldier's comfortable with

Annie to oversee! It was strange how much teaching he needed, and how often Annie was called to the rescue. The needle would stick so in the cotton, and he could not remember just how to tie that knot. So Annie, never dreaming that he knew how to tie the knot as well as she, would come to his aid, her hands sometimes touching his, and his black curls occasionally brushing her pale, brown braids as he bent over her to see how she did it so as to know himself next time! There was a world of mischief in Jimmie's saucy eyes as he demurely apologized to Mrs. Graham for the trouble he was giving her, but Annie never once looked up, neither did the color deepen in the least upon her cheek, and when Jimmie, on purpose to draw her out, suggested that "he was more bother than help," she answered that he "had better return to his reading, as she could get on quite as well alone."

After this, Jimmie thought proper to learn a little faster, and soon outstripped his teacher, who rewarded him with no word of approval save a cool "Thank you," when the comfortable was done and taken from the awkward frames. And this was a fair specimen of the nature of the intercourse existing between Jimmie and Annie. Secure now in the belief that she would never be recognized as the "Pequot of New London," Annie regarded Jimmie as any ordinary stranger, in whom she had no particular interest, save that which her kind heart prompted her to feel for all mankind. She could not dislike him, and she always defended him from the aspersions of the widow, who could not quite conquer her repugnance to a Rebel, and who frequently gave vent to her ill will toward Jimmie, whom she thought so proud.

"Stuck-up critter!" she said, "struttin' round as if he was good as anybody, and feelin' above his betters. Of course he felt above her, and Susan, and Annie, she knew he did; and if she's Annie she *vummed* if she'd stay there, and be looked at as Jim looked at her."

Although making due allowance for the widow's prejudice, these remarks were not without their effect upon Annie, who, imperceptibly to herself, began to feel that probably Jimmie did regard her as merely a poor dependent on his sister's bounty, and she unconsciously assumed toward him a cool reserved manner, which led him to fancy that she entertained for him a deep-rooted prejudice on account of his past error. Twenty times a day he said to himself he did not care what she thought of him, and as many times a day he knew he did care much more than was at all conducive to his peace of mind. Where this caring might end he never stopped to consider. He only felt now that he respected the Quaker-like Annie more than he ever respected a woman before, and coveted her good opinion more earnestly than he ever remembered to have coveted anything in his life, unless, indeed, it were his freedom when a prisoner in Bill Baker's power.

In this state of affairs it required all Rose's tact to sustain anything like sociability between her brother and Annie, and the little lady was perfectly delighted when the joyful tidings was received that *Tom* was coming home. Annie would like Tom, for everybody did; besides, Tom had written as if he were *almost* a good man himself, and Annie was sure to be pleased with that; they, at least, would be fast friends; and secure on this point. Rose, with her usual impulsiveness, plunged into the preparations for Tom's reception. Even Annie did not think any reasonable honor too great for him, particularly after Isaac wrote from Washington to his mother, telling her of Tom's generous sacrifice, and how he might have been home long before if he had not chosen to stay and care for a poor, sick boy. How the widow's heart warmed toward the Carletons, taking the whole family into its hitherto rather limited dimensions. Even Jimmie was not excluded, the widow admitting to Mrs. Baker, between whom and herself there had been many a hot discussion touching the so-called Rebel, that when he laughed, "he was uncommon handsome for a Secessioner," and she presumed that "at the bottom he was as good they would average."

But if the widow were thus affected by Tom's kind act, how much more were the mother and sister pleased to know how noble and good he was, while Annie, amid the tears she could not repress, said to Rose,

"You should be proud of such a brother! There are few like him, I am sure!"

How Jimmie envied Tom, as he heard, on all sides, praises for his noble unselfishness, and the resolution to welcome him and Isaac with military honors. Once more in his element, Bill Baker industriously drilled *his* clique, who were to answer no earthly purpose save to swell the throng and prolong the deafening cheers. Bill began to feel related to the Carletons, and regularly each day he called at the Mather mansion to keep Rose posted with regard to the progress of affairs. They were to bring out the new gun, he said, and as it was minus a name, the villagers had concluded to call it the "*Thomas Carleton*," asking "how she thought the '*Square* would like it, and how many times it ought to be fired. The band would serenade Tom in the evening," he said, "and *we* shall have bonfires kindled in the streets," talking as if instead of being merely cannon-tender, he were head manager of the whole, and that all the responsibility was resting on himself. Rose understood him perfectly, and with the utmost good nature listened to his suggestions, and scolded Jimmie for calling him her prime minister and confidant.

From the cupola of the Mather mansion the Stars and Stripes were to be hung out, and on the morning of Tom's expected arrival, Jimmie and Annie climbed the winding stairs and fastened the staff securely to its place. There were tears in Annie's eyes as the graceful folds shook themselves to the breeze, for she remembered the coming of another soldier when this same banner was wrapped around a coffin. Across the valley and beyond the confines of the village she could see where that coffin with its loved inmate was buried, and as the past came rushing over her, she suddenly gave way, and sitting down beneath the flag wept bitterly, while Jimmie, with a vague idea as to what might have caused her tears, stood looking at her, wishing he could comfort her. But what should he say? As yet they had scarcely passed the bounds of the most scrupulous politeness to each other, and for him to attempt to comfort her seemed preposterous, while to leave her without a word, seemed equally unkind. Perhaps it was the beautiful glossy braids of hair which brought him at last to a decision, causing him to lay his hand involuntarily upon the bowed head, while he said:

"I am sorry for you, Mrs. Graham, for I know how much the contrast between my brother's return and that of your husband must affect you, and gladly would I spare you the pain, if I could. I am not certain but the good people of Rockland, in their intended kindness to Tom, are doing you an injury, and surely Lieutenant Graham, having been a resident of this place, should receive their first thought with all pertaining to him."

There was no mistaking the genuine sympathy which thrilled in every tone of Jimmie's voice, and for a moment Annie wept more passionately than before. It was the first time he had ever spoken to her of her husband, and his words touched a responsive chord at once.

"It is not that so much," she answered, at last. "I am glad they are honoring your brother thus; he richly deserves it for his noble adherence to his country in her hour of peril, and for his generous treatment of poor Isaac Simms. I would do much myself to show him my respect; but oh, George, George, I am so desolate without him!" and covering her face with her hands, Annie wept again, more piteously than before.

Here was a point which Jimmie could not touch, and an awkward silence ensued, broken at last by Annie, who, resuming her usual calm demeanor, frankly offered Jimmie her hand, saying:

"I thank you, Mr. Carleton, for your sympathy. It has made me believe you are my friend, and as such I would rather consider you."

"Your friend! Did you ever deem me other than that?" Jimmie replied in some surprise, involuntarily pressing the little hand which only for an instant rested in his, and then was quietly withdrawn just as Rose from the foot of the stairs called out to know "what they were doing up there so long."

It was strange how differently Jimmie felt after this incident, and how fast his spirits rose. The few words said to him by Annie up in his sister's cupola had made him very happy, for he felt that a better understanding existed between himself and Annie, that she did not so thoroughly despise him as he had at first supposed, and that the winning her respect was not a hopeless task.

As early as two the crowd began to gather in the streets, and half an hour later Rose's carriage, with Jimmie in it, was on its way to the depot. Mrs. Carleton did not care to go, and so Rose, too, remained at home, and mounting to the cupola, watched for the first wreath of smoke which should herald the approach of the train.

"I see it,—he's coming!" she screamed, as a feathery mist was discernible over the distant plains, and in a few moments more the cars swept round the curve, while a booming gun told that Bill Baker was faithful to his duty.

There was a swaying to and fro of the throng at the depot, a pushing each other aside, a trilling of fife, a beating of drums, and then a deafening shout went up as Tom Carleton and John Simms appeared upon the platform, carefully supporting the tottering steps of the weak, excited boy, who stood between them. At sight of Isaac, there was a momentary hush, and then, with a shriek such as a tigress might give when it saw its young in danger, the Widow Simms rushed frantically forward, and catching the light form of her child in her arms, tried to bear him through the crowd, but her strength was insufficient, and she would have fallen had not Jimmie relieved her of her burden, which he sustained with one hand, while the other was extended to welcome the stranger who came near.

Half bewildered, Tom looked around upon the multitude, asking in a whisper what it meant. He could not think they had come to welcome him, and when assured by Jimmie that such was the fact, his lip quivered for an instant, and his tongue refused its office. Then, in a few well-chosen words, he thanked the people for the undeserved surprise, so far as he was himself concerned. *Isaac* was more worthy of such welcome, he said, and more than half of it was meant, he knew, for their townsman, who had shown himself equally brave in camp, in battle, and in prison, while, had they known that Lieutenant Simms, too, was coming, he was sure they would not have thought of him a stranger to them all.

The brief speech ended, and Rose, listening at home, clapped her hands in ecstasy as she heard the terrific cheers and caught the name of "Carleton" mingled with "Isaac Simms."

"Poor boy!" she said, "I wonder how he'll get home? I wish I had told Jimmie to drive that way, and take him in the carriage."

She need have given herself no uneasiness, for what she had forgotten was remembered by Jimmie, who, after a hurried consultation with Tom, insisted that both Isaac and his mother should take seats in the carriage, while he and Tom mingled with the crowd.

"And your other son, there's room for him," he said, looking round in quest of John, who, at the last moment, had obtained permission to visit his bride, and so came on with Isaac.

At a glance his eye had singled out *Susan*, and the young couple were now standing apart from the rest, exchanging mutual caresses, and words of love, the tall lieutenant kissing fondly the blushing girl who could not realize that she stood in the presence of her husband. After a little it was decided that Tom and Jimmie, Mrs. Simms and Isaac, should occupy the carriage, while John and Susan walked, and so from her lofty stand-point, Rose watched the long procession winding down the streets, amid the strains of music and the cannon's bellowing roar. It was very exciting to Isaac, and by the time the cottage was reached he was glad to be lifted out by Jimmie, who bore the tired boy tenderly into the house and laid him down on the soft, warm bed he had dreamed about so many nights in the dark, filthy prison corner. How faint and weak he was, and how glad to be home again! Winding his arms around his mother's neck, he sobbed out his great joy, saying amid his tears, "God was so kind to let me come back to you."

It was a very happy group the villagers left behind in that humble cottage, and neither John nor Susan thought it out of place when the mother called on them to kneel with her and thank the Giver of all good for his great mercy in granting them this blessing.

Meantime the procession passed on until it reached the Mather mansion, where, with three cheers for Captain Carleton, the crowd dispersed, leaving Tom at liberty to join the mother and sister waiting so impatiently for him, one on the steps, and the other in the parlor just where she had welcomed Jimmie.

"If *Will* were only here, it would be the happiest day I ever knew," Rose said, as, seating herself on Tom's knee with her chubby arm around his neck, she asked him numerous questions concerning her absent husband. Then, as she saw in him signs of weariness she said, "You are tired, I know. Suppose you go to your room till dinner-time. It's the one right at the head of the stairs," she continued, and glad of an opportunity to rest, Tom went to the room where Annie Graham just then chanced to be. She had discovered that the servant had neglected to supply the rack with towels, and so she had brought them herself, lingering a moment after they were arranged, to see if everything were in order. She did not hear Tom's step, until he opened the door upon her, and uttered an exclamation of surprise and apology. He had no idea who the little black-robed figure was, for though he knew the wife of George Graham was an inmate of his sister's family, he had her in his mind as a very different person from this one before him. Mrs. Graham was young, he supposed, and possibly good-looking, but she did not bear the stamp of refinement and elegance which this graceful creature did, and fancying he had made a mistake and stumbled into the apartment of some city visitor, he was about to withdraw, when Annie came toward him, saying:

"Excuse me, sir, I came in to see that all was right in your room. Mr. Carleton, I presume?"

This last Annie spoke doubtingly, for in the tall, handsome stranger before her there was scarcely a vestige of the "greyish haired, oldish, fatherly-looking man" she had in fancy known as Captain Carleton, and but for the eyes, so much like Mrs. Mather's, and the unmistakable Carleton curve about the mouth, she would never have dreamed that it was *Tom* to whom she was speaking. As it was, she waited for him to confirm her suspicions, which he did by bowing in the affirmative to her interrogation, "Mr. Carleton, I presume?"

Then holding the door for her to pass out, he stood watching her till she disappeared at the extreme end of the hall, wondering who she was, and why a mere visitor should take so much interest in his room. Once he thought of Annie Graham; but this could not be a widow, though the deep mourning dress told of recent bereavement. Still Annie Graham was a different personage, he knew; and thus perplexed, Tom, instead of resting, commenced his toilet for dinner, determining, as soon as it was completed, to go down and have the mystery unravelled.

Restless and impatient to know just what his brother thought of his late treachery to the Federal Flag, Jimmie paced the parlors below until he could wait no longer and knowing by the sounds which came from the chamber above, that Tom was not trying to sleep, he finally ran up the stairs, and knocking at the chamber door, was soon closeted with Tom. It was an awkward business to speak of the past, but Jimmie plunged into it at once, stating some reasons which had led him to abjure his own government, expressing his contrition for having done so, and ending by saying he hoped Tom, if possible, would forget that he ever had a rebel brother.

It had taken Tom a long time to recover from the shock of meeting his brother in the Virginia woods, and knowing he was a traitor to his country, but the same generous feeling which led him to refrain from any allusion to that meeting in the messages sent to his mother and sister from his Richmond prison, now prompted him to treat with kind forbearance the brother whom he had loved and grieved over since the days of his mischievous boyhood.

"I should have found it very hard to forgive you if you had staid in the Southern army," he said, "but as it is we will never mention the subject again."

Jimmie knew, by the warm pressure of Tom's hand, that he was forgiven, and with a burden lifted from his mind he was about leaving the room, when Tom, with a preliminary cough, said:

"By the way, Jimmie, who has Rose got here,—what visitor, I mean?" and Tom tried to look vastly indifferent as he buttoned his vest and hung across it the chain made from Mary's hair.

But the ruse did not succeed. Jimmie knew he had seen Annie, and with a sudden uprising of something undefined he answered in apparent surprise:

"Visitor! what visitor! He must have come to-day, then. Where did you see him?"

"I saw *her* in here," Tom replied, and Jimmie laughingly rejoined:

"A pretty place for a *her* in *your* quarters! Pray, what was she like?"

"Some like Mary, as she used to be when I first knew her,—a little body dressed in black."

"With large, handsome, blue eyes?" interrupted Jimmie, while Tom, without suspecting that his brother's object was to ascertain how closely he had observed the figure in black, replied:

"Yes, very handsome, dreamy eyes."

"And pale, brown *curls?*" was the teasing Jimmie's next query, to which Tom quickly responded:

"Curls, no. The hair was braided in wide plats and twisted around the head, falling low in the neck."

"Not a very white neck, was it?" Jimmie continued, with imperturbable gravity.

"Indeed, it was," Tom said, industriously scraping his thumb nail with his penknife. "White as snow, or looked so from the contrast with her dress. Who is she?"

"One question more,—had she big feet or little, slippers or boots?" and this time Jimmie's voice betrayed him.

Tom knew he was being teased, and bursting into a laugh, he answered:

"I confess to having observed her closely, but not enough so to tell the size of her slipper. Come now, who is she? Some lady you spirited away from Secessiondom? Tell me,—you know you've nothing to fear from steady old Tom."

For an instant the eyes of the two brothers met, with a curious expression in each. Both were conscious of something they were trying to conceal, while a feeling akin to a pang shot through Jimmie's heart as he thought how much more worthy of Annie Graham's respect was steady old Tom than a rollicking young scapegrace like himself.

"From your rather minute description I think you must have stumbled upon the *Widow Graham*," he said. "Rose has taken her up, you know, and as a word of brotherly advice, let me say that if you wish to raise Rose to the seventh heaven you have only to praise her protégée. We, that is the widow and I, do not get on very well, for she is a staunch patriot, and until this morning I verily believe she looked on me as a kind of monster. She's a perfect little Puritan, too, and if she stays here long, will make a straight-laced Methodist of Rose, under the garb of an Episcopalian, of course, as she is the strictest kind of a church woman."

"I shall not esteem her less for that," Tom said, and in rather a perturbed state of mind, as far as the Widow Graham was concerned, he went with Jimmie to the parlor, half hoping his brother had mischievously misled him, and that the stranger would prove after all to be some visitor from Boston.

But the first object he saw on entering the parlor was the dainty figure in black, standing by the window, and on the third finger of the hand raised to adjust the heavy curtain glittered the wedding ring. Tom knew now that Jimmie had not deceived him, and with a feeling of disappointment he addressed *Mrs. Graham*, when introduced by Jimmie, making some playful allusion to their having met before, but saying nothing to her then of George, for remembering his own feelings when Mary died, he knew that Annie would not thank him, a stranger, to bring up sad memories of the past by talking of her husband. Still, in his manner toward her there was something which told how he pitied and sympathized with her, and Annie, grateful always for the smallest kindness threw off her air of quiet reserve and talked with him freely, asking many questions concerning Isaac Simms and the condition of the Richmond prisoners generally.

"She was going round after dinner to call on Isaac," she incidentally said, whereupon Tom rejoined that wishing to know how Isaac bore the journey and the excitement, he had intended going there himself, and would, with her permission, time his visit to suit her convenience, and so accompany her.

Instantly Jimmie's black eyes flashed upon Annie a look of inquiry, which brought the bright color to her cheeks, for she knew he was thinking of the night when she had refused his escort, and she felt her present position a rather embarrassing one. Still the circumstances were entirely different. There was a reason why Tom should call on Widow Simms, while with Jimmie there was none, and bowing to Captain Carleton, she replied that "she presumed

Mrs. Simms would be glad of an opportunity to thank him for his kindness to Isaac, and that, though not in the least afraid to go alone, she had no objection to showing him the way."

"What! going off the first night, and they are coming to serenade you, too? You must not go, Tom. Shall he, mother?" cried Rose, who at first had been too busy with her duties as hostess, clearly to comprehend what Tom was saying to Annie.

"It will look as if you do not appreciate the people's attention," Mrs. Carleton replied, while Jimmie vehemently protested against the impropriety of the act, and so Tom was compelled to yield, thinking the while that a walk to the Widow Simms' might possibly afford him quite as much satisfaction as staying at home for a serenade.

"I always surrender to the majority," he said, playfully, while Jimmie's spirits rose perceptibly, and Annie had never before seen him so witty or gay since he came home from Washington as he was during the dinner.

It was joy at his brother's return, she thought, never suspecting that Tom's decision had anything to do with it, and Jimmie hardly knew himself that it had. He only felt relieved that Tom was not to receive a favor which had once been denied to himself, and glad also that Annie was to spend the evening with them. But in this he was mistaken. There was no necessity for Annie's deferring her visit. The serenade was not for her, and with that nice sense of propriety which prompted her to shrink from anything like intrusion, she felt that on this first night of their reunion, the Carleton family would rather be alone. This rule would apply also to Mrs. Simms, but Annie knew she was always welcome to the widow, and wishing to see the boy who had led her husband from the battle-field, she went to her room, and throwing on her cloak and hood, stole quietly down stairs just as Jimmie was crossing the hall. He guessed where she was going, and coming quickly to her side, said,

"I supposed you had given up that call, but if you persist in going, it must not be alone, this night of all others, when the streets are likely to be full of men and boys. You accepted my brother's escort, you cannot, of course, refuse mine," and seizing his hat from the hall stand he led her out upon the steps and placed her arm in his with an air of so much authority that Annie had no word to offer in remonstrance.

It was not a very comfortable walk to either party, or a very sociable one either, but ere it was ended Annie had reason to be glad that she was not alone, for as Jimmie had predicted, the streets were full of men and boys, following the band up to the Mather Mansion, and as they met group after group of the noisy throng, Annie timidly drew closer to her companion, who pressed more tightly the arm trembling in his own.

"I am glad you came with me," she said, when at last the friendly gleam of the widow's candle appeared in view, "but if you please I think you had better not go in to-night. You are so much a stranger to the family, and Mrs. Simms' boys have but just returned. John will see me safely home, and I'll excuse you now. You must feel anxious to rejoin your brother."

But Jimmie was not to be disposed of so easily. He had no intention of entering the house, but he should wait outside, he said, until Annie's visit was over. Annie had no alternative save submission, and parting from Jimmie at the gate, she hurried up the walk and was soon bending over the couch of the sick boy, whose eyes beamed the welcome his pale lips could scarcely speak. How many questions she had to ask him, and how much he had to tell her of that day when her husband received his fatal wound. Altogether it was a sad interview, and Annie's eyes were nearly blistered with the hot tears she shed while listening to Isaac's touching account of George ere the woods were gained, and Tom Carleton generously gave up his seat to the bleeding man, thereby becoming himself a prisoner. Much, too, was said in praise of Tom, and Annie felt that she could not do too much for one who had shown himself so generous and brave. Talking of *Tom* reminded her of Jimmie stalking up and down the icy walks, waiting patiently for her, and when at last the music of Tom's serenade had ceased she arose to go, wishing to get away ere the band came there, as she knew they were intending to do. As John arose to accompany her, she had to say that "Jimmie Carleton was waiting for her by the gate." Instantly the sharp eyes of the widow shot at her a curious glance, which brought the hot blood to her cheek, while John and Susan exchanged a smile, the meaning of which she could not fail to understand. Poor Annie! How her heart throbbed with pain as she guessed of what they were thinking! Could they for a moment believe her so heartless and cold? The mere idea made her dizzy and faint, and scarcely articulating her good-night, she hastened out into the cool night air, feeling half tempted to refuse outright the arm offered for her support. If she only dared tell him to leave her there alone,—leave her to flee away through the dark, lonely streets to the still more lonely yard, where on George's grave she could lay herself down and die. But not thus easily could life's heavy burden be shaken off, she could not lay it down at will,—and conquering the emotions which, each time she thought of John Simms' significant smile, threatened to burst out into a fierce storm of passionate sobs, she apologized for having kept Jimmie waiting so long, and taking his arm left the cottage gate just as the throng of serenaders turned into that street. Jimmie knew she had been crying, and conjecturing that she had been talking of her husband, he, too, began to speak of George, asking her many questions about him, and repeating many things he had heard in his praise from the Rockland citizens. It seemed strange that this should comfort her, but it did. The hard, bitter feeling insensibly passed away while listening to Jimmie, and by the time the Mather Mansion was reached the tears were dried on Annie's cheeks, and outwardly she was cheerful and patient as ever.

After that night Rose had no cause for complaint that Jimmie was rude to Annie, or Annie cool toward him, for though Annie talked to him but little, she did not forget the sympathy so delicately manifested for her, and treated him with as much respect as she awarded Tom, who grew each day more and more interested in the black-robed figure, reminding him so much of his lost Mary. Jimmie *knew* he did, and watched narrowly for the time when she would know it, too; but such time did not come, for Annie had no suspicion that either of the brothers regarded her with the shadow of a feeling save that of ordinary friendship. As much of her time as possible was spent with the Widow Simms, and a great part of Isaac's visible improvement was owing to her gentle care and the sunshine of her presence. John's furlough had expired, and now that he was gone, the disconsolate Susan turned to Annie for comfort, while Isaac watched daily for the sound of the little feet coming up the walk, and bringing with them so much happiness to the lonely cottage.

"I wish you'd stay home more; we miss you so much, and it's so dismal without you. Mother nods over her knitting, Tom just walks the floor, or reads some stiff Presbyterian book, while Jimmie thrums the piano and teases my kitten awfully," Rose said to Annie one night when the latter came in from a tour of calls, the last of which had been on Mrs. Baker, now a much happier, better woman, than when we first made her acquaintance. "It's so different when you are here," Rose continued, as Annie came and sat down by her side. "Tom is a heap more entertaining, while Jimmie is not half so mischievous and provoking."

"I did not suppose my absence could affect your happiness, or I would certainly have staid with you more," Annie replied; and Rose continued:

"Well, it just does, and now that both Tom and Jimmie are going so soon, I shall need you to oversee the things I must get ready for them."

"Captain Carleton and Jimmie going away soon!" Annie repeated, in some surprise. "Where are they going? The Captain's furlough has not yet expired."

"I know it," Rose continued, "but as he is perfectly well, he thinks it right to go back, and has fixed on one week from to-day."

"Yes, but Jimmie. You spoke of his leaving, too," Annie said, and Rose rejoined:

"Jimmie is going with Tom to join the Federal Army on the Potomac, and, as he says, retrieve, if possible, the character he lost by turning traitor once."

"Oh, I am *so* glad! and I like him so much for that!" Annie exclaimed, her white face lighting up with a sudden animation, which made it seem very beautiful to the young man just entering the door.

"I would brave the cannon's mouth for another look like that," was Jimmie's mental comment as he stepped into the room, and advanced to the ladies' side. "So you are glad I am going?" he said, half playfully, to Annie, who answered frankly:

"Yes, very glad."

"And won't you miss me a bit? Folks like to be missed, you know, if they are ever so bad. It makes one think better of himself, and consequently do better if he knows that his absence will cause a feeling of regret, however slight, to the friends left behind," Jimmie remarked, while in his eyes there was a peculiar expression which Annie failed to see, as he stood looking down upon her.

She would miss Jimmie, she knew, for she had become accustomed to his merry whistle, his ringing laugh, his teasing jokes at Rose's expense, and his going would leave them very lonely, and so she frankly admitted, adding that "it was not because she wished to be rid of him that she was glad; it pleased her to see him in the path of duty, even though that path led to danger and possible death."

"Oh, don't, Annie, don't talk of death to Jimmie!" Rose cried, with a shudder. "You can't begin to guess how it makes me feel, or how terrible it would seem if either he or Tom should die!"

"Can't I?" Annie asked, with such a depth of mournful pathos, that Rose's tears flowed at once.

Of course Annie knew how it felt, and every fibre of her heart was bleeding now, as she remembered one who left her as full of life and hope as either Tom or Jimmie, but who came back no more, save as the dead come back, shrouded and coffined for the grave. But Annie would not give way to her own feelings then. She would comfort Rose, and encourage the young man, who, she felt, shrank from the perils spread out before him. So she told how few there were, comparatively, who died on the battle-field, while the chances for life in the hospitals were greater now that better care and skill had been procured.

"Annie,—excuse me, Mrs. Graham?" and Jimmie spoke vehemently, while his eyes kindled with a strange gleam. "Why don't you go as nurse? You might be the means of untold good to the poor fellows who need such care as you could give."

"I have thought of it," said Annie, while Rose exclaimed:

"*You* turn hospital nurse,—ridiculous! You never shall, so long as I can prevent it. Shall she, Tom?" And she appealed to the latter, who had just come in. "Shall Annie go into those horrid hospitals?"

"I am not Mrs. Graham's keeper," Tom replied, "but I should be sorry to see her acting in the capacity of hospital nurse, even though I know that some of our noblest, best women are engaged in that work."

"Yes, old chap," and Jimmie laughed a merry laugh. "It's mighty easy talking that way now, but suppose *you* Captain Carleton, are some day among the terribly wounded, thigh shot through, arm splintered above the elbow, jaw-bone broken, and all that, wouldn't the pain be easier to bear, if the nurse should happen to be Mrs. Graham, or somebody just like her?"

"Undoubtedly it would," Tom answered. "Still I should be sorry to have her there amid the sickening horrors."

"Please stop, I can't bear to hear about it!" Rose exclaimed. "I know it would be nice to be a Florence Nightingale, and Annie would make a splendid one, but I'll never let her go, unless you, or Jimmie, or Will are wounded, and then we'll come together, won't we, Annie?"

There was no response from Annie, until Jimmie said:

"Say, Mrs. Graham, if I am ever wounded, and you hear I am suffering in some dismal hole, will you come and care for me?"

He did not join Will's or Tom's name with his own. It was "Jimmie Carleton" whom Annie was to nurse. But it did not matter. Lifting up her head so that her soft, blue eyes looked into his, Annie answered, unhesitatingly:

"Providence permitting, I will, and I would do the same for any brave fellow who follows, as my husband did, where duty to his country leads."

"So you see you will fare no better than I, after all," Tom laughingly rejoined, while Jimmie thought within himself:

"Why need she always bring that husband in? It's bad enough to know she's had one, without eternally hearing about him."

Foolish Jimmie. It was folly for him to lie awake so long as he did that night, or to dream, when at last he slept, of hospital walls expanding into a palace as an angel form with hair and eyes like Annie's bent over his feverish pillow, while soft, white hands dressed some gaping wound where the enemy's bullet had been. Sheer folly, too, was it for "dignified old Tom," to watch from his window the young moon, until it set in the western sky, thinking of *Mary*, as he tried to make himself believe, wondering why it was that Annie reminded him so much of her, and why he should be so deeply interested in one who, until a few weeks past, had been to him a stranger.

To Annie, Captain Carleton and Jimmie were nothing more than friends, and if, during the week preceding their departure, she was quite as busy as Rose, and apparently as much interested in the various preparations for their comfort, it was only because they were soldiers, and not, as Widow Simms once suggested to Susan, "because they were Carletons, and handsome and rich, and,—and,—well, there's no tellin' what will happen, when a widder's young and handsome, but this I know, *I've* never married, and my man's been dead this nineteen years! Nobody need tell me she'd be so busy for anybody but them Carletons. If 'twas the Cap'n, I wouldn't mind, but that *sassy*-faced *Jeems*. Ugh!" and in her ire at Annie's supposed preference for "sassy-faced Jeems," the widow spilled more than half of the spiced chocolate she was carrying to Isaac.

Never was the widow more mistaken. Annie Graham would have done for Eli, John, and Isaac Simms, or possibly William Baker, the same offices she was doing for "the Carletons," and her voice would have been just as sweet and hopeful when she bade them farewell, as it was that bright spring morning, when, in the parlor of the Mather mansion, Tom and Jimmie were waiting to say good-bye.

At the very last moment Bill Baker had announced his intention of going too.

"Thirteen dollars a month and dog's fare was better than layin' round hum," he said; "and livin' on the old gal, who was gittin' most too straight and blue for his notions. Besides that, he felt kinder 'tached to the Corp'ral, and wanted to be where he could see him and wait on him like any other nigger."

Jimmie would gladly have dispensed with such a singular attaché, but Bill could not be shaken off, and as he did in various ways evince a strong regard for his former captive, Jimmie was forced to submit to what he termed "his thorn in the flesh," giving from his own purse money for Billy's outfit, and furnishing the mother with means to repair her dwelling and make it far more comfortable than at present. This he was sure pleased Annie, and no sacrifice was too costly if it won her regard. She had prayed for him, he knew, for Rose had told him so, and prayers like hers, though they did not avail to save her George's life, would surely shield him from danger. *He* should come back again when the war was over,—come back to find an *older* grave by Rockland's churchyard gate, while the wife, who daily watered that grave with tears, would be as young, as beautiful, and far more girlish-looking than now, when, in her widow's weeds, she offered him her hand at parting, bidding God speed to him and the noble Tom, who stood beside him.

There were tears, and kisses, and blessings from Rose and her mother, a few low-spoken words of sympathy and good will from Annie, and then the two young men were gone.

Half an hour later, and the eastern train thundered through the town, bearing away to the fields of bloody carnage, three more young, vigorous lives, and leaving desolate two homes, one the lonely cottage, where Bill's mother wept alone, the other the Mather mansion, where Mrs. Carleton and Rose sobbed bitterly, while Annie strove in various ways to comfort them.

CHAPTER XX.
AT THE MATHER MANSION.

It was very lonely at the Mather mansion after the departure of the soldiers, and it required all Annie's tact to keep Rose from sinking entirely under the sense of desolation which crept over her as she began more and more to realize what the war meant, and to tremble for the safety of her husband and her brothers. They were still in Washington, but they might be ordered to advance at any moment; and, in a tremor of distress, Rose waited and watched for every mail which could bring her tidings of them. Next to her husband's letters, Jimmie's did her the most good, for Jimmie had in his nature a world of hopefulness and humor; and his letters were full of fun, and quaint description of the life he was leading. And still of the three young men,—Will Mather, Tom Carleton, and Jimmie,—the latter suffered the most acutely, for in addition to his dislike of military life he was compelled to endure the jokes and jeers which the coarser and more unfeeling of his comrades heaped upon him when, from Bill Baker, they heard that his first experience in arms-bearing had been learned in the army of the enemy. To one of Bill's instincts it seemed a great thing that he had captured and brought to Washington so illustrious a prisoner as the "Corp'ral," as he persisted in calling him, and the story was repeated with such wonderful additions, that Jimmie, when once by accident he was a listener to the tale failed utterly to recognize himself in the "chap who had run so many miles, *from*, and then fought so many hours *with*, the redoubtable Bill," who, while annoying his quondam captive so terribly, still, under all circumstances, evinced for him an attachment as singular as it was sincere. Everything which he could do for Jimmie he did, becoming literally his servant and drudge, and thus saving him from many a hardship which, as a private, he would otherwise have encountered. It was a fancy of Jimmie's that by serving as a private in the army against which his hand had once been lifted, he should in some way expiate his sin, and, perhaps, be surer of winning favor from Annie Graham, whose blue eyes were constantly before him just as they had looked when, in her dress of black, she stood in the spring sunshine, bidding him good-bye. Soon after his arrival in Washington, he had been offered a second lieutenancy in Captain Carleton's company, but he steadily declined the office, giving no explanation to any one except his brother and his sister Rose, to whom he wrote:

"Perhaps I was foolish to decline the offer, and for a moment I was horribly tempted to accept it, especially when, by doing so, I could to some degree escape my 'thorn in the flesh,' who, notwithstanding that he does me many a kindness, annoys me excessively. But I could not feel that I deserved that post. It ought to belong to some one who had never spurned the Old Flag, and so I stood firm, and suggested as a substitute that other Simms chap from Rockland, *Hophni*, or *Phineas*, or *Eli*,—hanged if I know what his name is. Any way, he is that crabbed widow's son, that used to pucker her mouth so when she saw '*that young reb* of a Carleton,' and snatch away her gown for fear it should hit me. I reckon he'll get the office, with its twelve hundred a year, which he can use for his mother's support. One of her sons, you know, is married, and as good as lost to her; while that boy Isaac is not long for this world. Prison life at Richmond did the business for him, or I'm mistaken, so let Eli be lieutenant, and James Carleton only a private. Do you think I did right, and will that paragon of yours, Mistress Graham, think so, too?"

This was what Jimmie wrote to Rose after he had been gone for three or four weeks, and what Rose, with her usual impetuous thoughtlessness, read to her mother and Annie, who were both in her room when the letter came. Annie had made an attempt to leave, but Rose had insisted that there could be no secret in Jimmie's letter. If there was, she would skip it, she said, and she read on, stumbling dreadfully, and mispronouncing words, for Jimmie's handwriting was never very plain: and this letter, written with a soft lead pencil, with a bit of slate-stone for a table, was his very worst. She made out, however, that he had declined the office of second lieutenant because he thought he did not deserve it; that he had named Eli Simms as a fitter person for it than himself, and that he had called the widow a "crab-apple," or something like it. All this was *very* clear; and, after exclaiming against Jimmie's morbid sense of justice in one breath, and pronouncing him "perfectly splendid" in another, she kept on till she reached the "paragon," which she rendered "Pequot," making the sentence read, "Will that Pequot of yours, Mistress Graham, think I did right?"

"What did he call me?" Annie exclaimed, her face turning very white, as she leaned toward Rose, who, startled at her vehemence, tried again to make out the word, which was strangely distorted, from the fact that just as Jimmie was writing it, his shadow, Bill, had struck him familiarly upon the shoulder, saying, with a laugh,

"Writin' to your gal, I s'pose? Give her Bill Baker's regrets."

"It looks like Pequot, and some like Patagonian," Rose said, deciding at last that it was *paragon*, and adding by way of an explanation to herself of Annie's evident surprise, "you did not like the idea of his calling you a Pequot, did you Annie? It wouldn't have meant anything if he had, and it was natural that I should make the blunder, for that's the name he gave the young girl at the Pequot House,—the one he liked, and to whom he passed himself off as Dick Lee. You remember I told you about her."

"Yes, I remember," and Annie's voice was a little husky—"the little girl who was not happy with her aunt, and so listened the more willingly to the boy's kind winning words."

Annie did not know why she said that, unless it were wrung from her by some sudden and bitter memory of what had been a bright sun-spot in her cheerless childhood. When the Pequot girl was mentioned in her presence once before, she had gathered that it was mostly Mrs. Carleton's pride which had taken the boy away from any more rambles on the beach or moonlight sails upon the bay, and perhaps it was a desire to defend and excuse the girl which prompted her to advance a reason why Dick Lee's attentions had been so acceptable. She would have given much to recall her words, which made Mrs. Carleton dart a quick, curious glance at her, while Rose exclaimed: "How do you know she was not happy with her aunt? Did Jimmie ever tell you about her?"

"Never," Annie replied, feeling glad that a servant appeared just at that moment, telling Rose a little girl was in the kitchen asking to see her.

It was a daughter of one of the soldiers whose mother was sick and had sent to Mrs. Mather for some little delicacy. Such calls were frequent at the Mather house, for the soldiers did not receive their pay regularly, and there was much destitution among their families, who, but for Rose's liberality, would have suffered far more than they did. As freely as water, her money was used to relieve their wants, and now, forgetting Jimmie and his Pequot, she entered at once into the little girl's story, and when told that the sick woman had expressed a wish to see her she said, "I'll go now; there's Jake just come in. I'll have him harness the horses and take you home. It must be a mile or more to your house."

Rose usually acted upon her impulses, and was soon in her carriage, with a huge basket at her feet and the little girl opposite, enjoying her ride so much, and enjoying it the more for the unmistakable signs of envy and wonder which she detected in the faces of her companions as she neared her humble home in the hollow. Rose had asked both her mother and Annie to accompany her, but they had declined, and for a time after Rose's departure they sat together in perfect silence, while a curious train of thought was passing through the minds of each. Annie's agitation when Rose read "Pequot" for "paragon" had surprised Mrs. Carleton, while what she had said of the girl and her aunt had awakened a feeling of disquiet and suspicion. Mrs. Carleton was proud of her own and her husband's family,—proud of her wealth, and proud of her position. Not offensively so, but in that quiet, assured kind of way so natural to the highly bred Bostonian. It was this pride which had prompted her to resort to so extreme measures with the boy Jimmie, when she found how much he was interested in the little Pequot, and when, during Jimmie's brief stay in Rockland, she, with a mother's quick intuition, detected in him signs of interest in Annie Graham, her pride again took fright, and she was half glad to have him go from the possible temptation. Something in the nobler part of the woman's nature told her how wrong the feeling was, while each day some new development of Annie's gentle Christian character, made the desolate young creature dearer to her. That she was superior to most people in her rank of life Mrs. Carleton knew, and she had more than once wondered how one like her had ever become the wife of a mechanic. She was not thinking of this, however, on the afternoon when she was alone with Annie, while Rose was away on her errand of mercy. She was thinking rather of the suspicion which had just found a lodgment in her mind, and was devising some means of testing its reality. To this end she at last made some casual remark about Rockland and its people, asking if Annie had always lived there.

"Only since I was married," was the reply. And Mrs. Carleton continued,

"You seem more like Eastern people than like a New Yorker. Were you born in New England?"

"Yes,—in Connecticut," Annie said. And then Mrs. Carleton made a great blunder by asking next,

"Were you born in or near New London? I have been there several times, and may know your family."

At mention of New London Annie's eyes flashed upon Mrs. Carleton with a startled look, as if she felt that there was a deeper meaning in the questioning to which she was being subjected than appeared on the surface, and her voice trembled a little as she replied,

"I was born in Hartford, and lived there till I was eight years old, when my parents both died of cholera in one day, and I went to live with my aunt in New Haven."

"Yes," Mrs. Carleton answered slowly.

Thus far there was quite as much to prove as there was to disprove the correctness of her surmise, and thinking to herself,

"I may as well go further now I have commenced with being rude," she continued, "Pardon me, Mrs. Graham, if I seem inquisitive, but I cannot help feeling interested in one to whom Rose is so greatly attached, and I do not remember that I ever heard any of your history before your husband went to war. I do not even know your maiden name."

Annie's heart beat almost audibly, and her cheeks were very red, as she replied,

"My father was Dr. Howard, and I was Annie Louise Howard. Excuse me, Mrs. Carleton, if I cannot talk much of my girl-life after my parents died. It was not a happy one. I was wholly dependent upon my aunt, who, while giving me every advantage in the way of education, kept before me so constantly the fact that I was an object of charity that it embittered every moment of my life, and when George offered me his love I accepted it gladly, finding in him the only real friend I had known since the day I was an orphan."

Annie was crying now, and excusing herself she left the parlor and repaired to her own room, where her excitement spent itself in tears and sobs as she recalled all the dreadful years when she was subject to the caprices of the most capricious of women, who had attempted to force her into a marriage with a millionnaire of sixty, and had driven her to accept the love which George Graham had offered her. George had *not* been her equal in an intellectual point of view, and none knew this fact better than Annie herself. But he was the kindest, tenderest of husbands, and she had loved him devotedly for the manly virtues which made him the noble, unselfish man he was. Capt. Carleton and Jimmie both could sympathize with her tastes and inclinations far better than George had done; but never once during her brief married life had she allowed herself to wonder what her lot might have been had it been cast with people like the Carletons. And since her husband's death anything which looked away from that grave by the churchyard gate seemed so terrible to her that now, as she recalled Mrs. Carleton's questionings, and guessed what had prompted them, every nerve quivered with pain, which could only be soothed by a visit to George's grave. There, on the turf which covered him, she had wept out many a grief, and she started for it now, the villagers watching her as she passed their doors, and curiously speculating, as people will, upon the time to come when the long black dress and graceful, girlish form would not be so often seen among the Rockland dead.

Already the gossips of the town were coupling her name with the Carletons, the majority giving her to Tom, the elder, and more worthy of the two. A whisper of this gossip had been borne to Mrs. Carleton, who, while pretending to ignore it, had felt troubled as she recalled all the incidents of Jimmie's visit at home. Then, when the suspicion came to her that the woman whom Rose had taken into her household was possibly identical with the girl of New London, whose name she could not remember, she felt for a moment greatly disturbed. There was a fierce struggle with her pride, a close reasoning with herself, and then her better nature triumphed, and her heart went out very kindly toward poor Annie, at that moment standing by her husband's grave, and wondering why her thoughts would keep straying away to the wayward young man who had been a traitor to his country, but was trying to atone by voluntarily bearing the hardships of a private's life when a better was offered him. He had asked if she would think he did right, and the question had shown that he cared for her good opinion. Yes, she did think he was right, and she resolved to send him a message to that effect when Rose wrote to him next. There was no wrong to the dead in the thought, and her tears dropped just as fast upon the marble as she stooped to kiss the name cut upon it and then left the silent graveyard.

Meantime Rose had visited her sick woman in the Hollow,—had fed the hungry children, and dropped upon the floor the six weeks baby which she tried to hold, then, gathering her shawl about her and holding up her skirts, just as she always did when in the homes of the poor, she re-entered her carriage and bade Jake drive her next to Widow Simms'.

Everything there was neat and clean as soap and sand and the widow's two hands could make it, while Susan made a very pretty picture, in her dark stuff gown with the scarlet velvet ribbon in her black hair. There was a saucer of English violets on the round deal table, and their sweet perfume filled the room into which Rose came dancing, her eyes shining like stars, and her cheeks so brilliant a color that the widow began directly to wonder "if there wasn't some paint there."

The widow was not in her best mood, for she was very tired, having done a heavy washing in the morning before Rose Mather had thought of opening her bright eyes; then, after the coarser, larger pieces were dried and ironed, she had tried to spin, a work to which she clung as tenaciously as if on every stream in New England there were not a cotton or woolen factory capable of doing the work so much easier and better than herself. The widow was fond of spinning, and she had turned the wheel with a right good will, until Isaac had complained that the continuous humming hurt his head, and made him think of the wind as it howled so dismally around the dreary prison in Richmond. Libby, they called it now, and Isaac always shuddered when he heard the name and thought of what he suffered there.

Isaac was very weak and pale, and his face looked like that of some young girl as he lay among his pillows, in the pretty dressing-gown which Rose had bought and Annie had made for him. He was sleeping when Rose came in, and the widow's "Hsh-sh," came warningly as a greeting, but came too late, for Rose's blithesome voice had roused him, and his glad, welcoming smile more than counterbalanced the frown which settled on the widow's face when she saw her boy disturbed. Rose was accustomed to the widow's ways, and throwing off her shawl and untying her hat, she sat down on the foot of Isaac's bed, and drawing Jimmie's letter from her pocket began:

"I've got such splendid news for you, Mrs. Simms,—at least, I think I have. Yes, I know it's sure to come true. Eli is going to be a lieutenant, with twelve hundred dollars a year. Such a heap of money for him; and it's all Jimmie's doings, too. He would not have the office because he did not think he deserved it. Listen to what he says."

Both the Widow and Susan were close to Rose now, the frown all gone from the widow's brow, and the pucker from her mouth; but both came back in a trice, as blundering Rose read on about "Hophni," and "Phineas," and "Eli," till she came to the "*crabbed*," which she called "*crab-apple*," and then stopped short, her face a perfect blaze, as she tried to apologize.

"'Tain't wuth while to soap it over," the widow said, fiercely. "I *be* a crab-apple, I s'pose, and a gnarly one at that, but I am as I was made, and I'd like to know if *crabs* wan't as good as *Secessioners*."

"Please, mother, never mind," Isaac said, pleadingly, and his voice always quieted the fiery woman, who listened while Rose read of Eli's good fortune, and made another terrible mistake by stumbling upon Jimmie's opinion of Isaac's sickness.

She only read, "He is not long for this world," but that was enough to bring a flush to his brow, and blanch his mother's cheek; while, with a gush of tears, Rose hid her face in Susan's lap, and sobbed:

"I wish I had not come. I'm always doing wrong when I mean to do the best. Oh, I wish the war had never been, and I don't believe Isaac is so sick. Jimmie has no right to judge. He don't know."

Rose's distress was too genuine not to touch the widow, who tried to appear calm and unconcerned, and even said something kind of Jimmie, who had so generously preferred Eli to himself. But there was a restraint over everything, and, after a few awkward attempts at something like natural conversation, Rose bade a hasty good-bye, and went out from the house to which she had brought more sorrow than joy.

CHAPTER XXI.
"NOT LONG FOR THIS WORLD."

The sick boy whispered the words a great many times to himself, as with his face to the wall, where neither his mother nor Susan could see it, he thought of what Rose had read, and wondered if it were true. He was not afraid to die. He had been very near death once before, and had not shrunk from meeting it *as* death. It was only the dying from home he had dreaded so much, asking to live till he could see his mother again, and the grass growing by the cottage door, and the violets by the well. And God had taken him at his word. He had lived to see his mother, to feel the touch of her rough hands upon his hair; to hear her voice, always kind to him, calling him her "Iky boy;" to see the green grass by the door, and the violets by the well. But this, alas! did not suffice. He wanted to live longer,—live to be a man, like Eli and John; live to do good; live to take care of his mother; live to hear the notes of victory borne on the northern breeze, as the Federal Flag floated again over land and sea. All this was worth living for, and Isaac was young to die,— only nineteen, and looking three years younger. It was very hard, and the dark eyelashes closed tightly to keep back the tears as the white lips tried to pray, "Thy will be done." That was what they meant to utter, but there came instead the first words of the prayer the Saviour taught, "Our Father!" that was all; but the very name of father brought a deep peace into Isaac's heart.

God was his father, and he had nothing to fear; living or dying, it would be well with the boy who would not tell a lie even for promotion. And so, while the mother whose heart ached and throbbed with this new fear, and still found time to feel a thrill of pride in Lieutenant Eli, moved softly around the room, preparing the dainty supper for her child, Isaac slept peacefully, nor woke until the delicate repast was ready, and waiting for him on the little table by the bed. There was spiced chocolate to-night, and nice cream toast, with grape jelly, and a bit of cold baked chicken, and the highly-seasoned cucumber pickles Isaac had craved so much since his return, and which the physician said were good for him. And the best china cup was brought out, and the silver spoons marked with the widow's maiden name, and a white napkin was on the tray; and Isaac, who enjoyed such things, knew why it was all done that particular night, just as the widow knew why, at bed-time, he asked Susan to read from Revelation, vii. 16, "They shall hunger no more, neither thirst any more; neither shall the sun light on them, nor any heat. For the Lamb which is in the midst of the throne shall feed them, and shall lead them unto living fountains of waters, and God shall wipe away all tears from their eyes."

He was thinking of his heavenly home, while the mother was thinking of the time when he, who Jimmie Carleton had said "was not long for earth," would be gone, and she could no longer do for him the little offices which gave her so much comfort. Since the dreadful days when she knew her boy was in prison, the widow had not felt so keen a pang as that which stirred her heart-strings now, when alone in her room she dropped in her quick, defiant way into the high-backed chair, and sitting stiff and straight, tried to face the future. It could not be that Isaac had only come home to die,—God would not deal thus harshly with her. He had spared Eli and John, He had promoted them both and He would not take Isaac from her. The boy was getting better, he was mending every day, or, at least, she had thought so, until Rose Mather came with her message of evil. Why could not Rose have stayed at home? Why need she come there and leave such a sting behind? The widow was growing very hard and wicked toward poor little thoughtless Rose, and her heart lay like a stone in her bosom, as for an hour or more she sat in her high-backed chair, thinking of the boy whose low breathings she could hear from the next room. He was sleeping, she thought, and she would steal softly to his side and see if it was written on his face that his days were numbered. But Isaac was not asleep, and he knew the moment his mother bent over him, and turning toward her, he whispered,

"I know why you are up so late, mother; and what you are here for. You are thinking of what Mrs. Carleton said, and wondering if it is true. I guess 'tis, mother, for I don't get any stronger, and my cough hurts me so. But I'm not a bit afraid to die now, with you beside me up to the very last minute. In Richmond it was different: and I prayed so hard that God would let me come back, if only to drink from the well and then die on the grass beside it. He did let me come, and now we mustn't say anything if He does not let me stay but a little bit of a while. I've been thinking it over since Mrs. Mather went away, and at first it seemed hard that Eli and John should both have such good luck, and only 'Stub,' be the one to suffer."

He said this last playfully, using his old nickname of "Stub," because he saw by the dim light burning on the table the bitter look of anguish upon his mother's face, and he would fain remove it. At the mention of the name which her more stalwart sons had given to her baby, the widow's chin quivered, and her rough hand smoothed the thin light hair, but she did not speak, and Isaac went on:

"Then, too, I want to live till the war is over. I want to hear the joyful shouts, and see the bonfires they will kindle in the streets. There's a big box in the barn. I hid it there the morning I went away, and I said when the peace comes we can burn that box, and mother will look out from the window, and the church bells will ring, and there'll be such rejoicings. Now I 'most know I shan't be here to see it. But, mother, you'll burn the box,—you and Susan, with Eli and John,—and you'll think of me, who did what I could to bring the peace."

There was a choking sound like the swallowing of a great sob, and that was all the answer the widow made; only her hands moved faster through the threads of light brown hair, and her rigid form sat up straighter, more rigid than ever. She was suffering the fiercest pangs she would ever know, for she was giving Isaac up. She was coming to the knowledge that he was really going from her,—that Jimmie Carleton was right, and Isaac was not long for this world. When at last her mind reached that point, the tension of nerve gave way for a little, and her hot tears poured over the white face she kissed so tenderly.

The moon was looking in at the low west window ere the widow went back to her own bed, and Isaac, nestling down among his pillows, fell away to sleep, dreaming of the bonfire in the street, when the hidden box was burned, and dreaming, too, of that other world which lies so near this that he could almost see the loving hands stretched out to welcome him.

After that night the widow's mouth shut together more firmly than ever, and the frown between her eyes was more marked and decided, while her manner to all save Isaac and Annie Graham was sharper, and crisper than before. When Eli's letter came telling of his promotion and lauding Jimmie Carleton, whose generous act was a by-word in the company, her face relaxed a little, and she said to Annie Graham: "The Lord is good to my two oldest boys, but if he'd give me Isaac I wouldn't care for all the titles in Christendom."

As the warm weather came on, Isaac did not get up any more to sit by the open door, but lay all day on his bed, sometimes sleeping, sometimes thinking, and sometimes listening while Annie read to him from the Bible. Isaac was very fond of Annie. She had been George Graham's wife, and he evinced so much desire to have her constantly with him that at last she stayed altogether with Mrs. Simms, only going occasionally to the Mather Mansion, where they missed her so much. Rose was nothing without her, and had at first opposed her going to the Widow Simms.

"If help was needed," she said, "she would hire some one, for Annie must not tire herself out just as she was beginning to grow plump and beautiful again."

But when Isaac said to her: "Please let Mrs. Graham come; it will not be long she'll have to stay, and she is so full of hope and faith that it makes me more willing to die and to go away alone across the Jordan," she withdrew her opposition, and Annie was free to go and come as she liked. It suited Annie to get away from the Mather Mansion just then, for she could not help feeling that there was a purpose in Mrs. Carleton's questioning her of her early history, and she hailed any excuse which removed her from the scrutiny with which since that conversation touching her early home and maiden name Mrs. Carleton had evidently regarded her. Jimmie had written to her once, inclosing the unsealed note in a letter to Rose, and Annie's cheeks had been all ablaze as she read it, for she knew the mother's eyes were fastened upon her. It was nothing but a simple acknowledgment of some article Annie had made and sent to him in a box filled for all three of the soldiers, Will Mather, Tom and Jimmie. There was also mention made of Annie's kindly message, to the intent that she did think he was right in giving the office to Eli, and a wish expressed that she would write to him.

"You don't know how much good letters from home do such scamps as we privates are, or how we need something from the civilized world to keep us from turning heathens."

Tom, too, had sent thanks to Annie Graham for the needle-book made for him, but he did not write to her, though every letter had in it more or less of "Mrs. Graham," and Mrs. Carleton, while saying to herself: "Both my boys have fallen under the spell," felt her pride gradually giving way and her heart growing warmer toward the woman whom she missed so much during the weeks spent at Isaac's bedside.

They were not many, for when the dry days of August came on, and the grass withered by the door, and the flowers drooped for want of rain, and the sun rose each morning redder, hotter, than on the previous day, the sick boy began to fail rapidly, and one night, just as the wind was beginning to blow from the west, where a bank of dark clouds was lying, he whispered to Annie:

"Call mother and Susan, for I know I am going now."

The widow was in the back yard, putting out the barrels and tubs to catch the rain if it came, for the well and the cistern were nearly dry, just as her dim eyes were, when a few minutes after she bent over her boy, and saw the change coming so rapidly. She could not weep, and Susan's sobs annoyed her. "'Twas like them Ruggleses to go into hysterics and make a fuss," she thought, with a kind of bitter scorn for her daughter-in-law, who loved Isaac as a brother, and wept that he was leaving them. Perhaps the dying boy detected the feeling, for he said, feebly:

"Go out, Susan and Mrs. Graham both. I want to be alone with mother a minute." Then when they were alone, he said: "I am dying, mother, and I know you won't be angry at what I say. I want you to be kind to Susan, and pet her some and love her for John's sake. She is a good girl, and Mr. Carleton's good too, the one they call Jimmie, I mean. Don't say harsh things of him because he was once a rebel. Don't speak against him to Mrs. Graham. Maybe she will like him sometime, and if so, help her, mother, instead of hindering it."

Jimmie Carleton, on his lone picket-watch that night on the banks of the Potomac, and thinking, alas! more of a black-robed figure, with braids of pale brown hair, than of a lurking foe, little dreamed of the good word spoken for him by the dying boy, whose eyes turned lovingly to Annie when she came back to him, and held his clammy hand.

"It is not dark; it is not hard; I am not afraid, for the Saviour is with me," he kept repeating, and then he sent messages to his absent brothers,—to Captain Tom Carleton, who had been so kind to him in prison, and to Jimmie, too, and all the boys who had been with him in battle; and then, just as the wind began to roar down the chimney, and the refreshing rain to beat against the windows, Isaac's spirit went out into the great unknown expanse beyond this life, and only the pale, emaciated body was left in the humble room, where the lone women stood looking upon the boyish face, which seemed so young in death.

The widow uttered no sound when she knew he was dead, and it was her hand which drew the covering decently about him, and then picked up from the floor a loose *feather*, which had dropped from the worn pillow.

Susan must speak to their next-door neighbors, she said, and ask them to care for the body. Then, when the men came in, she remembered an open window in the back chamber where the rain must be driving in, and stole up there on the pretence of shutting it; but she did not return till the men were gone, and Isaac was lying on the calico-covered lounge with a look of perfect peace upon his face, and the damp night air blowing softly across his light hair.

Kneeling at his side, and laying her hard cheek against the icy face of her last-born, the mother gave vent to her grief in her own peculiar way. There were no tears, or sobs; but loving, tender, cooing words whispered over the boy, as if he had been a living baby, instead of a soldier dead. And yet the fact that it was a soldier, lying there before her, was never lost sight of, and the bitter part of the woman's nature was stirred to its very depths as she remembered what had brought her boy to this. It was the *war*. And fierce were the mental denunciations against those who had stirred up the strife, while with the bitterness came pitying thoughts of the poor boys who died in the lonely hospitals, or on the battle-fields; and with her cheek still resting against the pale, clammy one, and her fingers threading the light hair, the widow vowed that all she was, and all she had, should henceforth be given to the war. She would work for the soldiers, give to the soldiers, deny herself food and raiment for the soldiers; aye, even *die* for them, if need be; and whispering the vow into her dead boy's ear, she left him there alone, just as the early summer dawn was breaking. And when, next morning, her friends came in to see her, they found her sitting by the body, and working upon the shirt she had a few days before taken from the Aid Society to make for some poor wretch.

She should not wear mourning, she said. She had other uses for her money; and so the leghorn of many years' date, with the old faded green veil, followed Isaac Simms to the grave, and the widow's face was still and stony as if cut from solid marble.

They made him a great funeral, too, though not so great as George Graham's had been; for Isaac was not the second, nor the third, nor the fourth soldier buried in Rockland's churchyard. But he was *Isaac Simms,*—"Little Ike,"—"Stub,"—whom everybody liked; and so the firemen came out to do him honor, and the Rockland Guards, and the company of young lads who were beginning to drill, and the boys from the Academy, and Rose Mather was chief directress, and her carriage carried the widow, and Susan, and Annie, and herself up to the newly-made grave, where they left the boy who once had sawed wood for the little lady now paying him such honor.

The war was a great leveler of rank, bringing together in one common cause the high and the low, the rich and the poor, and in no one was this more strikingly seen than in the case of Rose Mather, who, utterly forgetful of the days when, as Rose Carleton, of Boston, she would scarcely have deigned to notice such as the Widow Simms, now sought in so many ways to comfort the stricken woman, going every day to her humble home, and once coaxing her to spend a day at the Mather mansion, together with Susan, whom Rose secretly thought a little insipid and dull. Susan's husband was alive, and in the full flush of prosperity; so Susan did not need sympathy, but the widow did, and Rose got her up to the "Great House," as the widow called it, and ordered a most elaborate dinner, with soups and fish, and roasts and salads, prepared with oil, which turned the widow's stomach, and ices and chocolate, and Charlotte-russe, and nuts and fruit, and coffee served in cups the size of an acorn, the widow thought, as very red in the face and perspiring at every pore, she went through the dreadful dinner which lasted nearly three hours, and left her at its conclusion, "weak as water, and sweatin' like rain," as she whispered to Annie, who took the tired woman for a few moments into her own room, and listened patiently to her comments upon the grand dinner which had so nearly been the death of her.

Susan, on the contrary, enjoyed it. It was her first glimpse of life among the very wealthy, and while her mother-in-law was wondering "how Annie could stand such doins every day, and especially that 'bominable soup, and still wus *salut,*" Susan was thinking how she should like to live in just such style, and wondering if, when John came home with his wages all saved, she could not set up housekeeping somewhat on the Mather order. At least she would have those little coffees after dinner; though she doubted John's willingness to sit quietly until the coffee was reached.

It was a long day to the widow, and the happiest part of it was the going home by the cemetery, where she stopped at Isaac's grave, and bending over the turf, murmured her tender words of love and sorrow for the boy who slept beneath. There was a plan forming in the widow's mind, and it came out at last to Annie, who was visiting her one day.

The hospitals were full to overflowing, and the cry all along the lines was for more help to care for the sick and dying, and the widow was going as nurse, either in the hospital or in the field. She should prefer the latter, she said, "for only folks with *pluck* could stand it there."

And Annie encouraged her to go, and even talked of going too, but the first suggestion of the plan brought such a storm of opposition from Rose, that for a little time longer Annie yielded, resolving, however, that ere long she would break away and take her place where she felt that she could do more good than she was doing in Rockland.

CHAPTER XXII
THE WOUNDED SOLDIER.

Widow Simms was going to the army, and Jimmie Carleton, who was coming home for a few weeks, was to be her escort to Washington. During the summer Jimmie had seen a good deal of hard service. He had been in no general battle, but had taken part in several skirmishes and raids, in one of which he received a severe flesh wound in his arm, which, together with a sprained ankle, confined him for a time to the hospital, and finally procured for him a furlough of three or four weeks. Rose was delighted, and this time the Federal Fag was actually floating from the cupola of the Mather mansion in honor of Jimmie's return but there was no crowd at the depot to welcome him. That custom was worn out, and only the Mather carriage was waiting for Jimmie, whose right arm was in a sling, and whose face looked pale and thin from his recent confinement in hospital. Altogether he was very interesting in his character as a wounded soldier, Rose thought, as she made an impetuous rush at him, nearly strangling him with her vehement joy at having him home again. And Jimmie was very glad to see her,—glad, too, to meet his mother,—but his eyes kept constantly watching the door, and wandering down the hall, as if in quest of some one who did not come. During the weary days he had passed in the Georgetown Hospital, Annie Graham's face had been constantly with him, and as he watched the tall, wiry figure of the nurse, who always wore a sun-bonnet and had a pin between her teeth, he kept wishing that it was Annie, and even worked himself into a passion against his sister Rose, who, in one of her letters, had spoken of Annie's proposal to offer herself as nurse, and her violent opposition to the plan.

"If Rose had minded her business Annie might possibly have been in this very ward, instead of that old maid from Massachusetts, who looks for all the world like those awful good women in Boston, who don't wear hoops, and who distribute tracts on Sundays in the vicinity of Cornhill. Why can't a woman look decent, and distribute tracts, too? Annie, in her black dress, with her hair done up somehow, would do more good to us poor invalids than forty strong-minded females in paste-board bonnets, with an everlasting pin between their teeth."

Thus Jimmie fretted about Rose, and the Massachusetts woman, who, in spite of her big pin and paste-board bonnet, brought him many a nice dish of tea or bowl of soup, until the order came for him to go home, when, with an alacrity which almost belied the languor and weakness he had complained of so bitterly, he packed his valise and started again for Rockland. This time he wore the "army blue;" but the suit which at first had been so fresh and clean, was soiled, and worn, and hateful to the fastidious young man, who only endured it because he fancied it might in some way commend him to Annie Graham. Rose had written that she worshiped the very name of a soldier, especially if he were a *poor private*, her sympathies being specially enlisted for that class of people. And Jimmie was a poor private, and a wounded one at that, with his arm in a sling, and a cane in his hand, and his curly hair cut short, and his coat all wrinkled and soiled, and his knapsack on his back; and he was going home to Annie, who surely would welcome him now, and hold his hand a moment, and possibly dress his wound. That *would* be delightful; and Jimmie's blood went tingling through his veins as he felt in fancy the soft touch of Annie's fingers upon his flesh, and saw her head crowned with the pale brown hair bending over him. He felt a little disappointment that she was not at the depot to meet him, while his chagrin increased at the tardiness of her appearance after his arrival home, but she was coming at last, and Jimmie's quick ear caught the rustle of her garments as she came down the stairs and into the room, smiling and blushing, as she took his offered hand, and begged him not to rise for her.

"You are lame yet, I see. I had hoped your ankle might be well," she said, glancing at his cane, which he carried more from habit, and because it had been given him by an officer, than from any real necessity.

His sprained ankle *was* almost well, and only troubled him at times; but after Annie's look of commiseration at the cane, and her evident intention to pity him for his ankle rather than his arm, he found it vastly easy to be lame again, and even made some excuse to cross the room in order to show off the *limp* which had not been very perceptible when he first came in. And Annie was very sorry for him, and inquired with a great deal of interest into the particulars of his being wounded, and kindly sat where he could look directly at her, and thought, alas! how much he was changed from the fashionably-dressed, saucy-faced young man who went from them only a few months before. Short hair was not becoming to him,—neither was his thin, burnt face,—neither was that soiled blue coat; and he looked as little as possible like a hero whom maidens could worship. Some such thought passed through Annie's mind, while Rose, too, felt the change in her handsome brother, and, with a puzzled expression on her face, said to him, as she stood by his side:

"How queer you do look, with your hair so short, and the hollows in your cheeks! Does *war* change all the boys so much? Are Tom and Will such frights?"

"Rose!" Mrs. Carleton said, reprovingly, while Annie looked up in surprise, pitying Jimmie, whose chin quivered even more than his voice, as he said:

"Tom and Will have not been sick like me; and then,—there's no denying it,—officers have easier times, as a general thing, than privates. I do not mean, by that, that I regret my position, for I do not. Somebody must take a private's place, and it would better be I than a great many others; but, Rose, I shall regret it, perhaps, if by the means my looks become obnoxious to my sister and friends."

There was a marked emphasis on the word *friends*, and Jimmie's eyes went over appealingly to Annie, who remembered how proud the boy Dick Lee used to be of his beauty, and guessed how Rose's remarks must have wounded him. Rose suspected it, too, and winding her arms around his neck she tried to apologize.

"Forgive me, Jimmie," she said; "I did not mean anything; only your hair *is* so short,—just like the convicts at Charlestown,—and your coat is so tumbled and dirty; but Hannah can wash that, or I can buy you a new one," and Rose stumbled on, making matters ten times worse, until Mrs. Carleton succeeded in turning the conversation upon something besides her son's personal appearance.

Annie was very sorry for him, and her sympathy expressed itself in the soft light of her blue eyes which rested so kindly upon him, and in the low, gentle cadence of her voice when she addressed him, and her eager haste to bring him whatever she thought he wanted, and so save him the pain of walking!

Mrs. Carleton saw through that *ruse* at once. She had noticed no limp when Jimmie first came in, and she readily suspected why it was put on. But it was not for her to expose her son. From a lady who had spent a few days at the Mather House, and who once lived near Hartford, Mrs. Carleton had learned that the Dr. Howard, who had died of cholera in '49, was highly respected, both as a gentleman and a practising physician, and this had helped to reconcile her in a great measure to whatever might result from her son's evident liking for Annie Graham, *née* Annie Howard, and as she more than half suspected, the heroine of Jimmie's boyish fancy.

How very beautiful Jimmie thought Annie was, after he had had time to recover himself a little and look at her closely. She was in better health, and certainly in better spirits than when he saw her last. Her cheeks were rounder, her eyes were brighter, and her hair more luxuriant, and worn more in accordance with the prevailing style. This was Rose's doings, as was also the increased length of Annie's dress, which swept the floor with so long a trail that the Widow Simms had made it the subject of sundry invidious remarks.

"Needn't tell her that a widder could wear such long switchin' gowns, and think just as much of the grave by the gate. She knew better, and Miss Graham was beginnin' to get frillicky. She could see through a millstone."

This was Mrs. Simms' opinion of the long gored dress which Jimmie noticed at once, admiring the graceful, symmetrical appearance it gave to Annie's figure, just as he admired the softening effect which the plain white collar and cuffs had upon Annie's dress. When he was home before, everything about her was black of the deepest dye; but now the sombreness of her attire was relieved somewhat, and Jimmie liked the change. He could look at her without seeing constantly before him the grave by the churchyard gate, where slept the man whose widow she was. She did not seem like a widow, she was so young; only twenty-one, as Jimmie knew from Rose, who, delighted with the friendly meeting between her brother and friend, was again building castles of what might be. Could Rose have had her choice in the matter, she would have selected Tom for Annie. He was older, steadier, while his letters seemed very much like Annie. Tom had found the Saviour of whom Isaac Simms once talked so earnestly in the prison house at Richmond. He was better than Jimmie, Rose reasoned, and more likely to suit Annie. Still, if it were to be otherwise, she was satisfied, and in a quiet way she aided and abetted Jimmie in all his plans to be frequently alone with Annie. It was Annie who rode with him when Mrs. Carleton was indisposed, and Rose did not care to go,—Annie who read to him the books which Rose pronounced too stupid for anything,—Annie who brought his cane, and Annie who finally attended to his wounded arm. The physician did not come one day; Mrs. Carleton was sick; and Rose positively could not touch it and so Annie timidly offered her services, and Jimmie knew from actual experience just how her soft fingers felt upon his arm, his pulse throbbing and the blood tingling in every vein as she dressed his wound so carefully, asking anxiously if she hurt him very badly. He would have suffered martyrdom sooner than lose the opportunity of feeling those soft fingers upon his flesh, and so it came about that Annie was his surgeon, and ministered daily to the wound which healed far too rapidly to suit the young man, who began to shrink from a return to the life he had found so irksome.

Tom had written twice for him to come as soon as possible, and now only one day more remained of the month he was to spend at home. The Widow Simms was ready to go with him; Susan had gone to her mother, and the cottage was to be closed, subject to a continual oversight from Mrs. Baker and an occasional inspection from both Rose and Annie. The *box* which Isaac had hidden in the barn, waiting for the bonfire which should celebrate our nation's final victory, had been brought from its hiding-place, and baptized with the first and only tears the widow had shed since she went back to her humble home and left him in the graveyard. Sacred to her was that box, and she put it with her best table and chairs, bidding Annie Graham see that no harm befell it, and saying to her, "In case I never come back, and peace is declared, burn the box for Isaac's sake, right there on the grass-plat, which he dreamed about in Richmond."

And Annie promised all, as she packed the widow's trunk, putting in many little dainties which Rose Mather had supplied, and which were destined for the soldiers whom the widow was to nurse. She had been all day with Mrs. Simms, and Rose had been back and forth with her packages, curtailing her calls because of Jimmie, with whom she would spend as much time as possible.

Jimmie was not in a very social mood that day; the house was very lonely without Annie, and the young man did nothing but walk from one window to another, looking always in the direction of Widow Simms', and scarcely heeding at all what either his mother or sister were saying to him. When it began to grow dark, and he heard Rose speak of sending the carriage for Annie as she had promised to do, he said:

"I ought to see Mrs. Simms myself to-night, and know if everything is in readiness for to-morrow. I will go for Mrs. Graham, and Rose,—don't order the carriage,—there is a fine moon, and she,—that is,—I would rather walk."

Jimmie spoke hurriedly, and something in his manner betrayed to Rose the reason why he preferred to walk.

"Oh, Jimmie!" she exclaimed, "I'm so glad; tell her so for me. I thought at first you did not like each other, and everything was going wrong. I am so glad; though I had picked her out for Tom. I 'most know he fancied her, and then he is a widower. It would be more suitable."

Rose meant nothing disparaging to Jimmie's suit. She did think Tom, with his thirty-two years, better suited to Annie, who had been a wife, than saucy-faced teasing Jimmie of only twenty-four. But love never consults the suitability of a thing, and Jimmie was desperately in love by this time. It was not possible for one of his temperament to live a whole month with Annie as he had lived, and not be in love with her. Her graceful beauty, brightened by the auxiliaries of dress and improved health, and the thousand little attentions she paid him just because he was a soldier, had finished the work begun when he was home before, and he could not go back without hearing from her own lips whether there was any hope for him,—the scamp, the scapegrace, the rebel, as he had been called by turns. What Rose said of Tom brought a shadow to his face, and as he walked rapidly toward Widow Simms', not limping now, or scarcely touching his cane to the ground, he thought of Tom,—*old Tom* he called him,—wondering how much he had been interested in Annie Graham, and asking himself if it were just the thing for him to take advantage of Tom's absence, and supplant him in the affections of one whom he might, perhaps, have won had he an opportunity.

"But Tom has had his day," Jimmie thought. "He can't expect another wife as nice as Mary was, and it is only fair for me to try my luck. *I* never loved any one before."

Jimmie stopped suddenly here; stopped in his soliloquy and his walk, and looking up into the starry sky, thought of the boy at New London, and the hills beyond, and the hotel on the beach, and the white-robed little figure with the blue ribbons in the golden hair, and the soft light in the violet eyes, which used to watch for his coming, and look so bright and yet so modest withal when he came. *Louise* her aunt had called her, and he had designated her as *Lu*, or *Lulu*, just as the fancy took him.

"I *did* love *her* some," Jimmie thought. "Yes, I loved her as well as a boy of seventeen is capable of loving, and I deceived her shabbily. I wonder where she is? She must be twenty or more by this time, and a woman much like Annie. If I could find her, who knows that I might not like her best?" And for a moment Jimmie revolved the propriety of leaving Annie to Tom, while he sought for his first love of the Pequot House.

But Annie Graham had made too strong an impression upon him to be given up for a former love, who might be dead for aught he knew, and so Tom was cast overboard, and Jimmie resumed his walk in the direction of Widow Simms' cottage.

The widow's trunks were all packed and ready: every thing was done in the cottage which Annie could do, and with a tired flush on her cheek, a tumbled look about her hair, and a rent in the black dress, made by a nail on one of the boxes, Annie was waiting for the carriage, and half wishing, as she looked out into the bright moonlight, that she was going to walk home instead of riding. The fresh air would do her good, she thought, just as Jimmie appeared at the door. He had come to see if there was anything he could do for Mrs. Simms, he said, and to escort Mrs. Graham home.

Annie's cheeks were very red as she went for her shawl, and then bade good-bye to Mrs. Simms, whom she did not expect to see on the morrow. As soon as they were outside the gate, Jimmie drew her shawl close round her neck, and taking her arm in his, said to her: "The night is very fine and warm, too, for the first of November. You won't mind taking the longest route home, I am sure, as it is the last time I may ever walk with you, and there is something I must tell you before I go back to danger and possible death."

He had turned into a long, grassy lane or newly opened street, where there were but few houses yet, and Annie knew the route would at least be a mile out of the way, but she could not resist the man who held her so closely to his side. She must hear what he had to say, and with an upward glance at the clear blue sky where she fancied George was looking down upon her, she nerved herself to listen.

"Annie," he began, "I've called you Mrs. Graham heretofore, but for to-night you must be Annie, even if you give me no right to call you by that name again. Annie, I have been a scamp, a wretch, a rebel, and almost everything bad. I deceived a young girl in New London years ago when I was a boy. Rose told you something about it once. Her name was Louise,—*Lulu* I called her,—and I made her think I loved her."

"And didn't you love her?" Annie asked suddenly, her voice ringing clear in the still night and making Jimmie start, there was something so quiet and determined in its tone.

Still he had no suspicion that the woman beside him was the girl he had left on the beach at New London, and he continued: "Yes, Annie, I did, as boys of seventeen love girls of fourteen. She was pretty and soft, and pure and good, and I kissed her once on her forehead, and then I went away and never saw her after, or knew what became of her. And I am telling you this by way of confessing my misdeeds, for I've been a fast and reckless young man. I've gambled, and sneered at the Bible, and broken the Sabbath heaps of times, and flirted with more than forty girls, some of them not very respectable either, and none as pure as little Lulu. I ran away from home and nearly broke my mother's heart. I joined the rebel army and fought against my brother at the battle of Bull Run. I was captured by Bill Baker and led with a halter to Washington and there shut up in prison. A fine character I give myself, and yet after all this I have dared to love you, Annie Graham, and I have brought you this way to ask if you will be my wife. Not now, of course: not before I go back; but if I come through the war alive will you be mine then, Annie? Tell me, darling, and don't tremble so, or turn your face away."

Annie was shaking in every joint, and the face which Jimmie tried in vain to see was white as ashes. She had expected something like this when he led her down that grassy lane, but nevertheless it came to her with a shock, making her feel as if in some way she had injured her dead husband by listening to another's love. And still she could not at once repulse the young man whose arm was around her, and who had drawn her to a gap in a stone wall, where he made her sit down while she answered him. Strange feelings had swept over her as she heard Jimmie Carleton's voice telling her how much she was beloved,—how from the first moment he saw her he had been interested in her, and asking her again if she had anything to give the "recreant Jim."

He said the last playfully, but there was a great fear at his heart lest her silence portended evil to him.

"No, Mr. Carleton. I have no heart to give you. I buried it with George; I can never love another. Forgive me if in any way I have misled you. I was only kind to you as I would be to any soldier."

"Bill Baker, for instance," came savagely from Jimmie's lips.

He was cruelly disappointed, for he had not believed Annie would refuse him as she had done. He thought a good deal of himself as a *Carleton*. Nay, he believed himself superior to the man who was standing between him and the woman he coveted, and to be so decidedly refused by one who had been content with a person in George Graham's position angered him for a moment. Annie knew he was offended, and when he spoke of Bill Baker, she said to him gently:

"You mistake me, Mr. Carleton. If necessary, I could do for William Baker more than I have done for you; but it would only be from a sense of duty,— there would be no pleasure in it; while caring for you was a pleasure, because you are Mrs. Mather's brother, and because,—because—"

She did not know how to finish the sentence, for she could not herself tell why it had of late been so pleasant for her to do for Jimmie Carleton those little acts of kindness which had devolved on her. She was only interested in him as a soldier, she insisted, and she tried to make him understand that her decision was final; that were George dead a dozen years, she should give him the same answer as she did now. She could not be his wife. And Jimmie understood it at last, and by the terrible pangs of disappointment which crept over him, the Pequot girl was fully avenged for the many times she had watched from her window of the hotel, or walked sadly along the road by the bay to see if Dick Lee were coming. But Annie had no wish for revenge. She was only sorry for him, and she tried to comfort him with the assurance of her interest in him, and by telling him that, if ever he was sick in hospital or camp, and unable to come home, she would surely go to him as readily as if he were her brother.

Jimmie did not particularly care for such comforting then, and his face, when he reached home, wore so dark and sorry a look that Rose, knew at once that something was wrong; but she refrained from asking any questions then,— feeling intuitively that both Annie and her brother would prefer to have her do so.

It was a very grave, silent party which met at the breakfast table next morning, and only Annie was at all inclined to talk. She tried to be cheerful and appear as usual to the silent young man who never looked at her as she sat opposite him, with her smooth bands of hair so becomingly arranged, and her eyes so full of pity for him. She could not revoke her decision, but she was sorry to send him from her with that look upon his face; and when, after breakfast, she met him for a few moments alone in the library, she laid her hand timidly upon his arm, and said, "*Jimmie*, don't be angry with me. Try to think of me as your sister,—your best friend, if you like. It grieves me that I have made you so unhappy."

She had never called him *Jimmie* before, in his hearing, and as she did it now, the dark, handsome face into which she was looking, flushed with a sudden joy, as if he thought she were relenting. But she was not; she could only be his friend,—his best friend, she repeated, and her face was very pale, as she told him how she should remember him, and work for him, and pray for him, when he was gone. And then she gave him her hand, saying to him, "It is nearly time for you to go. I would rather say good-bye here."

And Jimmie took her hand, and, pressing it between his own, said to her:

"You have hurt me cruelly, Annie Graham, for I believed you cared for me; but I cannot hate you for it, though I tried to do so all night long. I love you just the same as ever, and always shall. Remember your promise to come to me when I am sick, and let me kiss you once for the sake of what I hoped might be."

She did not refuse his request; and when at last he left her there was a red spot on her cheek where Jimmie Carleton's lips had been. From her window she watched him going down the walk; and while with widow Simms he waited at the depot for the coming of the train, she on her knees was praying for him and his safety, just as, eighteen months before, she prayed for George when he was going from her.

CHAPTER XXIII.
TOM AND JIMMIE.

Jimmie's journey was performed in safety, and he won golden opinions from his traveling companion, for whom he had cared as kindly as if it had been his mother instead of the "crabbed widow" in her eternal leghorn, with the vail of faded green. He had left her at one of the hospitals in Washington, where she was to begin her work as nurse, and hastened on to join his regiment. Captain Carleton was glad to welcome back the brother whom he had missed so much, but he saw that something was wrong; and that night, as they sat around the tent fire, he asked what it was, and why the face, usually so bright and cheerful, seemed so sober and sad. Tom had made minute inquiries concerning his mother, and Rose, and Susan Simms, and even poor old Mrs. Baker. But not a word of Annie. He could not speak of her, with that unfinished letter lying in his little travelling writing-case,—that letter commencing "My dear Mrs. Graham," and over the wording of which Tom had spent more time by far than he did over the first epistle sent to Mary Williams. That had been dashed off in all the heat of a young man's first ardent passion, just as Jimmie two weeks ago would have written to Annie. But Tom was eight years older than Jimmie. His first love had met its full fruition, and Mary, the object, was dead. Tom had always been old for his years. He looked, and seemed, and felt, full forty now, save when he thought of Annie, who was only twenty-one. Then he went back to thirty-two, glad that he had numbered no more birth-days. He had made up his mind to write to her. A friendly letter the first should be, he said,—a letter merely asking if she would correspond with him, and hinting at the interest he had felt in her ever since he saw how much she was to Rose, and how constant were her labors for the suffering soldiers. If her answer was favorable, he should ere long ask her to be his wife, and this is the way he took to win the woman whose name he would not mention to his brother. He had been a little uneasy when Jimmie first went home, for he knew how popular the wayward youth was with all the ladies; but as Rose had never written a word to strengthen him in his fears, he had thrown them aside and commenced the letter which to-night, after Jimmie was gone, he was intending to finish for the morrow's mail. He changed his mind, however, as the night wore on, for in reply to his question as to what was the matter, Jimmie had burst out impetuously with,

"It is all over with me and the widow. I went in strong for her, Tom. I told her all my badness, confessed everything I could, and then she said it could not be. I tell you, Tom, I did not know a man could be so sore about a woman!" And with a great choking sob Jimmie Carleton laid his head upon Tom's lap, and moaned like some wounded animal.

Tom, who had been as a father to this younger brother, was touched to his heart's core, and felt as if by having that unfinished letter in his possession he was in some way guilty, and as a pitying woman would have done, he smoothed the dark curly hair, and tried to speak words of comfort.

"What had Annie said? Perhaps she might relent. Would Jimmie tell him about it?"

Then Jimmie lifted up his head, and looking straight in Tom's eyes, said,

"Forgive me, old Tom. I was inclined to be jealous of you. Rose said you were more suitable, and I know you are; but, Tom, I did love Annie so much, after I had swallowed the first husband, which cost me a great effort, for a widow is not the beau ideal I used to cherish of my future wife. Tom, you don't care for Annie, do you?" he continued, in a startled tone, as something in Tom's face affrighted him.

Tom would not deceive him then, and he replied,

"I have,—that is,—yes, I do care for her, and I had commenced a letter, but——"

"Don't finish it, Tom. Do this for me,—don't finish it!" Jimmie exclaimed, eagerly, knowing now how the hope that Annie might relent had buoyed him up, and kept him from utter despondency. "Don't send it, Tom; leave her to me, if I can win her yet. She may feel differently by and by: her husband is only one year dead. Let me have Annie, Tom," and Jimmie grew more vehement as he saw plainly the struggle in Tom's mind. "You've had your day with Mary. Think of your years of married life, when you were so happy, and leave Annie to me. At least don't try to get her from me,—not yet,— wait a year. Will you, Tom?"

Few could resist Jimmie Carleton's pleadings when they were so earnest as now; and generous Tom yielded to the boy, whom he had scolded, and whipped, and disciplined, and loved, and grieved over, ever since the day their father died and left him the head of the family.

"I will wait a year and see what that brings to us; and you, Jimmie, must do the same, then Annie shall decide," he said at last, and his voice was so steady in its tone, and his manner so kind, that Jimmie never guessed how much it cost the man who "had had his day," to unlock the little desk and take from it the letter intended for Annie Graham and commit it to the flames.

They watched it together as it crisped and blackened on the coals, neither saying a word or stirring until the last thin flake had disappeared, when Tom bent to pick up something which had dropped from the desk, when he took out the letter. It was *Mary's* picture, and in her lap the baby which had died when six months old.

"Yes, I have had my day," Tom thought, as he gazed upon the fair, sweet face of her whose bright head had once lain where he had thought to have Annie's lie. "I have had my day, and though it closed before it was noon, I will not interfere with Jimmie."

And so the compact was sealed between them, and Jimmie slept sounder on his soldier bed that night than he had slept before since Annie's refusal. Jimmie was not selfish, and as the days went by and he reflected more and more upon Tom's generosity, his conscience smote him for having allowed his brother to sacrifice his happiness for a whim of his. "She might have refused him, too, and then again she might not; at all events he had a right to try his luck," Jimmie reasoned, until at last his sense of justice triumphed and he wrote to Annie an account of the whole transaction.

"It was mean in me to let Tom burn the letter," he said, "but I could not bear the thought of his winning what I had lost, and so like a coward I looked on and felt a thrill of satisfaction when I saw his letter crisping on the coals. But as proof that I have repented of that selfish act, I ask you plainly, 'Would you have replied favorably to that letter, had it been sent?' If so, tell me truly, and without ever betraying the fact that I have written to you on the subject, I will manage to have Tom write again, and if the fates shall so decree I will try to forget that gap in the stone wall where we sat that night when I told you of my love."

His letter found Annie sick in bed from the effects of a severe cold which kept her so long in her room that it was not till just on the eve of the battle of Fredericksburg that Jimmie received her answer, "I should say No to your brother just as I did to you."

This was what Jimmie read, and with a feeling of relief as far as Tom was concerned, he crushed the few lines into his pocket and went on with his preparations for the contest at Fredericksburg, which seemed inevitable, with a kind of recklessness which characterized many of our soldiers. Jimmie had heretofore felt no fears of a battle. The bullet which might strike down another would not harm him, and he charged his preservation mostly to Annie's prayers for his safety; but in this, her last brief note, she had not said so much as "God bless you," and Jimmie's heart beat faster as he thought of the impending danger. Jimmie seldom prayed, but if Annie had failed him he must try what he could do for himself, and when the night came down upon that vast army camping in the woods and on the hillside, it looked on one young face upturned to the wintry sky, and the moaning winds carried up to heaven the few words of prayer which Jimmie Carleton said.

Oppressed with a strange feeling of foreboding, he prayed earnestly that God would blot out all his manifold transgressions, and if he died,—grant him an entrance into heaven where Annie was sure to go. Close beside him crouched

Bill, who listened with wonder to the "Corp'ral," a feeling of terror beginning to creep into his own heart as he detected the accents of fear in his companion.

"I say, Corp'ral," he began, when Jimmie's devotions were ended, "be you 'fraid of somethin's happenin' to you when they set us to crossin' that darned river, and if there does, shall I write to the folks and the gal you mentioned and tell 'em you prayed like a parson the night before?"

Jimmie was terribly annoyed with Bill's impertinence, and for a man who had just been praying did not exercise as much Christian forbearance as might have been expected. A harsh "Mind your business!" was his only reply, which Bill received with a good humored, "Guess you'll have to try agin, Corp'ral, before you get into the right frame;" and then there was silence between them, and the night crept on apace, and the early morning began to break and the wintry sky was obscured by a thick, dull haze, which hid for a time our soldiers from view, then a deadly fire of musketry from the opposite bank of the Rappahannock was opened upon them, till they fled to the shelter of the adjacent hills, where, forming into line, they again went back to the laying of the pontoon bridges, while the roar of the cannon shook the hills and told to the listeners miles away that the battle of Fredericksburg was begun.

CHAPTER XXIV.
RESULTS OF THE BATTLE.

The streets of Rockland were full of excited people when the news first reached the town of the terrible battle which had left so many slain upon the field, and desolated so many hearths both North and South. Rose Mather was nearly frantic, for Will she knew was in the battle, together with her two brothers, and it was not probable that all three would escape unharmed. Eagerly she grasped the paper to see who was killed, wounded, or missing, but neither of the three names was there, and she began to hope again, and found time to comfort poor Susan Simms, whose husband was also in the fight, and who had gone almost mad with the fear lest he should be killed.

Two days passed, and then there came a telegram from Tom, and Mrs. Carleton, who read it first, gave a low, moaning cry, while Rose, who read it next, uttered a piercing shriek, and fell sobbing into Annie's arms.

"Oh, Will!—oh, Will!—my husband!" was what she said, while Mrs. Carleton uttered Jimmie's name, and then Annie knew that harm had come to him, and placing Rose upon the sofa, she took the paper from Mrs. Carleton's hand, and read:

"Will was badly wounded,—lay on the field all night;—Jimmie missing,— supposed to be a prisoner. I am well.

"T. CARLETON."

"Poor Jimmie!" Annie whispered, sadly, her heart throbbing with pity for the young man who had gone back in time to meet so sad a fate.

Never had so dark a day dawned upon Rose Mather as that which followed the arrival of Tom's telegram, but ere its close there came a message of hope to her. Will had been taken to Washington, where he had providentially fallen into the hands of Mrs. Simms, who sent the joyful news that "no bones were broken, and he was doing well."

"Oh, Annie, God is so much better to me than I deserve; I must love Him now, and I will, if He will only send Jimmie back," Rose said, while Annie's heart went up in a prayer of thanksgiving for Mr. Mather's comparative safety, and then went out after the poor prisoner, whose destination was as yet unknown.

That night Rose started for Washington, and three days after there came to Annie a soiled, queer-looking missive, directed to "Miss Widder Anny Graam, At Miss Martherses," the name written at the top of the letter, and the superscription spreading over so much surface, that, had there been another word, it must, from necessity, have been written on the other side of the letter. It was from Bill Baker, and it read as follows:

"Army of Potomac, and about as licked out an army as you ever seen. To all it may concern, and 'specially Miss Anny Graam. I send you my regrets greetin', and hopin' this will find you enjoying the same great blessin'. Burnside has made the thunderinest blunder, and more'n a million of our boys is dead before Fredericksburgh. Mr. Mathers was about riddled through, I guess, and the Corporal,—wall, may as well take it easy,—I fit for him like a tiger, till they nocked me endways, and I played dead to save my life. But the Corporal's a goner,—took prisoner with an awful cut on his neck; and now what I'm going to tell you is this: the night before the battle I came upon him prayin' like a priest, kneelin' in an awful mudpuddle, and what he said was somethin' about Heaven, and *Anny*, whitch, beggin' your pardon, I think means you, and so I ast him in case of bad luck, if I should write and tell you. I don't think he could have ben in a vary sperritual frame of mind, for he told me to mind my bisiness, but I don't lay it up agin him, and when them too tall, lantern-jawed sons of Balam grabbed him as he was tryin' to skedaddle with the blood a spirtin' from his neck, I pitched inter 'em, and give 'em hale columby for a spell, till they nocked me flat and I made bleeve dead as I was tellin' you. Don't feel bad, Miss Graam. Trust luck and keep your powder dry, and mabby he'll come back sometime.

Yours to command,

"BILL BAKER."

"Tell the old woman I'm well, but pretty well tuckered out."

"God soften the hearts of his captors. God keep him in safety!" Annie whispered, and then, as Mrs. Carleton came in, she passed the note to her, and tried to comfort the poor mother, who, in Rose's absence, leaned on her as on a daughter.

Annie seemed very near the sorrowing woman, who wept bitterly for her poor boy, and in the first hours of her sorrow she spoke out what was in her mind.

"I believe Jimmie loved you, Annie, and that makes you very dear to me. We can mourn for him together, and, Annie, you will pray for him night and day, that God will bring him back to us."

Annie could only reply by pressing the hand which sought hers, for her heart was too full to speak. Had Jimmie been dead she would scarcely have mourned for him more deeply than she did now. The country was already rife with rumors of the sufferings endured by our prisoners, and death itself seemed almost preferable to months and years of privations and pain in the Southern prisons.

"Sent to Richmond, and probably from thence further South, probably to Georgia."

This was all the intelligence they could procure from him, until spring, when there came news direct that he was at Salisbury, and there for a time the curtain dropped, leaving his face shrouded in darkness, while in his Northern home tears were shed like rain, and prayers went up to heaven from the quivering lips of a mother, who was just learning to pray as she ought, and into Annie Graham's heart there gradually crept a wish that the poor, weary prisoner might know how much and how kindly she thought of him, feeling at times half sorry that she had not given him some little hope as a solace for the weary hours of his prison life.

CHAPTER XXV.
GETTYSBURGH.

Rose Mather had brought her husband home as soon as it was safe to move him, and with the good nursing of Mrs. Carleton and Annie, he grew strong enough to rejoin his regiment in May, and the last which Rose heard from him directly was a few words hastily written and sent off to Washington just as the Army of the Potomac was moving on to Gettysburgh. Then came the terrible battle, when the summer air was full of smoke, and dust, and flying splinters, with clouds of torn-up earth which blinded the horror-stricken men, who vainly sought for shelter behind the trees and the headstones of the graveyard, where the dead must almost have heard the fierce commotion around them as wail after wail of human anguish, mingled with the awful shrieks of dying horses, went up to the blackened heavens and then died away in silence. Where the battle was the hottest, and the carnage the most terrible, Will Mather followed, or rather led, and when the fight had ceased he lay upon his face, unconscious of the pitiless rain beating upon his head, or the two savage looking Texans bending over him, and turning him to the light.

Among the list of killed, the Rockland *Chronicle* of July 10th had the name of William Mather, while in another column, designated by long lines of black, was a eulogy upon the deceased, who was known to have fought so bravely. Then every blind of the Mather mansion was closed, and knots of crape streamed from the door-knob, and the villagers missed the roll of the carriage wheels which were wont to carry so much comfort and sunshine to the hearts of the poor soldiers; and the little airy, dancing creature, whose bright smile and rare beauty had done quite as good service as her generous gifts, lay in her darkened room, never weeping, never speaking, except to moan so piteously, "Oh, Will, my darling, my poor, poor husband."

They could not comfort her, for she did not seem to hear, or at least to understand one word they said, and the soft, dark eyes had in them a wild, scared look, which troubled the watchers at her side, and made them tremble for her safety.

The knots of crape were taken from the doors, and the blinds were opened at last, and the light of heaven let into the dreary house; but there came no change to poor little Rose, whose white face grew so thin that Tom, when in September he came home to see her, would scarcely have known the little sister, of whose beauty he had been so proud. As if the sight of him in his uniform had brought back the horror of the past, she uttered a piercing shriek, and hid her face for a moment in her pillows; then, with a sudden movement lifted her head, and shedding back her tangled curls from her pale forehead, she stretched her arms toward him and whispered:

"Take me, Tom; hold me as you used to do; let me be a little girl again in the old home in Boston, for Will, you know, is dead."

And Tom took her in his strong, brotherly arms, and laid her head against his breast, and caressed and smoothed her tumbled hair, and petted and loved her just as he did when she was a little child, with no shadow around her like that which enfolded her now. And then he spoke of Will, and the dark eyes fastened eagerly upon his as he told her how the very night before the battle, Will knelt down with him and prayed that whether he lived or died, all might be well with him.

"And Rose," he continued, "he bade me tell you, in case he was killed, that all was well, and you must think of him as in Heaven, not far, as some suppose, but near to you,—with you,—he said, and you must meet him there. You must bear bravely what God chooses to send; not give up like this when there is so much to be done. Will my darling little sister heed what poor Will said? Will she try to rally and be a brave woman?"

"Yes, Tom, I'll try," came gaspingly from the white lips, and Rose's voice was broken with sobs, as the first tears she had shed since she heard the fatal news, ran in torrents down her face.

Tom only staid a week, but he did them a world of good, and Annie felt she had never known one half how noble a man he was until she saw how tender he was with Rose, and how kind to his mother, whose heart was aching to its very core for her youngest son. He had been removed from Salisbury to Andersonville when they last heard from him, and was dead, perhaps, by this time. Poor Jimmie! The year he had asked Tom to wait would be up before very long, but Tom would still keep faith with him. Annie was sacred to Jimmie's memory, and once, when talking with her of the captive, he alluded to what would probably be when Jimmie came home again. And Annie did not turn from him now, as she would once have done had such a thing been suggested.

"God only knows how I might feel," she said, and by the look in her blue eyes, and the tone of her voice, Tom knew there was no hope for *him*.

With many kisses and loving words of sympathy, he bade his sister good-bye when his leave had expired, and then in the hall stood a moment while his mother whispered something to him which made him start, and turn pale as he said:

"Poor Will! he would have been so glad!"

Then, as if the news had brought Rose nearer to him, and made her more the object of his special care, he went back to her a second time, and wound his arms about her lovingly, as he said, "Poor little wounded dove! God's promises are for the widow and fatherless, and He will care for you;" and Rose guessed to what he referred, but there was no answering joy upon her face, and her hands were pressed upon her heart as she watched him from the window, going from her just as Will had gone, and whispered to herself, "It would have been too much happiness if Will had lived; but now I cannot be glad."

CHAPTER XXVI
COURSE OF EVENTS.

With a howl of despair, Mrs. Baker came rushing into the kitchen of the Mather mansion, one morning in November, startling Annie with her vehemence as she thrust into her hand a dirty, half-worn envelope, which she said was from Bill, who had been missing since August, and who, it now appeared, was at Andersonville.

"Might better be dead," his mother said, and then she explained that the letter she brought Annie had come in one to herself received that morning from Bill.

How he ever got it through the lines was a mystery which he did not explain; nor did Annie care, inasmuch as it brought news direct from Jimmie. He had written to her with the pencil and on the sheet of paper Bill had brought him, for Bill Baker was employed outside the prison walls, and allowed many privileges which were denied to the poor wretches who crowded that swampy pen. In short, Bill had taken the Confederate oath,—"had done some tall swearin'," as he wrote to Annie, giving as an excuse for the treasonable act, "that he couldn't *stan'* the racket" in that horrible place, where twenty thousand human beings were crowded together in a space of twenty-five acres, and part of that a marshy swamp, teeming with filth and scum, and hideous living things. Another reason, too, Bill gave, and that was pity for the "Corp'ral," to whom he could occasionally take little extras, and whom he would have scarcely recognized, he said, so worn and changed had he become from his long imprisonment.

"I mistrusted he was there," Bill wrote; "and so when me and some other fellow-travellers was safely landed in purgatory, I went on an explorin' tower to find him. But you bet it want so easy gettin' through that crowd. Why, the camp-meetin' they had in the Fair Grounds in Rockland, when Marm Freeman bust her biler hollerin', was nothin' to the piles of ragged, dirty, hungry-lookin' dogs; some standin' up, some lyin' down, and all lookin' as if they was on their last legs. Right on a little sand bank, and so near the dead line that I wonder he didn't get shot, I found the Corp'ral, with his trouses tore to tatters, and lookin' like the old gal's rag-bag that hangs in the suller-way. Didn't he cry, though, when I hit him a kelp on the back, and want there some tall cryin' done by both of us as we sat there flat on the sand, with the hot sun pourin' down on us, and the sweat and the tears runnin' down his face, as he told me all he'd suffered. It made my blood bile. I've had a little taste of Libby, and Bell Isle, too; but they can't hold a candle to this place. Miss Graam, you are the good sort, kinder pius like; but I'll be hanged if I don't bleeve you'll justify me in the thumpin lies I told the Corp'ral that day, to keep his spirits up. Says he, 'Have you ever ben to Rockland since Fredericksburg?' and then I tho't in a minute of that nite in the woods when he prayed about Anny; and ses I to myself, 'The piusest lie you ever told will be that you have been home, and seen Miss Graam, with any other triflin' additions you may think best;' so I told him I had ben hum on a furbelow, as the old gal (meanin' my mother) calls it. And I seen her, too, says I, Miss Graam, and she talked an awful sight about you, I said, when you orto have seen him shiver all over as he got up closer to me, and asked, 'What did she say?' Then I went on romancin', and told him how you spent a whole evenin' at the ole hut, talkin' about him, and how sorry you was for him, and couldn't git your natural sleep for thinkin' of him, and how, when I came away, you said to me on the sly, 'William, if you ever happen to meet Mr. Carleton, give him Anny Graam's love, and tell him she means it.' Great Peter! I could almost see the flesh come back to his bones, and his eyes had the old look in 'em, as he liked to of hugged me to death. I'd done him a world of good, he said, and for some days he seemed as chipper as you please; but nobody can stan' a diet of raw meal and the nastiest watter that ever run; and ses I to myself, Corp'ral will die as sure as thunder if somethin' don't turn up; and so, when I got the hang of things a little, and seen how the macheen was worked, sez I, 'I'll turn Secesh, though I hate 'em as I do pizen.' They was glad enuff to have me, bein' I'm a kind of carpenter and jiner, and they let me out, and I went to work for the Corp'ral. I'll bet I told a hundred lies, fust and last, if I did one. I said he was at heart Secesh; that he was in the rebel army, and I took him prisoner at Manassas, which, you know was true. Then I said his sweetheart, meanin' you, begging your pardon, got up a row, and made him jine the Federals, and promise never to go agin the flag, and that's how he come to be nabbed up at Fredericksburg. I said 'twan't no use to try to make him swear, for he thought more of his gal's good opinion than he did of liberty, and I set you up till I swan if I bleeve you'd a knowed yourself, and every one of them fellers was ready to stan' by you, and two of 'em drinked your helth with the wust whisky I ever tasted. One of 'em asked me if I was a fair specimen of the Northern Army, and I'll be darned if I didn't tell him *no*, for I was ashamed to have 'em think the Federals was all like me. I guess, though, they liked me some; anyway, they let me carry something to the Corp'ral every now and then, and I bleeve he'd die if I didn't. I've smuggled him in some paper and a pencil, and he is going to wright to you, and I shall send it, no matter how. The rebs won't see it, and I guess it's pretty sure to go safe. I must stop now, and wright to the old woman.

"Yours to command,

"WILLIAM BAKER, ESQUARE."

It was with great difficulty that Annie could decipher the badly-written scrawl; but she made it out at last, and then took Jimmie's letter next, shuddering as she saw in it marks of the horrors which Bill had described but faintly, and which were fully corroborated by Jimmie himself.

"My dear Annie," he wrote, "I do not know that this letter will ever reach you. I have but little hope that it will. Still it is worth trying for, and so here in this terrible place, whose horrors no pen or tongue can adequately describe, I am writing to you, who I know think sometimes of the poor wretch starving and dying by inches in Andersonville. Oh, Annie, you can never know what I have suffered from hunger and thirst, and exposure and filth, which makes my very blood curdle and creep, and from that weary homesickness which more than aught else kills the poor boys around me. When I first came here I thought I could not endure it, and though I knew I was not prepared, I used to wish that I might die; but a little drummer boy from Michigan, who took to me from the first, said his prayers one night beside me, and the listening to him carried me back to you, who, I felt sure, prayed for me each day. And so hope came back again, with a desire to live and see your dear face once more. My little drummer boy, Johnny, was all the world to me, and when he grew too sick to sit or stand, I held his poor head in my lap, and gave up my rations to him, for he was almost famished, and ate eagerly whatever was brought to us. We used to say the Lord's Prayer together every night, when a certain star appeared, which he playfully called his 'mother,' saying it was her eye watching over him. It was a childish fancy, but we grow childish here, and I, too, have given that star a name. I call it 'Annie,' and I watch its coming as eagerly as did the little boy, who died just as the star reached the zenith and was shining down upon him. His head was in my lap, and all there was left of my coat I made into a pillow for him, and held him till he died. His mother's address is ——, Michigan. Write to her, Annie, and tell her how Johnny died in the firm hope of meeting her again in heaven. Tell her he did not suffer much pain,—only a weakness, which wasted his life away. Tell her the keepers were kind to him, and brought him ice-water several times. Tell her, too, of the star at which he gazed so long as he had strength.

"It was all the companion I had after he was gone until Bill Baker came. I shall never forget that day. I had crawled up to my sand bank, and drawn my rags around me, and was beginning to wish again that I could die, when a broad hand was laid upon my shoulder, and a voice which was music to me then, if it never had been before, said to me cheerily, 'Hallo, old Corp'ral! Such are the chances of war! Give us your fist!' But when he saw what a sorry jaded wretch I was, his chin began to quiver, and we cried together like two great babies as we were.

"Oh, Annie, was it a lie Bill Baker told me, or did you really send me your *love*, and say that you meant it? He told me such a story, and I grew better in a moment. Have you relented, and if I could ask you again the question I asked a year ago, when we sat together beneath the moonlight, would you tell me *yes*? Darling Annie, Andersonville is not so terrible since I am kept up by that hope. I do not mind now if my shoes and stockings are all gone, and my trowsers nearly so, and I watch for that star so eagerly, and make believe that it is you, and when the dark clouds obscure it, and the rain is falling upon my unsheltered head, I say that it is Annie's tears, and do not mind that either. I pray, too, Annie,—pray with my heart, I hope, though my prayers have more to do with you than myself.

"Bill Baker said he should write and tell you about his taking the oath, which I believe he did almost solely for my sake, and greatly have I been benefited by it. Rough as he is, and disgusting at times, he seems to have gained friends outside, and he does us many a kindness, confining his attentions mostly to me, who am his especial care. It is a strange Providence that he who took me a prisoner at Bull Run and annoyed me so terribly, should now be caring for me here at Andersonville, and literally keeping the life within me, for I should die without him.

"I have not written half I want to say, but my paper is nearly used up, and not one word have I said to mother or Rose. Tell them they would not know me now, and tell them, too, that in my dreams, when I am not with you, I am with them, and mother's face is like an angel's, while Rose's sparkling beauty makes my heart beat just as it used to beat when I first began to realize what a darling sister I had. Dear Annie, you *did* send that message by Bill Baker, I *will* believe, and thus believing, shall gain strength maybe to bear up until the day of release.

"Good-bye, my darling. From my crowded, filthy, terrible prison I send you a loving good-bye."

Notwithstanding the sickening details of this letter the day succeeding its receipt was a brighter one at the Mather house than the inmates had known for a long time. Jimmie was still alive, and with Bill Baker's care he might survive the horrors of Andersonville and come back to them again. Annie showed both letters to Mrs. Carleton, who, when she read them, wound her arms around Annie's neck and whispered, "Is it wrong for me to be glad that Bill Baker told that lie, when by the means our prisoner boy is so greatly benefited."

Annie could not tell. She was not sorry that Jimmie should think of her as he did, and that night when the stars came out in the sky she looked tearfully up at them wondering which was the one watched for by the childish young man, and the little boy who died. Mrs. Carleton had taken it for granted that if Jimmie came back Annie would be her daughter, and she clung to her with a love and tenderness second only to what she felt for Rose. Poor Rose! She had listened with some degree of interest to such portions of Jimmie's letter as Annie chose to read to her, but it had no power to rouse her from the state of apathy into which she had fallen. She never smiled now, and rarely spoke except to answer a question, but sat all day by the window in her own room, and looked away to the southward, where all her thoughts were centered. It was very strange that nothing could be heard of her husband except that he was shot down dead. A dozen corroborated that fact, but his body had not been found on the field, nor was any mention ever made of him in any official accounts. Once Rose had been startled from her stupor by a soldier, who pretended to have seen her husband in one of the Southern prisons, but a closer examination proved that the man was intoxicated, and had told what he did in the hope that money might be given him for the intelligence, and then Rose sank back into her former condition, the same hopeless look in her eyes which had been there from the moment she heard her husband's name among the killed, and the same look of anguish upon her face which never relaxed a muscle, as she watched indifferently the preparations made by her mother and Annie for an event which under other circumstances would have stirred every pulsation of her heart. But when on Christmas morning, the bell from St. Luke's was sending forth its joyous peal for the child born in Bethlehem more than eighteen hundred years ago, there came a softer, more natural look to Rose's eyes, and her lip quivered a little as she said to Annie, who was bending over her, "What is that sound in the next room like the crying of a baby?"

"It is your baby, Rose; born last night. Don't you remember it,—a beautiful little boy, with his father's look in his eyes, and Jimmie's dimple in his chin?"

Annie hoped, by mentioning both the father and Jimmie, to awaken some interest in the little mother, whose eyes grew larger, and rounder, and brighter, as she whispered:

"My baby, I can't understand. It is all so strange and mysterious. How came I with a baby, Annie? Bring it to me, please."

They brought it to her, and laid it in her arms, and then stood watching her as the first tokens of the mother's love came over her face and crept into her eyes, which gradually began to fill with tears, until, at last, a storm of sobs and moans burst forth, as Rose rocked to and fro, whispering to her child:

"Poor darling! to be born without a father, when he would have been so proud of his boy. Poor, murdered Will! Poor, fatherless baby! I am glad God gave you to me. I did not deserve it. I've been so thoughtless and wicked, but I will be better now. Dear little baby, we will grow good together, so as to go some day where papa has gone."

She would not let them take the child from her. It was hers, she said. God had sent it to make her better, and she would have it. There was something in the touch of its soft, warm hands, which kept her heart from breaking. And so they left it with her, and from the day that little life came to be one in the household, Rose began to amend, and, in her love for her child, forgot in part the terrible pain in her heart. Once her mother said to her:

"Will you call your baby, William?" And she replied.

"No; there is but one Willie for me, and he is in Heaven. Baby will be called for brother Jimmie."

And so one bright Sunday morning in March, when St. Luke's was decked with flowers from the Mather hot-house, and the children of the Sunday School sang their Easter carols, Rose Mather, in her widow's weeds, went up the aisle, with her mother, Annie, and brother Tom, the latter of whom gave her bright-eyed, beautiful boy to the rector, who baptized him "James Carleton." And all through the congregation there ran a thrill of pity for the widowed mother, whose face, though it had lost some of its brilliant color, was more beautiful than ever, for there was shining all over it the light of a new joy, the peace which comes from sins forgiven, and, after the baptism was over and the morning service read, Rose knelt with her mother, brother, and Annie, to receive, for the first time, the precious symbols of a Saviour's dying love.

Rose had ceased to oppose Annie in her wish to join Mrs. Simms, who was then at Annapolis; and when Tom, a few days after the baptism, went back again, Annie would go with him as a regular hospital nurse.

It might be that Jimmie would be among the number of skeletons sent up to "God's land," as the poor fellows called it; and Annie's heart throbbed with the pleasure it would be to minister to him, to call the life back to his heart, to awaken an interest in him for olden times, and then, perhaps, whisper to him that the decision made that moonlight night, more than a year and a half ago, had been revoked and where she had said no, her answer now was yes. Between herself and Mrs. Carleton there had been a long talk, of which Jimmie and the little Pequot girl were the subjects, and the proud lady had asked forgiveness for the wrong done to that girl, if wrong there were.

"Something tells me you will find my boy," she said; "and if you do, tell him how freely I give him this little Lulu, and God bless you both!"

A few weeks later, and news came to the Mather House that when the battle of the Wilderness was over, Captain Tom Carleton was not with his handful of men who came from the field. "A prisoner of war," was the next report, and then, as if her last hope had been taken from her, Mrs. Carleton broke down entirely, and, secluding herself from the world without, sat down in her desolation, mourning and praying for her two boys,—one a prisoner in Andersonville, and one in Columbia.

CHAPTER XXVII.
THE HUNTED SOLDIER.

The sun was just rising, and his red beams gilded the summits of the Alleghany Mountains, which in the glory of the early morning seemed as calm and peaceful as if their lofty heights had never looked down upon scenes of carnage and strife, or their tangled passes and dark ravines sheltered poor, starving, frightened wretches, fleeing for their lives, and braving death in any form rather than be recaptured by their merciless pursuers. There were several of these miserable men hiding in the mountain passes now, prisoners escaped from Salisbury and other points, but our story now has to do with but one, and that a young man, with a look of determination in his eye, and the courage of a Samson in his heart. He had suffered incredible hardships since the day of his capture. He had been stripped at once of his handsome uniform by the brutal Texans, who found him upon the field. His gold, which he carried about his person into every battle, had been taken from him, and in this condition he had been sent from one prison to another, until Salisbury received him. At first he had suffered but little mentally, for the ball which struck him down had left him with his reason impaired, and to him it was all the same whether friend or foe had him in keeping. Deprived of everything which could mark his rank as an officer, and always insisting that his name was "Rose," he passed for a demented creature, whom the brutal soldiery delighted to torment. Gradually, however, his reason came back, and he woke to the full horrors of his condition. Then, like a caged lion he chafed and fumed, and resolved to be free. He could not die there, knowing that far away there was a blithesome little woman waiting for his coming, if, indeed, she had not ceased to think of him as among the living,—a state of things which he thought very probable, as he became aware of the fact that no one of his companions was acquainted with his real name. Rose was the only cognomen by which he was known, and the proud man shivered every time he heard that dear name uttered by the coarse, jesting lips around him. A horrid suit of dirty grey had been given him in place of the stolen uniform, and though at first he rebelled against the filthy garments, he began ere long to think now they might aid him in his escape, inasmuch as they were the garb of the Confederates. Day and night he studied the best means of escape, until at last the attempt was made and he stood one dark, rainy night, out on the highway a free man, breathing the pure breath of heaven, and ready to sell his life at any cost rather than go back again to the prison he had left. He had put his trust in God, and God had raised him up a friend at once, who had seen him leave the prison, and greatly aided him in his escape, just as he had aided others, knowing the while that by so doing he was putting his own life in jeopardy. But a staunch Unionist at heart, he was willing to brave everything for the cause, and it was through his instrumentality and minute directions that Will Mather had finally reached the shelter of the mountains which separate North Carolina from Tennessee. He had found friends all along the route, true, loyal men, who had periled their lives for him; brave tender women, whose hands had ministered so kindly to his wants, and who had so cheerfully divided with him their scanty meals, even though hunger was written upon their thin, haggard faces, and stared in their sunken eyes. And Will had taken down each name, and registered a vow that if ever he reached the North, these noble self-denying people should be rewarded, and if possible removed from a neighborhood where they suffered so much from privation and from the hands of their former friends, who, suspecting their sentiments, heaped upon them every possible abuse. Ragged, bareheaded, footsore and worn, he came at last, at the close of a June day, to the entrance of a cave in the hills to which he had been directed, and where, on the damp earth, he slept so soundly from fatigue and exhaustion that the morning sun was shining through the entrance to the cave, and a robin, on a shrub growing near, was trilling its morning song ere he awoke. The air, though damp from the water which trickled through the rocks, was close and stifling, and Will crept cautiously out from his hiding-place, and sitting down upon the ground drank in the beauty and stillness of the summer morning. Exactly where he was he did not know, but he felt certain that his face was toward the land where the Stars and Stripes were waving, and a thrill of joy ran through his veins as he thought of home and Rose, whose eyes by this time had grown so dim with looking for him. "God take me safely to her," he whispered, when up the mountain side came the sound of voices and the tramp of feet. Creeping to the farthest side of the cave, and crawling down beneath the shelving rock where the cool waters were dripping, he hoped to avoid being seen. Up to this moment Will's courage had never flagged, but now, when the Federal lines were not many miles away, and Rose and home seemed certain, he felt a great pang of fear, and his white lips whispered, "God pity me! God help me, God save me, for his own glory, if not for Rose's sake," then, knee-deep in the pool of water, he stood with his body nearly double, while the voices and the feet came nearer, and at last stopped directly in front of his hiding-place.

There were terrible oaths outside, and bitter denunciations were breathed against any luckless Union man who might be lurking near, and then the light from the entrance of the cave was wholly obscured, and Will saw that a man's back was against the opening, as if some one were sitting there. *Did* they know of the cave? Would they come in there, and if they did would they find him? Will kept asking himself these questions and his breath came gaspingly as he knew that the man whose back barred the entrance to his hiding-place was the bitterest in his invectives against the Yankees, and the most anxious to find them. Something in his voice and language indicated both education and position superior to his companions, who evidently looked up to him as their leader, calling him "*Square*," and acquiescing readily when, after the lapse of ten or fifteen minutes, he suggested that they go higher up the mountain to a gorge where some of the fugitives had heretofore taken refuge.

Five minutes more and the footsteps and voices were heard far up the mountain, and Will breathed more freely again, and kneeling down in the pool of water, thanked God who had turned the danger aside, and kept him a little longer. He did not dare leave the cave, but he came out from under the rock, and stretching himself upon the ground tried to wring and dry the tatters which hung so loosely upon him.

It was two days since he had tasted food, and the long fast began to make itself felt in the keen pangs of hunger. Surely he could venture out toward the close of the day, he thought, and see if there were not berries growing in the ledges, and when the sun was setting he crawled to the mouth of the cavern, where just in the best place for him to see it lay a huge corn-cake and slice of bacon, wrapped nicely in a bit of paper.

How it came there he did not stop to ask. That it was there was sufficient for him then, and never had the costliest dinner, served on massive silver, tasted to him half so well as did that bit of bacon with the coarse corn bread.

Refreshed and encouraged he went back to his hiding-place, intending to start again on his perilous journey when the mountain path grew dark enough to warrant him in doing so. But soon after the sunsetting a fearful storm came up, and in the pitchy darkness of the cave Will listened to the bellowing thunder roaring through the mountain gorges, and saw from the opening the forked lightning which struck more than one tall tree near the place of his concealment. Fed by the rain which had fallen in torrents, the stream under the projecting rock was beginning to rise and spread itself over the surface of the cave. It was up to his ankles now, and it rose so rapidly that Will was thinking of leaving the cave and groping his way as well as he could to the westward, when his quick ear caught the sound as of two or more persons coming stealthily up the mountain side. Whoever they were they seemed to move with the utmost caution, and Will's heart beat high as he hoped it might be some brother fugitives seeking the shelter of the cave. The gleam of a lantern, however, and the same voice he had heard in the morning cursing the Yankees so bitterly dispelled that illusion, and in a tremor of terror he drew back in his watery quarters, crawling in the darkness to the farthest end of the cavern, and feeling the rising water flow over his knees as he waited for what might come next.

"Stay here, Charlie, while I go in. I know he must be here, and if he isn't drowned by this time it's just a special Providence, that's all I have to say."

Surely that was no unfriendly voice, notwithstanding the oaths of the morning, but still Will did not move until the stranger, who evidently knew every turn and nook of the cavern, was so near to him that the light from the dark lantern fell full upon his face and betrayed him at once. There was a thought of Rose, and the freedom he had almost regained, and then forgetting the friendly tones, Will gave a low, bitter moan and stretching out his hands, said imploringly,

"Kill me here as well as anywhere, and let the suspense be ended."

"Kill you, my boy?" and the stranger spoke cheerily as he bent over poor Will and rubbed his clammy hands. "What should I kill *you* for? I've had my eyes on you ever since yesterday evening, when I saw you creeping under the brushwood, and knew you were hunting for this cave. The 'Refuge of Safety,' I call it, and it has proved so to many a poor devil who like yourself has taken shelter here. I have never known one to fail of reaching the happy land when once they got so far as this, so cheer up, my man. Paul Haverill can swear a string of swears about the Yanks which will reach from here to Richmond, if necessary, and then when the hounds are thrown off the track he can turn round and save the poor hunted rascal's life. You are among your friends, so come out from this puddle. You must be wetter than a rat. There's a spring under the rocks, and it rises in a rain so as to fill the cave sometimes. Here, Charlie, give us that shawl, his teeth are fairly chattering."

Thus talking, the stranger, who had announced himself as Paul Haverill, led Will out to where the boy Charlie stood, holding a bright plaid shawl in his hand, and looking curiously at the worn, drooping, sorry figure emerging from the cave. It was a woman's shawl, Will knew, but it was very soft and warm, and he wrapt it closely round him, for he was shaking with cold, and his tattered garments were wringing wet. Very few words were spoken, and those in a whisper, as they went cautiously down the mountain until they reached what seemed to be a road winding among the hills. This they did not follow, but, striking into the field or pasture land beside it, kept to the right, and at a safe distance from it, lest some straggler might be abroad, and meet them face to face. Will Mather was enough acquainted with Southern customs not to be surprised to find here in the mountain wilds a substantial and even handsome-looking building, which, with its white walls and green blinds, seemed much like the farm-houses in New England. There was a light shining from the windows, and a woman's brisk step was heard as they went toward the door; Paul Haverill coughing, to give warning of his approach.

"All right!" was the pass-word by which they entered, and Will soon stood in the wide hall which ran through the entire building, and opened in the rear upon a broad piazza.

"Better take him to Miss Maude's room," the woman said, and Will followed on to an upper chamber, which, he would have known at once belonged to a young lady.

It was not as elegantly furnished as his own sleeping apartment at home, but it bore unmistakable marks of taste and refinement; while the air of pure gentle womanhood, which pervaded it, brought Rose very vividly before him.

"This is my niece's room, Maude De Vere," Mr. Haverill explained, when they were alone, and Will was drying himself before the fire, kindled by the woman who had admitted them, and who, Will saw, was a mulatto. "My niece is not at home now," he continued. "She is in South Carolina; has been gone several months on a visit to old Judge Tunbridge, her mother's uncle. I'm her mother's brother, and she and the boy Charlie have lived with me since the first year of the war. Their father was Captain De Vere, from North Carolina, and was killed at the first Bull Run. Nelly, their mother, never held up her head after that. I was with her when she died, and brought the children home. Maude is twenty now, and Charlie fourteen. I am their guardian. Maude is Union, Charlie secesh, but safe. They have a great deal of property here and there, though how it will come through the war, the Lord only knows."

Will was glad to see that his host was inclined to talk on without waiting for answers, and he kept quiet, while Mr. Haverill continued:

"I dare say you wonder to find a chap like me among people who are so bitter against you Yankees, and I sometimes wonder at myself. I am South Carolina born, and ought to be foremost in the rebellion; but hanged if I can see that it is right. Why, *I* might as well set up a government of my own, here on the Oak Plantation, and refuse to come under any civilized laws. Mind, though, I don't think the South all wrong,—not a bit of it. The North *did* bully us, and the election of Mr. Lincoln was particularly obnoxious to the majority here, but we had no right to secede, and you did your duty trying to drive us back. For a spell I kept quiet,—didn't take either side; or if I did, I wanted the South to beat, as all my interests are here. But when our folks got to abusing their prisoners so shamefully, and told so many lies by way of deceiving us fellows who live among the hills and only get the news once or twice a week, I changed my politics, and after the day when I found one of my neighbors, and the best man that ever breathed, too, *hung* to a tree like a dog, with the word 'Abolitionist' pinned to his coat, I made a vow that every energy I had should be given to caring for and helping; just such wretches as you, and if I've helped one I've helped a thousand. Why, at least a hundred have slept in this very room,—Maude's room; for, as I told you, she is Union to the backbone, and led one chap across the mountain herself. She is a regular Di Vernon, and is not afraid of the very de'il. When she went away

- 206 -

she bade me put them in here, as the room least liable to suspicion. To the folks around me I am the roughest kind of a Secessionist, and I suppose nobody can beat me swearing about the Yankees, just to hoodwink 'em, you know. I suppose that's wrong; my wife would say so; she was a saint when she was here,—she is an angel now. She died five years ago,—before the war broke out; and *Lois*, the woman you saw, has been my housekeeper since. I shouldn't like the North to take her from me. They tried it once,—when a squad of 'em ransacked my house,—and I was sick in bed. Maude threatened to blow their brains out: and, sir, she would have done it, too, if the scamps hadn't let Lois alone.

"I don't agree with your folks on the nigger question, though none of mine has run away since the Proclamation, which I did not like. They know, too, they are free, or will be when the Yankees come, for I took pains to tell them, and gave them liberty to cut stick for the Federal lines as soon as they pleased; but they staid, and great help I find them in the business I'm carrying on. They are constantly on the lookout for runaways or refugees, and are quite as good as bloodhounds to scent one. They told me about *you*, and I watched and saw you go into that cave, which is on my land, and which few know about, or if they do they think it a springhole, and never dream that anybody can hide in there. Somebody else must have seen you, too, for word came that a man was hiding in the mountains, and as the acknowledged leader of as hard a set as ever hunted a Yankee, I went with 'em to find you, and carried in my pocket that bacon and corn bread which I managed to drop into the cave when I sat with my back against it. I knew you must be hungry, and it might be some time before I could come to your aid. We didn't find the chap; but to-morrow they'll be at it again, and so, while I help 'em hunt for a man about your build, you will stay in the room in Lois's charge. Maude has a good many gimcracks here, such as books and things, which may amuse you. She is coming home by and by. The house is very different then. You ought to see Maude. We are very proud of her. That's her picture, only not half so good-looking," and he pointed to a small oil painting hanging above the mantel.

It was a splendid head, and the glossy black hair bound about it in heavy braids gave it a still more regal look. The eyes, too, were black, but very soft and gentle in their expression, though something about them gave the impression that they might flash and blaze brilliantly under excitement. It was a beautiful face, and Will did not wonder that his host was proud of his niece,—prouder even than of the pale-faced, delicate boy, who next day, while the hunt for the runaway went on among the mountains, tried to entertain Will Mather by telling him of his old home in North Carolina, and how happy they were there before the war came and took his father away.

"I don't see it in the light Uncle Paul and sister do," Charlie said. "I don't want them to catch and torment the prisoners, or murder folks who don't think as they do; but I *do* want our side to succeed, and when I hear of a victory I say 'Hurrah for the Confederacy!' I can't help it when I think of father, who was killed by the Yankees, and all the trouble the war has brought. I'm willing to work like a dog for the refugees and prisoners, and I'd die sooner than betray one, but if I was a man I'd join Mr. Davis's army sure."

The pale face of the boy was flushed all over, and his dark eyes burned with Southern fire as he frankly avowed his sentiments, and Will Mather could not repress a smile at this noble specimen of a Southern rebel.

"I like you, my boy, for your frankness," he said, "and when the war is over, I shall have to send for you to come North and be cured of your treason."

"It is not *treason*," and the boy stamped his girlish foot. "It is not treason any more than the views held by the Revolutionary soldiers. Didn't the colonies secede from England, and does anybody call Washington a traitor now? I tell you it is *success* which decides the nature of the thing. If we succeed, future historians will speak of us as patriots, as a persecuted people, who gave our lives in defence of our homes and firesides."

"You won't succeed, my poor boy. The Confederacy is gasping its last breath. You will be conquered at the last, and then what have you gained?"

"Nothing,—nothing but ruin!" and the tears poured over the white face of this defender of Southern rights.

Soon recovering himself, however, he exclaimed, proudly:

"We may be conquered, but not subjugated. You can't do that with all your countless hordes of men, and your millions of money. The North can never subjugate the South. We may lay down our arms because we have no other alternative, but we shall still think the same, and feel the same as we do now."

Here was a curious study for Will Mather, who was surprised to find such maturity of thought and so strong determination in one so young and frail.

"No wonder it is hard to conquer a people composed of such elements," he thought, and he was about to continue the conversation when he was startled by a loud blast from a horn among the hills.

"They've caught some one. They always do that as a kind of exultation," the boy exclaimed, wringing his hands, and evincing as much distress as he had heretofore shown bitterness against the opposing party.

It was a poor refugee from a neighboring county, whom, in spite of Paul Haverill's precautions, they had found in a hollow tree, and whom they brought more dead than alive down to the Oak Plantation, amid vociferous cries of "Tar and feather him!" "Hang him to a sour-apple tree!" "Give him a taste of the halter!" "Make him an example to all other sneaking Yankee sympathizers!"

With his face as white as marble, and his lips set firmly together, Paul Haverill stood in the midst of the noisy group which he tried to quiet.

"Let us try him by jury," he said, and something in his voice reassured the frightened, haggard wretch, who had seen his house burned down and his son shot before his very eyes, and of course expected no mercy.

The trial by jury proved popular, and then Paul Haverill suggested that a judge be chosen in the person of some one who had lost a near friend in the war, and was of course competent to mete out full justice to the criminal— "Charlie, for instance," and his eye fell on the boy, who had joined the crowd and was standing close by the prisoner. The boy caught his uncle's meaning at once, and exclaimed:

"Yes, let *me* be the judge. My father was killed at Bull Run. My mother died of grief. Surely I may decide."

Charlie De Vere was a favorite with the men, who knew how staunch a Confederate he was, and, waiving the trial for want of time, they said:

"Charlie shall decide whether we hang, drown, whip, or tar and feather the prisoner at the bar."

Then, with far more energy and fire than had characterized his vindication of the South, Charlie De Vere pleaded for the criminal, that they would *let him go.* "Just this once, for father's sake, and mine, and Maude's," he said; and, at the mention of Maude, the dark brows began to clear, and the scowling faces grew more lenient in their expression, for Maude De Vere was worshiped by the rough men of the mountains, who, though they knew her sympathies were on the Union side, made an exception in her favor, and held her person and opinions sacred. For *her* sake, they would let their captive go, giving him warning to leave the neighborhood at once, nor let himself be seen again in their midst while the war lasted.

And thus it chanced that Will Mather had a companion in his wanderings, which were renewed the following day; the boy Charlie acting as guide through the most dangerous part of the way, and at last bidding him good-bye, with great tears in his eyes, as he said:

"I hope you won't be caught; but I don't know, the woods are full of our soldiers. Travel at night, and hide through the day. Trust no one, but the negroes; and if you are captured, ask for mercy in sister's name. Everybody knows Maude De Vere."

CHAPTER XXVIII
THE DEAD ALIVE.

It was the night of the third of July, the anniversary, as she supposed, of her husband's death, and Rose was sitting up unusually late. She could not sleep for thinking of one year ago, and the white-faced man who lay upon the battle-field with the rain falling upon him.

It was a clear starlight night, and she leaned many times from her open window and looked up at the kindly eyes keeping watch above her. But she did not see the figure coming down the street and up the walk to their own door; the figure of a worn-out soldier, who from the prison at Salisbury had escaped to Tennessee, and had come from thence straight on until the midnight train dropped him at the Rockland station.

The light was behind her, and Will saw *her* distinctly as he went up the avenue, and he stopped a moment to look at her. She was very pale, and much thinner than when he saw her last, but never, even on her bridal day, had she seemed so beautiful to him as then, when leaning from her window, and apparently listening for something.

It was the sound of his footsteps as he came up the walk which had attracted her attention, and when it ceased so suddenly as he stopped under the trees, she felt a momentary pang of fear, for burglars had been very common in the town that summer. Possibly this was one of the robbers, and Rose was thinking of alarming the house, when the figure emerged from under the shadow of the trees, and came directly up beneath the window, while a voice which made Rose's blood curdle in her veins, called softly,

"Rose, darling, is it you?"

Had the dead come back to life? Was that her husband's voice, and that his step in the lower hall? Rose had supposed the front door bolted. She had not heard it open, and now, when the steps sounded upon the stairs, her heart gave one throb of fear, as all the old superstitious stories of New England lore rushed to her mind. Perhaps on this anniversary of his death he *had* come back to see her. And perhaps——

Rose did not finish the sentence, for the opening of her own door disclosed the wasted figure of a man wearing the army blue, his face very pale, but lighted up with perfect joy as he stretched his arms toward the shrinking woman by the window, and said:

"Come to me, darling; I am no ghost."

Then she went to him, but uttered no sound. Her heart was too full for that, and seemed bursting from her throat as she laid her head upon the bosom of her husband, and felt his arms around her waist and neck. Her stillness frightened him, it was so unlike her, and lifting her from the floor, he took her in his lap, and said to her:

"Speak to me, Rose. Let me hear your voice once more. You thought I was dead, and you've been so sorry."

"Yes, killed at Gettysburgh," came gaspingly at last; and then a storm of tears and kisses fell upon Will's face, and Rose's arms were thrown about his neck as she tried to tell him how great was her joy to have him back again.

"I have been so lonely," she said, "for everybody is gone. Jimmie and Annie, and poor Tom, too, is a prisoner at last, so mother and I are all alone, except"——

Just then it occurred to her that her husband had no suspicion of the great joy in store for him.

"How shall I tell him?" she thought, and her eyes went from his face to the basket and chair where baby's clothes were lying.

The little white dress, with its shoulder knots of blue; the flannels and the soft wool socks were all there in plain sight, and Will saw them, too, as his eye followed Rose's.

"Rose, tell me, what is that? What does it mean?" he asked, and then, without a word, Rose led him into the adjoining room, where in his crib slumbered her beautiful boy,—*their* beautiful boy rather. He was hers alone no longer, for the father was there now, and the happiest moment he had ever known was that when he knelt by his baby's cradle, and felt how much he had for which to thank his Maker. He could not wait till morning before he heard the sound of his first-born's voice, and he took him at once in his arms, every pulse thrilling with pride and exquisite delight, as he felt the soft, baby hands in his own, and looked into the beautiful dark eyes which met his so wonderingly as baby awoke and gazed up into his face. It was not afraid of him, and Rose almost danced with joy as she saw it smile in its father's face, and then turn slily away.

"It was so terrible till baby came last Christmas," she said, beginning to explain how they believed him dead, and how much she had suffered. "Even baby did not make me as glad as it ought," she continued, "for I could not forget how happy you would have been to come home and find him here, and now you've come. God is very, very good; I love him now, Will, better, I hope than I love you, or baby, or anything. I've given baby to Him and given myself, too, but he had to punish me so hard before I would do it."

Then together the re-united couple knelt and thanked the Father who had remembered them so mercifully, and asked that henceforth their lives might be dedicated to his service, and all they had be subject to his will. There was no more sleep in the Mather mansion that night, for by the time Mrs. Carleton and the servants had recovered from their surprise and joy, the early morning was red in the east, and the sun was just beginning to show the returned soldier how pleasant and beautiful his home was looking.

The people of Rockland had not intended to have much of a celebration on that Fourth of July. The churchyard was too full of soldiers' graves, and the war-clouds were still too dark over the land, while the battle of the Wilderness, where so many had perished, was too fresh in their minds to admit of much festivity; but when it was known that Will Mather had come home the town was all on fire with excitement. Every bell was rung, and the cannon of Bill Baker memory bellowed forth its welcome, while in the evening impromptu fireworks attested to the people's delight. Then followed many days of delicious quiet in which Will told his wife and mother the story of his wanderings, but said very little of his life in Salisbury. That was something he could not mention without a shudder, and so he passed it over in silence, choosing rather to tell of his journey across the mountains, where so many friendly hands had been stretched out to help him. He had every name upon paper, and was only waiting for an opportunity to show his gratitude in some tangible form. Especially was he grateful to Paul Haverill, whose name became a household word, together with that of Charlie and Maude De Vere. Of her Rose thought so often, wishing she could see her, and resolving when the war was over either to write at once or go all the way to the Mountains of Tennessee to find her.

"Poor Tom!" she often sighed. "If he could only fall into so friendly hands."

But everything pertaining to Tom was shrouded in gloom. The last they heard he was in Columbia, while Jimmie still pined in Andersonville, if indeed he had not died amid its horrors. Exchanged prisoners were constantly arriving at Annapolis, where both Mrs. Simms and Annie were, and every letter from the latter was eagerly torn open by Rose in hopes that it might contain some news of her brothers. But there was none, and the mourning garments which, with her husband's return, were exchanged for lighter, airier ones, seemed only laid aside for a few weeks until word should come that one or both of her brothers were with the dead whose graves were far away beneath a Southern sky.

CHAPTER XXIX.
THE HEROINE OF THE MOUNTAIN.

Of the three captives, Will Mather, Jimmie, and Tom, the latter had suffered the least as a prisoner of war. A strong Freemason, he had found friends at Columbia, where chance threw in his way a near relation of his dead wife and a former classmate. Though firmly believing in the Southern cause, Joe Haskell from the first befriended Captain Carleton, whom he finally helped to escape, giving him money, and so far as he was able, directions where to go and whom to ask for aid. Tom's imprisonment had been of short duration, and thus it was, with vigor unimpaired and spirits unbroken, that he found himself free on that very night when Will Mather lay sleeping in the cave among the mountains of Tennessee. But that "Refuge of Safety" was many, many miles away, and Tom's route to the land of freedom was a longer and far more dangerous one than Will's had been. Still Tom had in his favor health and strength, together with a knack of passing himself off as a Southerner whenever an opportunity was presented, and so for a week or more he proceeded with comparatively little trouble; but at the end of that time dangers and difficulties beset him at every step, while more than once death or recapture stared him in the face, either from the close proximity of his pursuers, or the pertinacity of the bloodhounds which were set upon his track. Escape at times seemed impossible, and Tom's courage and strength were beginning to give way, when one night, toward the last of June, he found himself in a negro cabin, and an occupant of a bed whose covering, though impregnated with the peculiar odor of the sable-hued faces around him, seemed the very embodiment of sweetness and cleanliness to the tired and footsore man, who nearly all his life had slept in the finest linen, with lace or silken hangings about his bed. For linen now there was a ragged quilt, and the bed was festooned with cobwebs, while from the blackened rafters hung bundles of herbs and strings of peppers, alternated here and there with the grimy articles of clothing which old Hetty had washed that day for her own "boys," and in consequence of the rain had hung in her cabin to dry. Coarse, heavy shirts they were, but Tom, as he watched them drying on the pole, fell to coveting the uncouth things, and thought how soft and nice they would feel on his rough flesh. Then he thought of home and Rose, and wondered what she would say could she look in upon him in that negro hut, with all those stalwart boys sitting by, while Hetty, their mother, cooked the corn-cake, and fried the slice of bacon for supper. Two sat just where Tom could see them, while the third was near the door, keeping a constant watch on the circuitous path leading from the cabin to a large dwelling on the knoll,— "Marsr's house,"—where to-night a number of young people were assembled in honor of the return of the son and heir, Lieut. Arthur, who had been in so many battles, and had a taste of prison life at the North.

Though bitterly opposed to the Unionists, Arthur was truthful, almost to a fault, as some of his auditors thought to whom he was recounting the incidents of his prison life. Comfortable beds, decent bread, well-cooked meat, with plenty of pure air and water, *he* had received from the hands of his enemies; and once, when for a few days he was sick, he had been fed with toast and jelly, and tea quite as good as Hetty could make, he said. And while he talked more than one present thought of the Southern prisons, where so many men were dying from starvation and neglect; and one young girl's eyes flashed angrily, and her nostrils quivered with passion as she burst out with the exclamation:

"That's the story most of our prisoners tell when they come back to us. Think you a like report will be carried North, if the poor wretches ever live to get there! I think it a shame to allow such suffering in our midst."

This speech, which had in it the ring of Unionism, did not startle the hearers as much as might be expected. They were accustomed to Maude De Vere's outspoken way, and they knew that when she first came among them she was on the Federal side, and had opposed the secession movement with all the force of her girl nature. As yet no harm had been threatened her, for Maude was one to whom all paid deference, and her clear arguments touching the right of secession had done much toward keeping alive a feeling of humanity for our prisoners in the family where for months she had been a guest.

Squire Tunbridge—or Judge, as he was frequently called—was her near relative, and as his only daughter had died only two years before, and he was very lonely in his great house, he had invited Maude to visit him, and insisted upon her staying as long as possible. At first he had laughed at her Yankee preferences, but when the deaths at Salisbury and Andersonville increased so fast, he shook his head sadly and protested against the cruelty and neglect of the government. "He did not believe in killing men by inches," he said; "better shoot them at once." And still he would not willingly have harbored a runaway on his premises, for fear of the odium which would attach to him if the fact were known.

And so, when late that night, while Tom lay sleeping in Hetty's cabin, and Hetty, up at the big house, was waiting upon the guests and making secret signs to Maude De Vere, there came a band of men into the yard in pursuit of an escaped Yankee, the Squire roused at once, saying that no one could possibly be hidden on his plantation unless the blacks had secreted him. The negro houses were close by; they could look for themselves. He had supposed his servants loyal, but there was no telling in these perilous times; and the old man's face flushed as his Southern blood fired his zeal for the Southern cause.

In her evening dress of white, with her bands of glossy black hair bound like a coronet around her regal brow, Maude De Vere stood leaning upon the piano, her eyes shining like burning coals, and her lips slightly parted as she listened to the conversation, and then darted an anxious glance toward the spot where Hetty had been standing a moment before. But Hetty had disappeared, and under cover of darkness was running and rolling and slipping down the steep wet path, which led to her cabin door.

Arrived there, she seized the sleeping Tom by the arm, and exclaimed:

"Wake up, mars'r, for de dear lord's sake! De Seshioners is come, and will be here in a minute! I'm mighty 'fraid even Miss Maude can't save you!"

Tom was awake in a moment and fully alive to the danger of his condition. From the house on the knoll, he could hear the excited voices of his pursuers, and the sound made every pulse throb with fear.

"Tell me what to do," he said, and Hetty replied,

"Kin you bar smotherin' for a spell? If you kin, git under de ole straw tick, and lie right still and flat, and you, Hal, buckle into marsr's place, as if 'twas you who've been lyin' here all the time."

Tom did not hesitate a moment, and had just straightened himself under the straw bed, and drawn a long breath as he felt Harry's body settling down above him, when steps were heard coming down the path, and a young man's voice asked of Hetty if she had any strangers there—"any Yankees, you know; because if you have—" the young man paused a moment and peered out into the night to make sure that no one was listening, then, in a whisper, he added, "Keep them safe, and remember, Fleetfoot knows all the passes of the mountains between here and Tennessee."

A suppressed "thank God!" might almost have been heard beneath the straw bed, while old Hetty exclaimed,

"The Lord bless Mars'r Arthur, and Miss Maude, too! I know it is her doins."

And Hetty was right, for Tom Carleton owed his escape from that great peril, to Maude De Vere rather than to Lieutenant Arthur. "When the order was given to search the negro quarters, Arthur had seen that in Maude's face which constrained him to follow her when she beckoned to him to come out upon the piazza.

"Arthur," she said, putting her lips to his ear, "remember the kind treatment you received from your enemies, and be merciful. Don't let them find him, for there *is* a Yankee soldier down in Hetty's cabin. She told me to-night. Search her house yourself. Throw them off the track. Anything to mislead them. Be merciful. Do it, Arthur, for *my* sake."

Always beautiful, Maude De Vere was dazzlingly so now, as she stood before the young officer pleading for Tom Carleton, and Arthur Tunbridge was more influenced by her beauty, than by any party feelings. Assuming a fierce, determined manner, he went back to the pursuers and said,

"It's perfectly preposterous that one of those Unionists should come here for protection, when it is well known what we are. Still it may be. There's no piece of effrontery they are not capable of. I know them well, just as I knew every nook and corner of the negro cabins. Stay here, gentlemen, and take some refreshment while I search the quarters myself."

Arthur Tunbridge wore a lieutenant's uniform. He had been in the army from the very first; he had fought in many a battle; had been a prisoner for four months, while his father was known to be a staunch secessionist, who was ready to sacrifice all he had for the success of the cause he believed to be so just and righteous. There could be no cheating in such a family as this, and so, while Maude De Vere wore her most winning smile, and with her own hands served cake and coffee to the soldiers, Lieutenant Arthur went on his tour of investigation, and brought back word that not a trace of a runaway had he found, notwithstanding that every cabin on the premises had been visited. A savage oath was the answer to this report, but something in Maude's eyes kept the soldiers in check and made them tolerably civil, as they mounted their horses, and with a respectful good-night, rode off in an opposite direction.

With a feeling of security after hearing from Hetty of Maude De Vere, Tom came out from his hiding-place and ventured to the open door of the cabin, where he stood looking at the "big house" on the hill, from which the guests were just departing. He could hear their voices as they said good night, and fancied he could detect the clear, well-bred tones of Maude De Vere, in whom he began to feel so deeply interested. He could see the flutter of her white dress as she stood against a pillar of the piazza, with Arthur at her side, but her back was toward him, and he could only see her well shaped head, which sat so erect and proudly upon her shoulders. She was very tall, Tom thought, comparing her with Mary, Annie, and petite Rose as she walked across the piazza with Arthur, who, from comparison seemed the shorter of the two. Profoundly grateful to her as his probable deliverer, Tom went back into the cabin and began to question Hetty with regard to the young lady. Who was she, and where did she live, and how came she so strong a Unionist?

"She's Miss Maude De Vere, bred and born in the old North State, somewhars near Tar Run." Aunt Hetty said "Her father was killed at first Bull Run, and then her mother died, and she went to live with her uncle off toward Tennessee in de hills. She's got an awful sight of money, and heaps of niggers,—lazy, no count critters,—who jest do nothing from morn till night. She and Miss Nettie, Mars'r Tunbridge's gal, was great friends at school, and Miss Maude was here when she died, and has been here by spells ever since. Young mars'r think she mighty nice, but dis chile don't 'zactly know what Miss Maude do think of him. Reckon he's too short, or too sessionary to suit her."

This was Hetty's account of the young lady, who at that very moment was listening with a defiant look upon her face to Arthur Tunbridge's remonstrance against what he termed her treasonable principles.

"They will get you into trouble yet. The war is not over, as some would have you think. The North is greatly divided. Be warned of me, Maude, and do not run such risks as you do by openly avowing your Union sentiments. Think what it would be to me if harm should befall you, Maude."

Arthur spoke very gently now, while a deep flush mounted to his beardless cheek, but met with no reflection from Maude De Vere's face. Only her eyes kindled and grew blacker, if possible, as she listened to him, first with scorn, when he spoke of treason, and then with pity when he spoke of himself, and the pain it would cause him if harm should come to her.

Maude knew very well the nature of the feelings with which her kinsman, young Arthur Tunbridge, regarded her. At first she had been disposed to laugh at him, and his preference for an Amazon, as she styled herself; but Arthur had proved by actual measurement that in point of height he excelled her by half an inch, while the register showed that in point of age he had the advantage of her by more than four years, though Maude seemed the elder of the two.

"Don't be foolish, Arthur, nor entertain fears for me," she said. "I am not afraid of Gen. Lee's entire army, nor Grant's either, for that matter. My home at Uncle Paul's has been beset alternately by either party, and I have held a loaded pistol at the heads of both Federal and Confederate, when one was for leading away Charlie's favorite horse, and the other for coaxing off old Lois to cook the company's rations. No, I am not afraid, and if necessary I will guide that poor wretch down in Hetty's cabin safely to Tennessee."

Arthur's face grew dark at once, and he said, half angrily:

"Maude, let that man alone; let them all alone. It is not womanly for you to evince so much interest in such people. For your sake I'll help this one get away, but that must be the last; and remember, it is done for *your* sake, with the expectation of reward. Do you consent to the terms?"

Maude's nostrils quivered as she drew her tall figure to its full height, and answered back:

"I could not prize the love I had to buy. No, Arthur; I have told you once that you are only my brother, just as Nettie was my sister. Believe me, Arthur, I cannot give you what you ask."

She spoke gently, kindly, now, for she pitied the young man whose sincerity she did not doubt, but whose love she could not return. He was not her equal, either physically or mentally, and the man who won Maude De Vere must be one to whom she could look up to as a superior. Such an one she would make very happy, but she would lead Arthur a wretched, miserable life, and she knew it, and would save him from herself, even though there were many kindly, tender feelings in her heart for the young lieutenant.

She saw that he was angry with her, and as further conversation was useless, she left him and repaired to her room, the windows of which overlooked Hetty's cabin.

And there until daylight the noble girl sat watching lest their unwelcome visitors of the previous night, failing to find their victim, should return and insist upon another search. As Maude De Vere said, she had held a loaded pistol at the head of both Federal and Confederate, when her uncle was sick, and the house was beset one week by one of the belligerent parties and the following week by the other. She was afraid of nothing, and Tom Carleton, so long as she stood his sentinel, had little to fear from his pursuers. But she could not ward off the fever which for many days had been lurking in his veins, and which was increasing so fast that when the morning came he was too sick to rise, and lay moaning with the pain in his eyes and complaining of the heat, which, in that dark corner of the close cabin, and on that sultry summer morning, was intolerable.

"Mighty poorly, with face as red as them flowers in yer ha'r, and the veins in his forehead as big as my leg," was the word which Hetty brought up to Maude De Vere the next morning, and half an hour later Maude, in her pale buff cambric wrapper, with her black hair shining like satin, went down to Hetty's cabin and stood beside Tom Carleton.

He was sleeping for a few moments, and the drops of perspiration were standing on his forehead and about his lips. He was not worn and emaciated, like the most of the prisoners and refugees whom Maude had seen. His complexion, though bronzed from exposure, had not that peculiar greyish appearance common to so many of the returned prisoners, while his forehead was very white, and his rich brown hair, damp with the perspiration, clung about it in the soft, round curls so natural to it.

There was nothing in his personal appearance to awaken sympathy on the score of ill-treatment, and yet Maude felt herself strangely drawn toward him, guessing with a woman's quick perception that he was somewhat above many whom it had been her privilege to befriend. And Maude, being human, did not like him less for that. On the contrary, she the more readily brushed away the flies which were alighting upon his face, and with her own handkerchief, wiped the moisture from his brow, and then felt his rapid pulse.

"He ought not to stay in this place," she said, and she was revolving the propriety of boldly asking Squire Tunbridge if he might be removed to the house, when Tom awoke and turned wonderingly toward her.

He knew it was Maude De Vere, and something in her face riveted his attention, making him wonder where he had seen somebody very like her.

"You are sick," she said to him kindly, as he attempted to rise on his elbow, and fell back again upon the squalid bed. "I am afraid you are very sick, but you are safe here,—that is,—yes,—I know you are safe. None but fiends would betray a sick man."

She spoke rapidly, and Tom saw the bright color deepen in her cheek, and her eyes flash with excitement. She was very beautiful, and Tom felt the influence of her beauty, and tried to draw the ragged quilt over him so as to hide the coarse, grey shirt Hetty had given him, and which was as unlike the immaculate linen Tom Carleton was accustomed to wear as it was possible to be.

"You are Miss De Vere, I'm sure," he said, "and you are very kind. I shall not tax your hospitality long. I hope to go on to-night. Don't stay here, Miss De Vere; you must be uncomfortable. It's hotter here than in Massachusetts."

"You are from New England, then?" Maude asked, and Tom replied:

"From Boston,—yes,—your people hate us most of all I believe," and Tom tried to smile, while Maude answered him,

"It makes no difference to me whether you are from Maine or Oregon. You are sick and have come to us for succor. I'll do what I can to help you."

With the last words she was gone, her tall, lithe figure bending gracefully under the low doorway, and the rustle of her fresh, clean garments leaving a pleasant sound in Tom Carleton's ears.

"A sick Yankee down in Hetty's cabin,—a Boston one at that, with his Wendell Phillips notions, and you want me to let him be brought up to *this house*, the house of a Southern gentleman, who, if he hates one of the dogs worse than another, hates the Massachusetts kind, whose women have nothing to do but to write Abolition books about our niggers. No, indeed; he shall not come an inch, and by the Harry I'll send for the authorities and have him bundled off to jail before night, with his camp fever, and his Boston airs. Needn't talk. See if I don't do it, and I'll have Hetty strung up and whipped for harboring the villain. Treason under my very nose, and a Yankee, too! Go away,—go away, I tell you. I won't hear you. I hate 'em all for the cussedness there is in 'em."

This was Squire Tunbridge's reply to Maude De Vere, who had told him of Tom Carleton, and asked permission to have him moved up to the house. Nothing daunted, Maude went close up to him, and her beautiful eyes looked straight into his as she said:

"Think if it was Arthur sick among his enemies. They were kind to him, he says, and remember Nettie, too. Had she lived she would have married a Northern man. You liked Robert, and Nettie loved him. For her sake let this man be brought to the house. He will die there, where it is so close."

"Serve him right for coming down here to fight us; wish they were all dead. How are you going to get the rascal up that confounded hill? Can he walk?"

Maude had gained her point, and with Mrs. Tunbridge, who had a soft, kind heart, she hastened to make ready a large, airy chamber, somewhat remote from the rooms occupied by the family and their frequent guests. It was not the best room in the house, but he would be safer there than elsewhere, and Maude made it as inviting as possible, by pulling the bed out from the corner to the centre of the room, covering the plain stand with a clean, white towel, and the table with a gaily-colored shawl of her own. Then with Hetty and one of Hetty's sons she started for the cabin, followed by the Squire himself. Since the war began he had not seen a Yankee, and curiosity as much as anything took him to Tom Carleton, whom he assailed with a string of epithets, telling him "to see what he'd got by making war on people so much better than himself. Good enough for you," he continued, as, assisted by Hetty and Claib, Tom tried to walk up the winding path, with Maude in front and the Squire in the rear. "Yes, good enough for you, if you die like a dog, and I dare say you will. Fevers go hard with you Bunker Hill chaps. *Claib*, you villain, you are letting him fall. Don't you see he hasn't strength to walk? Carry him, you rascal!" And thus changing the nature of his tirade the Squire thrust his cane against Tom's back by way of assisting him up the hill.

He was human if he was not quite consistent, and his face was very red, and he was very much out of breath when the house was reached at last, and Tom was comfortably disposed in bed.

"For thunder's sake, Hetty, take that grey, niggery thing off from him," the Squire said, pointing to the coarse shirt Tom had thought so nice, when he exchanged it for his dirty uniform. "If you women are going to do a thing, do it decent. Arthur's shirts won't fit him, I reckon, for Arthur ain't bigger than a pint of cider, but mine will. Fetch him one, and for gracious sake souse him first in the bath-tub. He needs it bad, for them prison pens ain't none the neatest according to the tell."

In spite of his aversion to the Boston Yankees, the Judge had taken the ordering of this one into his own hands, and it was to him that Tom owed the refreshing bath which did him so much good, and abated the force of the fever, which nevertheless ran high for many days, during which time Maude nursed him as carefully as if he had been her brother. Arthur was absent when the moving occurred, but when he found that it was done, and the Yankee was actually an inmate of his father's house, he concluded to make the best of it, merely remarking that "they would be in a pretty mess if the story got out of their harboring a prisoner."

The Judge knew that, and in fancy he saw his house burned down, and himself, perhaps, ridden on a rail by his justly incensed neighbors. The fear wore upon him terribly, until a new idea occurred to him. Maude, as everybody knew, had long been talking of going back to Tennessee, and what more natural than for Paul Haverill to send an escort for her in the person of some cousin or other, who was foolish enough to fall sick immediately after his arrival. This was a *smart* thought; and as that very day at least a dozen people called at the Cedars, as the Judge called his place, so the dozen were told of "John Camp," sick abed up stairs, "kind of cousin to Maude, and sent to see her home, by her Uncle Paul."

"Right smart chap," the Judge said, feeling amazed at the facility with which he invented falsehoods when once he began. "Been a *guerrilla* there in the mountains, and done some tall fightin', I reckon."

This was the Judge's story, which his auditors believed, wondering, some of them, why the visitor should occupy that back chamber in preference to the handsome rooms in front. Still they had no suspicion of the truth. "John Camp" was accepted as a reality, and kind inquiries were made after his welfare, as, day after day, the fever ran its course, and Maude De Vere bent over him, bathing his forehead, smoothing his pillows, and brushing his hair, her white fingers insinuating queer fancies into his brain, as, half unconscious, he felt their touch upon his face, and saw the soft eyes above him.

At first Arthur had kept aloof from Tom, but as the latter grew better, he yielded to Maude's entreaties and went in to see him, feeling intuitively that he was in the presence of a gentleman as well as of a superior. He could not dislike him, for there was something about Tom Carleton which disarmed him of all prejudice, and many a quiet, friendly talk the two had together on the all-absorbing topic of the day.

"He is a splendid fellow, if he is a Yankee," was Arthur's mental verdict, "and fine looking, too,—finer a hundred times than I," and then there crept into his heart a fear lest Maude should think as he did, and ere he was aware of it, he found himself fiercely jealous of one who was at his mercy, and whom, if he chose, he might have removed so easily.

CHAPTER XXX.
ARTHUR AND MAUDE.

Tom Carleton was able to start on his journey westward. Twice he had left his room and joined the family below, making himself so agreeable, and adapting himself so nicely to all the Judge's crotchets that the old man confessed to a genuine liking for the *Yankee rascal*, and expressed himself as unwilling to part with him. He had inquired into his family history, and, to his infinite delight, found that the elder Carleton, Tom's father, was the very lawyer whose speech years ago, had been instrumental in sending back to bondage the Judge's runaway negro, Hetty's husband, whose grave was out by the garden wall, and whose wife and sons had rendered so different a service to the lawyer's son.

Tom's face was scarlet when he thought of the difference, and remembered how his father had worked to prove that the master was entitled to his property wherever it was found. The Judge suspected the nature of his thoughts, and with a forced laugh, said, goodhumoredly:

"You are more of an abolitionist than your father was, I see. Well, well, young man, times change, and we change with them. Old man Carleton did me a good turn, for Seth was worth two thousand dollars. I never abused him, nor gave him a blow when I got him back. I only asked him how he liked freedom as far as he had gone, and he didn't answer. He seemed broke down like, and in less than a year he died. He was the best hand I ever had, more'n half white. I cried when he died. I'll be hanged if I didn't. I told him to live and I'd set him free, and when I see how his eyes lighted up I made out his papers on the spot, and brought 'em to him, and he died with 'em in his hand, held so tight we could scarcely get 'em out, and I had 'em buried with him in his coffin.

"'Thank you, mars'r, God bless you for letting me die free, but it's come too late. I would worked for you, mars'r, all the same, if you'd done this before. I wanted to be a *man*, and not a *thing*, a brute. You have been kind to me mars'r; thank you, thank you for liberty.'

"These are Seth's very words. I got 'em by heart, and I said them so much that I began to wonder if freedom wasn't better than slavery. But, bless you, my niggers was about all I had. I couldn't give 'em up, though I used to go out to Seth's grave and think how he hugged the papers to the last, and wonder if the clause 'all men are born free and equal,' didn't mean the blacks. But the pesky war broke out, and drove all this from my head. I hate the Yankees,—I hate Lincoln. I hate the whole Union army, though I'll be blamed if I can hate *you*. Got a wife, hey?"

He turned abruptly to his guest, who had listened with so breathless interest to the story of poor Seth, that he did not see Maude De Vere, her eyes shining, and her cheeks flushed, as if she were under some strong excitement.

Between herself and Arthur there had been a long conversation concerning Captain Tom Carleton, and other matters of greater interest to Maude. The "John Camp" ruse had succeeded well, and Maude had a fancy for making it do still more, by taking her patient in safety as far as her Uncle Haverill's. She had received several letters from her uncle, urging her to come home, and in a week at most she was going. As one who had been expressly sent as her escort, Mr. Carleton would of course go with her, and in order to make the journey with perfect safety she would have Arthur go too, and it was of this that she had spoken to him that morning when she found him in a little summer-house at the rear of the long garden. There was a dark shadow on Arthur's face, as he listened to Maude's proposition, and when she had finished speaking, he replied:

"I intend to go with you, provided I am not ordered back to the army, but, Maude, I will not have that Yankee soldier hanging on to us. We have done that for him which imperils our lives, and now that he is able to go on, let him take his chance alone. If he is one half as keen as Yankees think themselves to be, he will get through unharmed. No, I won't have him in our way."

"But think of the dangers to be encountered, the hordes of guerrillas which infest the mountains," Maude pleaded, and in her earnestness she laid both her hands on Arthur's shoulder, and stood leaning over him.

"Maude De Vere," and Arthur spoke very decidedly, "*why* are you so much interested in this man? Tell me, and tell me truly, too,—have you learned to care for *him* more than you would for a *common soldier*, had such a one come to you as a runaway Yankee? If you have, Maude," and Arthur's face was white with determination, "if you have, by the heavens above us, I'll put a bullet through him myself, or worse than that, send him back to where he came from."

"That would be an act worthy of a Tunbridge and a Southern gentleman," Maude said, bitterly, and something in her tone warned Arthur that he had gone too far, so changing his tactics, he said more gently:

"Sit here beside me, Maude, and listen to what I have to say. You know that I have loved you ever since I knew the meaning of the word, and it is not in my nature to give up what my heart is set upon. You have refused me, but that does not matter. I want you for my wife; I must have you for my wife. I know you are my superior, and I am willing it should be so. You can fashion me into anything you like. I have screened, and hidden, and *lied* for that

Yankee Carleton, just to gratify you. And when I first consented to act the traitor's part, I supposed he was most likely some coarse, ignorant boor, but he is not. Returning health shows him to be a well-bred gentleman, and decidedly good-looking, so much so that I have been jealous of him, Maude, not knowing to what your strange opinions might lead you."

"You know of course he has a wife," dropped scornfully from Maude's lips, and Arthur started quickly.

"No, Maude, I did not know it. How came you by the knowledge? Did he tell you so?"

"Not directly, but when he was out of his head, or asleep, he talked of Rose, and Annie, and Mary, and he called the latter his wife. That is the way I know," Maude said, and Arthur's face cleared at once.

"Forgive me, Maude. I was a fool to be jealous of him. And now let us come to a final understanding. You have laughed at, and browbeaten, and queened it over me for years, but I have never despaired of winning you at the last. Once for all, then, will you be my wife? I must have you. I cannot be denied."

Arthur was in earnest now, and his pleadings were eloquent with the love he felt for the girl, who listened in silence, and then said to him:

"Arthur, it cannot be. I should make you very unhappy. We do not agree in any one point."

"But we will agree. I promise to conform to your opinions in everything. I'll guide this man to Tennessee, and give myself in future to the work of saving and helping the entire Yankee army. I'll be a second *Dan Ellis* if you like. I'll do anything but take the oath to the Union. I've sworn to stand by the other side. I cannot break my word even for you, Maude."

Maude did not like him less for that last. There was Southern fire in her heart as well as his, and Southern blood in her veins, and though she clung to the old flag, there were moments when she felt a flush of pride in her misguided brothers, who fought so like heroes and believed so heartily in their cause.

"Say, Maude," Arthur continued, "will you be my wife if I will do all this. Think how many lives I might save, and how much suffering relieve; there are so many chances where I could do good, for no one would suspect *me*. Give me some hope, Maude. Speak to me."

She was sitting with her face buried in her hands, as many another maiden has sat, "counting the cost." All her life long, Arthur Tunbridge had followed her with his love, till she was tired of the contest. Nothing she had ever said disheartened him. No rebuff, however severe, had availed to keep him quiet. She knew he loved her, and perhaps she might in time love him. It would make the old Judge and his wife so happy, while Charlie liked Arthur so much. Other people liked him, too. He was very popular, and she well knew that she was envied by many a proud maiden for the attentions of the agreeable Lieut. Tunbridge. Besides, if Arthur pledged himself to help the escape of prisoners, he would keep his word, and so through her much good might be done, and hearts made happy perhaps. Others had willingly sacrificed their lives for their country, and why should she shrink from sacrificing her happiness, if by it so many lives could be saved? Was it not her duty to cast self aside and think only of the suffering she could relieve with Arthur as her ally. Maude was selling herself for her country, and with one great throb of bitter pain, she said at last:

"I will deal frankly with you, Arthur, as I always have. You are not disagreeable to me. I like you very much as a friend. I miss you when you are away, and am glad when you come back; still, you are not just what I have imagined my future husband to be. I like you for the good I know there is in you, and I may learn to love you. I shall lead you a horrid life if I do not, for it is not in my nature to affect what I do not feel. If I cannot love you, I shall learn to hate you, and that will be terrible."

She was looking at him now, and though he winced a little beneath the blazing eyes, she looked so grand, so beautiful, that, foolish youth as he was, he fancied her hate would be preferable to losing her, and so he said:

"Go on, Maude, I am not afraid of the hatred if you always look as you do now."

Something like contempt leaped to her eyes then, but she put it aside, and continued:

"I will promise only on conditions. You shall see this Mr. Carleton safely to my Uncle Paul's. You shall befriend and help every runaway you chance to find. You shall relieve every suffering Union soldier when an opportunity occurs. You shall use your influence for the prisoners, and seek to ameliorate their wretched condition. If you do this, Arthur, and do it faithfully, when the war is over I will try to answer yes. Are you satisfied?"

It was a very one-sided affair, and Arthur knew it; but love for Maude De Vere was the strongest passion of which he was capable, and he answered:

"I am satisfied," and kissed the cold hand which Maude placed in his, and thought what a regal creature he had won, and thought, too, how implicitly he would keep the contract, even if it involved a giving up of Jefferson Davis himself into the enemy's hands.

CHAPTER XXXI.
MAUDE AND TOM.

It was then that Maude left him and went back to the house, where, standing in the door, she scanned the face and person of the man for whose safety in part she had pledged her heart and hand.

Tom's *tout ensemble* was good, and there was about him a certain air of grace and culture which showed itself in every movement. A stranger would have trusted him in a moment, and recognized the true manhood in his expressive face. And Maude recognized it, as she never had before, and the contrast between him and Arthur struck her painfully.

"If Arthur were more like him, I could love him better," she thought, just as the Judge asked the abrupt question:

"You have a wife, hey?"

"Of course he has," Maude thought, and still she listened for the answer.

"My wife died some years ago, before the war broke out. She was a Mary Williams, a near relative of the Williamses of Charleston. Perhaps you know them?"

"Know 'em! I'll bet I do!—the finest family in the State. And you married one of them?" the old Judge said, his manner indicating an increased respect for the man who had married a Williams of Charleston.

Maude knew the family, too, or rather knew of them, and remembered how, some years before, when she was at St. Mary's, she had heard a Charleston young lady speaking of a Mrs. Carleton from Boston, who had recently died, and whose husband had been so kind and patient and tender, and was "the most perfectly splendid looking man she ever saw."

Maude remembered this last distinctly, because it had called forth a reproof from the teacher who had overheard it, and who asked what kind of a man "the most perfectly splendid looking" one could be. Maude had not thought of that incident in years, but it came back to her now as she stood close to the man who had been so kind and tender to his sick, dying wife. He would be all that, she knew, for his manner was so quiet and grave and gentle, and then a great throb of pain swept over Maude De Vere as she thought of Arthur and the pledge she had given him. Maude could not analyze her feelings, or understand why the knowing who Tom Carleton was, and that he was also free, should make the world so desolate all on a sudden, and blot out the brightness of the summer day which had seemed so pleasant at its beginning.

"I did it in part for him," she said, feeling that in spite of her pain there was something sweet even in such a sacrifice.

She was still standing in the door, when Tom, turning a little more toward his host, saw her, his face lighting up at once, and the smile, which made him so handsome, breaking out about his mouth and showing his fine teeth.

"Ah, Miss De Vere, take this seat," and with that well-bred politeness so much a part of his family, he arose and offered her his chair.

But Maude declined it, and took a seat instead upon a little camp stool near to the vine-wreathed columns of the piazza.

It was very pleasant there that morning, and Maude, sitting against that background of green leaves, made a very pretty picture in her pink cambric wrapper, trimmed with white, white pendants in her ears, and a bunch of the sweet scented heliotrope in her hair, and at her throat where the smooth linen collar came together. And Tom enjoyed the picture very much, from the crown of satin hair, to the high-heeled slipper, with its bright ribbon rosette. It was not a little slipper, like those which used to be in Tom's dressing-room in Boston, when Mary was alive, nor yet like the fairy things which Rose Mather wore. Nothing about Maude De Vere was small, but everything was admirably proportioned. She wore a *seven* glove and she wore a *four* boot. She measured just twenty-five inches around the waist, and five feet six from her head to her feet, and weighed one hundred and forty. A perfect Amazon, she called herself; but Tom Carleton did not think so. He knew she was a large type of womanhood, but she was perfect in form and feature, and he would not have had her one whit smaller than she was, neither did he contrast her with any one he had ever known. She was so wholly unlike Mary and Rose and Annie, that comparison between them was impossible. She was Miss De Vere,—Maude he called her to himself, and the name was beginning to sound sweetly to him, as he daily grew more and more intimate with the queenly creature who bore it. He had buried his pale, proud-faced, but loving Mary; he had given up the gentle Annie, and surely he might think of Maude De Vere if he chose; and the sight of her sitting there before him with the rich color in her cheek, and the Southern fire in her eyes, stirred strange feelings in his heart, and made him so forgetful of what the Judge was saying to him, that the old man at last rose and walked away, leaving the two young people alone together. Tom had never talked much to Maude except upon sick-room topics, and he felt anxious to know if her mind corresponded with her face and form. Here was a good opportunity for testing her mental powers, and in the long, earnest conversation which ensued concerning men, and books, and politics, Tom sifted her thoroughly, experiencing that pleasure which men of cultivation always experience when thrown in contact with a woman whose intelligence and endowments are equal to their own. Maude's education had not been a superficial one, nor had it ceased with her leaving school. In her room at home there was a small library of choice books, which she read and studied each day together with her brother Charlie, whose education she superintended. Few persons North or South were better acquainted with the incidents and progress of the war, than she was. She had watched it from its beginning, and with her father, from whom she had inherited her superior mind, she had held many earnest argumentative discussions concerning the right and wrong of secession. Maude had opposed it from the first, but her father had thought differently, and carrying out his principles, had lost his life in the first battle of Bull Run. Maude spoke of him to Tom, and her fine eyes were full of tears as she told of the dark, terrible days which preceded and followed the news of his death.

"The ball which struck him down went further than that; it killed mother, too, and made us orphans," Maude said, and something in the tone of her voice, and the expression of her face, puzzled Tom just as it had many times before, and carried him back to Bull Run, where it seemed to him he had seen a face like Maude De Vere's.

"Was your father killed in battle?" Tom asked, and Maude replied:

"No, sir; that is, he did not die on the battle-field. He was wounded, and crawled away into the woods, where they found him dead, sitting against a tree, with a little Union drummer boy lying right beside him, and father's handkerchief bound round the poor bleeding stumps, for the little hands were both shot away. I've thought of that boy so often," Maude said, "and cried for him so much. I know father was kind to him, for the little fellow was nestled close to him, Arthur said. He was there, and found my father, though he did not at first recognize him, as it was a number of years since he had seen him."

Tom was growing both interested and excited. He was beginning to find the key to that familiar look in Maude De Vere's face, and, coming close to her he said:

"Were any prisoners taken near your father, Miss De Vere? Union prisoners, I mean?"

"Yes," Maude replied. "Arthur was a private, then, and, with another soldier, was prowling through the woods when they came upon father, and two Union soldiers near him,—one a boy, Arthur said, and one an officer, whose ankle had been sprained. In their eagerness to capture somebody they forgot my father, and carried off the man and boy. Then they went back, and Arthur found, by some papers in the dead soldier's pocket, that it was father, and he had him decently buried at Manassas, with the little boy. I liked Arthur for that. I would never have forgiven him if he left that child in the woods. When the war is over, I am going to find the graves."

She was not weeping now, but her eyes had in them a strange glitter as they looked far off in the distance, as if in quest of those two graves.

"Maude De Vere," Tom Carleton said, and at the sound, Maude started and blushed scarlet, "you must forgive me if I call you Maude this once. It's for the sake of your noble father, by whose side *I* stood when the spirit left his body, and went after that of the little drummer boy, whose bleeding stumps were bound in your father's handkerchief. I remember it well. I had sprained my ankle, and, with a lad of my company was trying to escape, when I heard the sound of some one singing that glorious chant of our church, 'Peace on earth, good will toward men.' It sounded strangely there, amid the dead and dying, who had killed each other; but there was peace between the Confederate captain and the Federal boy, as they sang the familiar words. As well as we could, we cared for him. I wiped the blood from your father's wound, and the boy brought him water from the brook, while he talked of his home in North Carolina; of his children who would never see him again; and of Nellie, his wife. It comes back to me with perfect distinctness, and it is your father's look in your eyes and face which has puzzled me so much. Two soldiers wearing the Southern grey came up and captured us, and we were taken to Richmond. Surely, Miss De Vere, it is a special providence which has brought me at last to you, the daughter of that man, and made you the guardian angel, who has stood between me and recapture. There is a meaning in it, if we could only find it."

Tom's fine eyes were bent upon Maude, and in his excitement he had grasped her hand, which did not lie as cold and pulseless in his as an hour before it had lain in Arthur's. It throbbed and quivered now, but clung to Tom's with a firm hold, which was not relaxed even when Arthur came up, his face growing dark and threatening as he saw the position of the two.

Maude did not care for Arthur then, or think what that look in Tom's kindling eyes might mean. She only remembered that the man whose hand held hers so firmly, had ministered to her dying father, had held the cup of water to his parched lip, had wiped the flowing blood from his face, and spoken to him kindly words of sympathy.

Here was the answer to her prayer, that God would send her somebody who could tell her of her father's last minutes. The somebody had come, and, in her gratitude to him, she could almost have knelt and worshiped him.

"Oh, Arthur!" she cried, "Captain Carleton is the very man you and Joe Newell captured at Bull Run. He was with father when he died; he took care of him, and was so kind until you came and took him."

And Maude's eyes flashed with anything but affection upon her lover, who for a moment could not speak for his surprise.

Curiously he looked at Tom, seeking for something on which to fasten a doubt, for he did not wish Maude to have a cause for gratitude to the Northern officer. But the longer he gazed the less he doubted. The face of the lame officer in the Virginia woods came up distinctly before him, and was too much like the face confronting him to admit of a mistake, especially after Maude repeated the substance of what she had heard from Captain Carleton. Arthur was convinced, and as Maude dropped Tom's hand, he took it in his, and said:

"It is very strange that my first prize, over whose capture I felt so proud, should fall again into my power. But this time you are safe, I reckon. I am older than I was three years ago, and not quite so thirsty for a Yankee's blood. You did Maude's father good service, it seems, and to prove that we *rebels* can be grateful and generous even to our foes, I will take you under my protection as one of my party, when I escort Maude home to Tennessee, as I intend doing in a few days."

Maude's face was white with passion as she listened to this patronizing speech, which had in it so much of assumed superiority over the man who smiled a very peculiar kind of smile, as he bowed his acknowledgment of Arthur's kind attentions. Not a hint was there that Maude was head and front of the arrangement,—that for Tom's sake she had pledged herself to one whose inferiority never struck her so painfully as now, when she saw him side by side with Captain Carleton. Arthur did not care to have Captain Carleton know how much he was indebted to Maude for his present pleasant quarters, and his prospect of a safe transfer to the hills of Tennessee. But Tom, though never suspecting the whole truth, did know that his gratitude for past and present kindness received from that Southern family was mainly due to Maude, whom he admired more and more, as the days wore on, and he learned to know her intimately. The shy reserve which since his convalescence she had manifested toward him, passed with the knowledge that he had stood by her dying father, and she treated him as a friend with whom she had been acquainted all her life long. Occasionally, as something in Tom's manner made her think that but for Arthur she might perhaps in time bear that relation toward him, which Mary Williams had borne, she felt a fierce throb of pain and a sense of such utter desolation, that she involuntarily rebelled against the life before her. But Maude was a brave, sensible girl. She had chosen her lot, she reasoned, and she would abide by it, and make Arthur as happy as she could. He was fulfilling his part of the contract well, as was proven by the terror-stricken creature, whom he had found hiding on the plantation, and had brought to Hetty's cabin, where he now lay so weak, that it was impossible to take him along on that journey to Tennessee.

"His time will come by and by," Arthur said, when Maude expressed anxiety for him. "I'll land him safely at your Uncle Paul's some night when you least expect it. My business now is with you and your Yankee captain."

Maude had asked that for the present nothing should be said with regard to their engagement. And so, though the Judge suspected that some definite arrangement had been made between his son and Maude, he did not know for certain, even when she stood before him attired for the journey.

The Judge was sorry to part with Maude, and he was sorry to part with Tom. He liked him because he was a gentleman if he *was* a Yankee, and because his father had sent *Seth* back, (poor Seth, with his free papers in his coffin,) and because he had been kind to Maude's father, and married Mary Williams, of the Charleston Williamses, and could smoke a cob-pipe, and enjoy it. These were the things which recommended Tom to the old man, who shook his hand warmly at parting, saying to him:

"I hate Northern dogs mostly, but hanged if I don't like you. May you get safely home, and if you do, my advice is to stay there, and tell the rest of 'em to do the same. They can't whip us,—no, by George, they can't, even if they have got some advantage. The papers say it was all a strategical trap, and we'd rather you'd have the places than not. You can't take Richmond,—no, sir! We will die in the last ditch, every mother's son of us; and what is left will set the town on fire, and let it go to thunder!"

The old Judge was waxing very eloquent for a man who had one Union soldier recruiting in Hetty's cabin, and was bidding good-bye to another; but consistency was no part of war politics, and he rambled on, until Arthur cut him short by saying they could wait no longer. With Arthur as a safeguard in case of an attack from Confederates, and Tom Carleton in case of an assault from the Unionists, Maude felt perfectly secure, and in quiet and safety she accomplished her journey, and was welcomed with open arms by Paul Haverill and Charlie. Arthur could only stop for a day among the hills. He might be ordered back to his regiment at any time, and if he got that *other chap* through he must be bestir himself, he said; and so he bade good-bye to Maude, in whom he had implicit faith, and whose sober, quiet demeanor he tried to attribute to her sorrow at parting with him.

"She does like me some, and by and by she will like me better," he said, as he went his way, leaving her standing in the doorway of her uncle's house, her face very pale, and her hands pressed closely together, as if forcing back some bitter thought or silent pain.

Turning once ere the winding road hid her from view Arthur kissed his hand to her gayly, while with a wave of her handkerchief she re-entered the house, and neither guessed nor dreamed how or when they would meet again.

CHAPTER XXXII.
SUSPICION.

Maude De Vere had insisted that Captain Carleton should have her room, inasmuch as he would be more secure there; for, if the house was suspected and searched, a catastrophe Paul Haverill was constantly anticipating, no one would be likely to invade the sanctity of her apartment.

And Tom found it so very pleasant, and quiet, and home-like, that he was not at all indisposed to linger for several days, particularly after Paul found an opportunity for sending to the Federal lines a letter, which would tell the anxious friends in Rockland of his safety. This letter, which was directed to Mrs. William Mather, had been the direct means of Tom's ascertaining that his brother-in-law was not only alive, but had once shared in the hospitalities now so freely extended to himself. After learning this, Tom could not forbear tearing open the envelope, and adding in a postscript:

"I have just heard that Will was, not many weeks since, a guest in this very house where I am so kindly cared for. God bless the noble man who has saved so many lives, and the beautiful girl, his niece. I cannot say enough in her praise. I do believe she would die for a Unionist any day. Will, it seems, did not see her, as she was away when he was here; and perhaps it is just as well for you, little Rose, that he did not. There is something in her eye, and voice, and carriage, which stirs strange thoughts and feelings in the hearts of us, savages, who have so long been deprived of ladies' society. She is a very queen among women."

That postscript was a most unlucky thought. The first part of Tom's letter had been so guarded with regard to the people who befriended him, that no harm to them could possibly have accrued from its falling into hostile hands; but in the postscript he forgot himself, and assumed forms of speech which pointed directly to Paul Haverill and his niece, Maude De Vere. And so the guerrillas, who caught and half killed the refugee entrusted with the letter, set themselves at once at work to find the "noble man who had the beautiful niece." It was not a difficult task; and Paul Haverill, who had been looked upon as so rank a Secessionist, was suddenly suspected of treason.

Paul was popular and dangerous; while Maude De Vere, whose principles were well known, was too much beloved by the rough mountaineers, to allow of harm falling upon her at once. But the writer of that letter,—the "Yankee Carleton"—should not go unpunished, and just at sunset one afternoon, Lois, who had been at a neighboring cabin, came hurrying home, with that ashen hue upon her dark face which is the negro's sign of paleness.

"Mass'r Paul was suspicioned of harborin' somebody," she said; and already the hordes of mountaineers were assembling around the Cross Roads, and concerting measures for surprising and entrapping the Yankee. "Chloe tell me she hear 'em say if they was perfectly sure 'bout mass'r, and it wasn't for Miss Maude, they'd set the house on fire; and they looks mighty like they's fit to do it. The wust faces, Miss Maude, and they does *swar* awful 'bout the Yankee. They's got halters, and tar and feathers, and guns"

Lois was out of breath by this time, and even if she had not been, she would have paused with wonder at the face of her young mistress. Maude had listened intently to the first part of Lois's story, but felt no emotion save that of scorn and contempt for the men assembled at the Cross Roads, and whom "Uncle Paul could manage so easily;" but when it came to the halter for the Yankee, her face turned white as marble, and in that moment of peril, she realized all that Captain Carleton was to her, and knew what had been the result of the last week's daily intercourse with one so gifted and so congenial. She knew too that he was not for her. Arthur Tunbridge stood in the way of that. She would keep her faith with him, but she would save Captain Carleton, or die.

"Lois," she said, and there was no tremor in her voice, "bring that dress I gave you last Christmas,—the one you think is so long. Your shawl and bonnet, too, and shoes; bring them to Captain Carleton's room."

Lois comprehended her mistress at once, and hurried away to her cabin after the dress, whose extra length she had so often deplored, saying "it wasn't for such as her to wear switchin' trains like the grand folks."

Meanwhile Maude had communicated with her uncle, who manifested no concern except for his guest, and even for him he had no fears provided he could reach the cave in safety. To accomplish that was Maude's object, and as the Cross Roads lay in that direction a great amount of tact and skill was necessary. But Maude was equal to any emergency, and half an hour later there issued from Paul Haverill's door, two figures clad in female garments, and whom a casual observer would have sworn were Maude De Vere and her servant Lois. Maude had a revolver in her pocket, and another in the basket she carried so carefully, and which was supposed to contain the cups of jelly and custard she was taking a poor sick neighbor, whose house was up the mountain path. At her side, with the shuffling gait peculiar to Lois, Tom Carleton walked, his nicely blackened face hidden in the deep shaker which Lois had worn for years, and his calico dress flopping awkwardly about his feet. Lois fortunately was very tall, and so her skirts did good service for the young man, whose powers of imitation were perfect, and who walked and looked exactly like the old colored woman watching his progress from an upper window, and declaring that she would almost "swar it was herself."

At her side stood Charlie, a round spot of red burning on either pale cheek, and his slender hands grasping a revolver, while occasionally his blue eyes looked eagerly along the mountain road, which as yet was quiet and lonely.

"I never thought to raise my hand against my own people," he said, "but if they harm Uncle Paul I shall shoot somebody."

The sun had been gone from sight for some little time, and the tall mountain shadows were lying thick and black across the valley, when up the road several horsemen came galloping, and Paul Haverill's house was ere long surrounded by a band of as rough, savage looking men as could well be found in the mountains of Tennessee.

Calmly and fearlessly Paul Haverill went out to meet them, asking why they were there, and why they seemed so much excited.

For a moment his old power over them asserted itself again, and they hesitated to charge him with treason, as they intended doing. But only for a brief space was there a calm, and then amid oaths and imprecations, and taunting sneers, and threats, they told him of the letter, and deriding him as a traitor, demanded the sneaking Yankee who had written that letter, and was now hidden in the house. To reason with such people was useless, and Paul Haverill did not try it. Standing upon his doorstep, with his grey hair blowing in the evening wind, and his hands deep in his pockets, he said,

"I admit your charge in part. There *has* been a Union soldier in my house,— an escaped prisoner from Columbia. I *did* care for him, and I am neither ashamed nor afraid to own it. Fear is a stranger to old Paul Haverill, as any of you who tries to harm him will find."

"Never mind a speech, Paul," said the leader of the men. "Nobody wants to hurt *you*, though you deserve hanging, perhaps. What we want is the Yankee. Fetch him out, and let's see how he'll look dangling in the air."

"Yes, fetch him out," yelled a dozen voices in chorus. "Bring out the Yankee, we want him. Hallo, puny face, are you a bad egg, too?" they continued, as Charlie appeared in the door.

"Shall I fire, Uncle Paul?" Charlie asked, and his uncle replied,

"By no means, unless you would have them on us like wolves. Friends," and he turned to the mob, which had been increased by some twenty or more, "friends, that man is gone; he is not here; he has left my house. You can search it if you like."

"Where's Miss De Vere?" a coarse voice cried. "We know her to be Union. She never tried to cover that as you, hoary old villain, did. She was out and out. Let her come and say the Yankee is gone and we will believe her."

"My niece, I regret to say, is not just now in either. She is gone with Lois to take some nicknacks to a sick neighbor."

"That's so, boys. I met her myself as I came down the mountain," called out a young man of the company, who seemed to be superior to his associates.

"Gone with Lois, hey? Then whose woolly pate is that?" responded a drunken brute, who, rising in his stirrups, fired a shot toward the garret window from which Lois in an unguarded moment had thrust her head.

Others had seen her, too, and as this gave the lie to the story that Lois was gone, the maddened crowd pressed against the house, declaring their intention to search it and hang any runaway they might find secreted here. It never occurred to them that the runaway could have been with Maude in Lois's clothes; but the young man who met the two lone women saw the ruse at once, and influenced by Maude's beauty and the remembrance of the sweet "Good evening, Mark," with which she had greeted him as he passed, he made his way to Charlie's side and whispered,

"If you know where your sister has gone, and can warn her, do so at once. Tell her if she is tolerably safe to stay there and not return here to-night."

Charlie needed no second bidding, and stealing from the rear of the house he was soon speeding up the mountain path in the direction of the cave. Meanwhile the search in Paul Haverill's house went on. Closets were thrown open; beds were torn to pieces; cellars were ransacked, and old Lois was dragged from the ash-house, where she had taken refuge, while, worse than all, Tom Carleton's boots were found in the chamber where he had dressed so hurriedly, and the sight of these maddened the excited crowd, which, failing of finding their victim, began to clamor for Paul Haverill's blood. But Paul kept them at bay. In the rear of the house was a small, dark room, to which there was but one entrance, and that a steep narrow stairway. Here Paul Haverill took refuge, and standing at the head of the stairs threatened to shoot the first man who should attempt to come up. They had not yet reached that state when they counted their lives as nothing, and so amid yells and oaths, and riding up and down the road, and drinking the fine grape wines with which the cellar was stocked, the hours of the short summer night wore on until just as the dawn was breaking in the east, the marauders put the finishing touch to their night's debauch by setting fire to the house, and then starting in a body up the mountain side in the direction of the cave.

CHAPTER XXXIII.
IN THE CAVE.

The cave was dry and comparatively comfortable, and Tom felt as he entered it almost like going home. Will Mather had spent a day and a night there, while better than all, Maude De Vere was with him, her bright eyes shining upon him through the darkness, and her hands touching his as she groped around for the candle her uncle had said was on a shelf in the rock.

It was presently found, and with the aid of the match Maude had brought with her a light was soon struck, its flickering beams lighting up the dark recesses of the cavern with a ghastly kind of light, which to Maude seemed more terrible than the darkness. She was not afraid, but her nerves were shaken as only threatened danger to Tom Carleton could shake them, and she felt strangely alone on the wild mountain side and in that silent cavern.

Tom did not seem like much of a protector in that woman's garb, but when, with a shake and a kick and a merry laugh, he threw aside the bonnet, shawl and dress, and stood before her in his own proper person, minus the boots, she felt all her courage coming back, and with him beside her could have defied the entire Southern army. There was water enough in the spring to wash the black from his face, and Maude lent her own pretty ruffled white apron for a towel, and then, when his toilet was completed, began to speak of returning.

"At this hour, and alone, with the road full of robbers? Never, Maude, never! You must either stay here with me, or I shall go back with you," Tom said, and he involuntarily wound his arm around the waist of the young girl, who trembled like a leaf.

She did not think of Arthur then, or her promise to him, for something in Tom's voice and manner as he put his arm about her and called her Maude, brought to her a feeling such as she had never experienced before. Perhaps Tom suspected that he was understood, for he held her closer to him, and passing his hand caressingly over her burning cheek, he whispered:

"Dear Maude, I cannot let you incur any danger which I must not share. You understand me, don't you?"

She thought of Arthur then, and the thought cut like a knife through her heart. She must *not* understand; she must *not* listen to words like these; she must not stay there to hear them, and with a quick gesture she was removing Tom's arm from her waist, when his wary "Hist!" made her pause and stand where she was, leaning against him, and heavily, too, as terror overcame every other feeling. Footsteps were coming near, and coming cautiously, too, up to the very entrance of the cave, where they stopped as some one outside seemed to be listening.

It was a moment of terrible suspense, and Maude could hear the throbbing of her heart, while Tom strained her so close to him that his chin rested on her hair, and she felt his breath upon her cheek.

"Maude,—sister Maude," came reassuringly in a low whisper, and with a cry Maude burst away from Tom, exclaiming:

"Charlie, what brings you here?"

He explained to her why he was there, and that she must stay all night, and with a shudder as she thought of what might befall her uncle, Maude acquiesced in the decree, feeling glad that Charlie was with them, a hindrance and preventive to the utterance of words she must not hear. A hindrance he was, it is true, but not a total preventive, for by and by the tired boy's eyes began to droop as drowsiness stole over him, and when Tom made him a bed with Lois's dress and shawl, and bade him lie down and sleep, he did so at once, after first offering the impromptu couch to Maude.

Seen by the dim candle-light, Maude's face was very white, and her eyes shone like burning coals as she watched Captain Carleton, and guessed his motive. Had there been no Arthur in the way, she would not have shrunk from Captain Carleton; but with that haunting memory she could have shrieked aloud when she saw the weary lids droop over Charlie's eyes, and knew by his regular breathing that he was asleep.

Tom knew it as soon as she did, but for a time he kept silence; then he came close to her, and sitting down by her side, said, softly:

"Maude, you and I have been very strangely thrown together, and as I once said to you, there is a meaning in it, if we will but find it. Shall I try and solve it for you, or do you know yourself what is in my mind?"

She did know, but she could not answer; and her face drooped over her brother, whose head she had pillowed upon her lap.

"Perhaps this is not the fitting place for me to speak," Tom continued, "but if the morning finds me in safety, I must be gone, and no one can guess when we may meet again. Let me tell you, Maude, of my early life before ever I saw or dreamed of you."

Surely she might hear this, and the bowed head lifted itself a little, while Captain Carleton told first of his home in Boston, of beautiful little Rose, and saucy, dark-eyed Jimmie, and then of the pale, proud Mary, his early manhood's love, who at the last had lost the pride and hauteur inherited from her race, and had died so gentle and lowly, and gone where her husband one day hoped to meet her. Then there came a pause, and Tom was thinking of a night when poor Jimmie sat by his side before the lonely tent fire, and talked with him of Annie Graham. Should he tell Maude of that? Yes, he would; and by the even beating of his heart, as he made that resolve, and thought of Annie, he knew he had outlived his fancy for one of whom he spoke unhesitatingly, praising her girlish beauty, telling how pure and good she was, and how once a hope had stirred his heart that he, perhaps, might win her.

"But I gave her up to Jimmie. Annie will be my sister, and I know now why it was so appointed. God had in store for me a gem as beautiful as Annie Graham, and better adapted to me. I mean you, Maude. God intends you for my wife. Do you accede willingly? Have you any love for the poor Yankee soldier who has been so long dependent upon you?"

He had her head now on his arm, and with his hand was smoothing her bands of satin hair, while he waited for her to speak. He had dealt honestly with her. She would be equally truthful with him, and she answered at last:

"Oh, Mr. Carleton, you don't know how much it pains me to tell you what I must. I might have loved you once, but now it is too late. I promised Arthur, if he would be kind to the poor prisoners and help the escaped ones to get away, and,—oh, I don't know what, but I am to be his wife when the dreadful war is over. Pity me, Mr. Carleton, but don't love me. No, no, don't make me more wretched by telling me of a love I cannot return."

"Could you return it, Maude, if there were no promise to Arthur?"

Tom spoke very low, with his lips close to her burning cheek, but Maude did not reply, and Tom continued:

"Maude, was the getting me here in safety any part of the price for which you sold yourself?"

She did not answer even then, but by the low, gasping sob she gave as she shed back from her hot brow the heavy hair Tom knew the truth, and to himself he said, "It shall not be." And then from his heart there went up a silent prayer that God would give him the brave, beautiful girl, who drew herself away from him, and leaning over her sleeping brother, sat with both hands clasped upon her face. They did not talk together much more, and once Tom thought Maude was asleep, she sat so rigid and motionless, with her face turned toward the entrance of the cave.

But she was not asleep, and her dark eyes were fixed wistfully upon the one bright star visible to her, and which seemed whispering to her of hope. Perhaps Arthur would release her from her promise, and perhaps,—but Maude started from *that* thought as from an evil spirit, and her white lips whispered faintly, "God help me to keep my promise."

The night was very still, and as the hours wore on, and the faint dawn of day came over the mountain tops, Maude's quick ear caught the echo of the fierce shouts in the valley below, and laying Charlie's head from her lap she went out of the cave, followed by Captain Carleton, who wondered to see how that one night had changed her. The brilliant color was gone from her cheek, which looked haggard and pale, as faces look when some great storm of sorrow has passed over them. Her hair had fallen down and lay in masses upon her neck, from which she shook it off impatiently, and then intently listened to the sounds which each moment grew louder. Shoutings they were, and tones of command, mingled with the distant tramp of horses' feet, while suddenly, above the tall tree-tops which skirted the mountain side, arose a coil of smoke. Too dark, too thick to have come from any chimney where the early morning fire was kindled, it told its own tale of horror, and Maude's eyes grew so black and fierce that Tom shrunk back from her, as pointing her finger toward the fast increasing rings of smoke and flame, she whispered:

"Do you see that, Captain Carleton? It's Uncle Paul's dwelling; they have set it on fire. I never thought they would do that, though I have watched more than one burning house in these mountains, and have almost felt a thrill of pride as I thought how dearly we were paying for our love to the old flag; but when it comes to my own home, the pride is all gone, the fire burns deeper, and one is half tempted to question the price required for the Union."

Tom was about to speak to her, when she turned abruptly upon him, and said:

"Captain Carleton, do you believe your Northern we men,—your Rose, your Annie would bear and brave what the loyal women of the South endure? They may be true to the Union,—no doubt they are, and they think they know what war means; but I tell you they do not. Did they ever see their friends and neighbors driven to the woods and hills like hunted beasts, or watch the kindling flames devouring their own houses, as I am doing now? for I know that is my Uncle Paul's, and whether he still lives, or is hung between the earth and heavens, God only knows, and perhaps *he* has forgotten. I sometimes think he has, else why does he not send us aid? Where are your hordes of men? Why do they not come to save us, when we have waited so long, and our eyes and ears are weak and weary with watching for their coming?"

She was talking now more to herself than to her companion, and she looked a very queen of tragedy, as, with her hair floating over her shoulders, and her hands pressed tightly together, she walked hurriedly the length and breadth of the long flat rock which bordered a precipice near to the cave

Tom was about to answer her, when a ball went whizzing past him, while the loud shouts of the men, whose heads were visible beneath the distant trees, told that he had been discovered.

To return to the cave and take Maude with him, was the work of a moment, and amid yells of fury the drunken mob came on to where Maude, forgetting everything now except Tom Carleton, stood waiting for them. They would not harm her, she knew, and like a lioness guarding its young, she stood within the cave, but so near the entrance that her face was visible to the men, who at sight of her stopped suddenly, and asked what she was doing there, and who she had with her.

"My brother Charlie and Captain Carleton, the man whom you sought at Uncle Paul's," she answered, fearlessly, as she held with a firm grasp the dangerous-looking weapon, which she knew how to use.

"And pray, what may you be doing with the Yankee? asked one of the coarser of the men; and Maude replied

"I am standing between him and just such creatures as you are."

While Tom, grasping her shoulder, said:

"Step aside, Maude; I cannot endure this. You, a girl, defending me! I must go out. Let me pass."

"To certain death? Never!" Maude replied, thrusting him back with a strength born of desperation.

Charlie, who had roused from his sleep, and fully comprehended what was going on, caught Tom around the neck, and nearly strangled him, as he said:

"Let Maude alone, Captain Carleton. They'll not harm her. They would only shoot you down for nothing."

Thus hampered and importuned, Tom stood back a little, while Maude held a parley with her besiegers threatening to shoot the first man who should attempt to pass her. She did not think of danger to herself, and she stood firmly at her post; while the men consulted together as to the best course to be pursued. And while they talked, and Maude stood watchful and dauntless the flames of Paul Haverill's house rose higher in the heavens, and strange, ominous sounds were heard in the distance,—sounds as of many horsemen riding for dear life, with shouts and excited voices; and Maude became aware of some sudden influence working upon the crowd around her.

Then a band of cavalry dashed into sight, and all was wild hurry and consternation. But, above the din of the strife without, Tom Carleton caught sounds which made his heart leap up, and springing forward past Maude De Vere, he exclaimed:

"Thank God, the Federals have come! We are saved! Maude, we are saved!"

As his tall form emerged into view, a brutal soldier, maddened by the surprise and unavoidable defeat, leveled his gun and fired, recking little whether Tom or Maude was the victim. The ball cut through the sleeve of Maude's dress, and grazing her arm enough to draw blood, lodged harmlessly in the rocks beyond.

At that sight all Charlie's fire was roused, and the shot which went whizzing through the air made surer work than did the one intended for Tom Carleton. Tom was out upon the ledge of rocks by this time, grasping the hands of the blue coats, who were a part of a company sent out to reconnoiter, and who had reached Paul Haverill's house just after the rebels had left it. At first they had tried to extinguish the flames, but finding that impossible, they had followed the enemy, most of whom were made prisoners of war.

Some months before, John Simms had been transferred from the Army of the Potomac to the Army of the Cumberland, and he it was who led his men to the rescue, doing it the more daringly and willingly when he heard who was in danger. *He* was a captain now, and he stood grasping Tom Carleton's hand, when a piercing shriek rose on the air, and turning round, the young men saw Maude De Vere bending over the prostrate form of a soldier, whose head she gently lifted up, as she moaned bitterly:

"Oh, Arthur, Arthur! how came you here?"

CHAPTER XXXIV.
POOR ARTHUR.

He had kept his word, and piloted safely across the mountains the prisoner left in Hetty's cabin. His arrival at Paul Haverill's burning home had preceded that of the Federal troops by twenty minutes or more, and when he heard of Maude's danger, he followed our soldiers up the hillside to where Maude held the entrance to the cave. He saw her, and tried to make his voice heard, but it was lost amid the strife and noise of the conflict, and she only knew of his presence, when Charlie, with chattering teeth, and a face as white as ashes, clutched her dress frantically, and said:

"Come, sister, come this way to Arthur,—somebody—shot him. Do you think he will die?"

Quick as lightning the remembrance of the thought, which had yet scarcely been a thought, of just such a contingency as this, flashed over Maude, sweeping away all the pain, the terror, the shrinking she had felt when she contemplated the fulfillment of her promise to Arthur Tunbridge. He was lying there at her feet, and the grass beneath him was all a pool of blood, while his dim eyes showed that the objects around him were now but faintly discerned. He saw Maude, though, and when her loud cry met his ear he smiled a glad, grateful smile, and said to her, as she knelt beside him and took his head in her lap—

"You are sorry, Maude. It was a mistake. You did love me some."

She pressed her quivering lips to his, and said again,

"Oh Arthur! Arthur! how came you here?"

Arthur knew he was dying, but, shaking off all thought of his own pain, he explained to Maude how he came there.

"The man,—you remember. I got him through, and I am not sorry, for he told me of a blind mother and six little children dependent upon him away off somewhere among the Ohio hills. Think if they had been left with out support. I am glad I saved him even if it cost my life. And still it is hard to die, Maude, just as you are beginning to love me, for you are, and if I had lived you would have kept your promise to me.

"Yes, Arthur, I would," and Maude's white fingers threaded the bloody hair and moved softly over the ghastly face. "Who did it, Arthur?" she asked, and Arthur's face flushed to a purple hue as with a moan he said:

"Don't ask me,—there was a *mistake*. I had taken no part in the fray, except to knock down the ruffian who fired at you. I was standing right behind him. Yes, there was a mistake. Oh Maude, it *was* a mistake."

He kept repeating the words, while Maude tried to stop the blood flowing so freely from the wound in his temple. The ball had entered there, but had not penetrated to the brain, and he retained his consciousness to the last, smiling once kindly on Charlie, who, half frantic, bent over him, and said:

"Yes, Arthur, it *was* a mistake, oh Arthur, oh Maude, and you two were engaged. I did not know it before."

Then a bright flush crept into Maude's white face, for she knew the tall shadow on the grass beside her belonged to Capt. Carleton, and he, she guessed, was thinking of last night in the cave. He did think of it, but only for a moment, and then his thoughts were merged in his great anxiety for Lieutenant Arthur, who he saw was dying. Arthur knew he was there, and smiled when he asked if he felt much pain.

"None with Maude beside me. She was to have been my wife, wern't you, Maude?"

"Yes, Arthur. I was to have been your wife."

She spoke it openly, frankly, as if by so doing she was seeking to atone for an error, and the eyes lifted to Tom's face had in them something defiant, as if she would say "I mean it. I would have been his wife."

But she met only pity in Tom's looks—pity for her, and pity for the young man dying among the mountains on that soft, summer morning, when the whole world seemed so at variance with a death like that. It was a strange scene, and one which those who witnessed it never could forget. The broad, level plat on the mountain side, the mounted horsemen, the group of prisoners, the beautiful, queenly girl, whose lap pillowed the head of the dying soldier, while her brilliant eyes wept floods of tears which, with quick, nervous movements of her fingers, she swept away. Beside her was Charlie, his face whiter than that of the dying man, and his muscles working painfully as if he was forcing back some terrible pang or cry of agony. Tom Carleton, too, and Paul Haverill, who had later joined the group and stood looking sadly on, while toward the south the smoke and flame of his own house was ascending, and in the east the early morning was bright and fresh with the summer's golden sunshine. And there on the mountain side they waited and watched, while the young lieutenant talked faintly of his distant home where the news would carry so much sorrow.

"Tell father I died believing in our cause, and were I to live my life over I should join the Southern army; but it's wrong about the prisoners. We ought not to abuse those who fall into our hands. I've loved you Maude, so long. Remember me when I am gone, not for anything brilliant there was about me, but because I loved you so well, and died in carrying out the work you gave me to do."

"Oh, Arthur! Arthur! speak some word of comfort to me or I shall surely die. It *was* a mistake," Charlie whispered, as he crept close to Arthur's side.

The dying man's eyes rested inquiringly for a moment in Charlie's face, then lighted up with a sudden joy.

"Charlie! Charlie! come close," he whispered. "Bend your ear to my lips. Maude must not hear me."

His head was still lying on Maude's lap, but he spoke so low to Charlie that she did not hear the question asked. She only knew that Charlie started quickly, and throwing one arm across her neck as if to save her from some evil, said, promptly, energetically:

"No, no, Arthur; no!"

Then the quivering lips went down again to Arthur's ear, and Maude caught the word "mistake," and that was all. She did not know or think what it really meant. It was *all* a mistake, the terrible war which had brought her so much pain and suffering.

"I die easier now. It was so horrible before. Poor Charlie! Don't let it trouble you. Care for Maude. She would have been my wife. Stick to our cause. You never forsook it," came faintly from Arthur, and his eyes, when again they rested on Maude's face, had lost the strange, frightened look which she had observed when she first came to his side. He was dying very fast, and his mind seemed groping for some form of prayer with which to meet the last great foe.

"Pray, somebody," he moaned, and Paul Haverill, who, wholly overcome with all he had passed through during the last few hours, had stood dumb and motionless, replied in a choking voice:

"I am not a praying man, but God be with you, my boy, and land you safely on t'other side, where there's no more fighting."

"Yes, but that isn't 'Our Father.' I used to say it at home," came feebly from the white lips, and then Tom Carleton knelt beside the youth whose path had crossed his own so often and so strangely, and with deep reverence and earnest entreaty commended the departing spirit to the God who deals more gently, and mercifully, and lovingly with his children than they dealt with each other.

Tom thought of Isaac Simms, and the noisome, filthy room in Libby where he had first learned to pray, and the thought gave fervor to his prayer, to which Arthur listened intently, his lips motioning the amen he could not speak, for he had no power of utterance. Once again they moved with a pleading kind of motion, and Maude stooped over to kiss them, her long hair falling across the pallid brow, where the blood stains were, and when she lifted her head up, and pushed back her heavy locks, there was the seal of death on Arthur's face.

CHAPTER XXXV.
THE DEAD AND THE LIVING.

Of all Paul Haverill's comfortable buildings, house, stables, barn and negro quarters, there was left him only one cabin which the fire had not consumed. That stood a little distant from the rest, and had been occupied by Lois before her husband died. It was superior to the other cabins then; it was neat and tidy now, and there they laid the dead lieutenant, in his grey uniform, with a little flag of stars and bars across his breast. This was Charlie's thought, and it was very mete that he who to the last had believed in the righteousness of the Confederacy should have her sign above him. There was no other spot except the cabin where Maude could stay, and the entire day and night she sat by her dead Arthur, whom, now that he *was* dead, she cherished in her heart as a martyr and a hero, questioning even the ground on which she had hitherto stood so firmly, and asking herself if, after all, the South was so very far out of the way, or if the Union were worth the fearful price the Southern people were paying for it. Maude did not know herself in this mood. It was so unlike all her former theories, and more than once she pressed her hot hands to her still hotter head, and asked if she was going mad.

Crouched beside Maude, with his blue eyes fixed upon her with a pitying, remorseful look, was Charlie.

"Poor Maude,—poor sister! I am so sorry. I never thought,—I did not know; you used to laugh about him so to Uncle Paul. I'd give my life to bring him back for you. Did you love him so very much?" Charlie said, in broken sentences, and then Maude shivered from head to foot, but made him no reply.

She had not loved him so very much, but his violent death and all the horrors attending it had shaken her terribly, and could he have come back to life she would have tried to love him, and with her iron will would have crushed that other love, the very knowledge of which had made her heart throb with so much joy.

But the dead come not to life again, and the next morning they buried Arthur Tunbridge in the grassy enclosure where Paul Haverill's wife was sleeping with the infant son who, had he lived, would have been just Arthur's age. The blue coated soldiery, who had been his deadly foes, paid him every military honor possible within their means, even marching to his grave behind the stars and bars which lay upon his coffin; but when they came back from the burial, they bore the national flag, whose folds that peaceful summer night floated in the breeze from the top of Lois's cabin.

Very kind, and gentle, and pitiful was Tom's demeanor toward Maude. During the day and the night, when she had sat by Arthur in Lois's cabin, he had not been near her; but, after all was over, he went to her, and, with the authority of a friend and brother, insisted that she should take the rest she needed so much. And Maude gave way at the sound of his soothing, quieting voice, and, with a flood of tears, did what he bade her do. And then Tom sat by her, and bathed her throbbing head, and smoothed her beautiful hair, and paid back in part the services she had rendered him when he lay sick in Squire Tunbridge's house.

Maude was not ill,—only exhausted,—both physically and mentally the exhaustion showing itself in the quiet, listless state into which she lapsed, paying but little attention to what was passing around her, and offering no suggestion or remonstrance when told of her uncle's plan to accompany Captain Simms and his men to Knoxville.

Over Paul Haverill, too, a change had passed. The attack upon him by his old friends and neighbors, though long expected, had been sudden and terrible when it came, and as he watched the burning of the house which had been his so long, he felt that every tie which bound him to the old place was severed. Then came swiftly the fearful tragedy of the mountains, when Arthur was brought to him dead. Stunned and bewildered by the startling events which had followed each other so rapidly, Paul was hardly able to counsel for himself, and assented readily to the plan which had really originated with Captain Carleton, who had another scheme underlying that, but who suggested both so skillfully that Paul Haverill fancied they were his own ideas, and gave them as such to Maude. They would go to Knoxville with the soldiers, he said; thence to Nashville. They had some relatives living there, and, after resting for a little, they would continue their journeyings North, going, perhaps, as far as New York.

"I always wanted to travel North," he said, "but my affairs kept me at home. Now I have no affairs. My neighbors have relieved me of such commodities and I want to get away from a spot where I have witnessed such dreadful things. We all need change. You, Maude, more than I, and Charlie more than either. I don't know what has come over the boy. That horrible night and morning were too much for him."

Maude knew that so far as Charlie was concerned, her uncle had spoken truly. Charlie was greatly changed, and his eyes had in them a scared look, as if every detail of the horrors of the fight on the mountain had stamped itself indelibly upon his mind, and was never for an instant forgotten.

He needed a change of place and scene; and as she could not return to Arthur's desolate home, whither the sad news had been sent at once, Maude assented to the Nashville arrangement, and in three weeks was comfortably settled at a Nashville hotel, with Lois as her attendant. Her uncle, Charlie, and Captain Carleton were with her, the latter constantly putting off his journey to Rockland, where they were so anxiously waiting for him. He had written to Rose immediately after his arrival at Nashville, telling her of all that had transpired, and speaking of Maude De Vere as one whom he hoped to make his wife. This time the letter went safely, and Rose replied at once, urging Tom to come, and insisting that Mr. Haverill, Maude and Charlie should accompany him.

"They saved Will's life as well as yours," Rose wrote. "I have a right to them all, and especially to the noble Maude. Bring her to me, Tom, and let me coax back the color to her dear face and the brightness to her eyes. I shall come myself and get her if she refuses."

Maude had never known the companionship of a sister,—had never had a single intimate girl friend except Nettie Tunbridge, who died. Independent, strong willed and self-reliant, she had cared but little for any society except that which she found with nature in the wild mountains of Tennessee; but now, broken and shocked, and shorn of some of her strength, she longed for sympathy and companionship, and something in Rose Mather's sprightly letter made her heart yearn toward the little lady who had written it, and the pleasant home which Rose described as beautiful with the summer bloom.

"I will think about it by and by," she said to her uncle; "but for the present it is nice to rest here in Nashville."

So for a time longer they lingered in Tennessee, while Rose waited impatiently for them and fretted at the delay.

CHAPTER XXXVI.
ANDERSONVILLE PRISONERS.

"This seems to be one of the worst cases we have had. I doubt if his mind will survive the horrors he has endured, even if his body does. Poor fellow! his mother would not recognize him now."

This was what the physician at Annapolis said to Mrs. Simms of a miserable, emaciated skeleton, which had come up from Andersonville with the last arrival of prisoners.

While we in the mountains of Tennessee were tracing the wanderings of Will Mather and Captain Carleton, Mrs. Simms and Annie had stood untiringly at their posts beside the sick and dying soldiers who had learned to bless and watch for the stern widow, and to love and worship the beautiful Annie Graham. And well had she earned such appreciation, for she had been most faithful to the wretched ones committed to her care,—faithful both to body and soul, and in the better world she knew there was waiting to welcome her more than one, whose darkened mind she had led to the fountain of all light. And Annie had made a vow to stay till from that foul Southern prison, where 28,000 men had died, there came to her *the one* for whom she always looked so anxiously when new arrivals came, her blue eyes running rapidly over each wasted form, and then filling with tears when the scrutiny was found to be in vain.

James Carleton had never been heard from since that letter sent to her so long ago, and hope had died out of Annie's heart, when at last, with Widow Simms, she stood by the cot where lay the insensible form of which the physician had spoken so discouragingly.

It was the figure of a young man, who must once have been finely formed, with handsome face and hair and eyes. The latter were closed now, and only the lids moved with a convulsive motion, as Annie bent over him. The dark hair, matted and coarse and filthy, had curled in rings about the bony forehead, but had been cut away when the bath was given, and the closely shorn head was like many other heads which Annie Graham's hands had touched, gently, tenderly, as they now moved over this one, trying to infuse some life into the breathing skeleton. He was to be her charge,—he was in her division and Mrs. Simms' keen grey eyes scanned Annie curiously as she bent over the poor fellow.

He was helpless as an infant, and Annie nursed him much as she would have nursed a baby whose life hung on a thread. He had been there four days, and only a faint, moaning sound had given token of life or consciousness. But at the close of the fourth day, as Annie sat chafing the pulseless fingers where the grey skin hung so loosely, the eyes opened for a moment and were fixed upon her face. There was no consciousness in them,—no recognition of her presence, nothing but the strained, hungry, despairing look Annie had seen in the eyes of so many of our prisoners, and which to a greater or less degree was peculiar to them all. Annie saw this look, and then underneath it all she saw something more,—*what* it was she could not tell, but it brought back to her those moonlight nights upon the beach at New London, and that other night of more recent date, when she sat with Jimmie Carleton beneath the Rockland sky and heard his passionate words of love, and saw his soft, black eyes kindle with earnestness and then grow sad and sorrowful with disappointment. There was no kindling in them now,—no ardent passion or heat of love,—but a certain softness and brightness, and even sauciness, lingered still and told Annie at last who it was.

"Oh, merciful Father! it is *Jimmie!*" she said, and unmindful of any who might be looking on, she bent down and kissed the sunken cheeks from which the flesh was gone.

She had expected him so long, and grown so weary and hopeless with expectations unfulfilled, that she could scarcely believe it now, or realize that the half dead wretch before her was once the lively, humorous, teasing Jimmie Carleton. How she pitied him, and how her heart throbbed as she thought of the suffering he must have endured ere he reached this state of apparent imbecility. Then, as she remembered what the physician said about his mind, she dropped upon her knees, and clasping her hands over her face, prayed earnestly that God would remove the darkness and wholly restore the man whom she loved so dearly.

"*Do* you think he will die?" she asked Mrs. Simms, who had come for a moment to her side.

"You know him, then. I was wondering that an old woman like me should see clearer than you. I mistrusted from the first," Mrs. Simms answered, and then to Annie's eager questioning she replied, "It will be almost a miracle if we do get any sense into that brain, or flesh upon these bones, but we'll do the best we can."

Her words were not very encouraging, and Annie's tears fell like rain upon the face of the man who gave no sign that he knew where he was, or who was bending over him. Oh! how he had longed for the air of the North, as his face daily grew thinner, greyer, and more corpse-like, while his flesh seemed shrivelling and drying on his bones. Bill Baker had done what he could to ameliorate his condition,—done too much in fact, and as the result he suddenly found himself shorn of his privileges, and an inmate again of the dreadful prison. Even then he clung to and cared for Jimmie, until the pangs of starvation and the pains of sickness made him forgetful of all but himself.

And there they pined and wept and waited until the day of their release, when Bill was too ill to be removed, and was left in charge of a humane family, who kindly promised to care for him until he was better. From a Rockland soldier who had been taken prisoner at the battle of the Wilderness, Jimmie had heard that Mrs. Graham was at Annapolis, and then! oh, how he longed for the time when it might be his fate to be tended and nursed by her. She would do it so gently, and so kindly and in his dreams the walls of his pestilential prison stretched away to the green fields of the North, where he walked again with Annie, and felt the clasp of her little hand, and the light of her blue eyes. She was always present with him,—she or the little Lulu, of Pequot memory. Somehow these two were strangely mixed, and when his mind began to totter as the physical strain on it became too great, the two faces were united in one body, and both bent lovingly over him, just as Annie Graham was doing now when he was past knowing or caring who ministered to him. A vague suspicion he had at intervals that in some respects there was a change, that his bed was not the filthy sand bank, nor his covering the pitiless sky. Gradually, too, there came a different look upon his face; the color was changing from the dingy gray, to a more life-like hue; flesh was showing a little beneath the skin, and the dark hair began to grow, and Annie watered the tiny curls with bitter tears, for, as proof of the terrible life whose horrors will never half be written, the once black hair was coming out streaked with grey. They knew in Rockland that he was at Annapolis, but Annie had peremptorily forbidden either Mrs. Carleton or Rose to come. "They could do no good," she wrote. "Jimmie would not know them; and they might be in the way."

They were constantly expecting Tom from Tennessee, with Maude De Vere and her friends, and so they remained at home the more willingly, enjoining it upon Annie to write them every day, just a line to tell how Jimmie was.

The summer rain was falling softly upon the streets of Annapolis, and the cool evening air came stealing into the room, where Annie Graham sat by her patient. There were not so many now in her ward, and she had more time for Jimmie, by whose bedside every leisure moment was passed. She was sitting by him now, watching him as he slept, and listening breathlessly to his low murmurings as he seemed to be talking of her and the dreadful prison life. Then he slept more soundly, and she arranged the light so that it left his face in shadow, but fell full upon her own.

Half an hour passed in this way, and Annie's head was beginning to droop from languor and drowsiness, when a sudden exclamation startled her, and she looked up to see her patient's eyes fixed upon her, while with his finger he pointed to the window opposite, and whispered,

"The star, it's risen again, when I thought it had set forever. I take it as a good omen, Bill. I shall see her face again."

Did he think himself in prison still, with that star shining over him, and did he take her for Bill Baker? The thought was not a very complimentary one, but Annie forgot everything in her joy, at this evidence of returning reason.

"Jimmie," she said softly, and she bent her face so close to his, that her lips touched his forehead, "Jimmie, don't you know that you are in Annapolis, with me, with Annie Graham. You remember Annie?"

She had many a time said these very words in his ear, hoping somehow to impress them upon him, and now she had succeeded, for he repeated them after her slowly and with long pauses, like a school-boy trying to say a half-learned lesson.

"Jimmie—don't you—know—that you—are here—in—Annapolis—with me—with—Annie—Graham—You remember—Annie?"

And as he said them consciousness began to struggle back,—the black eyes fastened themselves upon Annie with a wistful look; then they took in her dress, her hands folded in her lap, the decent covering on the bed the furniture of the room, and then throwing up his arms he felt of his flesh, and examined his linen, and patted the pillow, while still the look of wonder and perplexity deepened on his face. Suddenly he let his arms drop helplessly, then stretched them feebly towards Annie, and while both chin and lip quivered touchingly, and the tears streamed from his eyes, he whispered,

"Clean face, clean hands, soft pillow and bed, with the hunger, and thirst, and homesickness gone. This is—yes, this must be God's land, and *she* is there with me."

He fainted then. The shock of coming back to "God's land" had been too great, and for a week or more he paid but little heed to what was passing around him.

"Don't you know me, Jimmie? It's I,—it's Annie," Mrs. Graham would say to him, as his restless eyes turned upon her, and he would repeat after her,

"Don't you—know—me, Jimmie? It's I,—it's Annie."

This was a peculiarity of his, and it continued until Bill Baker, who had become strong enough to be moved, came to Annapolis, and asked to see the "Cop'ral."

At first the physician refused, but Annie approved the plan, hoping for a good result, and she waited anxiously, while Bill said cheerily,

"Hallo, old Cop'ral. Rather nicer quarters here than that sand bank down by that infernal nasty stream."

Bill Baker's voice was the last which in the far-off prison had sounded kindly in Jimmie's ears, and now as he heard it again his face lighted up, and his eyes kindled with something like their olden fire.

"You know me, Cop'ral. I'm Bill. We've been exchanged. We're up to Annapolis, and Miss Graam is nussin' you," Bill continued, and then Jimmie drew a long breath, and burst into a passionate fit of tears. "They'll do him good. They allus did to Andersonville. He'd hold in till he was fit to burst, and then he'd let 'em slide, and feel better. He'll know you, Miss Graam, after this."

Annie was called away just then, to attend to another patient, and Bill was left alone with Jimmie. There were a few broken sentences from the latter, and then Bill Baker was heard talking rapidly, but very gently and cautiously, and Jimmie lifted his head once and looked across the room where Annie was.

"Better leave him alone a spell, till he thinks it out, and gets it arranged," Bill said to Annie. "I made him understand where he was, and that you was here, and all right on the main question; and though he'd like to have bust his biler for a minute, he'll come all straight, I reckon."

It was more than an hour before Annie went to Jimmie again, but when she did, the eager, joyful look in his eyes told her that she was recognized.

"Don't speak to me,—don't talk," she said, laying one hand lightly upon the lips, which began to move, while with the other she smoothed the short curls of hair.

He kissed the hand upon his lips, and whispered, through the fingers:

"Tell me first, was it true, he told me? Do you"——

He did not finish the sentence, for Annie understood him, and bending so near to him that no one else could hear, she said:

"Yes, Jimmie,—I do."

He seemed satisfied, and something of his old manner came back to him when, later in the day, Annie tried to straighten the clothes about him, and wet and brushed his hair.

"Look like a hippopotamus, don't I?" he asked, touching his thick-skinned face.

"Not half as much as you did," Annie replied; and the first smile her face had worn for weeks glimmered around her lips, for she knew now the danger was past, and Jimmie Carleton would live.

CHAPTER XXXVII.
IN ROCKLAND.

The warm, bright November day was wearing to its close. The purple haze of the Indian summer lay around the hilltops, and the soft, golden sunlight fell softly upon the grass, and the few autumnal flowers which had escaped the recent storm. The grounds around the Mather mansion were looking almost as beautiful as in the early summer, for the grass, invigorated by the rain, was fresh and green again, and the brilliant foliage of the trees which dotted the lawn made up for the loss of the flowers. Even these last were not lacking indoors, for the hot-house had been robbed of its costliest flowers, which filled the whole house with perfume, and made Maude De Vere start with surprise when she first entered the parlors.

"It takes me back to my Southern home," she said to Rose, who, standing on tiptoe, fastened a half-open lily in her hair, going into ecstasies over the effect, and thinking to herself that Maude De Vere was the most regal creature she had ever seen.

Maude had been in Rockland three weeks, and Rose was already as much in love with her as if she had known her all her life. At first, she had dreaded a little to meet the fearless heroine of the mountains. A girl who had held a revolver at the heads of both Federal and Confederate; who, in the night, had ridden twenty miles on horseback to conduct a party of refugees to a place of safety, and had guarded the entrance of the cave in the face of a furious mob, must be something very formidable, or, at least, something unlike all Rose's ideas of what a lady gently born should be; and both Rose and her mother had waited nervously for the arrival of one who, they felt sure, was to be the wife of Tom. Nothing definite had been said upon the subject since Arthur died, but it was tacitly understood by all parties that Maude De Vere was, sometime, to be Maude Carleton; and Tom was allowed to pay her attentions which could only be paid to his *fiancée*.

In a great flutter of spirits, Rose had heard of Maude's arrival at the Monteur House, and immediately after dinner had driven down to see her, accompanied by Will, who, if possible, was more anxious than herself to pay his respects to Maude.

She was kneeling by Charlie's couch when the party entered, but she rose at once and came forward, with the most beautiful carnation staining her cheeks, and a look of modesty in her brilliant eyes. She wore a long, trailing dress of heavy silk, and stood so erect, and held her head so high, that she seemed taller than she really was,—taller than Tom, Rose feared; but as he stepped up to her, she saw he had the advantage of her by at least four inches, and thus reassured, she drew a long breath of relief; then, as thoughts of all her husband and brother had been saved from by this heroic girl came over her, she sprang toward Maude, and winding her arms around her neck, sobbed hysterically, but never spoke one word.

"What is it? What are you crying for?" Maude asked, petting her as if she had been a little child.

"Oh, I don't know. The sight of you who have done so much for the war, and been so brave, makes me seem so little, so small, so mean beside you, Maude De Vere," Rose replied, brokenly, and then Maude's eyes filled with tears, and she hugged the sobbing little creature, whom, from that moment, she loved so fondly.

She, too, had dreaded this meeting, for she knew that Rose Mather and her mother were both women of the highest culture, and she felt that they might criticise, and perhaps condemn one who had lived so long among the pines of North Carolina and the mountains of Tennessee. But Rose's manner divested her of all fear, and in a moment she resumed that unconscious air of superiority to all else around her, which was a part of herself. Queenly was the word which best suited her looks and her manners, and Rose paid homage to her as to a queen, and told her that she loved her, and how much she had thought of her, and how anxious her mother was to see her, and how happy they would all be when Jimmie and Annie came home.

There had been daily visits to the Monteur since then, and Mrs. Carleton had met the beautiful Maude, and mentally approved of Tom's choice.

Charlie too had been petted and caressed, and his blue eyes opened with wonder as he saw what Northern women were like, and remembered his prejudice against them. He liked the Northerners, he said, but he was loyal to the Southern cause, and listened, with flashing eyes and crimson cheeks, to all he continually heard of the sure defeat and disgrace of the Confederacy.

Matters were in this wise when the day came on which Annie was expected home with Jimmie. Great preparations had been made for that arrival. In Rockland there was more than one prisoner who had been nursed by Annie Graham, and her name was spoken with reverence and love by the veriest vagabond that walked the streets. They had not made a demonstration in a long, long time, but they were going to make one now, and the honors which poor George saw in fancy awarded to himself were to be given to his wife. Jimmie, too, whose terrible sufferings had excited so much commiseration, was to have his share of consideration. Bill Baker, who had been home for a week, and was as usual the most active spirit of all, suggested that when they flung out the banner on which was inscribed, "Honor and welcome to Annie Graham," they should give three cheers for Mr. Carleton too. "Bein'," as he said, "that they are about as good as one."

Prompt to the moment when it was due, the train swept round the Rockland curve and stopped at the depot where a large concourse of people was gathered. They had not expected the Widow Simms, and when her green veil and straw bonnet appeared on the platform, the foremost of the group looked a little disappointed, while the widow's face darkened as she saw the waiting multitude, and guessed why they were there.

Annie had appeared by this time, and at sight of her the tongues were loosened, and deafening shouts of welcome greeted her on every side. The flag bearing her name was held aloft, the cannon in the adjoining field sent forth its bellowing roar, and the band struck up the sweet refrain of "Annie Laurie;" while the voices of the Andersonville prisoners, who had been Annie's charge, sang the last line:

"And for bonnie *Annie Graham* I would lay me down and die."

Surely this was a coming home which Annie had never looked for, and with her face flushed with excitement, and her eyes shining with tears, she stood in the midst of the shouting throng, gazing wonderingly from one to the other, and realizing nothing clearly, except the firm clasp upon her arm.

It was Jimmie's hand, and Jimmie himself leaned upon her, as the crowd coupled his name with hers, and hurrahed for "James Carleton and Annie Graham."

"And the Widder Simms,—I swan if it's fair to leave her out. She did some tall nussin' down to Annapolis," Bill Baker said; and then the widow was cheered, and she acknowledged the compliment with a grim smile, and wondered when "folks would quit making fools of themselves, and if Susan wasn't up there, somewhere, in the jam. Of course she was; 'twas like them Ruggleses to go where the doins was."

And while she shook the hand of her neighbors, she kept her eyes on the watch for Susan, and felt a little chagrined that she did not find her.

Susan was at home in the neat little house which John had bought with his captain's wages, so carefully saved. The same house it was at which Annie Graham had looked with longing eyes, in the commencement of the war; and in the pleasant chamber which overlooked the town there was *a little boy* who had been in Rockland only a week, and whose existence was as yet unknown to the widow. They had purposely kept it from her, so she had no suspicion that he was expected; and the first genuine feeling of happiness she had known since Isaac died, she experienced when she was ushered into Susan's room, and the little red-faced thing was laid in her lap. She had looked askance at the new house, and neat furniture, and the pretty curtains, as so many proofs of "them Ruggleses" extravagance; but she was not proof against the white face which, from the pillows, smiled so kindly upon her, and called her mother. And she was guilty of kissing her daughter-in-law, even before she saw the baby, her first grandchild, whom Susan called *Isaac*, although she hated the name, and had tacked on to it *Adolphus*, with the hope that the future would adjust the name into *Adolph*, or something more fanciful than the good, plain Bible Isaac. And while the widow kissed and wept over her grandson, and felt herself growing young, and soft, and gentle again, the crowd around the depot had dispersed, a part going to their own homes, and a part following the soldiers and band which escorted Annie Graham and Jimmie Carleton to the Mather mansion, where everything had been made so beautiful for them.

It was a pleasant coming home, and a most ample compensation for all the weariness and privation which Annie, as hospital nurse, had endured, and she felt that far more was awarded to her than she deserved.

"Mr. Carleton was the one to be honored," she said, and her soft, blue eyes rested upon the pale, tired man, who, exhausted with his journey and the excitement, lay down at once upon the sofa, while his mother and Rose knelt beside him and kissed, and pitied, and cried over his poor white face, and long, bony hands, which were almost transparent in their whiteness.

Maude was not one of the party at the Mather mansion that night.

"You ought to be alone the first night," she said, when Rose insisted that she should join them. "To-morrow I will come round and call on Mrs. Graham and your brother."

She had been greatly interested in all the arrangements, and was curious to see the woman who had almost been her rival, while Annie was quite as curious to see her, the heroine of the mountains. In her letters to Annie, Rose had purposely refrained from mentioning Tom's name with Maude's, so that Annie was ignorant of the real state of things. But she did not remain so long.

"Is she so very beautiful?" she said to Rose, when, after supper, they were all assembled in the parlor, and Maude was the subject of conversation.

"Ask Tom; he can tell you," Rose replied, and by the conscious look on Tom's face, Annie guessed the truth at once.

That night, when the two brothers were alone in their room, Tom said to Jimmie:

"Well, my boy, I've kept my word,—I've waited a year and more. I've given you every chance a reasonable man could ask. Have you made a proper use of your privileges? Would it do me any good to try and win Annie now?"

"You can try if you like," Jimmie said, with a smile. And then Tom told him of his hopes concerning Maude De Vere, and Jimmie said to him saucily:

"Don't you remember I told you once you had had your day? But some lucky dogs have two, and you, it seems, are one of them."

CHAPTER XXXVIII.
THE LOVERS.

The next day brought Maude De Vere, looking so handsome in her black dress, with her coquettish drab hat and long drab feather tipped with scarlet, that she reminded Annie of some bright tropical flower as she came into the room with the sparkle in her brilliant eyes, and the deep, rich bloom upon her cheek. She had regained her health and spirits rapidly within the last few weeks, and even Jimmie, who seldom saw beyond Annie's fair face and soft blue eyes, drew a breath of wonder at the queenly girl who completely overshadowed those around her so far as size and form and physical development were concerned. But nothing could detract from the calm, quiet dignity of Annie's manner, or from the pure, angelic beauty of her face, and as the two stood holding each other's hands and looking into each other's eyes, they made a most striking tableau, and Mrs. Carleton thought, with a thrill of pride, how well her sons had chosen.

That night, as Maude was walking back to the hotel accompanied by Tom, he asked her again the question put in the cave of the Cumberland.

"I understand about Arthur," he said; "but he is dead; there is no promise now in the way. I claim you for my own. Am I wrong in doing so?"

That Maude's reply was wholly satisfactory was proved by the expression of Tom Carleton's face when at last he stopped at the door of the hotel, and by the kiss which burned on Maude's lips long after he had disappeared down the street.

The next afternoon, while Tom was with Maude, and both Mrs. Carleton and Rose were out on a shopping expedition, Annie sat alone with Jimmie in the pleasant little room which had been given to him as a place where he would be more quiet than in the parlor. Annie had been playing with Rose's boy,— the little Jimmie, a handsome, sturdy fellow of nearly a year old, whom the entire household spoiled. He was already beginning to talk, and having taken a fancy to Annie, he tried to call her name, and made out of it a tolerably distinct "Auntee," which brought a blush to Annie's face, and a teasing smile to Jimmie's.

"Come, sit by me a moment, Annie," Jimmie said, when the child had been taken out by his nurse. "Sit on this stool, so,—a little nearer to me,—there, that's right," he continued, in the tone of authority he had unconsciously acquired since his convalescence.

He was lying upon the couch, and Annie was sitting at his side and so near to him that his long fingers could smooth and caress her shining hair, while his saucy eyes feasted themselves upon her face, as he asked "when she would really be the auntie of the little boy who called her now by that name."

"Not till you are able to stand alone," was Annie's reply, and then, for the first time since his return from Andersonville, Jimmie spoke of that episode in his life at New London, when little Lulu Howard had stirred his boyish blood, and filled his boyish fancy.

Perhaps he wanted to tease Annie, for he said to her:

"I *did* like that little blue-eyed Lu,—that's a fact. I used to think about her all day, and dream about her all night. I wonder where she is now."

"What would you do if you knew?" Annie asked, and Jimmie replied:

"I believe I would go miles to see her, just to know what kind of a woman she has developed into. I trust she is not like her aunt. I could not endure her. She struck me as a hard, selfish, ambitious woman, terribly afraid lest the world generally should not think Mrs. Scott Belknap all which Mrs. Scott Belknap thought herself to be."

Annie's cheeks were very red by this time, and imputing her heightened color to a cause widely different from the real one, Jimmie drew her face down to his, and kissing the burning cheeks, said:

"Of course I should take you with me, when I went after little Lu."

"You would hardly find her if you did not," Annie said, while Jimmie looked inquiringly at her.

Annie had only been waiting for Jimmie to speak of the little Pequot, before making her own confession, and she now said to him abruptly:

"Did Lulu look any like me?"

"Why, yes. I've always thought so, only she was younger, and had short hair, you know, and short dresses, too. Annie, Annie, tell me,—was she,—do you,—are you"—Jimmie began, raising himself upright upon the couch, as something in Annie's expression began to puzzle and mystify him.

"Am I what?" Annie asked. "Am I little Lulu of the Pequot House? My name was *Annie Louise Howard* before I married George. My aunt called me Louise. You never inquired my maiden name, I believe. I suppose you thought I had always been a married woman, but I was a girl of fourteen once, and went with my Aunt Belknap to New London, and met a boy who called himself *Dick Lee*, and who was so kind to the orphan girl, that she began to think of him all day, and watch for his coming after his school hours. He was a saucy, teasing boy, but Lulu liked him, and when one day she waited for his promised coming till it grew dark upon the beach, and the great hotel was lighted up for the evening festivity, and when other days and nights passed, and he neither came nor sent her any word, and she heard at last from one of his comrades that he had gone home to Boston,—I say, when all this came about she began to think that she had loved the boy who deceived her so, for he did deceive her in more points than one, as she afterward learned. His name was not Dick Lee"——

"But, Annie," Jimmie began, and Annie stopped him, saying:

"Wait, Jimmie, till I am through. This is my hour now. I have delayed telling you all this, for various reasons. Your mother knew who I was before I went to Washington, and she excused you as far as was possible. That I have promised to be your wife is proof that I have forgiven the pangs of disappointment I endured; for, Jimmie, I did suffer for a time. There was so little in the world to make me happy, and you had been so kind, that I fully believed in and trusted you; and when I found I was deceived, my heart ached as hard, perhaps, as the heart of a girl of fourteen can ache from such a cause."

"Poor Annie! poor little Lulu!" Jimmie said, as he clasped one of Annie's hands in his own, and his voice expressed all the sorrow and tenderness he felt for Annie who continued:

"Such childish loves are usually short-lived, you know, but mine was the first pleasant dream I had known since my parents died, and I went to my Aunt Belknap, in New Haven. She meant to be kind, I suppose, and in a certain way she was. She gave me a good education, and every advantage within her means. She took me to Newport and Saratoga, and the New York hotels, and she turned her back on George Graham, whom we met at Long Branch, where he was making some repairs upon an engine. A mechanic was not her idea of a husband for her niece. She preferred that I should marry a man of sixty, who had already the portraits of three wives in his handsome house at Meriden; but then, for each portrait he counted over two hundred thousand dollars, and half a million covers a multitude of defects and a great many wives. I would not marry that man, and as the result of my persistent refusal, my life with my aunt became so unbearable that, when Providence again threw George in my way, and he asked me to be his wife, I consented, and I never regretted the step. He was very kind to me, and I loved him so much, that when he died, I thought my heart died too, for he was my all."

Annie was very beautiful in her excitement as she paid this tribute to her deceased husband, and Jimmie saw that she was beautiful, but felt relieved when she left George Graham, and spoke of Rose, who had come to her like an angel of light, and made the burden easier to bear.

"I had no suspicion that she was the *soi-disant* Dick Lee's sister, or that my boy-hero was not Dick Lee, until just before you came home for the first time, and then I thought I must go away, for I did not care to meet you. But Rose prevented me, and I am glad now that she did."

"And I am glad, too," Jimmie said. "Your staying has been the means of untold good to me, darling,—it was the memory of your sweet, holy life and character which led me, a wretch at Andersonville, to seek the Saviour whom you have loved so long. God has led us both in strange paths. We have suffered a great deal,—you mentally, I physically, and only what I deserved; but let us hope that the night is passed, and the morning of our happy future dawning upon us. We are both young yet,—you twenty-three, and I only twenty-six. We have a long life to look forward to, and I thank God for it; but most of all, I thank Him for giving me my darling Annie,—my dear little Lulu! Does Rose know that you are Lulu?"

Mrs. Carleton had thought it better not to add to Rose's excitement by telling her who Annie was, while Jimmie's fate was shrouded in so much gloom; then, after his return, she decided that Annie should have the satisfaction of telling herself, and thus Rose was still in ignorance with regard to Annie's identity with the Pequot. But Annie told her that night, and Rose's eyes were like stars, as she smothered Annie with kisses, and declared it was all like some strange story she had read.

CHAPTER XXXIX.
CHARLIE.

He did not improve as his sister and uncle hoped he might; and as the cold weather increased, they began to talk of taking him to a warmer climate, but Charlie said:

"I am as well here as I could be anywhere. I don't want to be moved about. Let me stay here in quiet."

So they made him as comfortable as possible at the hotel, and Rose and Annie came every day to see him and he learned to watch and listen for their coming, especially that of Annie, to whom he took the kindliest. She knew just how to nurse him, and as she once cared for the poor prisoners, so she now cared for the Southern boy, who, while acknowledging the kindness of the Northern people, was still as thorough a Secessionist as he had ever been. Anxiously he waited for daily news of the progress of Grant's army, refusing to believe that Lee was so closely shut up in Richmond that escape was impossible. Blindly, like many of his older brethren, he clung to the hope, that underlying the whole was some hidden motive which would in time appear and work good to his cause. Maude never opposed or disputed with him now, but read him every little item of good for the South. But when, in the spring, the fighting at Petersburg commenced, there were no such items to read, and Charlie asked no longer for news. Then there came a never-to-be-forgotten day, when through the length and breadth of the land, the glad tidings ran that Richmond had fallen; that Lee with his army was flying from the city, with Grant in hot pursuit. The war was virtually over; and from Maine to Oregon the air was filled with the jubilant notes of victory. For three long hours the bells of Rockland rang out their merry peals, and at night they kindled bonfires in the streets; and on the grass-plat by the well in Widow Simms' yard, they burned the box, which, four years before, poor Isaac had put away for just such an occasion as this.

All the morning of that memorable Monday, while the bells were ringing, and the crowds were shouting in the streets, Charlie De Vere had lain with his white face to the wall, and his lips quivering with the grief and mortification he felt, that it should have ended thus. Occasionally, as the shouts grew louder, he stopped his ears, so as to shut out what seemed to him like exultations over the death of so many hopes; but when Annie came in, and told Maude of the bonfire they were to have that night in Mrs. Simms' yard, and asked her to come for the sake of the boy whose box was to be burned, Charlie began to listen. And as he listened, he grew interested in Isaac Simms and the grass-plat by the well, and the box hidden in the barn, and he expressed a wish to be present when it was burned. Maude, too, had heard of Isaac Simms before. She knew that he had been captured by Arthur Tunbridge, but she did not know the particulars of his prison life, or how generously Tom had sacrificed his chance of liberty for the sake of the poor, sick boy, until Annie told the story, to which she listened with swimming eyes and a heart throbbing with love and respect for her lover, who had been so noble and unselfish. She would go to the bonfire on the grass-plat, she said; and Charlie should go too. *He* had wept passionately at the recital of Isaac's sufferings in Libby, but still found some excuse for the South generally.

"It was not the better class of people," he said, "who did these things; it was the lower, ignorant ones, whose instincts were naturally brutal."

And neither Maude nor Annie contradicted him, though the eyes of the former flashed indignantly, and her nostrils quivered as they always did when the sufferings of our prisoners were mentioned in her presence.

That night, when the stars came out over Rockland, a party of twelve or more was congregated at the house of the widow Simms, where, but for the sad memory of Isaac, whose soldier-coat hung on the wall, with the knapsack carried into battle, all would have been, joy and hilarity at the prospect of certain peace. But death had been in that household, just as it had crept across many and many another threshold; and mingled with the rejoicings were tears and sad regrets for the dead of our land, whose graves were everywhere, from the shadowy forests of Maine, and the vast prairies of the West, to the sunny plains of the South, where they fought and died. There were twenty-five buried in the Rockland graveyard; and others than the party assembled at Mrs. Simms, thought of the vacant chairs at home, and the sleeping dead whose ears were deaf to the notes of peace floating so musically over the land. Charlie's face was very white, and there were tears in his eyes as he laid his thin, white hands reverently upon the box, examining its make, and bending close to the name, and date, and words cut upon it.—"Isaac Simms, Rockland, April 25th, 1861. This box to be burned——" There was a blank which the boy, who had cut the words with his jack-knife, could not supply. He did not know *when* the box would be burned. Then it was April, 1861; now it was April, 1865. Four years of strife and bloodshed, thousands and thousands of desolate hearth-stones, and broken hearts, and lifeless forms both North and South, and the end had come at last. But the boy Isaac was not there to see it. It was not for *him* to fill up that blank; but for the Southern boy, Charlie De Vere, who took his pencil from his pocket, and wrote, "April 3d, 1865, to celebrate the fall of Richmond, and the end of the Confederacy. Charles De Vere."

"Who shall light the pile?" Tom asked, when all was ready. And Charlie answered, "Let me, please. Surely I may light the fire!"

And he did light it, and then, with the rest, looked on while the smoke and the flames curled up toward the starry heavens where the boy Isaac had gone, and where Charlie in his dreams that night saw him so distinctly, and grasped his friendly hand.

After that night, Charlie failed rapidly, and often in his sleep, he talked to some one who seemed to be Arthur, and said it was "a mistake, a dreadful mistake." At last, as Maude sat by him one day, the fifth after the bonfire on the grass-plat, he said to her suddenly:

"Maude, if a man kills another and didn't mean to, is it *murder*?"

"No, it is manslaughter. Why do you ask?" Maude said; and Charlie continued:

"Don't hate me, Maude, nor tell any body, for *I* killed Arthur, myself. I shot him right through the head, and—Maude, he thought it was *you*!"

"Oh! Charlie! Charlie!" and Maude shrieked aloud as she bent over her brother, who continued:

"Not when he died, but at first, when he lay there on the grass, moaning and looking at you so sorry and grieved like, don't you remember?"

"Yes!" Maude gasped; and Charlie went on:

"You know that one of the ruffians fired at Captain Carleton and hit you, and then I could not help paying him back. He was taller than Arthur, who stood behind him, and knocked him down in time to take the ball himself. He knew you had a revolver, and he thought it was you, though an accident, of course, and it made him so sorry that you should be the one to kill him. But I told him different; when I whispered to him, you know. I said it was I, and his eyes put on such a happy look. I know he forgave me, for he said so; but my heart has ached ever since with thinking about it. I could not forget it; and I've asked God to forgive me so many times. I think he has; and that when I die, I shall go where Isaac Simms has gone. I like him, Maude, if he was a Yankee, and fought against us; and I like Mrs. Graham so much; and Mr. James Carleton, and the Mathers, and Mrs. Simms, some; but I can't like that dreadful Bill Baker, with his slang words and vulgar ways; he makes me so sick, and I feel so ashamed that we should be beaten by such as he."

"You were not beaten by such as he! You are mistaken, Charlie! The Northern army was composed of many of the noblest men in the world. There are Bill Bakers everywhere, as many South as North. It is foolish to think otherwise."

Maude was growing hot and eloquent in her defense of the Northern army, but Charlie's gentle, low-spoken reply, stopped her:

"Perhaps it is. I got terribly perplexed thinking it all over, and how it has turned out. I think—yes, I know I am glad the negroes are free. *We* never abused them. Uncle Paul never abused them. But there were those who did; and if slavery is a Divine institution, as we are taught to believe, it was a broken down and badly conducted institution, and not at all as God meant it to be managed."

Charlie paused a moment, and when he spoke again, it was of *Tom*, who had been so kind to him.

"He is like a brother to me, Maude, and I am glad you are to be his wife. And Maude, don't wait after I am dead, but marry Captain Carleton at once. You will be happier then."

With tears and kisses Maude bent over her brother, who after that confession seemed so much brighter and more cheerful, that hope sometimes whispered to Maude that he would live. Annie was almost constantly with him now. He felt better and stronger with her, he said, and death was not so terrible. So, just as she had soothed, and comforted, and nursed many a poor fellow from Andersonville, Annie comforted and nursed Charlie De Vere, until that dreadful Saturday when the telegraphic wires brought up from the South the appalling news that our President was dead,—murdered by the assassin's hand.

"No, no, not that. We did not do that," Charlie cried, with a look of horror in his blue eyes when he heard the dreadful story, and that the Southern leaders were suspected of complicity in the murder.

"It would make me a Unionist, if I believed my people capable of that; but they are not,—it cannot be," Charlie kept repeating to himself, while the great drops of sweat stood upon his white forehead, and his pulse and heart beat so rapidly, that Maude summoned the attending physician, who shook his head doubtfully at the great change for the worse in his patient.

"I had hoped at least to keep him till the warm weather, but, I am afraid those bells will be the death of him," he said, as he saw how Charlie shivered and moaned with each sound of the tolling bells.

"Perhaps they would stop if you were to ask them, and tell them why," Annie suggested to Maude; but Charlie, who heard it, exclaimed,

"No, let them toll on. It is proper they should mourn for him. The South would do the same if it was our President who had been murdered."

So the bells tolled on, and the public buildings were draped in mourning, and the windows of Charlie's room were festooned with black, and he watched the sombre drapery as it swayed in the April wind, and talked of the terrible deed, and the war which was ended, and the world to which so many thousands had gone during the long four years of strife and bloodshed.

"I shall be there to-morrow," he said, "and then perhaps I shall know why all this has been done, and if we were so wrong."

Maude and Annie, Paul Haverill and Tom Carleton watched with him through the night, and just as the beautiful Easter morning broke, and the sunlight fell upon the Rockland hills, the boy who to the last had remained true to the Southern cause, lay dead among the people who had been his foes.

At Maude's request they buried him by the side of Isaac Simms, and Capt. Carleton ordered a handsome monument, on which the names of both the boys were cut, Isaac Simms, who had died for the North, and Charlie De Vere, who, if need be, would have given his life for the South, each holding entirely different political sentiments, but both holding the same living faith which made for them an entrance to the world where all is perfect peace, and where we who now see through a glass darkly shall then see face to face, and know why these things are so.

Six months had passed since Charlie De Vere died. Paul Haverill, Will Mather, and Captain Carleton had been together on a pilgrimage to Paul's old neighborhood, where the people, wiser grown, welcomed back their old friend and neighbor, and strove in various ways to atone for all which had been cruel and harsh in their former dealing toward him. The war had left them destitute, so far as negroes and money were concerned; but such as they had they freely offered Paul, entreating him to stay in their midst and rebuild the homestead, whose blackened ruins bore testimony to what men's passions will lead them to do when roused and uncontrolled. But Paul said no; he could never again live where there was so much to remind him of the past. A little way out of Nashville was a beautiful dwelling-house, which, with a few acres of highly cultivated land, was offered for sale.

Maude had spoken of the place when she was in the city, and had said:

"I should like to live there."

And Tom had remembered it; and when he found it for sale, he suggested to Mr. Haverill that they buy it as a winter residence for Maude. And so what little property Paul Haverill had left was invested in *Fair Oaks*, as the place was called; and Tom gave orders that the house should be refurnished and ready for himself and bride as early as the first of November.

As far as was possible, Will and Tom found and generously rewarded those who had so kindly befriended them in their perilous journey across the mountains.

But some were missing, and only their graves remained to tell the story of their wrongs.

This trip was made in June, and early in August, the whole Carleton family went to New London, where Jimmie improved so fast that few would have recognized the pale, thin invalid, of Andersonville notoriety, in the active, red-cheeked, saucy-eyed young man, who became the life of the Pequot House, and for whom the gay belles practiced their most bewitching coquetries.

But these were all lost on Jimmie, who was seldom many minutes away from the fair, blue-eyed woman who, the girls had learned, was a widow, and of whom they at first had no fears. But they changed their minds when day after day saw the "handsome Carleton" at her side, and night after night found him walking with her along the road, or sitting on the rocks and watching the tide come in, just as he had done years ago, when both were younger than they were now. They lived those days over again, and, in their perfect happiness, almost forgot the sorrow and pain which had come to them both since they first looked out upon the waters of New London bay.

Tom and Maude were there, too, together with Rose Mather and Will, and Susan Simms and John.

A well-timed investment in *oil stock*,—a lucky turn of the wheel,—and Captain John Simms awoke, one morning, with one hundred thousands dollars! He did not believe it at first, and Susan did not believe it either. But when John, who, with all his good sense, was a little given to show, or, as his mother expressed it, "to making a fool of himself," brought her a set of diamonds, handsomer than Rose Mather's, and bought her a new carriage, and took her to Saratoga, with an English nurse for little Ike, she began to realize that something had happened to her which brought Rose Mather's envied style of living within her means.

She soon grew tired of Saratoga. She was too much alone in that great crowd, and when she heard that the Carletons were at New London she went there with her diamonds and horses, and, patronized by Rose, who took her at once under her protection, she made a few pleasant acquaintances, and ever after talked confidently of her "summer at the sea-side." She did not care to go again, however. "She and John were not exactly like people born to high life," she said, and so she settled quietly down in her pretty home, and made, as the Widow Simms said, "quite a decent woman, considerin' that she was one of them Ruggleses."

Bill Baker was astir very early one bright, October morning, his face indicating that some important event was pending in which he was to act a part. It was a double wedding at St. Luke's, and Maude and Annie were the brides. There was a great crowd to witness the ceremony, and Annie's "boys" whom she had nursed at Annapolis, were the first to offer their congratulations to Mrs. James Carleton, who looked so fair and pure and lovely, while Maude, whose beauty was of a more brilliant order, seemed to sparkle and flash as she bent her stately head in response to the greetings given to her.

Upon Bill, who had turned hack-driver, devolved the honor of taking the bridal party to and from the church, and his horses were covered with the Federal flag, while conspicuous in his button-hole was a small one made of white silk and presented to him by a girl whom he called "Em," and who blushed every time she heard Bill's voice ordering the crowd to stand back and his horses to "show their oats," as he drove from the church with the newly-married people.

Their destination was Nashville, where, in Maude's beautiful home, Jimmie and Annie passed a few delightful weeks, and then returned to Boston to the old Carleton house on Beacon Street, which had been fitted up for their reception.

Mrs. Carleton, senior, divides her time between her three children, Tom, Jimmie and Rose, but her home proper is with Annie, in Boston, where there is now a little "Lulu Graham," six months old, and where Rose and Will often go, while each summer Tom Carleton comes up from Fair Oaks with his beautiful Maude, the heroine of the Cumberland Mountains.

THE END.

Booksophile
Your Local Online Bookstore

Buy Books Online from
www.Booksophile.com

Explore our collection of books written in various languages and uncommon topics from different parts of the world, including history, art and culture, poems, autobiography and bibliographies, cooking, action & adventure, world war, fiction, science, and law.

Add to your bookshelf or gift to another lover of books - first editions of some of the most celebrated books ever published. From classic literature to bestsellers, you will find many first editions that were presumed to be out-of-print.

Free shipping globally for orders worth US$ 100.00.

Use code "Shop_10" to avail additional 10% on first order.

Visit today
www.booksophile.com